Praise for War

"Warren Adler writes with skill and a sense of scene."

— *The New York Times Book Review* on *The War of the Roses*

"Engrossing, gripping, absorbing... written by a superb storyteller. Adler's pen uses brisk, descriptive strokes that are enviable and masterful."

— *West Coast Review of Books* on *Trans-Siberian Express*

"A fast-paced suspense story... only a seasoned newspaperman could have written with such inside skills."

— *The Washington Star* on *The Henderson Equation*

"High-tension political intrigue with excellent dramatization of the worlds of good and evil."

— *Calgary Herald* on *The Casanova Embrace*

"A man who willingly rips the veil from political intrigue."

— *Bethesda Tribune* on *Undertow*

Warren Adler's political thrillers are...: "Ingenious."

Praise for Shannon McKenna

"An intensely terrifying psychic thriller..."

Library Journal, on *Fade To Midnight*

"Blasts readers with a highly charged, action-adventure romance..."

Booklist

"Pulse-pounding... with raw emotions."

Romantic Times

"Shannon McKenna introduces us to fleshed-out characters in a tailspin plot that culminates in an explosive ending."

Fresh Fiction

"A suspense vehicle on overdrive!"

RT Book Reviews

"Her books will take readers on a nonstop thrill ride and leave them begging for more when the last pages are devoured."

Maya Banks, *New York Times* bestselling author

"This action-packed novel is sure to be a crowd pleaser."

NOBODIES

WARREN ADLER
SHANNON MCKENNA

Published by Adler Entertainment Trust
Cover design by Jane Dixon Smith
Title Production by The BookWhisperer.ink

Also by Warren Adler

FICTION

Banquet Before Dawn

Beneath the Ivory Tower

Blood Ties

Cult

Empty Treasures

Finding Grace

Funny Boys

Heart of Gold

High Noon in Hollywood

Little Black Dress (coming 2025/2026, posthumously revised and edited)

Madeline's Miracles

Mother Nile

Mourning Glory

Natural Enemies

Nobodies - written by Shannon Anderson & Warren Adler

Private Lies

Random Hearts

Residue

The Casanova Embrace

The David Embrace

The Henderson Equation

The Housewife Blues

The Norma Conquest

The Serpent's Bite

Treadmill

Twilight Child

Undertow

We Are Holding the President Hostage

THE ROSES: A DARK COMEDY SERIES

The War of the Roses

The Children of the Roses

The Curse of the Roses (coming 2025/2026, inspired by Warren Adler's The Roses *series)*

CHURCHILL'S SHADOW: A HISTORICAL THRILLER SERIES

Mission Churchill - Written by Alex Abella, Inspired by Warren Adler's Target Churchill

Target Churchill - written by Warren Adler & James C Humes

FLANAGANS ANTIQUES COZY MYSTERIES SERIES

Flanagan's Dolls

Flanagan's Strings by Andrew Frothingham & Warren Adler

THE FIONA FITZGERALD MYSTERY SERIES

American Quartet

American Sextet

Death of a Washington Madame

Immaculate Deception

Senator Love

The Ties That Bind

The Witch of Watergate

Washington Masquerade

Chapter One

At 10:19 AM, Henry Devlin was distracted by a flash of movement in the corner of his mental grid of the Rose Reading Room. Without moving his head, he lifted his gaze from the screen he'd been staring at and swept the room, cataloging every change.

He'd always had a talent for single-minded concentration, but in these strange days, he'd been forced to apportion smaller and smaller pieces of his attention to multiple tasks at once, forcing them all to work in parallel. Not optimal or efficient, but a fugitive had no choice. He had to be constantly on the alert.

The disturbance on his grid was a hunched, elderly woman who was entering the Rose Reading Room. She had long, unkempt gray hair under a puffy knit hat with a bill, and wore a tired wool coat of dingy gray that used to be black. She shuffled forward, thick ankles bulging over heavy black orthopedic shoes that clumped and dragged. She had shiny brown compression stockings, a dowager's hump, a hooked nose, heavy glasses, and hanging jowls. He focused his attention, to see if maybe…

Yes. It was the costume girl. Jubilant certainty filled him as he admired her disguise. Incredible, how she upped her game with each new persona.

It felt like a game now, even a friendly duel. The rush he got from spotting her was also cause for worry. He was walking a tightrope. Any strong feeling, positive or negative, could knock him off it.

To survive, he had to be blank, gray, empty. The actions of a person who had no feelings, opinions or preferences could not be predicted. So he had to be invisible even to himself. He had to be not there.

He had to be nobody.

Nostalgia still overtook him whenever his guard faltered. For the way he used to be. Not so much for life with his former wife, which in any case had been a lie.

Then again, from the start he'd had the uneasy sense that Belinda was just too good to be true. Part of him had been braced for disaster all along. Unwilling to let go of the fantasy, but at the same time, always waiting for the other shoe to drop.

And then it dropped. Right on top of him, like a ton of broken rock.

A year and a half ago, he'd been Belinda's husband, the father of a perfect baby girl. He'd been making good money. He had a nice house, a good car, a great sex life. An enviable existence by all standard markers of American manhood. Incredible luck for a shy, socially awkward, nerdy guy like himself. Improbable, if you thought about it. So he'd tried not to. He'd just embraced his luck, because why not?

In prison, he'd had all the time in the world to ponder why not.

What he really missed now was the way he'd worked before. Focusing so completely that the world went away. He couldn't get to that place anymore, even alone in his studio sublet. He was too tense for deep dives. It was only brief, shallow dives now, and he always came up quickly, anxious, scared, gasping for air.

It used to be that when he sat down to work, a big hand reached up out of the screen, grabbed his brain, and yanked him down to where the magic happened. Nothing touched him when he was in that state, not hunger or thirst or the body's demands. Not an alarm wailing, a phone ringing, a baby crying.

He craved those brainwaves the way other people craved food.

Belinda had scolded him for that. *Get out of la-la land. Join the real world.*

She'd gotten her wish. By framing him for fraud, Belinda and Victor, her sociopathic boyfriend, had catapulted him headlong into a world that was terribly real. The clang of prison doors closing still echoed in his mind. It didn't get much realer than that.

But he shouldn't think about Victor and Belinda at all. He exhaled, replacing thoughts of them with blank gray. Invisible. Empty. Nothing. He clung to nothing, and called nothing his own. Not his memories, not even his anger. It was all fiction, all suspect, all up for debate.

Except for Faith. Memories of his baby he would keep, even though they burned like an ulcer.

Henry focused on the costume girl as she shuffled along leaning heavily on her cane, precisely as an old lady with badly swollen ankles would. Liver spots. Raised veins. She had incredible skill.

He'd noticed her a few weeks ago, but she may well have been coming in for a while before that. One day, while organizing his mental images of the Rose Reading Room occupants, he cross-referenced her with the memory of a woman he'd seen four days before. The first woman had been slim, with a black Metallica sweatshirt, star-spangled active-wear spandex pants, auburn dreads, rimless glasses, and facial piercings. The second woman had chipmunk cheeks, pink-rimmed sparkling glasses, a perky gray bob, a heavy bosom, and a big belly. Body shape, haircut and color, skin tone, eye color and age were all different, but there were too many similarities to overlook.

Henry had been so alarmed that he had actually considered walking away from the Rose Reading Room, even leaving New York City altogether. But he loved the big, loud, anonymous city, and the Rose Reading Room soothed him. Yes, it was dangerous to have habits, but he'd given up so much already. He needed one constant in his life. Just one, for baseline sanity. A safety rope to keep him moored to the world.

He felt suffocated in his studio apartment. He needed the outdoors, movement, a destination, and public libraries were the only sheltered place where a person could take up space without paying for the privilege.

His mom had been a librarian, so libraries felt like a haven to him.

Still, he kept going, and kept watching the costume girl, growing more fascinated with her by the day. Nothing bad had happened yet. And she didn't act the way a person stalking him would act. A cop, a Fed, a P.I., any one of them would have made a move by now.

He'd begun anticipating the challenge. He felt flat and somewhat cheated when she didn't show up. Over time, she'd become his entertainment. His guilty pleasure. It was as if they had a secret little outlaw club with a membership of two. A brief flash of connection every day. All of that was probably all in his head, but he enjoyed it. And his enjoyments were few these days.

He caught her glancing over to see if she'd fooled him, and lifted his coffee cup, giving her a slight, deliberate nod, almost a bow, in homage to her skills. Thanking her for another magnificent performance.

Great try. But no.

The costume girl looked away. Her lips seemed to tighten, but she had somehow created so many lip wrinkles that he couldn't be sure. He wished he could ask her how she did it, but he wouldn't have been capable of an overture like that even before his life exploded and he became a fugitive, indebted to criminals. An outlaw with no name, no past, no future. No self.

In any case, she'd bolt if he tried it. Normal people didn't hide under elaborate disguises. She was on the run, hiding from something or someone, just like him. He'd bet money on it. He watched as she pulled out a tablet. He ought to tell her to switch out that cover. She always used the same grubby pink thing, though only a detail-crazy geek like him would notice.

Henry forced his attention back to the screen. He was working for a hardened criminal, which made him tense, but he had no choice other than prison, which was no choice at all. No matter who he was working for, he was grateful to be out. He could exist off the grid and make enough money to survive, and it was all thanks to Ivar, a contact he'd made in prison.

Henry had met Ivar Schull soon after he arrived at the Rock Ridge Correctional Facility for Men. Ivar was in for mail fraud, and up for parole very soon. Ivar was fiercely intelligent, a born hustler with an entrepreneurial mindset. When he learned how Victor and Belinda turned Henry's technical skills against him, he'd started dreaming up ways to monetize Henry's talents in the criminal underworld. It started as a joke. It didn't stay one for long.

Before he was released, Ivar quietly suggested that, in return for a long-running commitment for some trifling technical services, he could arrange for Henry to break out. Ivar would take care of the details. Once Henry was on the outside, he would hide him, outfit him, find him serviceable

ID. It would be expensive. But Henry could work off his debt with his special skills.

At first, Henry laughed him off. At the time, he still hoped that he could prove his innocence and get his life back. Then, slowly, he began to realize the extent of the trouble he was in. The evidence against him was rigged, and the judge was prejudiced.

In the end, he realized that the indentured servitude Ivar was offering was actually his best bet.

According to the prosecution, Henry had defrauded his three biggest clients of a combined six-point-five million dollars using cutting edge tech tools he had inserted into databases he had designed for them. The prosecutor offered clemency if he cooperated, a slap on the wrist. Two to five years in a minimum security facility, out early for good behavior. All he had to do was give back the money. But since he had not stolen the money, he was useless in recovering it, much to the disgust of his lawyers.

He'd never been a bitter, cynical person, but the events of the past eighteen months had changed him. He was like a lump of coal subjected to massive geological forces. He'd become a diamond, but not the bright, glittering kind. More like the practical, un-beautiful kind. The ones they used for drill bits.

The prosecution had presented videos of him buying diamonds. Security cameras from jewelers all over the tri-state area had recorded him. Receipts had been produced bearing his signature, from places he'd never been, generated by people he'd never met, spending money he'd never touched. Over and over, there he was, brazenly laundering his ill-gotten gains right out in front of God and everyone. He would have been more intelligent about it if he had actually done the crime. He'd said as much to his lawyers, but as a defense strategy that didn't go over very well.

As Mom had always gently tried to remind him, nobody liked a smart-ass.

His wife, Belinda, had stolen a copy of Mirror, Mirror, a deep-fake program Henry had written himself. He'd done it for fun, delving into deep-fake tech to see if he could make videos that would fool a forensic expert. He'd pulled it off, too. And like a kid with a new toy, he'd run right off to show his creation to Belinda.

Henry had never meant to sell or use Mirror, Mirror. It was clearly a tool for bad actors. He'd simply wondered if the logistical difficulties of a deep-fake were solvable, and when his brain posed a question like that, he had to answer it. By showing Mirror, Mirror to Belinda, he had exposed himself, like a fawning idiot. He had handed her a rope and begged her to hang him with it.

Belinda had asked for his signature all the time when they were married, usually while he was concentrating on some other project. He'd always given it. Absently, trustingly. Innocuous things, permissions for Faith to have her picture taken at the child-care center, releases for vaccinations, tax stuff, banking stuff. He'd been grateful to leave the busywork of life to her so he could focus on more important things. Hurray for the division of labor that liberated him to leverage his true talents, right?

He'd been so stupid. Not in the obvious ways in which they had made him seem stupid, which were bad enough. He'd been stupid in deeper, more humiliating ways. He'd been emotionally callow, blind, with holes in his head. Belinda and Victor had used every one of those holes, and he had no one to blame but himself.

After the trial, Henry let go of any hope of justice. If he reached for justice, he'd get smacked down so hard, he'd never see the light of day again. But revenge was a more flexible proposition.

During sleepless nights in the prison, surrounded by the

miserable nocturnal noise and stink of his cellmates, he'd decided he wanted every penny they had accused him of stealing. He'd never cared about money until he married Belinda, but it had taken on a new importance now. Money meant freedom, high-quality ID, travel, the chance to build a life somewhere else. Money meant seeing the sunrise, the breeze on his face.

He needed a large sum of money to crawl out of the hole he was in now. Ivar sent him a steady stream of work, and bit by bit, he was paying off his debt for the prison break. But it was slow going. What Henry really needed was a new passport. A real one. Ivar had assured him, somewhat cagily, that this was doable. Ivar dealt in secrets and favors. The bigger the secrets, the bigger the favors, and he had secrets on people in government agencies who could make it happen. Or so he claimed.

But it was not in Ivar's best interest to hand such a document over until Henry had paid off his debt, and maybe not even then. The prison break and all the help he'd been given afterward, the housing, electronics, bank accounts, credit cards with driver's licenses to match them, had already run up a tab of close to a million. A genuine American passport, Ivar said, would be another million. It would take years, working night and day, to pay that off. And even if Ivar did get him that passport, he could always tip off the authorities himself, and Henry would be back to square one, in prison.

So in a way, he was still inside. Still stripped of any real identity. Still a nobody.

He could sell Mirror, Mirror to Ivar outright. But he was living proof of the harm that Mirror, Mirror could do.

The only other solution was the money Victor and Belinda had stolen, if they still had it. That would be plenty to both pay off his debt and leave enough extra to start over.

Among the other favors he had bestowed upon him, Ivar had put Henry in touch with people who sold test-taking services and the writing of scientific masters and graduate theses. Henry churned these out with such ease, the man who found him the jobs had asked him to dumb them down, just to make them more believable. It was a unique challenge for him, dialing it down and not up. But the extra cash that he earned from those gigs covered his basic expenses.

Even if he took back what Victor and Belinda had stolen in his name, it could never make up for what he'd lost. His reputation, his identity. And Faith. His baby girl.

Even so, destroying Belinda and Victor was a way to even the score. He'd ruin them, just as they'd ruined him. He would bully and hassle and torment them. They would not have a moment's peace until he got that money back, paid his debt, and left the country.

The only problem was Faith, stranded out there with them on the firing range.

Movement on the screen caught his eye. Henry studied the flicker on one of the thumbnail monitors. The one that had been activated was in Belinda and Victor's garage. Belinda had taken to doing her grocery shopping in the mornings after dropping Faith off at the daycare center. She brought it home, unpacked it, and then went to work. Coming into work a couple of hours late was evidently one of the perks of sleeping with the boss.

He watched as she sat in the garage in her Toyota Gamma for so long that the motion-activated light snapped off, leaving her in total darkness. A tiny flickering glow wavered in front of her. A cigarette. She'd quit while she was pregnant with Faith, but picked it up again. Maybe having her husband thrown into prison was stressful. Maybe she felt guilty, conflicted. Maybe a life of crime exhausted her. Maybe it was just having a toddler.

Belinda took her time finishing her cigarette and then tucked behind some boxes. Then she grabbed her reusable shopping bags from the back. Classic Belinda, always thinking of the planet, with her hybrid SUV, her eco-sustainable body care products, her free-range eggs, grass-fed beef, organic produce and hemp sneakers. Hyper-conscious of her carbon footprint.

But she'd stomped all over him without a shred of remorse.

The monitor enlarged as she entered the frame, then reduced to a thumbnail as she left. Now the kitchen monitor dominated his screen. Her new kitchen was more impressive than the one in the house Henry had bought for her. Now he watched her via the video camera of the cutting-edge electronic butler. Belinda and Victor had a smart house, which made it all the easier for Henry to hack into their systems. This particular gizmo was fortuitously angled to encompass the entire kitchen. It even afforded a glimpse through the entryway into their living room. Thanks to the almost too easy hacking of all their monitors and security systems, Henry had broken in a couple of months ago and loaded a sleek little key-logging bit of malware into their computers. If they tried to change their passwords, all he had to do was access the logger, and he was right back inside.

Thanks to the house's smart-hub, he had access to everything. Their electronic butler. Their computers. Their smart TVs, the Bluetooth, the security cameras, the smart appliances, the baby monitor, Belinda's phone. He hadn't compromised Victor's phone yet, but he could listen to all Victor's conversations in his car through his Bluetooth connection. It had been easy to hack the cyber-connected cars. If he wanted to, Henry could seize control of those cars at any time he liked.

He hadn't played that card yet. For now, he just enjoyed holding it. Little pleasures.

The Bluetooth connection had proved especially useful when Victor set up extracurricular sex parties with escorts in the city, a thing he did frequently. It had taken Henry a while to figure out how to collect video evidence of these encounters, and when he did, watching it had been extremely distasteful. But he had what he needed now. Another stick to beat Victor with. And soon.

Belinda hoisted the grocery bags onto the granite-topped central island. The island had a sink and a stovetop. There was another sink and stovetop against the wall, below a big window with decorative lace curtains. Beyond the window, Henry saw rolling knolls of green uniform grass, and a glimpse of the artificial lake at the center of Victor's gated community, the Chilton Estates.

Belinda went back and forth, grimly putting her groceries away, her carefully shaped dark brows knotted into a frown. Her collagen-plumped lips were pursed tight. Items piled up. Pre-washed organic salad greens. Frozen pizzas. Frozen dinners. Baby carrots. Yogurt, baby food, frozen chicken tenders. Belinda had never been a very inventive cook. Henry had done most of the cooking during their marriage. Belinda unpacked wipes and diapers. She plonked two large packs, sized for an eighteen-month-old, on the counter.

Henry frowned. Eighteen months? Faith was well over two and a half. She had not been underweight back when he had been bathing her, feeding her, changing her.

He swiftly opened the monitor that showed the daycare center's play rooms, looking for Faith. Belinda had recently, and conveniently, moved her to Busy Bees Day Care, a facility that offered continuous video monitoring for anxious helicopter parents.

Henry finally found Faith sitting in a corner on a rubberized mat decorated with the letters of the alphabet. She showed no interest in the toys scattered around her, just sat hunched over, sucking her small fist, looking pinched and hollow-eyed.

Henry didn't like this at all. The listlessness, the dullness in her eyes, her shrimpy smallness. Not that he was one to judge if she was undersized. But she certainly did not look like the bouncing, alert baby he remembered. The baby fat on her wrists and ankles was gone. Her little arms and legs were spindly now.

Henry swallowed the rebellious clutch of emotion in his throat. *No*. Faith was someone else's kid. She had never been his to begin with. A genetic test, demanded by Victor's angry ex-wife, had revealed that she was Victor's biological child. Faith was definitely someone else's problem now. Just another unlucky kid who had drawn shit parents from the great lottery in the sky. It was a big shame, but there it was. All he could do was wish her luck and get as far away from her as he could.

Faith had been nine months old when they dragged him away in cuffs. He still remembered her screaming in Belinda's arms, holding out her arms to him, her little face purple with yelling, wet with tears and snot. Howling in bewilderment.

Henry had given Faith his mother's name, over Belinda's protests. Belinda thought the name was old-fashioned and stodgy, but Henry had insisted. So Victor Shattuck's child bore Henry's mother's name. Not that it mattered. Faith was Victor's now, to neglect, disappoint, damage.

Every time he looked at her, he had to remind himself that she was no longer his responsibility. Even if he could do something so crazy, taking a little kid with him on the lam would be doing her no favors. The chances of that ending well were slim to none. The kindest thing he could do for her was to somehow take her worthless parents off the playing board. Let her roll the dice again with a fresh set of adoptive ones. After all, she couldn't possibly do worse than those two ghouls.

He switched off the Busy Bees monitor and checked back on Belinda, who was still putting away yogurt cups and pureed soup. She pulled out two tubs of caramel praline ice cream, her favorite, and one of chocolate almond fudge. Henry and Belinda had always had a dish of ice cream after sex. Belinda had been struggling to stop smoking at the time, so the ice cream took the place of nicotine.

Henry favored simple French vanilla. To his mind, ice cream should be creamy, plain, and perfectly uniform in texture. He didn't get why anyone would mar that with chunks or nuts, or gummy fudges, or crystals that crunched, crackled, and stuck in your teeth.

Belinda had teasingly called him her "vanilla man." He hadn't known what that meant. He'd been a virgin when they met. Dazzled by sex. Pathetically enthusiastic. Later, he'd run across the term in a magazine in prison, and learned that being "vanilla" meant you were dull, boring, and predictable in bed. No spice, no kink.

A painful revelation, but relatively speaking, other things had hurt him more.

So Victor was a chunky almond fudge kind of guy. Henry stared at the tubs of ice cream, wishing he could return to his previous state of blissful ignorance.

Once she'd finished putting away her ice cream, Belinda shrugged on her coat. Henry followed her progress back out into the garage. Then he switched the GPS tag on and followed her Gamma through town. She veered off to stop at the coffee shop for her usual sugary expresso drink. Bel was a creature of habit.

While she ordered, Henry clicked into the smart house control hub, found the refrigerator, and turned it off. By the time Victor and Belinda got home that night, their ice cream would be liquid slop.

Maybe it was a petty gesture, but Henry preferred to think of it as thorough. And a harbinger of things to come.

Chapter Two

Amber pulled out her haul from last night's nightclub run, displaying it piece by piece for Angus, the fence. She'd gotten Angus's name from an old friend from her grifting days, before her stint as a Vegas showgirl, but she wished she had some other option to unload her loot. Angus was stingy and dislikable.

Tricked out in her sexiest finery, Amber had spent last night cruising three nightclubs, slow-dancing and making out with her drunken marks in corridors, shadowy booths, and bathroom stalls. Now, she laid a Rolex watch, a Philippe Patek watch, a diamond tennis bracelet, and a dangling diamond pendant in white gold. Not a bad haul for a Thursday. Angus surveyed the pieces, his thick, heavily jowled face blank and unreadable before looking her over with beady, suspicious eyes.

Amber was glad she was facing him as Betty Lipschitz. Betty's persona was a bullet-proof shield against unwanted masculine attention.

Amber always gave her personae names. It helped to mentally organize their details and backstories. Betty was old, shabby and unkempt, her teeth distorted by a jaw prosthetic which gave her a tragic overbite. Amber had packed Betty's pallid, wrinkled cheeks to match the hunch-backed fat suit she wore under the voluminous, stale-smelling black coat. The costume was heavy and uncomfortable, but she'd been going all out to fool the black-bearded guy in the Rose Reading Room. Not that it had worked all that well. The dude homed right in on her every time, like he had X-ray eyes. What the hell was up with that?

"I'll give you two thousand-five for all of it." Angus took a long drag on his cigarette and blew smoke into her face.

Damned if she'd give him the satisfaction. Amber resisted the urge to cough. "It's worth ten times that."

Angus shrugged. "Go get ten times for it somewhere else, then."

Amber hesitated, but not for long. She didn't have the energy to make the rounds of other fences. The results would likely be the same, anyway, and Angus knew it.

The problem was partly the costume. Betty Lipschitz looked too desperate to get a fair deal out of an asshole, like Angus. She should have gone home, changed, and come back as sexpot Trix. Looking like a call girl or a burglar would have worked way better.

But she was too tired and broke to hold out for more cash tonight. The house-sitting gig she had landed provided a free place to stay, but she still had to eat, get around the city, and buy costumes and incidentals. Even thrift-store shopping added up. Makeup and good wigs were costly.

She took the money Angus counted out and tucked it into the inside pocket of her coat. Betty Lipschitz's coat, which she'd picked out at the thrift store specifically for its mildewed smell. Details mattered, and Amber knew every detail of Betty's sad story. She was seventy-eight, but looked and felt ten years older. She took a lot of medication. She'd lost her husband thirty years ago. She was estranged from her one son, who now lived in California somewhere. Betty eked out her lonely existence in a small, squalid rent-controlled apartment that reeked of cabbage and mold, which exacerbated her respiratory allergies. She favored game shows and reality TV.

Betty/Amber stumped out of the basement thrift shop and onto the street. An icy gust swept down the long wind tunnel, making her big coat billow and flap. The one good thing about fat suits was that they were great insulation, against both unwanted attention and biting cold.

It hadn't fooled Blackbeard, though. She'd gotten up early and spent over three hours on this get-up, and he had seen through it like glass. Damn the guy.

The orthopedic shoes had thick, rubbery treads that were good on icy sidewalks. Shoes make the outfit. A friend of hers in Vegas had taught her that years ago when she was young and green, and she'd taken the advice to heart. These shoes were as ugly as turds. Perfect for Betty.

She'd been so sure Betty would fool him. The protruding teeth, the chalky wrinkles created using glues and liquid latex. She'd pulled out all her tricks, deployed all her arts. But Blackbeard had an eye for her now. The harder she tried, the quicker he spotted her.

She'd noticed him the very first day. He was memorable, in a subtle way, with that intense look in his bright blue eyes as he constantly scanned the room with swift, laser-sharp sweeps. She counted on people focusing mainly upon themselves, and for the most part, they obliged her. Blackbeard paid far too much attention to his surroundings. When Blackbeard began to take notice of her personally, she should have decided the Rose Reading Room was no longer a safe haven, and left.

Instead, she'd doubled down. She should have her head examined.

Still, Blackbeard didn't seem like a U.S. Marshal or a Fed, and he seemed even less like someone Leon or DiAngelos would send. One of the reasons she'd chosen the Rose Reading Room was because it was the last place either of them or their minions would ever go. Proponents of high culture they were not. Nor would they think to look for her there. What would a piece of simpering blond arm candy like her be doing in a place like that?

Amber also chose it because she loved the Reading Room's lush, nineteenth-century vibe, its high ceilings, big windows, fuss and frescoes and curlicues, gleaming brass lamps and glowing chandeliers. All of it was extravagantly beautiful. Even better, it was a place where nobody was buying or selling or ripping anybody off. The Rose Reading Room was just a quiet, mellow place to read or think or simply be alone. All those people together, politely minding their own business. Demanding nothing from her but that she be quiet. Such civility. It soothed the soul.

It reminded her a little of her grandmother's house in Buenos Aires. Nonna Sofia had come from Italy as a bride after the Second World War, and her old palazzo had seemed impossibly fancy and luxurious to Amber's child-self. In reality, the place had been shabby, faded and peeling, a mere ghost of its former splendor, but still so beautiful.

No, she thought. No way was Blackbeard with Leon or the DiAngelos. For starters, if he were, she would be dead. But mostly, he just wasn't the type. Not that he was easy to categorize. Blackbeard was youngish, mid-thirties, maybe, with shaggy black hair, an unkempt matching beard, a hooked nose, and bad glasses. She had an eye for a home dye job, but this man was neither old enough nor well-groomed enough to be dying his hair for reasons of vanity.

No, he was hiding out, just like her. Took one to know one.

The umpteenth cab zoomed past, slinging icy slush over her compression stockings. No cabbie in his right mind was going to stop for poor old Betty, lurching along in her turd shoes. Funny how, when she glammed up and put the goods on display, cabs shrieked to a stop at the mere flick of her hand. Men responded like dogs to the dinner bell.

Blackbeard saw something else in her. The more frowsy she looked, the more intrigued he got. So it wasn't sexual.

Of course, the way her life was going lately, it was probably something worse. So what was it that interested him? Amber didn't understand it, and that made her extremely curious.

But Blackbeard was not her mission, she reminded herself. Forget about Blackbeard. She needed to find Michael's mystery haul before Leon hunted her down and killed her. That was how she stayed alive. Because the alternative, staying in Idaho, being Leon's bed toy, opening her legs when he told her to…that would kill her. Particularly now that she knew what Leon was capable of. What she'd seen him do in his Vegas penthouse five months ago. It haunted her dreams. Her waking hours, too.

She couldn't grit her teeth and stay put until Leon got bored and decided to trade her in for a newer model with fewer miles on it. At which point he'd probably just slit her throat and dump her in the boneyard.

Stealing wallets, watches, and jewelry had jacked her anxiety level so high, she barely slept anymore, leaving her jumpy and nervous. There were drugs for that, of course. But she didn't dare blunt her edge, even if that sharp edge was bleeding her out.

That was why she liked The Rose Reading Room. Just being there relaxed her. Like Nonna Sofia's old palazzo.

She'd spent a wonderful summer there when she was eight. Then Mamma had a screaming fight with Nonna Sofia, and back they went to Albuquerque, onto the grift again. Amber had been grifting with Mamma since she was five days old. She started out as a cute little prop, but she grew up fast, and got good at it in her own right. She was not Ofelia DeGennaro's daughter for nothing. She'd learned her makeup tricks from Mamma. Then she'd learned still more from other crews as she got older. Those skills had served her well as a showgirl in Vegas. Those skills kept her alive and hidden now.

She went down the stairway to the A train. She should save that cab money, anyway. Picking pockets in nightclubs was risky. If the cops caught her, someone would hear about it, whether it was the Feds, the US Marshals, Leon, or the DiAngelo crew. And it would be lights-out for Amber Dixon.

The train was crowded. She had to look for a seat. No one was getting up to give poor, tired Betty a break tonight. Settling in a corner so she could study the other subway goers, she wondered if Blackbeard had picked New York City for the same reasons she had. Constant chaotic motion. And it was so visually dense, one could never be certain what one had seen. That made it easy to disappear, with her skills.

Arriving at her stop and emerging from the subway, Amber trudged toward the Chelsea townhouse owned by Robert and Rayna Grudberg, currently off on a six-month sailboat trip. The house-sitting gig was a stroke of pure, God-given luck. An accidental gift from her best girlfriend and colleague, Trix.

Like Amber, Trix had been a showgirl at the Magnum Theater in Las Vegas. Amber had called Trix to warn her after she saw Leon murder Michael, Trix's secret number-two boyfriend. She warned her friend that Leon would come after her to collect whatever Michael had stolen from him, the mystery object that had ruined everyone's lives. Told her that she had to run like hell.

Trix had listened, and flown off to Japan with Kenji, her main man, thank God. Amber had sneaked over to Trix's apartment afterward just to make sure Trix hadn't left anything behind that could lead Leon back to her. In her panic-packing, Trix had left behind her New York driver's license.

That license saved Amber's ass many times over. It had

been her working ID ever since. It had also made her eligible to house-sit in New York.

Before Vegas, Trix used to house-sit in Manhattan to get away from her pain-in-the-ass mom in Jersey. When Amber checked online, she found that Beatrice Graziano's profile on the Trusted House-Sitters site was, amazingly, still current. Trix had good reviews from home owners. As Trix, Amber could find comfortable places to stay in exchange for feeding a cat, scooping some poop, watering some ferns.

Becoming Trix hadn't been a challenge. Amber was older than her friend by a good eight years, but she was about the same size and shape. A long, curly black wig, colored contacts, some cheek stuffing, and she matched that license just fine.

Trix's biggest problem now was being bored to death and miserable in Kenji's lonely penthouse in Tokyo, so much so that Amber worried she might do something stupid. Amber had only persuaded her to go in the first place by promising that if she found whatever Michael had stolen, they could share it. If it could be turned into money, Trix would get half. Which would give her options, freedom, agency.

It was just a fantasy, of course, and Amber knew it. But Trix needed something to cling to. Hell, so did she. The stakes were so high, and the odds so low.

Amber had known the minute she laid eyes on the smooth-talking Michael that Trix would crash and burn with him. Not that she was in any position to criticize. She'd hooked up with Leon, after all, and she'd been a fool to think she could manage him. Amber wasn't stupid. She'd known that Leon had mob connections, but he'd kept the details to himself.

Leon was loaded, generous, and even courtly at the start. He'd been her best prospect at the time, especially as the feeling grew ever keener that she needed out of Vegas life before her tits sagged definitively, and her ass and jowls along with it. She would be thirty-seven on her next birthday. She was the oldest girl in the show. It was time for an exit ramp, and the sooner the better.

Amber had meant Leon to be her last professional liaison, just to top up her nest egg before she retired. To some place quiet and green, maybe, since she'd always lived in dry, sundrenched deserts. Someplace far from men's expectations, and their rages and their appetites and their fantasies about themselves. She'd made a living flattering and soothing men, pumping up their egos and various other parts of their anatomy. Now she just wanted to be left the hell alone.

She couldn't wait to get home and get this damned glue off her face. It itched and pulled. But she slowed as she noticed the butcher's shop and the bodega, belatedly remembering about food. She wasn't much of a cook, but even she could toss a chop into a pan and slice a tomato. Maybe she would get a potato and bake it in the Grudberg's' air fryer. A regular little Suzie Homemaker.

Amber went into the butcher's and got in line. A guy in a bloody apron was chopping ribs. The sound of the cleaver jolted her, slicing through meat, bone—

She stared at the white kitchen, spattered with blood. Michael was stretched out naked on the counter, writhing, pleading. Leon stood over him, his white shirt soaked with red, a spatter of blood on his chin, grinning. His eyes lit up as he lifted the cleaver. It flashed down…thunk. Michael shrieked…

"Ma'am? Ma'am! Are you all right?" Someone's hand touched her shoulder.

She was on her knees, gasping. Staring down at the dirty tile floor, making involuntary gasping and whistling sounds. There were shoes all around her. A forest of legs. A hand patted her back timidly. "Ma'am, are you ill? Should I call an ambulance?"

"No, no, no," she mumbled. "I'm fine. Just give me some air. Outside. Please."

They scrambled back to make way for her as she stumbled

21

out the door, cold smacking her in the face. Amber leaned over the gutter, retching. But there was nothing much in her stomach to heave. It just twitched and cramped. Staggering, she turned and took off, running for the shelter of the town-house. Flat out, top speed. Not limping and hobbling like Betty.

The fat suit chafed and bounced. The orthopedic shoes slapped the sidewalk. The big wool coat flapped in the cold wind. Betty's hat flew off, but Amber did not stop to retrieve it.

Chapter Three

Church of St. Anthony
Pasadena, California
Six Months Earlier

L eon shifted on the hard pew. Catholic funerals were a pain in the ass, literally. But the funeral of Ferdinando Sallustio, aka Fat Ferdie, could not be missed. His right-hand man, Michael Basile, sat next to him, one foot crossed over his knee, his gleaming black Italian leather shoe bouncing with so much wound-up nervous energy that if Leon grabbed that shoe, the twitch would burst out somewhere else. An eyelid would start to quiver. His fingers would drum, or his toe would tap, or he'd start humming. Leon was tempted to pistol whip the guy just to make him be still.

What was left of Fat Ferdie's family sat in the pews ahead of them, Tommy DiAngelo, Leon's boss, the head of the DiAngelo crime family in the center. Domi D'Amato, his numbers guy, the one who had taken over Fat Ferdie's job after his stroke, sat on one side of Tommy. Tommy's slut trophy wife, Claudia, a cold-eyed blonde, sat on the other.

Claudia was a looker, tall, regal and stacked. Leon felt a pang of regret that he hadn't brought Amber along. Stripper or not, Amber was a bombshell. Put her next to Claudia, and she would leave that frigid DiAngelo bitch in the dust. But, then again, Leon thought, hauling his piece around while conducting business cramped his style. Besides, who knew what the night might bring? He liked to leave his options open.

Which was why he'd been stringing along the two Feds who had been working on him, Special Agents Larry Wojniac and Steve Daly. For weeks, they had been playing Good Cop, Bad Cop, brandishing carrots and sticks. Promising him immunity, and a new start in the Witness Protection program if he would just turn on Tommy DiAngelo and tell them where all the bodies were buried. Truth was, he was tempted, and soon, he'd have to decide. When he did, a lot of options he had now would vanish. It was a tough call.

Leon had always thought of himself as a loyal soldier. Not a traitor or a rat. But he'd been knocked back down the ladder of success for the last two decades, and knocked hard, especially after what happened to Fat Ferdie. Tommy had never stopped punishing him for that, and he was sick of it. Unrewarded loyalty eventually went sour. Sad but true.

That casket up front was a hell of a thing, wide as a grand piano. It must have been custom made for Fat Ferdie. One would think being paralyzed and bedridden for twenty-six years would shrink a big guy down. Evidently not. There were no pallbearers. The casket rested on a rolling cart, probably also custom made. A casket like that would give the pallbearers hernias, if it didn't kill them outright. At the end of the service, four of Tommy DiAngelo's highest ranking guys rolled the casket solemnly down the aisle.

They stopped halfway so Stefy, Fat Ferdie's unmarried sister, could wail and sob and fling herself across the thing.

Dumb, grandstanding bitch. She should be happy for the poor guy that he had finally managed to kick the bucket. Death was a kindness for Ferdie. What kind of life had it been, staring at the ceiling, immobilized, wires cut, for twenty-six fucking years? Who even knew if he could see through those dim, cloudy eyes, or think at all? It had been a shit card to draw, no question about it. But Leon still hadn't forgiven Fat Ferdie for what his ill-timed stroke had done to Leon's career. Ferdie had fucked him so hard.

Stefy was winding up to her grand finale, howling and slapping at the casket, *thump, thump, thump.* He'd never liked that bitch. So cold and judgy, with her squinty dark eyes, pinched nostrils, and sour, puckered lips. The feeling was mutual. Stefy hated his guts after that bad night long ago, after Fat Ferdie's stroke. Not that Leon could blame her. Not his best moment.

Stefy's niece, a scrawny stick of a girl, tried to put her arm around her aunt. Stefy knocked her arm away and redoubled her wailing. Claudia stood up and made her way to the sobbing woman, murmuring in her ear. Finally, she pulled Stefy away so the casket could proceed, because for fuck's sake already.

The condolences line was stupidly long and slow. After an eternity of inching forward, Leon finally got to the top. Stefy and her even less attractive niece stood in front of him. Grabbing Stefy's hand, he murmured, *"Condoglianze."*

Stefy's swollen, red-rimmed eyes opened wide as she recognized him. Before Leon knew what was happening, she had snatched her hand away and slapped his face, shouting, "You? Pig! Take your *condoglianze* and stick them up your ass! How dare you come here after what you did? You bastard!"

"Stefy!" Claudia hissed, patting her shoulder and scowling at Leon. "A little decorum, please! This is a house of God!"

"That filthy animal threatened to cut me!" Stefy's voice

was shrill. "And I'm supposed to make nice? At my own brother's funeral? It's too much, Claudia! Too much!"

As Leon opened his mouth to defend himself, Tommy slid between him and Stefy. Knocking Leon out of line, the boss herded him swiftly to the other side of the pews.

"You shoulda known better than to get near her, Leon," Tommy muttered, *sotto voce*. "What the hell were you thinking, coming here?"

Claudia left Stefy sobbing in her niece's arms and minced toward them, her spike-heeled black patent pumps clicking on the stone floor. She crossed her arms and looked him up and down. The pose made her tits bulge. "Mad dogs should be kept on a shorter chain," she said. "He shouldn't be allowed around here, ever. It's not seemly. Poor Stefy shouldn't have to look at his face."

"Hey," Leon protested. "I just wanted to pay my respects to Ferdie."

"By ruining his funeral?" Tommy turned on him. "Get out of LA. Stay in Vegas, where I put you."

"That's the thing," Leon said. "I need to talk to you. I've been putting together some new business opportunities. Any chance we could find time for a meet?"

"No. I got too much going on." Tommy waved toward the door. "Go home and do your fucking job. If I want you to drum up new business, I'll tell you to do it. Now get lost, before Stefy comes over here and whacks your balls off. Nobody wants to see that."

Leon nodded, backing away. Tommy held his gaze and jerked his chin. And just like that, Leon was dismissed. As if he was some low-level chump asshole who didn't know shit. Some clueless dickhead, not a guy who'd busted his ass for thirty years for this motherfucker. Jesus. After all the things he'd done and seen. All the things he'd risked. All the things he knew.

As Leon backed toward the door, Michael sauntered over,

smiling and joking, oblivious to the undercurrents. He chatted with Tommy, flattering him, laughing dutifully at some stupid thing Tommy said. Not that Leon could hear what it was because the roaring in his ears was too loud. Then he realized that even if he could have heard it, he wouldn't have understood it, because they were speaking Italian. No, not even. Tommy and Michael were yukking it up in some Southern dialect, thick and fast and percussive.

Leon's Italian was weak. He'd come to it late, so he was always trailing, hoping he hadn't missed something crucial. His father was from the old country, but Papà had been the sullen type. And when he wasn't being sullen, he'd been out on the big oil tankers. He'd taken off for good when Leon was ten.

Mom had been a Pole, and she never shut up. If these goatfuckers had been speaking Polish, Leon would have been fine.

"Come on," he said, finally swatting Michael on the shoulder. "Let's go."

Michael hesitated, looking at Tommy, waiting for the boss to give him permission. Tommy gave it with a subtle chin thrust. *Go on. Humor the dumb bastard. Keep a close eye on him.* Leon read the silent instructions as if they were flashing neon.

Lying little fucker. So, Michael was managing him. Spying on him. Keeping tabs. And probably had been from the very fucking start. From the moment Tommy had paired them off, over two years ago. Now, Michael followed him out of the church with obvious reluctance. Two-faced little dipshit, with his lying lips and his shiny shoes and his designer suits. Talking shit about Leon to the boss. Making him look stupid.

He tossed Michael the keys. "You drive. Nata's. You know it, right?"

"Hell, yeah," Michael said, catching them single-handed.

Nata, also known as Natalya, was a whore Leon had frequented back in the day, when he'd been tight with Tommy, before the bad stuff went down. A time he remembered fondly. He'd been on the rise back then. Close to the boss. Life had been sweet.

Nata had moved on since then. She was now the madam of an exclusive brothel. Leon hadn't seen her in well over a decade and had never been to her most recent establishment. Tommy had exiled him from LA for that long.

Turning out of the church lot, Michael sped up to catch a green light. The prospect of a whorehouse jazzed him even more than usual. "So what's the story with Stefy?"

Leon shook his head. "Nothing. She's just a crazy bitch."

Michael shot him a look. "Fine. I'll ask the guys later on."

The thought of the guys talking about his shit behind his back made Leon's skin crawl. "Get fucked," he growled.

"I definitely will, at Nata's." Michael grinned. "Come on, Leon. Spill it."

Watching Michael out of the corner of his eye, it occurred to Leon that it might be better if the story came from him, rather than from one of the condescending fuckwits on Tommy's crew. They'd make him out to be the village idiot. Which he wasn't.

"It was twenty-six years ago," he said. "Tommy was making a killing with some big coke deals, and he needed ways to move money. I'd been grooming this banker guy who had a stash of bearer bonds and a big gambling problem. He owed Tommy over ten mil, so I arranged for him to pay with the bonds. Fat Ferdie was Tommy's accountant back then, so I gave them to him for safekeeping. Ten-point-four million."

Michael whistled.

"Then Ferdie had a stroke," Leon went on. "A bad one. He was alone in his house. By the time they found him and got him to hospital, he was too far gone to be helped much. He couldn't talk, couldn't move. Massive brain damage."

"Oh, my God. And nobody knew where those bonds

were? And Ferdie couldn't tell anyone? Shit! Couldn't they just cut open his safe?"

"They did, of course. But they weren't in Ferdie's safe. Or in Tommy's safe, or anywhere else that we could find. We tore Ferdie's place apart. Stefy was living next door. I questioned her. I pressed her pretty hard, I guess she hasn't forgiven me. Vengeful old hag. It's been twenty-six years, for fuck's sake."

"And since then? No one had a clue?"

"No," Leon said. "They stayed lost. Ferdie had logged all the serial numbers, and we had that list, but it wasn't like Tommy could go knock on the door at Fort Knox and ask for duplicates. He was pissed, and he needed someone to blame. So he blamed me."

"But it wasn't your fault! You couldn't have known Ferdie would have a stroke. And he was Tommy's accountant, not yours. It was Ferdie's fault for not telling Tommy or you where the money was! Why would anybody blame you?"

Leon shook his head. "It didn't matter. He couldn't get satisfaction out of Ferdie. So he sent me away so he wouldn't have to look at me."

"That sucks," Michael said forcefully.

Leon's teeth ground. Having this ass-kissing weasel feel sorry for him was the cherry on top of his day. "Yeah," he said. "So Fat Ferdie's bearer bonds passed into legend. Domi, the new accountant, set something up with an IT guy who works for the US Treasury, Frank Holland, or Holstein, something like that. Some loser Tommy had his hooks into. This Holstein sneaked in some code, so if someone cashes in one of the bonds, he gets a ping, and he tells Domi. But no one ever cashed one. They're still lost."

They pulled over in front of the large, somewhat decaying house in South Pasadena where Nata's girls plied their trade. Two burly, flint-eyed younger guys stationed at the front door waved them in. Leon had never met either of them, but he knew they were Tommy's guys, since Tommy owned the house. Nata was just the madam, though he'd been told that she swanned around like she owned the place.

A handful of girls lounged on display downstairs. Leon swept an appraising eye over them, deciding against redheads. He had that at home. What he wanted right now was a tall blond. An ice-princess type, like Claudia, to bend over and bang until she squealed.

When he looked around, a full-figured brunette in her fifties was gliding toward them, her heavily made-up face wreathed in smiles. "Leon!" She held out her arms. "So good to see you! So many years!" The familiar Russian accented voice was husky.

"Nata?" he said, startled.

She gave him a seductive smile as she stroked his cheek with her fingertips. "Am I so different?"

"More beautiful than ever," he said dutifully.

"Ahh. Sweet man. And who is your handsome friend?" She turned toward Michael. "I have seen him here before, but I did not know he was your friend, or I would have given him special treatment!"

"This is my associate," Leon said. "Michael."

"Michael." Nata ran an appraising eye over him. "Very good. We take good care of you both. Beautiful girls for you tonight. Beautiful. Come to my office! I give you a cognac while girls prepare? Or perhaps you would prefer whiskey?" She laughed. "Or very fine Russian vodka?"

A few minutes later, they were seated in a wood-paneled library. The room was decorated with erotic art, some fancy, some trash.

"So why you come to LA?" Nata asked, turning to hand Leon a glass. "They tell me you go to Vegas."

"I came back for Ferdie's funeral." He accepted the single malt and swirled it in the heavy crystal tumbler.

Nata's smile faded. "Ah, yes. Very sad. He was sweet man, Ferdie. Very kind. When he had stroke, I cried for him."

"You knew Ferdie?" Michael asked. He'd opted for the vodka.

"Oh yes. Many years ago, before he had stroke. Yes," Nata said, her voice softening. "He was very good client. He call me all the time."

"Called you where?" Leon asked. "Didn't you work for Rosa then?"

"Yes," Nata nodded, settling herself behind an ornate fake ormolu desk. "But Ferdie did not like Rosa's. He felt that girls laughed at him there, and he hated going up stairs. Remember those awful stairs? It took him long time to recover from stairs before we could, well, you know. So he would send car to bring me to his house. I tried to convince him to eat good." She sighed wistfully. "He was good man. Not pig, like others." She caught herself and lifted her glass, which Leon noticed was sparkling water. "Except you two, of course!"

Michael leaned forward. "Nata, did you ever see if Ferdie had some sort of secret hiding place in his house? You know, back in the day, when you were there?"

The hairs on the back of Leon's neck prickled. Of course, he would have asked Nata that question himself. It didn't really matter a damn who asked the question. But that in-your-face bastard. Stepping on Leon's toes, buzzing ahead a hundred miles an hour like a busy little boot-licking bee.

Sensing tension, Nata's dark eyes sharpened, darting from one to the other of them. "No," she said, finally. "It was many years ago. I go there, I take off my clothes, we fuck, I leave. Who cares now, anyway? The house was sold. Years ago. The sister sold it."

Leon stared at her. "You know me pretty well, right?"

"Right," Nata agreed. "Very well." She took a sip of her water. "Of course I know you. You are old friend."

"So you know my rep, right?"

"Yes," she said, her voice getting smaller. "Right."

"So you know that lying to me would not be good for your health?"

Color drained from her face, making her lipstick harsh against her suddenly ashen skin. "Yes," she muttered.

"So," Leon drained his glass. "I'll ask Michael's question again." He leaned forward, dropping his voice to make Nata work to hear him. "Did you ever see a hiding place in Ferdie's house when you visited him?"

Nata blinked. Seconds ticked by. "Yes." Her voice was a faltering whisper. "Maybe. In floorboards."

Leon sat very still, not taking his eyes off her face. Excitement exploded inside him. "Yeah? Which room?"

"His office. Back of house. Under radiator. I saw him put something down there. He yelled at me to go out when I came in. But I saw him there on floor, and thought he had fallen down. That he needed help to get up. Such a big man. And I see this hole in floor. Only time he was ever angry with me."

"What was in the hole?"

Nata had put down her drink, and was twisting her hands together. "I did not see." Her accent deepened. "Papers. Passports, maybe. I left to go do adult films at studio in San Diego after. I never saw Ferdie again. Or his house."

Leon stared at Nata, trying to picture it. Fat Ferdie, doing the deed with a beautiful Russian whore. Wonders never ceased. "What other girls besides you went to that house?"

Nata shook her head. "I recommended Carla when I knew I was leaving. But I don't think she ever went there. Ferdie had stroke very soon after. And then, well." She shrugged. "You know how it was for him."

Leon and Michael exchanged a glance. Michael looked pleased with himself. Taking credit for thinking of it all. Arrogant shithead.

A knock sounded. Nata jumped up. "The girls. Come in," she called. "Come in!"

Four women filed into the room. Two were tall blondes.

Another was a lush, golden-skinned Pacific Islander. The fourth was a waif-slender Asian girl with long black hair.

Leon kept his eye on Nata. The woman was no fool. She knew she'd bumped into something lethal. His body buzzed with a furious elation. He was closer than he'd been in twenty years. He looked at the blondes. "Both of them," he said.

"And you?" Nata turned to Michael.

Michael gave her a predatory smile. "You," he announced.

"What?" Nata's eyes widened. "Me? I don't take clients anymore."

"I'll pay. Double. I want you."

"What the hell, Michael? You got Mommy issues?" Leon was already on his feet, already following the blondes into the hallway. He was in a hell of a mood, he thought, banging the door behind him. After that funeral and Tommy's tongue-lashing, which had rubbed salt into old wounds, he was looking to take it out on somebody. Anybody. Or two.

And then, he was finally going to get his hands on those bonds.

The blondes, who had been giggling, stopped giggling quickly. By the time Leon was done, they were cowed, silent and shaking, makeup running down their faces. He would have to pay the house extra for damages, since neither of these girls would be working for the next few days. But it was worth it. A man had to blow off steam. Or else he would blow up completely.

Maybe, he thought as he reached for his clothes, if the Feds sent that prick Tommy away, he'd pay a visit to Claudia. Set some things straight. Teach her how the world worked, and what her place was in it.

"Get the fuck out," he snarled at the whores.

When the weeping girls had stumbled out, he shrugged on his shirt and stepped out to the balcony. Leon pulled the burner Wojniac had given him out of his pocket. He'd carried that thing around for a month. It was programmed with a single number.

Leon hit 'call.' Wojniac answered on the first ring. "Yeah?"

"It's me," Leon said. "I'm in."

"Good." He heard Wojniac let out a breath. "Good. Let's meet. Tonight."

"Not tonight," Leon said. "I'm out of town."

Wojniac grunted. "Okay." Leon could almost see him running his hand through his hair, or what was left of it. "Monday. The Bradley Arms. Suite 5005. Seven PM."

"Got it," Leon said, as he closed the call.

Surely by now Michael would have worked through his Oedipus complex, or whatever the fuck it was. But there was no answer when he knocked at Nata's office. He knocked again, then thudded the door with his palm.

"Mike!" He yelled, "Mikey, come on!"

When there was still no response, he turned the handle and pushed the door open.

Nata was sprawled on the library's red velvet couch. Her naked body was covered in blood. Her throat had been cut. Her dark, empty eyes looked dull and unsurprised.

That piece of shit. Michael didn't have mommy issues. That sneaky son of a bitch had tortured the address of Ferdie's old house out of her.

He pulled a tissue from the box on Nata's desk. Her purse was by the chair. Using the tissue, Leon rummaged around until he found her key fob. That fucker would have taken the car, so he'd need to use hers. He dropped it in his pocket. As he was leaving, he noticed the two glasses, one empty of whiskey, the other still half full of vodka and melting ice. He turned back to the desk, pulled another Kleenex, grabbed his own glass, shoved it in his jacket pocket, and left Michael's. Plenty of prints all over it.

Leon let himself out and went down the back staircase and into the yard. He clicked the fob in the alleyway outside until the headlights of a black BMW blinked back at him. The car was nice. Nicer even than his. Settling into the seat, he let the engine purr for a second, then he put the car in gear and headed for Ferdie's.

The house was in Fair Oaks. Leon parked a block away. The neighborhood had come down since he'd been here last. The trees were bigger and shaggier; the bushes overgrown. Plenty of cover.

He had no idea who had bought Ferdie's old house, nor did he care. All he cared about was that it hadn't been torn down and gentrified, or some shit. But it still looked the same. The lights were on.

Circling the house, Leon saw that the back door hung wide open. He slipped inside like a shadow.

The first body was in the kitchen. A big, pot-bellied man in a bathrobe lay in a pool of blood. Splatter was everywhere. Leon tip-toed around, keeping his shoes clean. The second body was in the bedroom. A woman. Michael had snapped her neck.

What had been Ferdie's office was now a yoga room that stank of essential oils and scented candles and mindfulness shit. Yoga gear was strewn over the back of a chair. Leon had no idea where Michael was. He dropped to his knees where he thought Ferdie's desk had been. Someone had rolled back a yoga mat. There was a blood smear on the molding. Leon pried at the floorboard, finding it loose, already knowing what wouldn't be there. Sure enough, the hole was empty.

The rage that had been brewing in Leon for years, ever since Fat Ferdie's stroke and Tommy deciding to blame him for all the shit on God's earth, exploded into something monstrous. He was furious that two stiffs out there were already dead. He wanted to tear them apart himself. Leon got to his feet, wishing he had torn Fat Ferdie's slack, drooling jaw right off his skull years ago, when he had the chance. That bastard could have found a way to communicate where the bonds were somehow. But, no. He hadn't, out of pure fucking spite. And now, death had put him beyond Leon's reach.

Ferdie, yes. But not Michael. Michael, that little sneaky two faced bastard, was still on this mortal plane.

Something Tommy had said many years ago flashed through his mind. How Leon had potential, but was too slow on the uptake. That he needed to sharpen up.

Those fuckers were about to find out how razor sharp he could be.

Chapter Four

Milton, Connecticut
Present Day

"For fuck's sake, could you get that kid to shut up?"

Victor's voice came from the living room. Belinda could hear the muted clink of ice cubes in his scotch as she jiggled Faith, cuddling and cooing with increased desperation. 'That kid,' he always called her. Like she wasn't his kid.

She wanted to say that to him, but she didn't dare. It would be stupid, destructive, and a waste of energy. Besides, she understood where he was coming from. It had been a long day. He was under so much stress with these strange hassles they'd been having, and on top of it all, he hadn't experienced the mental and emotional preparation of pregnancy, birth and infancy. Henry had done all that. So poor Victor had inherited this huge responsibility all at once, in a sort of intensive shock therapy. It was no wonder he wasn't very paternal with Faith yet.

They just had to get through this period of adjustment. She was sure it was only a matter of time. Faith was his child, after all. There had never been any doubt. But the genetic test that Eleanor, his ex, had demanded had clinched it. Which was fortunate, since she'd been married to Henry for three years. Victor had needed some convincing that the baby was his. Science had spoken, thank God.

"What the hell is wrong with that kid?" Victor appeared in the nursery doorway, his face flushed. "She never stops screaming." He tossed back the last of his drink. "It can't be normal. This constant whining is driving me out of my mind."

"She's not whining." Belinda was careful to keep her voice low and even. Victor hated it when she was shrill. "She's just hungry. She was too fussy at the daycare to eat anything. Holly told me she just spat everything out."

She laid Faith down in the crib. The child proceeded to wail and writhe. Victor grabbed the bottle of formula from the outside pocket of the diaper bag and stuck it, ungently, into Faith's mouth.

"C'mon, kid. Eat."

Faith squirmed away, making choking sounds. Belinda snatched the bottle. "Stop!" She snapped. "You're making it worse!"

"How could it possibly be any worse?"

Taking a deep breath, Belinda narrowly avoided rolling her eyes. How could it be worse, her ass. It could always be worse, particularly with him just standing there with that look of disgust in his eyes while she stumbled her way through mothering a fussy, nervous toddler. He didn't need to tell her that his own daughter repelled him. That he hated everything about her; the food, the smells, the noise, the clutter, and the confusion. The pharmacy and the daycare, and the doctors and the pink plastic sippy cups. The growth chart, and the vitamin gummies, and the toys, and the bibs, and the laundry.

All of it, every bit of it, was Belinda's problem. Victor didn't lift so much as a finger. Not once. Not ever. He just wouldn't do it. The car seat requirements alone drove him crazy. He refused outright to fit a car seat into his car. So, apart from everything else, Belinda did all the driving, too.

She would never dare say such things out loud. But part of her couldn't help but compare. Henry, for all his clumsy strangeness and odd tics, had been all over baby Faith. No detail had bored him, however small. At the time, it had struck her as a little weird. But then again, most things about Henry had been weird. The whole situation had been weird from the start.

Victor had taken notice of Henry after Henry designed a brilliant database for him years ago, back when Victor was just starting the long, drawn-out process of divorcing his wife. Belinda and Victor had already been together, of course. She'd been crazy about Victor. Ready to do anything for him, literally.

Even to seduce Henry. And eventually, to marry him. All of it had been Victor's idea. Henry married to Belinda meant Belinda could control him, and all the weird tech shit he made. Which they could then steal. And use to steal even more.

Victor liked it when she had sex with Henry in front of the cameras they'd hidden all over the house. He had particularly liked critiquing Henry's performance, in detail, then showing her how much better he was at whatever Henry had done with her.

Afterward, Victor would light up a cigarette and ask her if she'd faked an orgasm with Henry. Or was she really a bad, dirty little girl who liked it? Especially when she knew he was watching.

I'm doing it for you, she told him over and over. *Because you asked me to and I love you.*

Yeah, but I didn't tell you to like it, bitch.

Victor was the one who had liked it. He'd get so worked up watching her have sex with Henry that when he got his hands on her, he'd practically brain her against the head-board. When Belinda furnished their new master suite, she'd made sure to choose a fully upholstered bed.

Getting pregnant had been an accident, one she didn't have a chance to correct because Henry had noticed right away. He'd been incredibly excited, so Victor had told her to continue the pregnancy. She wondered sometimes if it had ever even occurred to Victor that her being pregnant meant him becoming a parent.

Pushing the unhelpful thought aside, she asked, "Did you talk to the private investigator you told me about?"

Victor rattled the ice-cubes in his now empty glass. "You still think it's Henry who's messing with us? Come on. You give him too much credit. He escaped eight months ago. If he wanted to hurt us, he would have done it by now. Why mess around with our credit rating? He's a fucking fugitive, for Christ's sake. Why would he waste his time bugging us?"

"Revenge," Belinda said. "I know you hate it when I say this, but he's brilliant. He's trying to break us. Drive us crazy. Death by a thousand cuts, and all that."

"Death? You think that geek Henry Devlin is capable of killing? Pussyface Henry, who changes diapers and asks you nicely before he fucks you? Is that what you want, Bel? Do you want me to beg like a dog?"

"Oh, for God's sake, Victor," she said, teeth clenched. "Please, don't start. Things are bad enough as it is. Anyway, I only did all that because you asked me to."

"Yeah, Bel. I could see how you were suffering, when he was pounding you from behind. I was watching. Remember?"

"Victor. Please." Her voice caught. "I can't deal with this right now."

"For fuck's sake!" He slammed the glass down on the changing counter. "Don't fall apart on me now! Get a grip! Stop seeing boogeymen in dark corners. Henry is a dumb-ass. He has nerd-smarts, yes. But he's not world-smart."

"He escaped from prison," she said. "That's not dumb-ass."

"Yeah. Did it turn you on? Did it, Bel? That big brain? Was it stimulating for you?"

"Don't," she snapped. "Let's be serious. Yes, it's been eight months since Henry disappeared out of that prison van. But our problems didn't start until five months ago. When did the first identity thing happen? The thing with the bank?"

"Five months ago," Victor said, his voice sullen.

"Right," Belinda said. "He had to find his feet. At first, he'd be busy just figuring out how to stay alive. He'd have to find somewhere to live. Get ID. Find a way to make money. Get the right stuff, computers, whatever. Internet. Routers. VPNs. Everything he needs to do his thing."

"Get real, Bel," Victor was clearly bored with this conversation. "You really think he'd be angry enough to kill us?"

Belinda bit her lip. Henry had never been aggressive to her. Just an enigma. The way his mind worked was unfathomable to her. "I don't know," she said, finally. "But if I were him, I would be. You said he'd be behind bars for thirty years. I thought that part of it was over. That he was gone. We'd never have to deal with him again."

"Well, I didn't expect him to bust out of prison. In any case, we have passports for you and Faith now. So if it comes to it, and Henry the Bogeyman does come for us, we can take off at a moment's notice."

"And go where?" Belinda had never left the country. She was deathly afraid of flying. The one time they had flown to San Francisco on a romantic escape for two, she'd thought she was going to die.

Victor had just laughed at her. Told her to take some beta-blockers and suck it up.

"We'll figure something out," he said. "Diamonds are great for travel. And Mirror, Mirror could come in handy, too.

Everybody loves a deep-fake. I could sell the service anywhere. Ecuador. Brazil. Shit, Europe, too.'

Ecuador? Belinda tried to smile, but it didn't come easily. She'd been in on the whole thing from the start, of course. She'd installed the keystroke logging software on Henry's computer so Victor and his tech guys could get the passwords and take control of the system. She was the one who let them into the house when Henry was out so they could load the malware that had to originate from Henry's IP address. She'd been a regular Mata Hari, right at the heart of all of it.

But she hadn't enjoyed it. Not like Victor did. She got no particular kick out of destroying Henry. He had never hurt her. All he'd done was love her and Faith and be so damn trusting and innocent that at times it infuriated her. It was like he was on his knees, just begging to get screwed over.

So, what did he expect? With Victor breathing down her neck, what else could she do?

So, yeah. Would Henry figure it all out and would Henry be angry? Yes, he would. Murderously angry. She didn't get why Victor didn't understand that, but she'd taken some precautions herself. She'd planted tracking devices on both the stroller and the car seat, just in case Henry decided to punish her through Faith.

Victor didn't need to know. He would say she was overre-acting, and maybe she was. After all, Victor was also brilliant, in his own way. The delicious glow she got from Victor's approval was worth any moral misgivings. She lived for those moments. Though Victor had been very stingy with praise since Henry broke out of prison.

She was weak, and she knew it, but she just had to have him. Victor pushed her to a place she craved. He brought her to her knees, which was exactly where she needed to be to get off.

Having sex with Henry while Victor watched had excited her. She'd felt she was giving Victor something darkly erotic, something only she could provide. It was undignified, kinky, dirty, wrong. But there was nothing she could do about it. Self-loathing didn't change it, so why bother hating herself?

"Let's go out to eat," Victor said suddenly.

Belinda looked around the nursery, bewildered. "How?" She asked. "With her in this state and no babysitter? I can't get someone at this hour, and we can't bring her to a restaurant."

"We'll just leave. She's in the crib, right? She can't get out. The house is warm and safe, the door is locked. She'll cry and fall asleep while we eat prime rib and grilled asparagus with a nice Bordeaux at Flannery House. Followed by crème brûlée. Just the two of us. Like old times."

Belinda felt a sharp pang of longing at the thought of snowy tablecloths and wine glasses glinting in the candlelight. The gleam of the silver. And Victor's ice-gray eyes, watching her hungrily as she slipped a foot out of her high heels so she could stroke his erection under the table.

Her reverie was shattered by an ear-splitting wail. "We can't just leave her here," Belinda said bleakly.

The smile of invitation faded from Victor's eyes as suddenly as it had appeared. "Get that kid to shut up and get into the bedroom. You have five minutes."

It was more like twenty-five by the time she got Faith down, programmed her favorite lullaby at just the right level, dimmed the lights so the projector could send pink ponies dancing and blue bunnies hopping across the walls so she could finally tip-toe away.

Belinda hurried into the bathroom, fingers shaking as she freshened up. She splashed her face, brushed her teeth, slicked on lip gloss, and struggled into a cami and panties. She knew Victor would make her pay for waiting. It was just the way Victor was.

He was on the bed, stroking himself in preparation, when

Belinda finally walked into the bedroom. His face was hard. "You're late," he said.

It's not my fault, and you know it, goddamn it. I'm trying so hard and you are not helping. You aren't doing shit for me, or for your baby. Even before the words sprang up, she swallowed them down.

"I'm sorry," she said instead, in her best wispy, little-girl voice.

"Get over here!" Victor thumped the side of the bed.

It hurt, as it always did when he was in one of his moods. Victor sealed his hand over her mouth. "Ah, ah, ah," he warned. "Don't make a sound, or you'll wake up your brat."

When he finally rolled off, they lay there panting for a long time. Eventually, Victor turned to her. "Well?" he said, already impatient. "What are you waiting for? Go get the ice cream."

Belinda flinched. The ice cream had been hers and Henry's thing. Henry had been trying to help her quit smoking. Victor had seen it on the cameras, and taken it, just like he took everything else, because he was voracious. It had been one of the things about him that made her tremble with excitement, longing to be devoured.

Padding barefoot into the kitchen, Belinda grabbed a couple of bowls, found some spoons, and pulled open the freezer drawer. But no cold puff wafted up to soothe her hot, chafed face. Looking down, she realized water was seeping across the floor and pooling around her feet. She put her hand in the freezer. Everything was wet, soft. Melted.

"What the fuck is taking so long?" Victor appeared in the kitchen entryway, naked and scowling.

A howl of misery came from the nursery. Faith was awake.

Something squeezed in her chest, like talons tightening around her lungs. No breath even to sob. She shook her hair forward to hide her face.

Victor hated tears.

Chapter Five

"Just park right here, under the tree."

The driver glared at Amber over his shoulder. "You shoulda told me we was driving all the way to Jersey, lady. You pickin' someone up here, or what?"

"Not exactly," she said.

"Well," He huffed. "Are we waitin' long?"

"Not too long. A few minutes."

He huffed again, but she caught him checking her out in the rearview, and gave him a big, wide 'what-the-fuck-are-you-looking-at' smile. Complete with bold lipstick. Donna's favorite.

Amber was proud of today's persona. Donna DePilato, wife of a very successful building contractor, lived in a cul-de-sac of gaudy McMansions in South Cambrook, New Jersey. In her late forties, Donna had bobbed, bouncing dark hair, and liked things that sparkled. Big earrings, sequins, spangles, anything metallic. Including her generously applied eye shadow, which combined so nicely with smoky liner and straight-out-of-the-nineties dark lip-lining pencil, filled out with pink, pearly gloss. She also liked Zumba and Aqua-gym and drinks with her girlfriends. Lots of drinks. Which, combined with the fact that she was a very good cook, did nothing to reduce the size of her impressively large ass.

Amber wondered how Donna would hold up under Blackbeard's scrutiny. Of course, Blackbeard was no normal observer. And he was actively scanning for her now, so he hardly counted. Still, Donna just might fool him for a few minutes longer than usual.

Aw, crap. The whole point of this insane project was to build some kind of life where she would never have to seek a man's approval. And here she was, obsessing about some laser-eyed rando freak who haunted public libraries.

A clot of SUVs had pulled up in front of the Cheltenham Academy. She needed to get closer to them. Closing the back door, she rapped on the front window. "Can you wait right here for me?" The driver gave her a long-suffering look, and she blew him a kiss. "No more than ten minutes, promise," she assured him.

Girls and boys dressed in dark blue school uniforms were swarming into the academy. Amber picked up the bakery box she'd brought along for cover and followed them up the steps. At the top, she stood smiling indiscriminately, scanning the kids and the cars until she saw a big black Navigator nose its way up the drive and double-park right in front of the school. A big thick-necked guy in a suit got out and opened the door for Ettore Graziano, Trix's nephew. Tori was twelve and skinny, with pallid skin and limp dark hair and shadows under his eyes, all of which made the poor little guy look totally miserable.

The Navigator idled, as the driver, whom Amber could see now had a heavy fold of fat around his neck, slammed the door and walked Ettore up the steps to the school. As they passed her and disappeared inside, the Navigator suddenly backed up. Someone yelled. Several people jumped as the big black car jerked to a stop and just as suddenly pulled forward again. Amber hustled back to her ride.

"See that big black SUV turning in the parking lot down there? Follow it!" she barked, jumping into the back seat. "But hang back a little."

"Lady, I don't want to be part of some creepy stalking thing."

"It's not like that." The Navigator was in danger of disappearing. "Please, just do it. I'll tip very generously."

The driver huffed, but they took off, staying a conservative half-block behind the Navigator. Which was essential, because Amber had found records of all sorts of properties owned by the Graziano family, but she'd had no way of knowing which of them Tori and his grandmother lived in right now.

A couple of times, the driver let too many cars get between them and the Navigator. Once Amber even thought they had lost it. But the Graziano's SUV was big enough and slow enough to keep in sight, and after about fifteen minutes, she had a pretty good idea of which house they were heading for. Thanks to Google Earth, she'd studied every Graziano property until she knew them intimately. The drives, the grounds, the outbuildings.

South Cambrook itself had a pokey, small-town feel. After doing time in Idaho with Leon in the WITSEC safe-house, any small town made her feel like someone was holding an arm over her windpipe. Thank God for the constant churning noise of New York City.

Amber leaned forward. "Slow down."

The driver obliged as the Navigator turned into a driveway. It stopped at a big iron gate, which was opening. The Navigator went through as they drove by.

"Stop here," Amber said, after a few hundred yards. "Wait for me. I won't be long."

The driver gave her a slit-eyed look. She sighed and pulled three twenties from inside her coat. "Another sixty when I get back," she said. "Promise. If you wait."

"You casing the joint, or what?" He snatched the bills.

Amber slammed the door on that rude question and started back toward the Graziano house. The champagne pink sweat suit was warm enough in the cold wind if she race-walked. She picked up her pace, lifting her knees and twitching her foam-enhanced ass as she approached the spiky, wrought-iron gate.

Beyond it, a long, curving driveway led to a big, carefully manicured, Tudor-style house. A high wall surrounded the property. Video cameras were trained on the gate and mounted at various intervals, watching the street. The place was a fortress. Which should have been no surprise. Trix had frequently complained that the Grazianos were a deeply nervous and suspicious family.

Amber hustled. Knees up. Chop-chop. Someone was probably paid to monitor those cameras, so she didn't dare display any overt interest. A white van passed her, then slowed as it approached the gate to the Graziano property. It stopped and the driver's door opened. An older woman leaned out and pushed the buzzer. Green and blue lettering along the van's side read MENZIES & SONS. DEEP CLEANING SINCE 1967. FEEL THE DIFFERENCE FOR YOURSELF.

The gate ground open, and the van disappeared inside. Amber walked on, noticing more cameras on the wall.

Serafina Graziano, mother of Trix and grandmother of Tori, was the matriarch of a family with ties to organized crime all over the tri-state area. The old lady was a ball-breaker extraordinaire, and the Grazianos were a family not to be messed with. Not that she was proposing to mess with them, or even take anything that genuinely belonged to them.

All she wanted was what Michael had hidden here. Whatever that might be.

This thing had evidently belonged to Leon. Or Leon certainly thought it did. He was murderously angry that it had been stolen from him.

Right before all the trouble began, Trix had come back to

visit her mom and Tori. She'd brought Michael with her so she could introduce him to her family, but it had gone very badly. Serafina Graziano sent them packing with harsh words. Trix got on a plane and flew back to Vegas to lick her wounds. Michael went off to conduct some mysterious business in Florida. He was supposed to be on his way home that fateful night that Leon intercepted him.

Tigre di Tori! Tigre di Tori! Tigre di Tori! Amber had heard Michael say it over and over while Leon was hacking at him. Those had been his last words. Tori's tiger.

Trix had talked all the time about Tori, her maladapted little nephew. She and Amber had even had a few laughs about his unfortunate name. Even back in the old country, nobody inflicted "Hector" on a kid anymore. According to Trix, the Grazianos specialized in clunky, antique names. Her own name was Beatrice, which she hated. Her mother's was Serafina. Her brother was Ignazio. Saddling their kids with unbeautiful names was a Graziano family tradition.

Hector. Ettore. Tori. That's what Amber had heard Michael saying. She was sure of it. Leon, on the other hand, had heard "*torri*." Towers. She'd snooped on his laptop and seen the internet searches. Tigre Torri, Torri Tigri. Tiger Towers, Tower Tigers. Leon couldn't hear the difference between a single and a doubled consonant. Thank God. He had been on the wrong track, which was where he had to stay if little Tori Graziano was going to survive. Sad-eyed, clueless, twelve-year-old Tori didn't stand a chance against a mad dog like him.

Sadly, neither did Amber. Not on her own, with no money, no identity other than Trix's borrowed license, and the Feds and the US Marshals on her trail. To say nothing of the DiAngelo crew, who were all fired up to kill her, too. Whatever Leon had been trying to pry out of Michael, she needed it for herself, and for Trix. If only to keep them alive and out of Leon's grasp. That was all she had to work with. No Plan B.

Trix should have avoided Michael like the plague. She should also have stayed in Jersey, protected by her family. She should never have run off to Vegas to try to make it as a dancer. Trix had no real talent for dancing. Neither did Amber. Showgirls and kept women, that's what they had come down to.

Trix had a particular talent for landing bad boyfriends, though Amber understood why she had been attracted to Michael. Trix was officially kept by rich, stodgy Kenji, who bored her. Michael was forty years younger than Kenji. He was dashing and funny and flashed a lot of money around.

Just thinking about that night in the kitchen made Amber's stomach lurch. It still astonished her that Leon hadn't killed her right then for seeing him do what he'd done. Instead, he'd dragged her to a wedding chapel on the Strip a few days later, and after witnessing how handy he was with a meat cleaver, she'd clearly understood that 'no' was not an option.

Then, to her shock, he turned on Tommy DiAngelo, and before Amber knew what was happening, the US Marshals showed up, and she'd been escorted to Waylon Mills, Idaho, to live that dull, stifling little ranch house with her husband, Leon. Whose name had been changed to Jeff Hinkley, of all things.

Overnight, all her savings, all her plans, gone. Witness Protection took her old credit cards, her old passport, her old everything. Even if she could have figured out how to access her own money, the DiAngelo family would have heard about it, found her, and killed her. She didn't think they'd listen if she tried to explain that she had nothing to do with ratting on Tommy.

They'd still kill her. And if he found her, Leon would kill her, too.

The burner she kept in the inside pocket of any coat she wore vibrated against her chest. She stopped and pulled it out. The country code was 81. Japan. Hoo-boy.

Trix. Talking to her friend was dangerous, but Amber hadn't spoken to a single person she knew in the three months since she'd said goodbye to Leon on her way to work and gotten the hell out of Idaho. She raised the phone to her ear. "Yeah?"

"Amber?" Trix's teary voice wobbled.

"It's dangerous for us to talk. And I still don't have any news." She lowered her voice, even though she was alone in the street.

"I couldn't stand it anymore!" Trix wailed. "I know! I'm sorry. But I had to know what was going on. And things aren't good with Kenji. He hates it when I cry, and he hates it when I drink, but I can't just be happy on command, just because someone wants me to, you know?"

"Uh huh," Amber said. Then, guilty, added. "Yeah. Yes. I do know."

"How am I supposed to just act normal?" Trix's voice caught. "God, I just miss Michael so much. He was going to marry me, you know? He was going to get me away from all that fake, crazy Vegas bullshit. He was going to get me out of the life. We were going to go off and live someplace beautiful. Maybe even have a kid. The whole deal."

Amber had her doubts about that dreamy, soft-focus plan. Not that it mattered now. Michael was dead. No need to burden Trix with her cynicism. "You have to be tough," she said. "Hang on."

"After my mom had her freak-out, we went to the airport," Trix's voice waterlogged with tears. "I didn't want to go back. To Vegas, I mean. I just wanted to stay with him, leave it all behind, right away. But he said he had to go down to West Palm Beach to take care of a thing. I was crying too hard to even go through the security line, and do you know what Michael said to me?"

Amber let out a silent sigh. "What did he say, honey?"

"He said, he was going to work for our future," Trix forced

out, between sobs. "He said, there was a bridge leading to a happy ending for us, but someone was standing in the way, so he had to go take care of it so we could be free. Then Leon just kills him. Just like that. Boom! My future. My life. Gone. Just gone."

"Baby, I'm so sorry. I would have stopped it if I could."

"Please. Just tell me. Does Leon know about me? Or Tori?"

"Listen, Trix," Amber said gently. "Listen carefully, okay? I split from Leon more than three months ago. I don't know what he's thinking or planning, or what he's found out about you, or anybody. All I know is, if he can find me, he will kill me. I didn't know his thoughts before, when I was living with him, either, to be honest. He's just not the confiding type."

"You must have seen something," Trix pleaded. "Or heard something! You were the only person he had to talk to in that place! Tori's just a helpless kid. He can barely survive my mom, let alone Leon Gambelli. Just tell me if you think he'll make a move!"

"I don't know, Trix. I'm thousands of miles away from him now."

Trix was silent for a moment. Then she asked, "Where? Are you on the East Coast?" Her voice hardened. "That's real close to Tori. You could draw Leon there if he hunts you down. You shouldn't have gone to the East Coast, Amber!"

"I can't talk about that now, Trix. Look, are you sure you can't just ask your mom to look around? See if she can find anything that's out of place? It makes sense, right?"

"God, no." Trix's voice was vehement. "If she found whatever Michael left at the house, no matter what it is, she'd keep it from me just to punish me. She'd convince herself she was doing the right thing by taking it herself, just to teach me a lesson. She just can't help herself. She's that angry with me."

"Okay, okay. Just wondering if there was a simpler solution to all this."

"Well, duh." Trix sounded like her old self for a minute. "If there was, I'd come home and look for whatever it was Michael left myself. But Mom threw me out."

"I know. That's why I told you to go with Kenji," Amber reminded her.

"But I can't stand it here! Michael's dead, poor little Tori's on the block. And I'm halfway around the goddamn world in this fucking apartment, listening to clocks tick! I'm going fucking nuts!"

"I'm sorry," Amber soothed. "I'm so sorry babe. I am. I know it's hard. I was only trying to protect you and Tori both. But how long do you think you'd last if Leon came at you? Want to take a guess?"

Trix began to cry. "I can't do this," she said. "You know, like, be professional with Kenji. Not when I feel this bad. And Kenji's so sick of it, he might cut me loose."

"No!" Amber was alarmed. "Pull yourself together, Trix! Give him the old razzle-dazzle."

"I can't," Trix whimpered.

Amber thought furiously. She had to throw Trix a bone, or she was going to snap. "I don't think Leon knows Tori even exists, babe," she said. "Really, I don't. I think he misheard what Michael said. A lot of it was in Calabrese. I barely understood it myself."

"But how can you be sure?"

"I looked at Leon's internet searches. He was looking for *Torre Tigre, Tigre Torre, Torri Tigre*. A tower, Trix. Not Tori. He's barking up the wrong tree."

"But didn't you hear Michael say Tori's name?" she asked, her voice small.

"Yeah, I did. But Leon never knew Tori was a person. So he's still safe."

"Well, I don't know about any tiger stuff," Trix sniffed. "I didn't see anything like that in Tori's room when I was home.

But I have to find a way out of this place. Amber, I just have to."

"We will," Amber said. "Come on, Trix. We're the femme fatale squad. No mortal man can withstand our blazing power, right? Just do your thing. Kenji won't know what hit him. You run the show. You decide. You're the boss. That's how we do it. Remember?"

"Yeah," Trix said faintly. "Yeah. I remember."

Amber was almost at the main street, so she turned around and headed back toward her ride. "I gotta go," she said. "Hang in there, and don't call. It's not safe. I'll call you when I can, okay?"

"Okay." Trix sounded lost. "Bye," she whispered.

"Keep it together, Trix. Be strong. You can manage Kenji." Amber closed the call, staring down at the burner phone.

Trix wasn't the brightest bulb. At times Amber had felt more like an exhausted babysitter than a girlfriend. But it had been nice to feel needed by someone who actually knew who she was as a person.

It had probably been stupid to give Trix that number. She should get rid of the phone. But if she did, she'd be all alone, spinning through empty space like a stray meteor that no one cared about enough to name or even map.

Am I invited to your pity party? Mamma's sharp, accented voice popped into her head. Mamma had always hated it when Amber moped.

She was almost back at the car. Dropping the phone into her pocket, she pulled open the door, slid in, and dug out three more twenties. Passing them to the driver, she said, "Let's go back to the city."

"Where in the city?"

Amber considered the question. Getting inside the Graziano house was going to be a real ordeal. If Serafina had been a man, she might have been able to employ her womanly wiles, but no.

What she needed was a team. Unfortunately, people with talent commanded top dollar. She could try to get a legitimate job at the cleaning company that had gone to the Graziano house. What had it been called? Menzies. That was it. But there were too many variables. Were they hiring? Would her ID hold up? Beatrice Graziano had no demonstrable experience as a cleaner. No references, no employment record. If she were running the Menzies outfit, she wouldn't hire Trix. And even if they did, even if, by some miracle, she could get the cleaning people to hire her, how long would it take to inveigle herself onto the Graziano house crew?

All those things were out of her control. It would be a long game with an entirely hypothetical prize. Pie in the sky. Which she didn't have time for. Because her time was running down, grain by grain.

"Take me to the Rose Reading Room at Forty-Second and Fifth," she said. She'd just see how long it took Blackbeard to spot Donna DePilato.

That was more fun than sitting around moping.

Chapter Six

The Harry Reid International Airport
Las Vegas, Nevada
Five and a half months earlier

I n the end, it had been easy to take Michael down.
Almost an insult to Leon's skills.
Michael had come back to Las Vegas only two weeks
after robbing him in LA, and he'd come without taking any
precautions or even using a fake ID. Leon got a call from his
guy in the airport when Michael's name turned up on the
flight manifest for a flight from West Palm Beach. And the
dumb twat had even gotten himself good and toasted on the
flight. He was so busy flirting with a cute flight attendant; he
saw and noticed nothing else.

Michael was playing the big man now, offering to wine
and dine her. Show her around, but he couldn't even get that
right. The flight attendant refused a ride to her hotel. Instead,
she stuck with her co-workers. The decision saved her life and
simplified Leon's. Small favors.

Disguised with a hat, fake beard and long coat, Leon had
picked Michael up as soon as he came through baggage claim.

He'd been so close he'd even heard the woman blowing him off. That was how out of it that dumb shit was. Michael barely waited until the flight attendant took off before he'd pulled out his phone and called his girlfriend.

"Yeah, babe…my flight was delayed…yeah, so sorry…oh, me too, doll. I wanted to get back to you. I'll make it up to you as soon as possible, okay?…yeah, yeah. I know. First thing tomorrow. The first flight I can get to Vegas, okay? I'll be on it. You bet."

Leon had been vaguely aware of the girlfriend. It wasn't like he gave a shit about Michael's love life, but he had no idea how serious it was, or how much Michael might have confided in her, or even who she was. Those were among the many questions he would have for Michael tonight, when they got down to talking. Or he could just look her up on Michael's phone log. There would be no loose ends this time.

Fingering the hypodermic in his coat pocket, Leon followed Michael, who still hadn't noticed him, into the parking garage. Leon pretended to head for the car beyond Michael's as he pried the plastic cap off the needle. His eyes swept the place to make sure they were alone. Then he walked up behind the guy as he popped the trunk. "Hey, Michael," he said in a casual tone.

Michael spun around. He had just time to make a thin squeak as the needle stabbed into his neck.

Michael sagged fast. It was no trouble at all to tip him into the trunk.

Leon dug the car keys out of Michael's coat pocket and threw his carry-on into the back seat after searching it swiftly, just to make sure Michael wasn't stupid enough to carry the bearer bonds around with him. The little shit had been stupid enough to take them in the first place, then run around drunk in an airport chasing tail. So really, who knew?

Unfortunately, Michael was not stupid enough to have the bonds on him. That would have been too easy. Leon swore softly as he slid behind the wheel of Michael's girly little black sports car. He should have been on the other side of the world by now. The Feds, the DiAngelo's, Michael, they all underestimated him. That jerk Wojniac and his sidekick actually believed that he, Leon Gambelli, had agreed to fuck over Tommy and pit himself against a criminal syndicate in exchange for some bullshit Witness Protection life in Nowheresville, USA.

His plan had been more along the lines of silk pillows, cold drinks, and sea breezes with Amber, tanned and smiling, dressed to the nines. Or, better yet, undressed. All he needed was the bearer bonds to make it happen. And Michael was going to give them to him, if it was the last thing he did.

Which it definitely would be.

Leaving the airport, Leon drove carefully, at the legal speed limit, to the derelict warehouses in North Las Vegas where he'd left his car. Slogging it on foot to a convenience store where he could get a cab to collect him and drop him at the airport had been a pain, but worth it. No one would find Michael's car here for a good long while. Digging that hole out near Lake Meade had been a pain, too. His hands were blistered. That was the downside of secrecy. No grave-digging grunts to do the scut work. Leon had considered having Michael dig his own grave, of course, but that would have been a whole fucking drama, and would have taken more time than he wanted to spend. Besides, it was too risky. Michael was a quick little fucker, and not always stupid. Arming him with a shovel wouldn't have been a good idea.

So, he dug the hole himself. Just like he had to do everything himself, if he wanted it done right.

Pulling up beside his own car, Leon killed the engine, got out and dragged the huge rolling suitcase out of his own trunk. Michael was a short guy. He probably weighed less than one-fifty soaking wet. It was still a challenge to wrestle him in the suitcase, get him all folded up and zip-tied and gagged.

Then he had heaved that motherfucker into the back of his car.

Amber was out with her girlfriends tonight at a bachelorette party, probably getting wasted and tucking twenties into the G-string of some male exotic dancer. He didn't love that scenario, but the party was well-timed. There wasn't all that much he loved about Vegas, Leon thought as he pulled out of the warehouse complex and headed toward home, but he was going to miss his penthouse on the Strip. It was a showplace, the best apartment in a brand-new building, and their dedicated elevator would come in handy tonight. All he needed was to be jammed in with a bunch of nosy neighbors, or worse, their dogs, in that inevitable moment that Michael came to and started to wiggle or moan in the big suitcase.

For once, everything went smooth as butter. Leon even got a parking space right next to their elevator door. Maybe, just maybe, his luck was finally changing. After the private elevator cab opened into the apartment, he rolled the suitcase into the kitchen, opened it and heaved the smaller man's body up onto the counter. Leon was in his fifties, but as strong as a bull.

Michael's eyelids were starting to flutter. He made feeble noises through his gag.

Leon hummed to himself as he stretched Michael's body out on the kitchen island, legs and arms still bound. When that was done, he buckled an oversized dog collar around Michael's neck and attached it with a zip tie to the sink spigot. Then he studied the knife block. Big knives, small knives. Serrated knives, boning knives, flaying knives, kitchen shears. And a big, shiny, well-sharpened meat cleaver.

Michael came to abruptly. Eyes widening with terror, he started to writhe and gurgle behind his gag. Leon selected a pair of boning shears and started cutting Michael's pants off. *Snick, snick, snick,* as Michael's body arched in panic, flopping like a freshly caught fish. When he reached Michael's groin, Leon gave him a toothy smile and cut his underwear off, exposing the hardworking tool that lay shriveled and cowering against his thigh.

"Well, look at that. I wouldn't have taken you for a guy who shaved his balls. So you're used to having sharp blades near the family jewels, eh? That's good." Leon pulled the gag out of Michael's mouth.

Michael coughed and rasped, dragging in desperate breaths. Then he started to yell. "Help! Help me! Help—"

Smack. Leon punched him until he had blood in his teeth. Michael looked dazed, but he shut up.

"Now," Leon said. "We're going to talk about Fat Freddie's bearer bonds."

Michael licked his quivering lips. "I...but...but I—"

"You're gonna tell me everything. But first, I want you to understand what a little shithead you were. You'll know when I start to cut. So, where do I start? Your hands? Your feet? Your balls? Your cock? It's all gonna go, Michael. Say goodbye to all your precious parts. You're in Leon's chop shop tonight, buddy."

"No! *Ti dirò tutto! Ti dirò tutto! Ti giuro!*" Michael started babbling in Italian.

Oh, for fuck's sake. Not this Italian shit again. Michael was messing with him. Trying to make him feel stupid. Make him feel like a dickhead and a loser.

"Speak English, dumbass." Leon smacked Michael again, his signet ring bashing out a tooth.

Michael was hysterical now, letting out a shrill stream of nonstop Italian, too panicked to remember the English he had only learned as an adolescent.

The dumb bastard was regressing. And the more Leon went at him with the filleting knife, the worse it got. Soon, he was wailing in high-pitched, childish cadences. Yelling for mamma, for fuck's sake.

"Stop your whining!" Leon bellowed.

Michael flinched, whimpered, and spewed another flood of desperate, pleading words. Dialect, now. For fuck's sake. Later, after it was too late, it occurred to Leon that he should have recorded all that dialect blathering. He might have been able to get someone to translate. But it would have been tough to find someone expendable, who could be quickly disposed of. It was risky to leave an incriminating artifact, even for a short time.

What a fucking mess. He hadn't expected Michael to fall apart so quickly. Unless Michael was faking it, of course. Making a fool of him, like Tommy, Fat Ferdie, and all those shitty bastards.

He smoked a cigarette as he stared at the shaking, bleeding man before him. Michael's hands were zip-tied and roped to the zip-tie at his ankles, but he had enough play to jerk his feet up in a vain attempt to protect his balls.

Enough. Leon seized Michael's hand. His own hand was slippery with Michael's blood, which made it tough to get a grip. "Speak English, fuckwad!"

But Michael just kept repeating *Torre. Tigre. Tigre di Torre Tigre di Torre.* On and on in a rapid, ceaseless babble. Leon didn't even know what order the words were in. Tiger, tower? Tower Tiger? "What's is that?" he demanded. "Speak English, asshole!"

Snot and blood burbled in Michael's mouth as he repeated the phrase, breathless and slurred.

Leon seized Michael's hand, bracing his thumb against the granite countertop. "English now, or I take your thumb. You're right-handed, right? This is your gun hand? That's excellent. Say goodbye to it."

Michael let out an inarticulate howl of terror and convulsed desperately. Leon lost his grip on Michael's wrist, and it shifted, sliding forward—

Thunk. The cleaver chopped through Michael's wrist. His hand slid and spun on the bloody granite countertop. Hot arterial spray hit Leon's face and his chest. It spattered the cupboards and drawers and tiles as the severed hand slid and spun on the bloody granite counter top before sliding off and plopping wetly onto the floor.

"Oh, fuck me!" Leon grabbed a stray zip-tie and whipped it around Michael's arm in a makeshift tourniquet. He wrapped a dishtowel around the stump. What a shitshow. Michael's lips were white. His eyes rolled up. His body shuddered. He was going into shock.

Leon slapped Michael's face. He swore and punched and squeezed Micheal's balls, but it was useless. Michael was gone. That lightweight had croaked on him. Out of spite, just like Fat Ferdie. He'd been reamed once again by fate. Cheated by the goddamn Grim Reaper. Again.

After that, he barely knew what he was doing for a while. It was just a loud, red, blood-streaked blur, the meat cleaver chopping wildly, making wet thudding sounds. At one point, Michael's head rolled off the countertop and hit the floor with the dull, hollow thud of a melon.

Leon stood, covered in blood and sweat. He was panting, adrenaline coursing through him when he registered a sound. A tiny electronic burp. He prowled, cleaver in hand, from the kitchen to the dining room to the living room. Blood dripped down onto the pale beige rug. Leon peered around the couch.

And there was Amber. Huddled in a ball on the floor, staring up at him with big, wide, blank eyes. She was all made up, her lips stark and red, her hair piled in a puffy, messy up-do. Her dress was one he particularly liked. A slinky, pale green filmy thing that cupped her tits. A bunch of sheer, floaty panel things, like fucking Tinkerbell. "Hey, baby," he said. "You been here long?"

She tried several times to reply. Nothing came out but a dry clicking sound.

Long enough, Leon thought. Shit. This was a hell of a thing. She should have been off at that fucking party. Now he had some fast decisions to make, and Leon hated being rushed. Either he brought Amber in right now, or he buried her with Michael. Both options were problematic.

"I know it looks bad," he told her. "But that son of a bitch had it coming. Believe me. He set me up. Robbed me, betrayed me. It had to be done. Do you understand me, Amber? He screwed me over. I had to put him down. Like a mad dog. You got me?"

Amber gave him a jerky nod. She flinched away when he reached to pull her to her feet. All the blood, probably. Dropping his hand, Leon stepped back. "Get up."

She was trembling so hard it took her several tries. Finally, she gripped the couch, staggering and tottering on high heels.

"Amber, listen good," he said. "I'm going to need you to help me. You up for it?"

Yes. She formed the word, but still made no sound.

"Good." Leon nodded and smiled. "First thing? Swear to me that you will never say a word to anyone about what you just saw. Not one goddamn word. Not to anyone. Ever. Understand?"

She nodded and kept nodding.

"What the fuck are you doing here anyhow?" he demanded. "I thought you were at that party for your girlfriend. Why'd you come back so early?"

"I, ah…I got a headache." Her voice was thin and breathless.

"Huh." Leon glanced at the cleaver. He had only just realized that he was still holding it. "Okay. If you say so. Take off that dress." Her mouth dropped open. He let out a sharp little laugh. "Oh, no. Not for that, babe. Not yet, anyway. I like to get a job all wrapped up with a bow before I celebrate. I just don't want you to get blood on it. I like that dress. It looks great on you. You don't want to mess it up. Get it off. Quick."

Still nodding, Amber fumbled with the zip. Watching a woman peel off her clothes was a spectacle that never lost its charm, even in these conditions. Finally, there she was, a sight to behold in nothing but an ivory lace thong, matching balcony bra, and thin silver peep toes.

"Can you clean?" he asked her.

She just stared at him, uncomprehending. "Huh?"

"Clean," Leon repeated. "You know. Like a maid."

"Yeah. I, ah…yes," she said faintly. "But I've been hiring someone to do it for a long time."

"Well, that's not an option here," Leon said. "Nobody can see this. Or know about it. Not a cleaning lady. Not your girl-friends. Nobody. You got that straight in your head, baby?"

"Yes. Yes." Amber nodded frantically, her chest heaving.

"Calm down, babe," he soothed. "You'll hyperventilate. It's all gonna be all right. Michael had it coming. If people are respectful and treat me right, I'm nice. Like I'm nice to you. Am I not nice to you, Amber? When have I ever not been nice to you?"

Her teeth were chattering now. "You are. You're, ah, nice to me."

"Yes. I am. So I want you to be nice to me and help out with this mess. Then I want you to forget it ever happened. Just push it all right out of your pretty head. Get this cleaned up, clap a lid on it, lock it, and think pretty thoughts. That's the trick to staying sane. You just put bad stuff out of your mind, like it's a bad dream that never happened. And life goes on. Life with me. You like being with me, right, Amber?"

"Ah…y-y-yes," she quavered.

"Good," he said. "Because you're in the inner circle now. I never meant for you to have to know any of this stuff. It's my job to know it, not yours. But now that you do know it, we can be, well, you know. Closer. Would you like that? Being closer to me?"

"Y-y-yes. I'd…I'd like that." She gulped. "I'd…I'd like it a lot."

"Okay, then. Good. You're my woman now. You help me

when I need help, and I can trust you with anything. And you don't let me down. Ever. Got it? Are we crystal?"

"Yes," she gasped. "Yes. Never. Never. Crystal."

She looked terrified, but it was good to scare the shit out of a woman from time to time. Then they knew exactly who they were dealing with. They didn't get uppity, start getting ideas, playing power games. Besides, he was going to have to go off grid and lie low in Bumfuck Nowhere, USA, while they waited for the DiAngelo trial, at least until he figured out what Michael's fucking Tigre Torre was. He would prefer to have a woman with him for that stint. It was going to be boring as hell.

Then, it occurred to him that wives didn't have to testify. Whores, mistresses, girlfriends, yes. But wives, no. Something to think about while shoveling dirt over that suitcase.

Amber got to work with impressive swiftness. She pulled a bunch of stuff from under the sink, bottles and sprays and sponges. She found a bucket, a mop and some rags in the utility room. She got right to it, wiping down the cupboards and counter tops, washing the floor, her stunning ass on full display as she swabbed and spritzed and scrubbed.

It was a soothing sight. This time, Leon thought, he'd chosen well. Amber was strong. Tough. And she understood him. She had not cheated him or robbed him, or made a fool of him. Amber was a gem. A treasure. They worked together, side by side, like a team. Her cleaning up the mess, and him packing pieces of Michael into the suitcase. It was old-school domestic, the way things used to be. The little woman doing her feminine thing while he took care of the men's business. He liked this. It worked.

Leon grabbed a garbage bag and went to strip off his blood-drenched clothing. He had to be presentable for the drive to Lake Meade. He stuffed the clothes into the plastic bag, pulled on fresh pants and a shirt, and went back to the kitchen, giving it a critical once-over. Not bad. The place looked almost normal. And Amber was cute as hell in her microscopic skivvies, with those big yellow rubber gloves smeared with blood, and those spiked heeled peep toes. Before, the place seemed like a spatter film. Now, with her dressed like that, it looked like the set of some kinky porno.

"Floor still needs some work." He pointed to some pinkish smears.

She nodded. "I'll take care of it."

Watching Amber mop, it occurred to Leon that he had a new dilemma. What should he do with her while he took the suitcase out to the desert? He needed to keep an eye on her, but if he brought her along, she'd know too much.

Besides, she looked done in. Shaky, blue-lipped, wobbling. So not a good idea. Still, leaving her felt dangerous. She might do something panicky and dumb while he was gone.

She had finished the floor, and was washing her hands in hot water and dish soap. When he touched her shoulder, she jerked as if he had struck her.

"Hey, relax," he said. "I'm going to go take care of some stuff. You go into the bedroom. Take a hot shower and lie down while I take care of this."

"Okay," she whispered. But she didn't move.

"Come on, Amber. Move it."

"I'll go in a little while," she said. "I'm still washing up in here."

"You'll go when I say you go." Leon seized her shoulders, turned her around and gave her a little slap. Just a warning snap. Just his fingertips. So she'd understand how things were going to work with them going forward.

"Just let me get my dress," she said. "I don't want it to get ruined."

She sidled around him and trotted into the living room, gathering up the dress she'd left crumpled on the sofa. She clutched the wad of pale fabric to her chest as he herded her into the main bedroom. It had an attached bath, a balcony that did not communicate with any of the other rooms or balconies, and a lock that he could engage from the outside. Leon always made sure the places he lived in had at least one room with a door he could lock from the outside.

"Stay in here," he said. "And give me your phone."

"My…my phone?" He gave her a little shove. She staggered forward.

"Yes, your phone. Just hand it over, babe. Don't make me wait."

Amber nodded, plucking her phone from the crumpled pale green fabric. She'd put a pale green cover on it so it would match her dress. Women.

"You locking me in here?" Her voice quavered as she dropped the phone into his outstretched hand.

Leon nodded. "Just for tonight. For your own protection. If you're a good girl, I won't have to do it again. So show me how good you are, babe. Okay?"

He shut the door in her face and engaged the lock. Then he went back down the hall to the kitchen, and the suitcase. It was gruesome to open it, but it had to be done. As Leon tucked the plastic bag filled with his own bloody clothing into a corner, it occurred to him he didn't have Michael's phone. He went through the pockets of the guy's jacket. Felt around for possible hidden pockets. Nothing. *Shit.*

Michael must have dropped it under the car at the airport. Or maybe it was still in the trunk of his car, parked back at the warehouse. That was unfortunate.

He tucked Michael's head carefully into the space between the bend of his knees and angled it so that Michael's empty eyes looked straight back at him. *Gotcha, asshole.*

It was so much easier to fit a guy into a suitcase when he was disassembled.

Chapter Seven

The waitress filled Henry's coffee cup and gathered his breakfast plates. The diner was a popular spot, and they were busy. Henry was supposed to be having breakfast with Anselm, an associate of Ivar's. Anselm had been passing test and grad thesis jobs to Henry for the last couple of months.

He was late, though. Which meant Henry would be late getting to the Rose Reading Room, which he disliked intensely. He needed his favorite seat in the back to work effectively. His concentration was never as good with anyone seated behind him.

He wondered if Victor had seen the sex tape yet. It had been delivered the day before. He'd be able to tell by the level of Victor's general viciousness once he tuned in to monitor it. He sipped his coffee, adjusting the baseball cap he always wore outside the house. His mother would have been horrified to see him wearing it in a restaurant. He apologized to her in his mind. These were desperate times. The bill of the hat had tiny infrared LEDs embedded in it which projected dots of light, neutralizing facial recognition software. All that the facial recog tech would see would be a random male face, generated with AI.

Henry looked up in time to see Anselm crossing the street. His long quilted coat billowed around him like a cloak. Wispy, thinning blond hair whipped in the wind. He spotted Henry through the window and beamed, flapping his arms like a windmill.

For God's sake. The guy knew Henry was trying to lay low. He did it on purpose.

Henry insisted on anonymity, but Ivar had arranged for Anselm to sublet him his studio apartment in Hell's Kitchen, so this guy knew what he looked like and where he lived. Not ideal. But he got a lot of work from Anselm, so he gritted his teeth and endured the buzz of anxiety that had become his constant companion.

Anselm shambled over, grinning, and slid into the booth. "Hey, there, Raymond! You're a hard man to contact! What, you ate already? You didn't wait for me?"

"I've been here for a while. Gotta go soon." Henry shrank down into the booth, trying to disappear. Raymond was the name on the fake ID he'd used to rent Anselm's apartment.

"Pancakes!" Anselm yelled to the waitress across the room.

"Why did you need to see me?" Henry asked. "Why not just text?"

Anselm shrugged. "I prefer the personal touch. I have a real bonanza for you, man! Three new jobs. Good ones. One doctoral thesis in mechanical engineering, one in organic chemistry, and one in neurolinguistics. Great stuff, Raymond. You'll really cash in with these gigs."

"Did you have them collect all their source material for me?"

"Just like you said." Anselm produced a handful of files and pushed them across the table.

Henry leafed through them, doubting it. He wasn't sure

what bothered him more, using Mirror, Mirror to create alibis to let criminals get away with their crimes, or helping people cheat academically and professionally. What was the point of that, in the long run? How could these idiots live with themselves? Then again, neither their consciences nor their futures were his problem. Nobody had asked him, and his judgment meant nothing. Rent needed to be paid, and the kind of high quality ID he needed to travel abroad cost a fortune. He wasn't free to say no to a well-paid gig, even if someone as loud and grating as Anselm was providing it.

Henry tossed back his coffee and slid out of the booth. "Thank you, Anselm. I'll get right on it. I'll send you quotes and turn-in dates as soon as I can look at the material."

"Do the mechanical engineering one first. He needs it really soon!"

"He should have planned his life better."

"Yeah, well, what are you gonna do?" Anselm said breezily. "Our clients aren't the brightest stars in the firmament. If they were, they wouldn't need you. So how are things, my friend? What? You're leaving already? But I just got here!"

"Sorry," Henry mumbled. "Gotta go. I'll be in touch." He paid and fled, walking fast toward the library, fighting the urge to look over his shoulder.

At the Rose Reading Room, Henry found he was in luck. There was one seat left in the back row. He settled into it and glanced through the mechanical engineering doctoral candidate's source material. It wasn't going to be a problem. He tucked it away for later. Work on Ivar's deep-fake videos took top priority. That was the deal he had made.

As soon as he flipped open his laptop, Henry noticed activity on Belinda and Victor's kitchen monitor. Joggling Faith on her hip, Belinda was pulling food out of the fridge and sniffing it. She put eggs and milk on the countertop while Victor paced around. They were both obviously agitated.

Henry slid his earphones on. Faith whimpered. Bacon hissed in a frying pan.

"...turned it off again?" Victor snarled. "Didn't you turn it on last night?"

"Yes! Of course I did!" Belinda snapped. "You saw me do it! We did it together!"

"Well, evidently you didn't do it, Bel, because on the smart hub, it's clearly toggled off. For fuck's sake, get your head in the game!"

Yes. The edge in Victor's tone definitely suggested that he'd received and viewed the sex tape.

"I did!" Belinda shifted Faith to the other hip . "I'm going to have to get to work later today. I've got to drop her off at Busy Bees, then deal with the rest of this food. We'll have to throw it away. We can't eat stuff that's been unrefrigerated for twenty-four hours. Certainly Faith can't."

"Just get in as soon as possible because I made an appointment with Joseph Knox. That P.I. I told you about. The meeting is this afternoon at two-thirty. You need to be there."

Belinda rounded on him. "What? No! I can't! I told you about Faith's appointment this afternoon at one-forty-five, with that pediatric gastroenterologist!"

"Cancel it," Victor said. "The P.I. is more important."

Faith's whimpers turned suddenly into wails, making it difficult to follow the conversation. Henry strained to hear Belinda. "...pediatrician urged me to make an appointment with a specialist as soon as possible, Victor! She's way behind in all her milestones, and we have to figure out what's going on, if there's some underlying problem that we—"

"It can wait, Bel. The kid's not dying."

"We have waited! The guy's been booked solid! We've waited over seven weeks for this appointment! And 'not dying' is a pretty low bar to set for your kid!"

"Watch your tone, Bel." Victor's voice had a sting to it that made Belinda back away. "And do something about that bacon. You must have splashed water in the pan. The fat's spitting everywhere. It's gotten all over the curtains. It's making a godawful mess. For Christ's sake, deal with it."

Muttering an obscenity, Belinda held Faith out to Victor. "Take her, then," she said. "I can't have her near hot grease."

Victor recoiled. "No way. I just had this suit cleaned. I don't need it covered with spit or shit or vomit. Or bacon grease, for that matter. The bacon is scorching, Bel. Hurry."

Shaking her head, Belinda strapped the wailing, flailing kid into a high chair and grabbed a plate from the cupboard. Her lips were tight and pursed as she forked the overcooked strips of bacon onto the plate as the pan sputtered hot grease across her bare arms. She turned the burner off, grabbed paper towels to wipe up the mess, then wiped her hands.

"Don't forget the curtains," Victor said. "We have to get them cleaned, or the kitchen will stink of bacon."

"Later for that," Belinda said. "Just meet with this guy without me. Tell me all about it after Faith's appointment. You know everything I know. You don't need me."

"Use your head. I know it's not your forte, but try, okay? He'll need you to tell him about Henry. Not really something I can do, since I haven't fucked him."

"Please," Belinda snapped. "Not in front of the baby."

"Oh, don't worry. She's still pre-verbal. Which I doubt she'll ever get beyond. All she can manage is incoherent screaming, for Christ's sake. My mom said I spoke at eight months. And you say she's mine."

"I know she's yours! The genetics lab says she's yours! The test your own ex-wife demanded we do! What, don't you believe the results?"

Victor narrowed his eyes. He plucked up a piece of bacon from the plate, took a bite, and made a face. "Scorched," he said, tossing it onto the counter. "Watch the tone, Bel. Gotta go. I'm late. Make sure you're at the meeting."

The door slammed shut behind him. Henry brought up

the garage monitor and watched Victor pulling out. In the kitchen, Faith continued to wail. Belinda pressed her hands to her face, then spun around, facing the high chair. "Shut up," she shouted, her voice shaking.

Faith flung her head back and shrieked louder. Belinda leaned forward, hands up, fists clenched. "Would you just … shut … up!" she bellowed, right into Faith's face.

Henry braced himself, but no blow fell. He couldn't breathe. He watched as Belinda rocked back, panting, and put her hands over her face. A few seconds later, she unstrapped the toddler, yanked her out of the chair, and hurried into the other room.

In the back row of the Rose Reading Room, Henry listened to the baby monitor. But there was nothing to hear except Faith's ceaseless crying. Belinda changed and dressed her, then left her wailing in the crib while she packed the diaper bag. By the time they left, the baby was quiet, red-faced and exhausted, sucking her thumb as Belinda carried her into the garage and muscled the little girl into the car seat.

Releasing his white-knuckled fists, Henry let out a shaking breath.

So today, they met with the P. I. He hoped he would be able to listen through Bel's phone, since he could turn on her microphone. Victor had changed his tune rather abruptly about the investigator, and he was no longer telling Belinda that she was being paranoid. In fact, he was rushing a meeting, which suggested that he had watched the sex tape either late last night or sometime this morning.

That was all good. But a painful conviction was growing inside Henry. Faith wasn't going to make it. Not with that sociopathic bastard for a father. Victor didn't care if she lived or died, and Belinda wasn't strong enough to protect her.

And? So? a cold voice in his head asked. It was a disgrace, a tragedy. But still not his problem. They'd robbed him, framed him, shamed him, cuckolded him, humiliated him, imprisoned him. He had to save himself. Protect himself. Any way he could. He couldn't protect Faith, too.

Henry clicked into the smart hub. Victor had turned the fridge back on, so he toggled it off again. The frying pan was still on the stove. Henry turned on the burner, dialed it up to its top setting, and disabled the security failsafe.

Movement at the entrance of the Rose Room caught his eye. He felt only a second or two of disorientation. Then she slipped into focus. It was the costume girl in all her glory. Lately she'd been dressing down, trying not to attract attention. Today, she was big and shiny in a magnificently puffy pink coat with fluffy white fake fur trim. Her wig was a gleaming, top-heavy brown bob of the kind favored by well-heeled suburban women of a certain age, complimented by overdone makeup and big, gaudy earrings.

She shrugged off the coat to reveal a very pink sweat suit. Costume girl was impressively wide in the beam today, and it was very believable, right down to the way she seated herself. Henry liked to imagine that at this point, he could see through any disguise she tried. Even a burqa or a hazmat suit couldn't fool him now. He'd see her switched-on energy shining through whatever disguise she wore. Like a star.

Her gaze flicked his way from behind rhinestone-studded cat-eye glasses. Henry's coffee cup was long empty by now. But he raised it anyway, giving her a respectful and appreciative nod. *My compliments.*

He thought he caught the briefest frown in reply, and it gave him a glow of pride. As if she'd trotted her shiny new disguise into the Rose Reading Room just to test him. To impress him.

Wow, that was quite the fantasy. The kind of thing only a lonely, unbalanced guy starved for dopamine and company would indulge in. He dragged his eyes back to the monitor, and was startled to see Belinda and Victor's grease fire well underway, blazing up big and bright. It had ignited the grease-soaked paper towels, which had in turn set the curtains on fire. The video image began to vanish as the kitchen filled with smoke. Tapping on the sound, Henry heard the shrill squealing of the fire alarm. Damn. That had gone better and faster than he'd hoped. Excellent.

He clicked out of Victor and Belinda's video monitors, and returned to the deep-fake security video feeds he was doing for Ivar. When Henry had told Ivar how Belinda and Victor framed him, it had given Ivar the idea to provide top-shelf, bespoke deep-fake video alibis. Do you need to prove you were somewhere else when a crime occurred? Check out the security video feed at this convenience store! There you are, buying condoms and cigarettes at exactly the time the burglary/assault/abduction/whatever took place. Let the forensic techs pick it over all they wanted. Mirror, Mirror would fool them all.

Since Henry was paying him back for the prison break, Ivar took the lion's share of the fees. The modest sum for his expenses that Henry got for each video was deposited directly into one of the bank accounts Ivar had organized for him. The irony was not lost on Henry. Using the very weapon that had destroyed him to facilitate still more crime? It was a bad choice. But he had only bad choices now.

He was the poster child for bad choices. Driven by spite and rage, at Victor, for using, humiliating, and framing him, and at Belinda for doing all of that, plus pretending to love him.

He should have known better. He'd been so bewildered when Belinda started coming on to him. He'd already decided that any guy as peculiar and awkward as he was not destined for the sex/love/procreation thing. In his inexperience, he'd mistaken lust and dazed confusion for love.

She'd been so patient with him while he babbled about his algorithms, the technical details of back-end database design. And she was so pretty. When she aimed that thousand-watt smile at him, he kept turning around to see who was standing behind him. She drew him in, dazzled him, seduced him. She had been the one to propose, too. He'd been amazed at his luck. Wishing that Mom was still alive to see him actually married, just like she'd dreamed of. Giving her a grandchild, even.

Henry had thought Faith's birth was proof this was for real. Surely Belinda wouldn't compromise her life so completely if she were not genuinely invested in the relationship, right? He'd seen Faith not just as his baby girl that he adored, but also as a promise from Belinda. A guarantee that this wasn't a mirage.

The costume girl stood up, putting on her long, puffy pink coat. Leaving already? She'd barely been here an hour, tapping away at her tablet. She didn't usually leave this early, but there she was, packing her things into a pink leather purse. Heading toward the door like a big pink ship in full sail.

He didn't want her to leave. He liked having her there, even if they'd never exchanged a word, or been closer to each other than twenty yards.

They were both invisible. Both starving to be seen. Maybe he was projecting his own feelings onto her, but he would bet good money that it was true. That she felt that way, too.

This hunger to be seen was stupid and dangerous, but that didn't keep him from getting up, sliding his laptop into his satchel, and following her.

Her coat helped. He could hang far back and still keep her in sight as she bobbed along the sidewalk like a bright pink bubble. Then she plunged down into the crowded rush-hour subway at Columbus Circle.

Henry followed her onto the Uptown 1 train all the way up to 125th Street. He ambled after her down the sidewalk, staying as far back as he dared. He attracted no attention. There were countless guys looked like him in New York City. Mid-thirties, nondescript, overgrown, bearded, ball-cap, down-at-heel, unwilling to make eye contact. There was nothing about him that stood out.

He lost her for a moment as they approached another subway station, and was overcome with an irrational panic. Then he spotted her again among a crowd of Japanese tourists climbing up the stairs to the elevated train. She had spotted him. He knew it. She was leading him around, punishing him for having seen through her disguise. *You want to chase me? Then run.*

He raced for her train, jumping in just as the doors closed. She got off at 42nd Street and flounced down the tunnel toward the A train. Then, instead of heading downstairs to the track, she darted through the turnstile and ran up to the street.

Henry followed, bursting out onto the sidewalk just in time to hear a car door slam. She looked directly at him, giving him the finger and a frown as her cab pulled away.

A deep sense of loss swamped him as he stood watching the taillights disappear, followed by an even more uncomfortable sense of having been very foolish. He'd killed this delicate moth-wing flicker of human connection by being his usual clumsy self. Chasing her like a grabby, creepy, grasping perv.

Not that he'd have known what to do with her if he had caught her. Like he'd ever had jack squat say to a woman who interested him. Much less now, when he didn't even exist. Any woman with half a brain would be terrified of what he had just done. And Henry was sure that she had plenty of brains.

He turned homeward, filled with new resolve. Monitoring Victor and Belinda's meeting with the P.I. was a much better use of his time than playing with his imaginary friend.

Especially since his imaginary friend had just made it crystal clear she didn't want to play.

Chapter Eight

Waylon Mills, Idaho

"No," Leon said. "My wife wouldn't just leave me. I'm telling you, she'd never do that!"

Agent Daly looked down and played with his water glass. Wojniac, who had been digging enthusiastically into his Dutch apple pie, looked up and gave Leon a cool, assessing look that just burned his ass.

"Think it through," Wojniac said. "If DiAngelo's men had taken her, they would have done something flashy with her to hurt you. Something you would have heard about on the news. But it hasn't happened. She's been gone for over three months now, and nobody's heard a peep about her." He forked up another piece of pie. "She flew the coop, buddy."

Buddy? Leon studied the other man. He was FBI, all the way from his starched shirt with the collar cutting into his double chin to his pinched lips and pink-rimmed, rabbity eyes.

Rage crackled inside him. He'd kept his part of the bargain, delivered Tommy DiAngelo, his two sons, his son-in-law and six of his made men. The whole kit and caboodle. Bail denied. All inside, awaiting trial. Surely that was worth a lot more than this. What, did Wojniac and Daly specifically ask the US Marshals to pick the dullest, ugliest place on earth to stash him and Amber? Then she fucking disappeared three months ago, and all these do-nothing FBI assholes could do was insult her.

"You don't know Amber like I do," Leon said.

"Call her Mary Agnes," Wojniac corrected. "Make a goddamn effort, Jeff."

Jeff, his hairy ass. Hah. Jeff Hinkley? And giving Amber a name like Mary Agnes Hinkley? For fuck's sake. It sounded like a name for some old, sphincter-mouthed nun.

"She didn't have any money," Daly said. "Or skills, to speak of. I think she just panicked and ran. She's hiding. But DiAngelo's people will find her. And when they do, she'll give you up. In a heartbeat." Daly looked at Leon and shook his head. "You know what the DiAngelos are like, man. She won't have a choice. She'll talk, and everything will go straight to shit."

Leon glared at the two men. "Amber's not the independent type. She shook her stuff in Vegas to make a living. But she's my woman now. She does what she's told, then expects a pair of diamond earrings."

Wojniac looked around the faded, grubby diner. "Not a lot of diamond earrings in Waylon Mills. Or places to wear them, either."

No shit, Sherlock. If only he'd gotten the info he needed out of Michael before he croaked. If he had his bonds, he'd be way far away from here, being expertly blown by his beautiful bride. New names, new credit cards, new life.

"Maybe she got homesick," Daly said. "I mean, we get it. This isn't easy. Was there trouble in Paradise? Were you two fighting? It's stressful, leaving the past behind. Friends, family, everything."

"She didn't have any family," Leon said. "And her friends

were a pack of worthless strippers, pimps and whores. She's better off without all those losers."

"Maybe so," Daly nodded. He was playing Good Cop today. "But still, it would be disorienting for her. Could she have met someone, in her work, at the store? She's a fine looking woman, even dressed way down. She probably attracted some attention in a place like this."

"You're saying you think my wife ran off with some redneck clown?"

Wojniac shrugged and pushed his plate away. "It happens. And the lady wasn't famous for her attention span. Or her good judgment." He chortled at his own joke.

Leon felt the noise, the rattling roar, the haze of red. He wanted to throttle the cocky shit-weasels, right here and now. "So, what?" he asked through clenched teeth. "You're just going to wipe Amber off the books, then? She's just some dumb slut who ran off with a trucker or a biker?"

"A religious cult, maybe?" Wojniac looked around the diner, lip curling. "People who live in backward places like this are different. People under stress do strange things."

Leon laughed. It was not a nice sound. "Not Amber. No Jesus stuff for her. She's a party girl."

Wojniac looked dubious. "Waylon Mills is a tough sell to a Vegas party girl who likes her diamond earrings."

"She did not run away," Leon repeated. "That's not my Amber."

"Whatever you say." Wojniac wiped his mouth and threw the napkin on the table. "Another thing. A colleague of mine from Vegas had some interesting things to say about your associate, Michael Basile."

"Former," Leon said. "Former associate Michael Basile. We parted ways. Haven't spoken in a couple months."

"Yeah." Daly leaned forward, resting his elbows on the table. "See, that's the thing. No one has. Spoken to Michael Basile in a couple of months, I mean. There was a murder in a brothel in Pasadena. Natalya Luchenko, killed on the same day you agreed to testify, which was also the day of Ferdinando Basile's funeral. Two men fitting yours and Michael's descriptions were seen at that same brothel that same day. There was also a home invasion that night, in Fair Oaks. An older couple were brutally murdered in a house they bought from Ferdie's sister, Stefania Sallustio, twelve years before. Did you hear about any of that?"

"News to me," Leon shrugged. "I kinda fell off the map when I agreed to testify."

"Michael's fingerprints were found at the scene," Wojniac said.

Leon spread his hands. "Strange. But I can't help you. I don't know anything."

"Too bad there were no cameras in the whorehouse," Wojniac mused. "But a couple girls described a customer who was very rough with them. A man who could have been you."

Leon laughed. "Hey. I was traveling back to Vegas to meet with you two. Remember? And I'm a perfect gentleman with fairer sex."

"Interesting, how Ferdie's house got hit that night," Daly said. "We even heard a wild story about ten million dollars in bearer bonds. Lost forever because Ferdie hid them before he had his stroke. Ever hear that story?"

"Yeah," Leon said. "That's a nice one. Kind of like the Easter Bunny and Sasquatch."

"I heard you got demoted after that," Wojniac said. "Rank stripped. Like a little bitch."

Leon's hands clenched under the table. "Are you fucking with me, Wojniac?"

"Larry," Daly chided, frowning. "Don't be an asshole. No, he's not fucking with you. He just has no people skills. We just wondered if you had any info, any ideas about Michael. Or people he associated with. Or Ferdie's lost stash. That would be useful to us."

Leon just fucking bet it would be. "Michael," he said slowly, as if talking to a stupid child, "had shit for brains. I imagine he got his incompetent ass kicked by someone who lost patience with him. And if I had ten million bucks in bearer bonds, do you think I'd be in the ass end of nowhere talking to you two losers in some shit diner?"

Daly's teeth glinted. "Always the charmer."

"Just stay the course, Jeff," Wojniac said.

"Don't call me that," Leon snarled. "It's a dumb name. Who picked that name?"

"Just try not to draw attention to yourself. We're trying to keep you alive, okay? And, be ready to move at any time. You could already be burned, with your wife on the loose out there."

"I don't want to leave until you locate Amber." Leon said through his teeth. "Can't you use facial recognition, or some shit like that, to find her?"

Wojniac shook his head. "Nah. It's not like in the movies. But if we hear of her, we'll tell you. We promise. She can always come back into the fold if she reaches out to us. As of now, she hasn't popped up in the system anywhere, under either name. She hasn't gotten a job, unless it's off the books. She hasn't tried to access her old bank account, or applied for a driver's license or a credit card. Maybe she got herself some fake ID under some other name. Did she have computer skills?"

"Does," Leon snapped. "Not did. And, no. Not that I ever saw. She was the ornamental type, if you know what I mean."

"Yeah, I do," Wojniac said. "I saw her at the Magnum once. Wow."

Leon stared at him, picturing the many ways he would enjoy making Special Agent Wojniac die screaming. Wojniac stared back.

"Good talk, Jeff," Daly said, getting to his feet. "We'll be in touch. Come on, Larry."

After they left, Leon sat staring at the table. It was almost time for him to go back to work. Landscaping, for Christ's sake. Work he hadn't done since he was nineteen, when he learned that busting heads was both easier and more profitable. And Amber's job, clerking in the big box store. In housewares, for fuck's sake. What did he expect her to do? She was in this shit town because of him, living in a drab split-level ranch house on a yellowed lawn spotted with dog turds. It made it worse that Amber was a crappy cook, and there wasn't any decent takeout in a radius of two hundred miles.

Leon. I love you so much. I would never leave you.

Bullshit, she wouldn't. Those big golden eyes. That wispy doll-baby voice. Telling him she had his back. That they were in this together. Then, boom! She vanished. Sneaky, treacherous little whore. Maybe she was one step ahead of him, too. Just like all the others.

He couldn't just wait for the Feds to track Amber down. They didn't have a clue.

But Amber didn't have any family. The only friends she had were that flock of flashy sluts who performed with her at the Magnum. He needed to talk to some of them.

Going to Vegas was going to be tricky. But he was not getting fucked over by a little two-bit sexpot.

He realized his fingers were drumming the table, hard enough that people looked around to see what the sound was. It made him think of Michael's constant nervous twitching.

Fine. He would need all the nervous energy he could get for what was coming.

Chapter Nine

Belinda hated Joseph Knox on sight.

It was the calculating once-over he gave her as soon as she joined them in the conference room. Those cold, pale eyes, the thin, faintly sneering lips. The way his gaze lingered on her chest before that unpleasant smile twitched the corner of his mouth. He'd assessed her, pinpointed her fault lines and shaky spots, already picked out which weaknesses he could exploit.

Victor was oblivious to the disrespectful way Knox looked at her. Victor had no fault lines or weaknesses. Belinda loved that about him. Or rather, she marveled at it.

Victor had launched into his spiel when Knox held up his hand and said, "Stop."

"What is it?" Victor was not used to being interrupted.

"Have you got cell phones on you?"

"Of course. Why?"

"You need to leave them in another room."

Victor looked incredulous. "My phone is completely secure."

"I'm sure it is," Knox said. "It's just protocol."

"What about your phone?"

"It's in a Faraday box in my car. You may think you're ahead of the game, but there's always someone three steps ahead of you. Assume that they are, and you won't ever get in trouble."

"I'll take them." Belinda stood up, glad to leave the conference room, and the odious presence of Joseph Knox, even if only for a moment. She held out her hand. Victor frowned, but he gave her his phone.

When Belinda came back in, Victor was well into his recitation for the private investigator.

"...figure out if these things that are happening to us, the security breaches, the identity stuff, can be traced back to Henry Devlin."

Knox looked up from the notebook he had opened, his pen pausing in mid-air. "How long ago did he break out of Rock Ridge?"

"Eight months," Victor said. "He escaped on the way to his sentencing hearing. Someone put a rumble strip on the road. Tased the guards and the driver. Very slick. He had expert help."

"I see. Tell me again what was his crime was?"

"Fraud," Victor said. "He defrauded three of his clients of six-point-seven million dollars, and turned it into diamonds. I assumed, after his escape, that he'd just take the diamonds from wherever he hid them and disappear. But based on what's happening to us, it looks like he's stayed all too close to home."

Knox grunted under his breath. "Of course, you've strengthened and updated your home and device security? New passwords, more encryption, all that?"

"Of course," Victor said. "Several times over."

Knox turned his pale, fishy gaze on Belinda. "So you were married to Henry Devlin?"

Belinda tugged her blazer closed. "Yes," she nodded. "For three years. We have a daughter together."

"And you've been working for Mr. Shattuck for how long?"

"Almost six years." Belinda's voice was tight and too high.

"And you two are together now. Right?" He nodded toward Victor. "Have I understood that correctly?"

Belinda blew out a breath. "Yes. After it happened, Henry being arrested. Well, you can imagine. I was just shattered. Victor was a rock."

Knox smiled, slowly. Belinda wondered if the oily insinuation was all in her head. She looked at Victor. For God's sake. They were paying this guy to disrespect her, and he hadn't even noticed.

"We became a couple after Henry went to prison," Victor said. "It looked like he would be in for decades. No one could blame Bel for moving on with her life."

"Henry might." Knox made a note in his book. "So, just to recap. The two of you think this guy is angry enough to waste his time and money and risk being exposed so he can hang around and mess with your heads instead of taking his diamonds and fleeing the country? I mean, staying here to turn off your freezer and melt your peas and carrots? Seriously?"

"We think these things are messages," Belinda said stiffly.

"Maybe. If so, what do you think the messages mean? Why is he so angry, do you suppose? Any insights?"

Victor shrugged. "It's obvious. I assume he's jealous because Belinda is in a relationship with me. That's understandable."

"Yes, it is," Knox agreed. "And you've been her boss for what, six years?"

"We've been friends for a long time," Belinda said. "When my life fell apart, I was beside myself, all alone with a tiny baby. And Victor was…"

"A rock," Knox supplied as her voice trailed off.

There was a charged silence. Belinda felt her lacquered nails digging into her palms. She was being judged by this smirking asshole. She had canceled Faith's appointment with the pediatric gastroenterologist for this? He was looking at her like he thought she was a scheming tart. *Well, aren't you?* She blanked the thought out, fast. She wasn't the problem, Knox was. He had no right to make assumptions about her, or Victor. He knew nothing. Zero.

"The kid?" Knox looked at Victor. "Is she his? Or yours?"

Victor hesitated for an instant too long, and Knox's smile widened. "Understood," he said. "It did seem strange. I mean, if a guy has a bag of diamonds, why isn't he on a beach somewhere with some babe in a bikini? Why stay here and bust your balls?"

"That's what we wanted you to find out," Belinda said sharply.

Knox stared at her, drumming his fingers on the table. "Here's the thing, Ms. Devlin," he said. "My effectiveness is directly related to how forthcoming you are. If you guys are blowing smoke, I can't see my way, and I'll just waste your money. You might want to keep that in mind. I promise you, the only principle I adhere to is profit. I am discreet, and I don't judge."

The hell you don't, you arrogant dipshit. Belinda pasted on a thin smile.

"So," Knox said. "How about you tell me everything?" He picked up his pen. "Everything you know about Mr. Devlin."

It was difficult to talk about Henry with Victor listening avidly. Every cutting comment, and there were plenty of them, that Victor would have made if Knox had not been sitting here, scribbling in his god damn note book, ran through her head. She'd hear them anyway. Later. At home. She had no doubt.

Belinda struggled to describe Henry's work. Henry had talked about it all the time, but she had only pretended to listen. She knew nothing about the particulars of the databases he created. Victor had been the one who hired Henry four years ago to do whatever it was that Henry did for the hedge fund. This was all Victor's fault, not hers. It had been Victor who had seen Henry's potential. Victor, who had been the architect of the entire plan.

"Family?" Knox persisted, after she came up blank on work. "Hobbies? Pastimes? Bucket list destinations? Dreams, obsessions, pet peeves? Dig deep, Mrs. Devlin. It's the only way I can help you."

"As far as family goes," Belinda said, "he doesn't have any. At least that I'm aware of, and he would have told me. He never knew his dad and his mom died when he was in college. She was a librarian in North Carolina, he was an only child, and she raised him alone. As far as I know, there were no aunts or uncles or grandparents or second cousins. Nobody else."

Knox's lip curled. "So sad to be all alone in the world, huh?"

Belinda paused. "Is this funny to you, Mr. Knox?"

"No, no," he said. "Not at all. Serious as death. Though I do like to see the lighter side of things. Moving on. How about friends?"

"Not close ones. A few people he gamed with online. People he sub-contracted work to, I guess. He didn't really have a group of friends, per se."

"A real loner, then?"

"Yes. He was an unusual person. Shy. Not socially graceful."

"Somewhere on the spectrum?"

Belinda shrugged. "I guess. Maybe. He was an innocent in some areas, incredibly brilliant in others. And he had an amazing ability to concentrate. Super focused. Almost pathological."

"What kind of things did he concentrate on?"

"He liked to study emerging tech, then fiddle with it until it was ten times more powerful than before." Belinda shook her head, remembering. "I'd say, why not sell this and make a fortune? And Henry would just laugh and say it would only be useful to crooks, and that he didn't need more money. He had everything he needed now that he had me and Faith."

Knox raised his eyebrows. "Interesting stance on money. I'm guessing you two weren't entirely in agreement?"

"Well, it did seem like a waste," she admitted. "All that money left on the table. All that talent left undeveloped."

"Like his deep-fake program," Victor broke in. "Tell him about Mirror, Mirror, Bel."

Belinda threw him a startled look. Mirror, Mirror was way too close to the bone. But the damage was done. Knox was looking from one to the other of them.

"Mirror, Mirror?" he asked. "What's that?"

Belinda waved her hand dismissively. "Henry got fascinated by making deep fakes for a while. It was just a phase."

"What? Like doctoring video? Putting people in places where they weren't, making them say things they didn't?"

Belinda shifted as Victor watched her with a faint, taunting smile. She could have killed him. He'd brought this up to punish her and put her on the spot. Now she had to get them out of it, all alone. And if she screwed it up, they would both go down in flames. Knox was looking at her expectantly.

"Yes," she said. "Like that. Sort of. Henry got all obsessed by it. Like a little boy. He did that kind of thing often. He wrote a deep-fake program that was souped up to the max in some way that I never quite understood. He claimed that even a forensic expert wouldn't be able to tell that the video wasn't real. Something about the number of pixels. It was nothing to him. He did it for fun."

Knox looked fascinated. "Tell me more."

"I don't know more." Her voice had a sharp edge. "I didn't understand it. It was just a thing he did to see if it would work. He liked to challenge himself that way. He'd speed-read a manual or textbook, and then take random tests for fun. The LSATs, or the MCATs, stuff like that. I told you. He was weird that way."

"And he never used this, what was it called? Mirror, Mirror program? For anything?"

"Other than to show it to me, no. He genuinely didn't care about using it."

"Something like that could be dangerous in the wrong hands," Knox murmured. "Valuable, too, I bet."

"I guess," she said stiffly. "But it was his main hobby. That, and Faith. Henry was extremely focused on her. He memorized every book he could get his hands on about infancy." Belinda shook her head. "It was crazy. He probably knew more about pediatric illnesses than an actual doctor."

Knox scribbled into his notebook. "Did they ever find the money he stole?"

"No," Victor said. "He pleaded not guilty. Insisted he didn't do it."

"Interesting," Knox murmured as he reviewed his notes. "So." He put the pen down again and looked up. "I'm guessing you two can pay my fees, no problem."

Victor's eyes sharpened. "What are you insinuating?"

"I don't insinuate," Knox said. "I say it right to your face. You're in no position to take offense." He turned to Belinda. "Does he know that the baby isn't his?"

Belinda flinched. "He didn't the last time I talked to him. He might know now."

Knox nodded. "He knows. Seems like a lot has been taken from this guy. His wife. His child. His job. His reputation, and his freedom. A real clean sweep."

"We didn't take anything from him," Victor snapped.

"Right," Knox waved a hand. "Of course you didn't. It's

what he thinks that's relevant. And, he thinks you did. So, I'm not at all surprised that he's angry. Or that he's fucking with you. Frankly, I'm surprised he's not fucking with you harder. Was he a hacker?"

"Not really," Belinda faltered. "I'm sure he could have been. Could be though, if he had to. But it wouldn't be a natural thing. Henry didn't have a malicious bone in his body."

Knox gazed at her. "People change."

Before Belinda could say anything, there was a knock on the door.

"What part of I told you not to disturb us don't you understand!" Victor yelled as

Iris, Victor's secretary, poked her head through the door of the conference room.

"This is important," she said apologetically. "Like, really."

"What?" Victor rolled his eyes.

"The Fire Department is at your house. There was a fire, and they're putting it out now."

Belinda leapt to her feet. "Oh, my God! How bad is it?"

"He didn't say, but I—"

"Victor, we have to go home! Right now! Let's go!"

Victor waved her down. "We're in a meeting, Bel. The fire department has it covered. What do you think you could do when you get there? Hold the hose yourself?"

She stared at him, taken aback. Even the thought of his own home in flames didn't rattle him. "But, I want to see what's going on! It's our house, Victor! Our home! Faith's home! How can you just not care?"

"Of course I care," he said. "But there's nothing I can do. Let's divide and conquer. I'll finish our chat with Mr. Knox. You check out the damage, and report back."

Belinda stared at him. "You're not coming with me?"

"No," Victor said coolly. "This situation is just as urgent. Call me when you get there. I'll join you as soon as I'm free."

Belinda backed out. Her throat burned as she retrieved her phone and coat, fighting back tears. Getting in the car, she could barely see the road. All she could see was the look in Victor's eyes.

Or, more to the point, what wasn't in his eyes.

Chapter Ten

Victor sighed as the door shut. "Women. They get so worked up."

Knox's non-existent eyebrows lifted. "You are one cool customer, Vic. I'm a pretty detached guy. But if I found out my house was burning down, my heart rate might kick up a notch or two. Sure you don't want to keep your wife company? We can reschedule."

"She's not my wife," Victor said.

"Ah." Knox smiled. "So, that's how it is."

"That's how it is," Victor agreed. "Actually, I wanted to take this opportunity to speak to you alone. I have another issue to discuss regarding Henry."

Knox crossed his legs, and waited, his pale eyes attentive. "So? Tell me."

Victor looked at the private investigator, still hesitating. He hated exposing himself to anyone. But he'd called Joseph Knox precisely because he'd been assured that the man was a pragmatist. Someone open to unorthodox solutions to complicated problems. For a salty price. And something unorthodox, say a meat mallet to Henry Devlin's overheated brain, would be very refreshing right now.

Victor had made a classic mistake. He had underestimated Henry. Now Henry was ruining a perfect plan. The fraud had been designed to snare Henry like a sacrificial goat. He would take the blame for everything while Victor got rich. It had been fucking brilliant. Now, Henry was dismantling it piece by piece.

He plucked a padded mailer from his briefcase and threw it on the table. "This was delivered to my office yesterday. There was nothing on it except my name printed on a label. There is a thumb drive inside. I watched it this morning, before I called you."

"What's on it?"

"Video," Victor said. "Of me and some other people. Occasionally I have encounters in the city. When I feel the need for some variety, or want to blow off steam. I book a room. I make a few calls. I relax."

"I see. And someone filmed you relaxing in your hotel room, I take it? With girls? I assume they're girls?"

"Yes, girls. Two cameras. One in the smoke detector, another in the bathroom vent."

"No blackmail note?"

Victor shook his head. "He doesn't need one. I know what he's getting at. He's angry at me for being with Belinda."

"So why did he not send this to Belinda?"

"Oh, hell, I don't know. To drag it out? Make me sweat? Who the fuck knows? It's an inter-office envelope. From the building. He was right here, where Belinda and I work. Probably at the same time we were."

"So, he's letting you know he can reach out. Any time he wants." Knox leaned back and steepled his fingers. "He's telling you that he doesn't care how dangerous it is for him. That he doesn't care about the risk of getting caught again because thanks to you, he has nothing left to lose."

"Yeah. I figured that out all by myself."

Knox's non-eyebrows lifted again. "Ah. Then I guess you don't need me."

"Don't dick around," Victor snapped. "This is serious."

"Oh, yes," Knox agreed. "It is serious. This guy is definitely a problem. He is motivated, patient, extremely angry, and a lot smarter than you are." They stared at each other for a long moment before Knox spoke again. "Luckily for you, I'm here."

"Let's stay on topic," Victor said, through clenched teeth.

"Absolutely. I assume the sex tape hasn't been seen by your wife?"

"She's not my—"

"Wife," Knox said. "Yes, I get it. Does she know about these encounters?"

"No, she does not. And she can't."

"Understood. I will keep that in mind when I deal with the two of you."

"No, you won't have to. After today, you'll only deal with me," Victor said. "The sex tape is a big escalation from playing games with the freezer."

"So is the fire. I'm assuming that's him, too."

"So am I," Victor said. "He's declared war. My relationship. My house. At this point, I don't even want the cops to drag him back to Rock Ridge. I want that shithead gone. For good."

Knox's eyes narrowed. "That will be expensive," he said after a moment. "But I'm guessing you're flush, and you have cash to hand. Unless of course, your assets are tied up in, I don't know, gemstones?"

"I'm not paying you to speculate about me," Victor said. "I want this problem dealt with."

Knox steepled his fingers again. "I'll need money. Cash up front. Subcontracting is expensive."

"You hire other people—"

"You don't really want to know the details, do you, Vic?"

Knox's teeth flashed. "I can't imagine you want me to send you an itemized bill?"

"No," Victor said. "And cool the attitude. I've had a shitty day."

"I get that a lot," Knox said. "It's one of the reasons I get results. So listen up. Unless he got someone else to do it, which I doubt, Henry Devlin was here, in this building, to deliver the thumb drive. He was monitoring you when you set up your encounter. He knew which hotel, and which room you were going to be in. He probably planted the hardware himself. So he's not far away. What phone did you use to contact the women and book the room?"

Victor thought about it. "My cell."

"At home? Or at work?"

"I was in the car," Victor said. "Same with the hotel reservation."

Knox nodded. "Okay. It's hard to say where he's watching. Definitely at home, what with the fire and the fridge. But you didn't call the women or the hotel from home. So, this is what we'll do. Call me from your car, and give me details for a meeting. Make it for tomorrow night. That gives me time to line up the right person, and gives Henry time to get to the city from wherever he might be hiding. Pick a restaurant in New York, and ask me to make the reservation. Be specific, including about the table. He'll hear everything. And say we need privacy. He won't be able to resist that. I'm betting that he'll try to record us. To see if you incriminate yourself."

"You're baiting a trap?"

"You don't want the details, Vic," Knox said. "Just picture a mugging gone tragically wrong."

"Great," Victor said. "Great. The sooner the better."

"Which brings us to my fee," Knox scribbled a number in the notebook and slid it to Victor. "That includes my expenses."

Victor's eyes widened. "That's outrageous."

Knox shrugged. "It's more than reasonable. Shop around if you want to."

Victor stared at the number on the paper. He wanted to kick someone. Preferably Henry Devlin, who had made such a goddamn mess of everything.

It was a lot. But Knox was right. This was his best bet. Shopping around meant more exposure.

He could just take matters into his own hands. He was tempted. But it simply was not practicable. He wasn't a trained assassin, though that might have been a good career choice for him, he sometimes thought. It would have exploited almost as many of his talents as the hedge fund did.

Anyway, at this point, Knox knew too much and had guessed a lot more. If he didn't get his own hands dirty, he'd have no incentive to keep quiet.

Victor nodded in bad grace. "Fine. Half up front. Half when it's done."

"Fine." Knox stood again, his voice brisk. "I'll make some calls. Plan on driving down toward the city tomorrow evening. He's probably put a tracker on your car, and he'll be watching it."

"I found it already," Victor said. "Fucking bastard."

Knox nodded, picking up his briefcase as he turned to the door. "You think you found it, but you didn't find them all. Same with your wife's car—oops, sorry. Your baby mama."

Victor ground his teeth as the door fell shut behind the man.

Chapter Eleven

Bingo. There he was, the man himself, coming out of the library. Even from all the way down the block at the bus stop where she lurked, Amber recognized Blackbeard's tall, lanky silhouette and the baseball cap, oversized coat, and the cross-body computer bag he always carried. She also recognized the way he stopped at the top of the steps and did a slow one-eighty, scanning the entire street. She'd seen him do it before because she'd actually lingered more than once to catch a sneak peek.

She couldn't see his face from here, which was a shame. Because she liked his face, though someone should teach him to groom his facial hair. The guy needed help.

But he wouldn't get any from her, not after that stunt he pulled yesterday. Chasing her through the subway like some maniac stalker. Jesus. It had brought back all her worst fears. Amber had difficulty sleeping at the best of times. Blackbeard dogging her up and down the length of Manhattan had really done a number on her nerves. She'd been buzzing all night. Still was buzzing, in point of fact.

She'd been skulking in the bus stop for a couple of hours now, wearing an N95 mask, a hat with the brim tugged low and tinted glasses. The baggy, shapeless black fake fur coat she was huddled in was warm enough for brisk walking, but not for stationary lurking. She was freezing her ass off out here. She should have built an outfit around one of her fat suits. All the other times she had waited to peek at him, Blackbeard had come out not long after she'd left. Her arrival and departure times were random by design.

It was almost like once she was gone; he lost interest in being there, too.

But she couldn't read his mind. She didn't know if he was thinking about her. She knew absolutely nothing about him, except that he had chased her tired ass all over town yesterday, so he'd definitely been thinking about her then. And she wasn't going to sleep again until she knew why.

Bad enough that he saw through her kick-ass disguises. The only reason she had concluded that his interest was benign was because he'd never tried to follow her. Until, suddenly, he did.

So now what was she supposed to think? Was Blackbeard on her trail, after all? Was he with the US Marshals, or the Feds, or working for Leon, or the DiAngelos? Was he out to get her? Or just too curious for his own good? She knew a little something about that herself. Two could play this game.

Amber was tired of being at a disadvantage. As soon as he copped to her disguises, he instantly became someone who knew a lot about her. He had no context for the info, but he still had it. She, on the other hand, knew absolutely nothing about him.

This was not okay, so she would fix it. She'd follow him back to his lair. Find out where he lived and anything else she could glean about him. What she'd do with the information was anyone's guess. But hey, one small, shuffling step at a time. The whole point of this was to do, well, something. Not nothing.

Blackbeard took off, walking fast, heading downtown. He

WARREN ADLER & SHANNON MCKENNA

ate so much ground that she had to scramble to keep him in sight, bumping and jostling through the crowded Midtown sidewalks. At least the pursuit warmed her up. Small mercies. The crowd gave her cover, but it gave him cover, too, and he almost got away from her at least a half a dozen times. Once, she was sure she'd lost him. She paused on the sidewalk outside a big electronics store, just panting and staring around herself, when Blackbeard pushed out through the doors, carrying a plastic shopping bag and moving so fast, he didn't even notice her.

Amber waited a decent interval, heart thudding, then followed him once again.

He was heading west now, then south. He made another stop at a little bodega on a cross-street. Amber watched him pick out his groceries. An orange. An apple. Two bananas. He ducked inside and came out with another bag. She could see a cornflakes box and a quart of milk through the thin recyclable plastic. Blackbeard apparently shared her minimalist culinary sensibilities. Maybe her miniature grocery budget, too.

She decided he was probably on his way home. People didn't usually get groceries unless they were going to offload them soon. She hung back as he headed farther south and west, into Hell's Kitchen, finally stopping in front of an unprepossessing twelve-story building. It was soot-stained, shabby, and encrusted with scaffolding. Blackbeard pulled out a key and vanished through the front door.

Amber stood there, feeling dispirited, tired, and more than a little stupid. All this drama, all this subterfuge, all this effort, and for what? She had a street address now. But no apartment number. Hundreds of people probably lived in that building.

She should be at work on her own project. Making bold decisions, clever plans, and finding the money to execute them. Not wasting her time getting yet another pointless door slammed in her face. Blackbeard's hidden agenda was yet another mystery, as impenetrable as Tori's tiger. Which might as well be in Fort Knox, given how unlikely it was that she'd get into the Graziano house to search for it.

She had to top up her money stash, starting tonight. Time to go home and make herself look smashing. Then it was off to the bars and clubs to relieve people of their wallets and their bling. That at least she could do on her own, without expensive expert help.

She was pushing her luck, doing it, and pushing it hard. But what choice did she have? Getting any kind of real job would require ID and references she didn't have in the new name. She needed money if she was going to storm Fortress Graziano. Social-engineering her way into the place would require the help of professionals like the ones she and Mamma worked with back in their grifting days, and they didn't come cheap. And she couldn't promise to cut them in, either. Even if she could find the damn thing, she had no idea what was in Tori's tiger. Or if anything was in it at all. Poor Michael had probably been delirious by the time he started yelling about it. She could be shooting at the moon.

Amber was beginning to have an unsettling sense of déjà vu. This was exactly the kind of high-pressure situation that had ruined Mamma. A person had to be cool and steady to grift, and Mamma had not been, at the end. She had needed a stake to get away from Sid, who was throwing his weight around, getting drunk, stealing Mamma's money and grabbing the fourteen-year-old Amber's ass. So Mamma had taken some risks, and she'd gotten herself busted. Eight to ten in the women's prison, leaving Amber to Sid's tender mercies.

Mamma hadn't had any illusions about what that would mean for her daughter. Sid was a pig and a shithead loser. Mamma could have written the script herself. When the inevitable happened, Amber confessed it tearfully in one of her phone calls. Mamma tried to organize for someone to take Sid out. But before she could follow through, she slipped in the showers, hit her head, and died.

Or so they said. A hothead like Mamma, mean as a snake. She'd run off her big mouth, pissed someone off, and run herself off a cliff. She'd run Amber off a cliff, too.

Sid had his depraved fun with her for a while. Then he got the bright idea of renting her out to his buddies. That was Amber's cue to dissolve some of his Valium into his whiskey. As soon as he passed out, she cleaned out his wallet. She had thought about killing him before she left. A knife in the belly. A frying pan to the skull while he lay there, snoring. She'd stood staring at him, thinking about it. Imagining it. Staring holes into the useless bag of skin that lay on the couch. But in the end, she didn't have the stomach for it. She'd hoped maybe the Valium would kill him, but there hadn't been enough pills in the bottle.

Amber trudged toward Chelsea, her steps slower and heavier now. Chasing Blackbeard had worn her out, and she had a long night of being sexy and scintillating ahead of her. The thought exhausted her. Maybe because she'd let herself think about Sid. She usually slalomed around those memories.

Part of her had hated the rest of her for not following through on killing him. But that would have turned her into a completely different person. Set her on a different path. Who could say if it would have been a better one, or a worse one? She had no clue.

She picked up the pace, giving herself a pep talk. Mamma had tried to save her, after all. Even if she had fallen short, Amber still appreciated the effort. And the fact that Mamma had thought she was worth saving. That had to mean something.

Even if that bitch Fate rolled right on over the two of them anyway.

Chapter Twelve

H enry paced back and forth in front of the restaurant where Victor was meeting his investigator. Kavanaugh's was his least favorite kind of place, a big noisy bar crowded during post-work happy hour, fronting a big noisy dining room. He'd gone inside when he arrived, but he hadn't been able to come up with a plausible reason to approach the table Victor had told the man to reserve. Victor had been very specific about that. Henry had no idea why, but it was useful info. Or would be, if Henry could get anywhere near it.

Right now it was occupied by a couple who were taking their time, giggling and kissing each other's hands. He stuck an earbud in and tapped his phone, listening again to the clip he had intercepted.

"Let's meet tomorrow evening. I'll drive down to the city. I need to talk to you in private. I was thinking Kavanaugh, on Eighth Avenue. Could you make the reservation for me?"
"Sure, no problem. Nine-thirty good?"
"That's fine. Do it soon. The place is hot right now, so it'll be busy. There's a booth in the back corner of the dining room, a two-header with

a wine bar on one side and a condiments bar on the other. Ask for that.
It'll give us a little space. And it's private. I don't want anyone listening
in by accident."
"I hear you, and I'm on it. See you there."

Henry felt weirdly exposed in the get-up he'd bought for
the occasion, a business suit, dress shirt, and a tie. He'd
trimmed his hair and even bought the right shoes. All of it felt
so wrong. He'd gone to great lengths to organize his life so he
would never have to dress like this, choked by a stiff collar,
bound by a suit jacket pulling across his shoulders. He'd fitted
the bill of his flat cap with his anti-facial recognition LEDs.
Some kind of billed hat was necessary when he was out in
public, but the flat cap made him feel like he was fresh off the
boat, as out of place as his Irish ancestors must have felt back
in the nineteenth century.

He'd spent the afternoon listening to Belinda carry on
hysterically about the fire, but the damage had not ultimately
been all that bad. The house was waterlogged from the sprin-
klers, the kitchen would have to be cleaned and repainted, and
some of the cabinets needed replacing. But it was just a matter
of spending money, being inconvenienced. Alas. Poor them.

Victor had cut through the tearful harangue and
demanded that Belinda go to the bank and get cash out of
their safe deposit box. He had heard them talk about that
particular bank before. The one in Weybourne, over thirty
miles away from where they lived. It was not the bank Belinda
had used when Henry had been married to her. Henry
suspected that the diamonds were there, too.

He also had a hunch that this meeting was a trap. They
knew that any chance to gather more information, especially
possibly incriminating information, would be irresistible to
him. They could be setting him up. But he still couldn't let this
chance go by.

Standing around and waiting was driving him out of his

mind. Or maybe he was already there. The things he found himself doing these days were not hallmarks of a healthy psyche. Like trailing the costume girl. He was still kicking himself for that. She hadn't even shown up in the Reading Room today, which made him ridiculously, inappropriately, miserable. He'd blundered plenty of times with women before, making an ass of himself in various ways too painful to think about. But nothing had ever made him so angry at himself as yesterday's performance. Except for believing Belinda's declarations of love.

He decided to check back inside. Sidling through the crowded bar, he saw that the lovers at Victor's table had finally reached dessert, and were feeding each other tiny, teasing bites. His was something chocolate. Hers was something orange, maybe pumpkin. Henry hated pumpkin. He turned around and elbowed his way outside again. The street was a cacophony of traffic and the sidewalk was jammed. No one was likely to notice him pacing up and down like some kind of maniac.

A few minutes later, he glanced through the restaurant window and saw the couple. The guy was helping the girl put on her coat. He leaned down to kiss the nape of her neck. Which tickled, judging from her laughter. If someone did that to him, he'd scream and hit the ceiling. As Belinda had learned, to her cost.

Before he could head them off, Henry was swamped by an embarrassing flood of memories. How he'd acted when Belinda came on to him, even after they were married. He'd been as romantic and tender as he knew how to be, but he'd always felt she was amused by his awkward efforts. He'd been so overcome by his luck. A woman like that, the envy of other men, with him? Wow! He'd never even let himself question it.

It would never have occurred to him to kiss the nape of her neck. Certainly not in a restaurant. It had been a big deal to hold her hand in public. Intimate moments were none of the world's business.

The couple were making their way out of the bar and onto the sidewalk. This was his chance, before they seated another party. After that, it would be time for Victor and the P.I.'s date. He went back into Kavanaugh's, elbowed through the crush of people in the bar, and barreled into the dining room.

"Sir?" The hostess hurried after him, alarmed. "Sir, do you have a reservation? Excuse me! Sir!"

Henry smiled over his shoulder without breaking stride. "My girlfriend forgot her phone," he explained. "She's double parked out on a cross-street. I need to see if it fell under the table. I'll be just a second."

The woman hustled after him. "I'll do it, sir! Let me check that for you, and I'll—"

"Two seconds, and I'll be out of your way."

He wound his way around tables, catching a few puzzled glances, as he felt in his pocket for a small listening device he'd bought earlier. The table Victor had specified, back corner, wine bar on one wall, condiments bar on the other, was right in front of him.

Sliding into the booth, Henry leaned down, pulled out the listening gizmo he'd already programmed to his phone, and stuck it under the table. Then he rummaged theatrically around on the floor. After a few seconds, he got up, brushing his pants and straightening his jacket. The hostess was watching him, tight-lipped, her arms crossed over her chest.

He shrugged, putting on his best apologetic look. "Not there. Sorry. I had to cover all the bases, you know? Thanks." He added, sidling past her. "Have a great night."

As he left the dining room, he was uncomfortably aware that he'd just impressed himself into that woman's long-term memory. She would have no trouble at all recognizing his mugshot. He pushed through the bar, trying to catalog everyone he saw, but the lights were low, and suddenly he felt dizzy.

It was a trap. All at once, he was sure of it. The sex video had been his message to Victor. And right afterward, Victor tossed out a lure like this. What else could it be? And he'd leaped for it. Like an idiot.

The noise in the bar swelled until it was grotesquely loud in his head. He smelled garlic, armpit, wet wool and wet feet. Henry's stomach flopped in revulsion. He could barely breathe. Panic rose in him as he shouldered his way outside and took off down the sidewalk, ducking and dodging through the crowd, moving as fast as he could without flat-out running.

Chapter Thirteen

Amber sipped her lemon drop. She was listening with half an ear to the guy chatting her up at the bar while keeping an eye on Blackbeard in the mirror behind the bar's liquor bottles. For what purpose, she could not imagine.

If tailing him earlier had been a waste of time, following him tonight was doubly pointless. All he'd done was lurk here. She might as well ignore him and get to work. This place was full of perfectly good marks, for God's sake. But was she working them? No. She was too busy monitoring Blackbeard.

She couldn't figure it out. What, did she have some sort of crush on this guy? An obsession on a man? It was so out of character. She needed to focus, and having Blackbeard take up all her bandwidth made it really freaking hard.

She'd been minding her own business earlier this evening, cabbing up to one of her best hunting grounds when she'd realized she was at Blackbeard's cross-street, and yelled at the driver to stop, on impulse. What had she hoped to accomplish by that? Staking out Blackbeard's building in the icy darkness, while wearing an outfit calculated to give her frostbite and to attract maximum male attention? Really?

Her IQ was falling before her very eyes. Draining out like water from a bathtub.

She had been standing there berating herself when all of a sudden, Blackbeard strode into the light of a streetlamp right across the street. He'd been walking her way. The only reason he hadn't seen her was because she was in the shadows under a storefront awning.

He looked different tonight. All dressed up in a fancy wool coat and suit, a jaunty flat-cap on his head. He looked nervous, though. Jittery and distracted. What was it about this guy? For fuck's sake, they'd never even exchanged so much as a word, and already he was making a fool out of her.

But her cab was long gone, so what the hell. She stepped out of the shadows and followed him.

If he turned and caught a glimpse of her, he'd probably assume she was a working girl. Amber was decked out as Trix tonight. She had given the end of her nose a little silicone cap to make it squarer, more upturned, and she'd crafted a small bump right where the bone met cartilage. Trix had bitched and moaned about that bump. She'd talked about fixing it, but never had the nerve.

Amber had gold-toned foundation covering her freckles. Her wig was dark. Night-black ringlets fell to the small of her back. She'd used dark contacts. Her red lips tingled from the inflammatory lip-plumping goo. Long fake lashes enhanced Trix's signature smoky eye-makeup and heavy brows. Amber's own eyes were more wide-set than Trix's. But it wasn't like she was trying to fool anyone tonight.

Fortunately, she didn't need to change her body much. She and Trix had often used the same costumes. Trix's tits were bigger, but Amber's were higher, thanks to a little help from one of the showgirls' favorite boob doctors. Not an implant, just a lift, to slow down the inexorable march of time. Tonight, they popped abundantly out of the black corset-style leather top she wore with an above-the-knee black leather skirt. High black boots with square heels and thick rubber soles completed the outfit. No spikes tonight, in case she had to run like hell.

Like yesterday, when Blackbeard chased her across hell's half-acre. She still felt affronted about that. After weeks of those shy, delicate gestures, that barely perceptible nod that said *yes. I see you* all of a sudden. Out of nowhere, he was chasing her all over the city. It was jarring. Rude. Unlike him.

But how did she know what he was like? She didn't. She knew nothing.

But whoever and whatever he might be, by God, he had seen her. He was the only person in this teeming city who had. And, stupid or not, she liked being seen. At least by him.

Maybe that was why she'd spent the afternoon trailing him back to his den. Because he'd actually noticed her. He was smart and observant, she could tell that much. Even kind of cute, if you liked the wound up, laser-eyed types. And he wasn't stalking her for sex. Neither Donna nor Betty nor any of her other recent alter egos were likely to tickle any man's fancy.

No, Blackbeard saw things through different eyes. She hadn't been curious about a man in a long time. Except for Leon, who didn't count, at least that way. She had to pay attention to Leon just to keep from getting chopped into chunks.

In her book, mostly, men were a known quantity. Their minds all ran on similar tracks. The same tired scripts came out of their mouths with very little variation. In all fairness, she had been a showgirl, shaking tits and ass, so perhaps she had only encountered a certain class of man, ranging in quality from trash to barely mediocre. Bad boys out to party. Playing in Vegas in the convention hotel on the boss's expense account. Their wives didn't understand them, their kids were spoiled, ungrateful shitheads, all women were gold-digging bitches. But not you, oh, no. You seem so different from those cheap whores. Gimme something good to think about. Show me your tits.

The Kavanaugh was hopping tonight. The bar was packed with of out-of-towners. Businessmen drinking. Weekend adventurers from Jersey. People giving themselves permission to do things they wouldn't do back home. It felt a lot like Vegas.

The guy next to her informed her that his name was Armand. She nodded and smiled, but he was too busy gawking at her cleavage to notice. If it was quick money she wanted, the obvious solution was staring her in the face. But oh, God. She was sick to death of her future clients before she even solicited them. Death was almost preferable.

Or maybe not. Leon had redefined her fear of death when she saw what he'd done to Michael. That was not how she wanted to check out when her time came.

She'd been so close to packing it all in when she met him. Getting out of the scene for good. She'd been saving money for years. She didn't have a fortune by any stretch, but she'd socked away a few CDs. And now, thanks to Leon, the fruits of all that labor were out of her reach. If she even tried to withdraw them, she was cooked.

Armand was still talking. Amber murmured something that passed for a response and kept an eye on Blackbeard, who was still pacing up and down on the sidewalk. She decided she liked his flat-cap way better than the baseball cap. He'd even trimmed up the beard, wonder of wonders. If not for the tension on his face and those weird-ass glasses of his, Amber would have definitely have called him cute.

She felt a jolt of adrenaline as he turned off the sidewalk, pushed through the doors, and started elbowing his way through the bar. She was right in his line of vision, but he looked right past her.

What the hell? He'd spotted her as a shambling oldster, as a chubby pink-clad soccer mom, as a dried-up old gray-cardigan-wearing librarian. He'd seen through fake noses, prosthetic jaw inserts, buck teeth, over-bites, under-bites, wigs and stains, glued-on facial hair, dowager humps, fat suits. Now she was tarted up into full bombshell and all she got was crickets? Fuck that. It was not to be borne.

Blackbeard headed into the dining room. Armand was still talking, but Amber wasn't even pretending to listen anymore. She sidled away, trying to see what Blackbeard was doing. He was a man on a mission, weaving between tables and heading for a back booth. The hostess was chasing him.

Amber lost sight of Blackbeard when Armand jumped in front of her, desperate to reclaim her attention. She dodged, trying to look around him, and suddenly the thought hit her.

Blackbeard must be going on a date. That would explain everything; the nerves, the suit, the coat. Of course. Of course. She didn't have reason to have any emotions about that. It was a stranger's intimate life. A man she'd never spoken to, whose name she did not know. It was none of her goddamn business.

But then suddenly, he was back again, alone. He sped through the crowded bar and ran out onto the sidewalk.

Dumping her drink on the bar, Amber followed without a second thought. The last thing she heard was Armand, shouting something hostile after her. Picking up speed, she dashed through the door. The sidewalk was so crowded, she could lose Blackbeard in a heartbeat.

But there he was, striding purposefully away. So tall, with that jaunty hat. She set off after him, bobbing and weaving through the crowd, trying to keep the swift-moving form in sight.

Soon, the crowds began to thin. Blackbeard glanced back over his shoulder a couple of times, as if he was afraid of being followed. The third time he did it, Amber noticed the other guy.

He was big. Huge, actually. Black knit cap. Forest camo

coat. Jeans, boots. He was faster than she was, darting behind the back of a parked car as Blackbeard looked back. And yes, he was definitely following Blackbeard. Amber hadn't been sure at first. But when Blackbeard looked back again, and the guy dodged into a bus stop shelter, she knew that something was up.

She should turn around, she thought. Right now. Walk the other way. But she didn't. She kept moving.

What was her goddamn problem? Leave him to his fate. Who knew, maybe Blackbeard was the bad guy, and Camo Coat was a wronged victim seeking justice. Not that he looked like a wronged victim. He looked like a thug, and she should know. Even so, this was not her problem or her responsibility. Blackbeard's trouble was of his own making. She had bad choices of her own to sort out.

Then Blackbeard turned right, crossed the street, and headed west. He was going straight back home after his jaunt to Kavanaugh. No hot date, evidently. A second later, Camo Coat crossed, too.

Timing a break in the traffic, Amber sprinted. A horn blared as she jumped onto the opposite sidewalk. A taxi screeched. She hurried around the corner, boots pounding. Heart pounding.

Halfway down the block, she saw Camo Coat. Then she caught a glimpse of Blackbeard, now just a dark silhouette far ahead. He disappeared under some scaffolding. After the bright, disorienting chaos of Times Square, the street was eerily deserted. No one to call for help if whatever this was went sideways.

As Amber caught up, she saw Blackbeard fumbling with the key to his shabby apartment building. He finally got it right and vanished inside. Camo Coat walked up, stepping aside as a young man in earphones and a long scarf came out. Camo Coat caught the door just before it swung shut. As he went in, Amber darted forward. But she was too late. The door closed with a *thunk*. All she could do was watch through the glass as Camo Coat entered the stairwell and started up the stairs.

"Excuse me, miss." An old lady carrying a canvas bag of groceries was waving at Amber to get out of the way with her cane. Amber stepped aside with a smile and then stuck her booted foot in the door.

Halfway across the foyer, the old lady looked back at her and muttered some version of 'there goes the neighborhood'. Amber ignored her and went to the stairwell. She peered up.

Two shadows moved in a spiral above her, one on the second floor, one on the fourth. *Stupid, stupid, stupid.* That refrain played on a loop in her head as she ran up the stairs, staying flush to the wall, trying not to make noise, thankful for the thick rubber soles of her boots.

She was far beyond curiosity now. Curiosity was not a good enough reason to do something that might get her killed. She was acting as if Blackbeard belonged to her. As if he was someone she knew, or cared about, or needed, or felt responsible for. But the man was nothing to her. He was nobody.

She didn't even have a goddamn weapon. Not even a stupid, makeshift one. She could have at least grabbed a bottle from one of the recycling bins. The shadow flickering on the wall closest to her began to slow down. She did, too. Camo Coat was sneaking up on Blackbeard. She had to decide what to do about it.

Amber put on a burst of speed. The stairwell was unevenly lit. Some of the fluorescent bulbs were burnt out. If Camo Coat saw her before he made his move on Blackbeard, she would chug indifferently on past like any disgruntled woman who lived on the ninth floor of a building with a broken elevator, and just hope he didn't stab her as she went by. She could only hope that the presence of a witness would stop the guy from attacking. But that was a lot of weight to pin onto something as fragile as hope.

If she succeeded in thwarting Cam Coat's initial attack, she would look for an opportunity to warn Blackbeard without compromising herself. Maybe she could harangue him for playing his stereo too loud. Bitch about how she was sick of listening to Metalhead at three AM. He would be very confused by this. So would Camo Coat. And then?

Yeah. And then nothing. That was the best plan her rocket-scientist brain could come up with.

She climbed faster. Peering upward to see what was happening, she glimpsed Camo Coat slipping his hand into his pocket. On the floor above, Blackbeard's shadow wavered, then stopped in front of a door. Over the pounding of her own heart, Amber heard the click and rattle of keys. She saw the gleam of a blade. Camo Coat's shadow, tall and distorted like the Grim Reaper, oozed forward—

"Watch out!" she shrieked.

Time stretched like pulled taffy as Amber burst up out of the stairwell and Blackbeard spun around, his arm whipping up to block the blade that would have stabbed him in the neck.

Amber leaped onto Camo Coat's back with a yell, clawing at his face, trying to knock him off his feet, but he seemed rooted to the ground. Camo Coat stabbed at her thigh, then flung her off with ease. Amber smacked against the wrought-iron railing of the stairwell, bashing her head, shoulders, and back. Camo Coat followed up with a kick to her belly, and for some unmeasurable interval it was just pain. Shadows and blazing light, gasping and choking, more pain...

As she dragged in a rasping teaspoonful of air, then another time began to move forward again. But she couldn't tell what was going on the blur of movement. Grunts and shouts, gasps and thuds, shadows forming and re-forming. Someone's boot stomped at her wig. Another boot clipped her wrist.

Light shone down as one of the guys was flung to the

other side of the corridor, but there was so much blood in her eyes she couldn't tell which guy. Then she saw Camo Coat grinning down at her maniacally as he wound up to kick her in the face.

Amber flinched away, and the blow glanced off her shoulder. Blackbeard barreled into Camo Coat, and they were at it again, grappling over the railing. Blackbeard got a punch to the gut and a knee to the groin that made him gasp, but he kept pressing Cam Coat to the railing. The big man's feet stuttered and dragged on the floor, fighting for purchase. As he head-butted Blackbeard, who rocked backward, Amber grabbed Camo Coat's ankles and yanked them hard.

Camo Coat's feet lost their purchase and slipped. She let go. Camo Coat tipped. Blackbeard heaved, and Camo Coat went over the railing in a horrifying slow-motion somersault.

There was a long, despairing wail, followed by a *whump.* And silence.

Blackbeard hung over the railing, his mouth wide in disbelief.

Chapter Fourteen

Henry stared down in shock and denial. This could not have just happened. It was a dream, a hallucination. The crumpled form below was like a comma on the dingy white and gray tile in the bottom of the stairwell. Blood pooled around the man's head, spreading to form a gruesome mandala surrounded by the spiraling squares of flights of stairs. Henry's mind spun horribly. Like his stomach.

"Hey? Mister! No. Don't do it."

He spun around at the low, authoritative voice and was confronted by the keen gaze of the mysterious siren, still on the ground, her forehead streaming with blood. She was struggling to get up but kept thumping back down. Her leg was bleeding, too.

"Huh?" he said helplessly. "What?"

"You were about to hurl down on a crime scene, buddy. I urge you not to."

Crime scene? "But…but I…but he…he attacked me!"

"Sure, I know that. But tell it to the cops. They didn't see."

Oh shit. Cops would be all over this soon, and all over

him, too. She saw the horrified dismay in his eyes and nodded. "Yeah. It's just like I figured."

"What?" he said in bewilderment. "What are you figuring? Who are you? Do we know each other?"

She wiped the blood off her forehead. "Guess not," she murmured.

Whoever she was, she had been hurt defending him. She had saved his life. Oddly, he heard Belinda's disapproving voice in his mind. *Wake up, Henry. Get out of la-la land.*

He knelt beside her. "You're hurt," he said. "Your leg and your nose. And it looks like your nose is—what on earth is on your nose?" It seemed absurd, but the tip of her nose seemed to have peeled right off. As she plucked at it, Henry realized it was a prosthetic silicon extension. Then it hit him, like a brick in the face. "Oh, my God, of course! It's you!"

Her eyebrows climbed up. "Meaning what? Who am I?"

"The costume girl from the Rose Reading Room," he said. "You're very different tonight. I've never seen you so, ah…"

Sexy. He didn't say it, but she heard it anyway. Her full, painted red lips curled in amusement. "Yeah. I mostly like to disappear, but you've been making that hard lately, buddy. Not tonight, though. You were way out in space. You didn't see me at all in the bar. The lengths I have to go to get your attention, man. Whew. That guy almost had you."

He looked around wildly. It seemed so strange that, after what had just happened, that no people were pouring out of their doors on every floor to gawk at the nightmarish spectacle and point accusing fingers at him. "Thanks for saving me," he said. "But why were you following me to begin with?"

She tried once again to clamber to her feet, grabbing the wrought-iron railing with her bloodied hand, but she lost her balance again. Henry caught her and steadied her. She pulled a tissue out of her pocket, clapped it over her thigh, and looked up right into his eyes. "That's my question," she said. "Why were you following me the other day?"

"Sit down," he urged her. "Please. You'll fall over."

"Just tell me why, right now. Before you say one more word."

He let out a breath, trying to think of something, anything, to say. He didn't really know the answer to her question, but something about the switched-on look in her eyes shocked the awkward truth right out of him.

"First, I was just curious," he said. "And I was afraid you were trailing me. Then, when you kept coming, wearing all the different costumes, I figured you must be hiding, too. I wanted to ask you, but I knew you'd bolt. And you did." He hesitated for a second. "I thought I'd ruined it. That I'd never see you again. And that made me sad."

A baby cried somewhere in the silence, from an apartment down the hall.

"Well, damn," she said. "That's weird, but okay. Now listen up. You have a series of decisions to make real quick. What's your name?"

"Henry," he blurted before he could stop himself. He had given no one his real name since the day he'd been sprung out of prison. He hadn't even spoken it out loud.

"Henry," she repeated. "Okay. Someone's going to find that asshole downstairs any minute, and I don't want to be here when they do. I'm assuming you don't either."

"No, but you need a doctor. Your leg, and your——"

"No doctors. And you're bleeding, too." She pointed at his forearm. He suddenly noticed the heat, the sting, the sticky hotness of blood seeping down the sleeve into his hand.

"I can't call the cops," he told her. "Or go to the emergency room."

"Me neither. But whoever has it in for you knows where you live now, so you'd better blast out of here permanently. Help me get up, okay?"

"I'll help you get home. I'll call a ride share. Just let me grab my computer and my go-bag. It's all ready."

"Good man. Hurry. I'm going to start down the stairs."

"Let me help you—"

"No! Not together. If someone sees us or stops us, there's no use in both of us getting busted, right?"

Henry picked up the keys from where he'd dropped them when the guy jumped him and went inside. The bag and the laptop were ready to go, and he was grateful for the paranoia that had impelled him to keep them that way. On his way past the kitchen, he seized a roll of paper towels. Tearing off a big handful, he ran some water over his bloodied hand, then stuffed the wad of paper towels up his sleeve. He dampened another handful, slung his go bag over his shoulder, and walked out the door. It hurt, viscerally, to leave thousands of dollars in electronic equipment behind, but he'd been steeling himself for the possibility. He wiped up the blood on the floor, and ran down the stairs, wiping up blood drops as he saw them.

Joining the costume girl on the landing, Henry handed her a clean wad of paper towels. "Here," he said. "Hold these against your leg."

She pressed the makeshift bandage to her thigh as Henry tapped his location into the ride share app. He found one thankfully nearby. "Can I pull up your hood?" he asked. "To hide the blood?"

She blinked, her eyes bleary, and nodded, fumbling with her bloodied hand. He tugged the hood over her head then put an arm around her, lifting her almost off her feet as he hustled her down the many flights of stairs. In the foyer, they were careful not to look at the body sprawled below in the basement level.

The rideshare was waiting at the corner, a battered old Jeep. Henry opened the door and helped her into the seat, then ran around to climb in on the other side, hoping the guy wouldn't notice the shape they were in.

"Where to?" the driver asked.

Henry nudged the costume girl. "Hey," he prompted. "Where can I take you?"

She coughed out a Chelsea address. The Jeep surged forward, and the more speed they picked up, the more oxygen went into his lungs. The costume girl's eyes had closed. Her face seemed gray and stiff beneath the streaks of blood. The driver was lost in his own thoughts, thank God.

A half an hour of crawling crosstown traffic later, the rideshare stopped in front of a modest townhouse. Henry sent the payment with a thirty percent tip, and hurried around the car, pulling the woman out and onto her feet. The bloody wad of paper towels fell into the gutter as the Jeep accelerated away, leaving Henry holding her braced against his body, but she had gone limp, sagging against him.

"Hey," he urged. "Let me get you inside. Do you have keys? Please, stay with me. Help me out." He patted her cheek, which was sticky with blood. "Miss? Your keys?"

Her eyelashes fluttered as she groped at the pocket of her coat. Henry dug his hand into the pocket the costume girl was feebly patting and pulled out a bunch of keys.

There was a video camera over the door. He looked down, hiding his face behind his hat brim and the costume girl's shiny black ringlets. His computer bag was slung securely over his shoulder, so he scooped her into his arms.

A memory flashed through his mind, of the last and only time that he had ever carried a woman. He'd carried Belinda over the threshold of their house after they were married. He had been flustered and embarrassed, but she had insisted.

This was easier. The costume girl seemed lighter, or maybe he was just stronger after all those months of push-ups, sit-ups, and running. Plus, he was hopped up on adrenaline, so she seemed almost alarmingly light. He practically bounded up the steps to the front door, trying to keep her steady while also managing the keys.

They got inside before anyone walked past, fortunately.

The scene would have been memorable and suspicious to anyone watching, but somehow, they had evaded casually curious eyes tonight. He hoped he hadn't been caught by any electronic ones.

Henry stopped in a large, elegantly furnished living room. The furniture was cream-colored, and they were both still sticky and oozing with blood.

"Where will I find some first aid gear?" he asked her. "Disinfectant, gauze?"

Her improbably long, dark lashes fluttered open. "Upstairs," she said faintly. "Front bedroom. It has an attached bath. There's stuff in there. Lemme take this off." She shrugged out of the coat, letting it plop onto the carpet runner.

He left it, and picked her up again. Once upstairs, he flicked on lights as he went through doors. Henry found the front bedroom and bathroom, and set her down gently onto the edge of the bathtub. "Can you stay sitting up?"

She nodded.

"How do you feel?" he asked. "Still with me?"

"Peachy," she forced out. "Never better."

It occurred to him that if she had the energy to be sarcastic, that had to be a good sign. Though it could just be a reflex. He pulled out the roll of paper towels he'd shoved into his go-bag and unwound a few, folding them into a fresh pad. "I'm just going to wash my hands," he told her. "Keep that pressed against the wound."

He washed in the hottest water the sink would produce with the hyacinth scented soap until the water swirling in the big porcelain sink no longer ran pink. The costume girl was deathly pale, but her hand still pressed the pad over her leg.

Henry knelt on the fluffy bath mat and folded up the edge of the blood-soaked black leather skirt so he could look at the wound. It was still oozing, but slowly now. He cleaned and dressed it as best he could, glugging betadine onto cotton balls he'd found in the medicine cabinet. He pulled the skin together with butterfly bandages and slathered the whole thing with antibiotic ointment. Then he put a wad of gauze on it, and taped it down onto her pale, freckled thigh.

He wished sharply that he'd done something useful and practical with his life, like become a doctor. Having taken the MCATs on a dare was useless. He should have at least done a course in emergency medicine. He had meant to, after Faith was born. It was a good way to fend off the anxiety that came with being too acutely aware of the dangers to a baby or toddler. Choking, fevers, poison, convulsions, fractures, punctures, insects, dog bites, cars, antibiotic-resistant pathogens of all kind. So many things could hurt those tender, helpless, bumbling little things before they developed faculties of reason.

Plenty of things could hurt them afterwards, too.

Henry turned his attention to her bloody forehead, using a washcloth to clean away the mess so he could see the damage. Her eyes opened. "Henry," she said softly.

"Yes?"

"Is that your real name?"

He hesitated, but only for a moment. "Yes." It was a relief, to say it. To have someone know it.

He swabbed disinfectant gently over the contusion on her hairline. She hissed and flinched away. "Ow," she muttered.

"Hold on a sec."

"I need to clean it."

"Yeah, yeah. I know. Just one second."

To his astonishment, though he should not have been so surprised, she reached up, fiddled around her ears, and lifted the curly mass of black curls right off her head.

She stared up at him, eyes defiant, looking so much smaller without it. Reddish blonde hair was coiled on her head and flattened beneath a nylon cap. Fuzzy pale wisps escaped around her temples and her nape. "Easier to clean this way," she said. "Right?"

"Ah, yes," he replied, bemused. "It definitely will be."

The wound was uglier than he'd anticipated. A raised knot was forming on her hairline. Blood matted the soft, strawberry-blonde locks. He cleaned it, disinfected it, and covered it with a bandage. "What about your nose?" He asked when he was done. "It was bleeding, too."

"No biggie. It just got bumped." She touched it gently. "It'll swell, and I'll have some bruises under my eye, but that's all. Nothing some makeup won't cover."

"You could have a concussion. And you need a tetanus shot for that stab wound," he said. "Maybe a stitch or two. And he kicked you in the stomach. I saw it."

She shrugged. "I've taken worse and been fine. I can't go to a hospital, so don't give me a hard time. And you got cut, too, right? How's that arm?"

"It's fine."

Her eyes narrowed. "Don't be a dick, Henry. Take off the jacket. Let me see."

He reluctantly shrugged off the jacket. The wads of blood-soaked paper dropped on to the floor. The cut was oozing. It looked messy and horrible.

"Well, well. You need stitches and a tetanus shot, too. Give me that disinfectant."

"I can do it," he protested. "It's fine."

"Shut up, Henry. You're bugging me."

In the end, they compromised. He leaned over the sink to wash the wound and she washed her own hands in the bathtub. Then he let her dab on various disinfectants and tape on the gauze. Afterward, they just sat there together, exhausted and speechless among the litter of bloodied paper towels and bandage wrappings.

"What's your name?" Henry asked.

She hesitated, then let out a soft huff of laughter. "Amber."

That was fitting, he thought, looking at her hair. "Is that your real name?"

"As real as any other name. It's definitely my favorite name. My enemies know it, too, though, so please keep it to yourself."

"Of course," he said hastily. "And please, return the favor."

"Sure. So since we're letting our hair down and all, pass me the white case on that shelf next to you. And the bottle of saline solution, too."

He did, and watched as she popped open two little caps in a long series of lids along the length of the case. She took contact lenses out of her eyes, rinsed them in saline solution and left them to float in little pools of salt water. When she was done, she snapped the contact cases closed, and looked up at him and smiled. Her eyes were topaz gold. Beautiful.

"That's a kit?" he muttered, dazzled. "With all those different color eyes? Wow."

"Yeah." She shrugged. "You switch them out, like clothes or wigs. These lenses are hard, though. I'd rather use soft ones, but they're too expensive. I can only stand to wear these for a few hours. Any longer and my eyes puff up and I look completely baked."

Next, she peeled off her false eyelashes. Dropping them in the trash, she gave him a crooked smile. "I have blonde eyelashes," she said. "Big beauty flaw. Pass me the blue packet of makeup wipes on that shelf."

He'd learned about makeup wipes during his time with Belinda. It took Amber a good bit of swabbing to get off the gold-toned foundation, the smoky eye shadow, the lip-liner, the eyebrows. Beneath the cosmetics she was very pale, with reddish brown eyebrows and a spattering of freckles.

Finally, she peeled off the nylon cap, plucked out a few

hairpins, and loosened the coils of red gold corkscrewing curls with her fingers. Her hair swung just shy of her shoulders. Without makeup, she looked soft. Vulnerable. Lovely.

Panic jolted him as he realized he had been staring at her. Like a creep.

"This is Amber, with no tricks," she said, her voice light. "You might be the only man on earth who's seen me at such a disadvantage. And you might never see it again."

"Sorry I was staring." He looked away. "I was kind of, ah, hypnotized. It's been a weird night. I didn't mean to gawk at you."

"It's okay," she said. "I'm used to it."

I just bet you are. He stopped the words from bursting out just in time. He had no idea if that was an offensive thing to say to a woman, but he didn't dare risk it. Still, he couldn't look away. She was unlike anything he'd ever seen. She reminded him of what he thought a wood nymph might look like, or a sprite. There was something unearthly about her, right down to the thin green tendril, a tattoo of a vine that curled over her shoulder and spread perfect little purple flowers across the shimmery paleness of her back.

She was loosening the tie of her corset top, giving him a lopsided smile. "So Henry. I don't want to wear this leather thing to bed. It's time to take it off. And I really hope you're not expecting a full frontal. Because it's not happening."

"Oh, God, no. I'm so sorry." He leaped to his feet, tipping over the bottle of disinfectant and knocking a pile of towels off the shelf.

Righting the bottle, he screwed on the lid, and picked up the towels. "Sorry. I'm out of here. Right away. Just let me clean up this mess."

Amber gave him a little, teasing smile as he mopped up the disinfectant, and nudged the wastebasket with her foot so he could stuff everything inside it.

"Could you pass me some fresh stuff to change into?" she asked.

"Sure. Of course." He backed hastily out.

"Look in the tall dresser near the window," she called through the door. "Second drawer. There's a pair of pale blue jersey shorts, and a long navy T-shirt. And grab me some fresh underwear while you're there. Top drawer."

Oh, God. He found the shorts and tee-shirt without incident, but the top drawer was a shock. Every item in it was skimpy satin, or silk, or lace. No plain cotton in sight.

It felt like a trap, and he was mortally afraid of this kind of trap. But he had to power through this for her sake. She had warned him, and saved his life, twice. He could hand her a pair of underwear through a bathroom door. It wouldn't turn him to stone.

He grabbed something silky at random. Wrapping the tee-shirt and shorts around it, he passed it through the door, face averted.

She took the clothing. "Thank you," she said, sounding amused.

After that, Henry just stood there at a total loss, wondering what his duties and obligations were to this strange and terrifying creature who had just inexplicably saved his life. The dilemma was resolved for him when the bathroom door opened a few minutes later. She stood in the doorway clad in the blue cotton jersey, her slim, graceful form backlit by the bathroom light. "You still in there, Henry?"

"Yes," he replied, flustered. "Sorry. I don't want to intrude. I just wanted to make sure you didn't need any more help. Let me get you to the bed."

She let out another soft huff of laughter. But as he angled his body so he could pick her up again, she made no sound of protest. He paused, looking down at her. "May I?"

A puzzled crease appeared between her fine red brows. "Sure. Thanks for asking."

It wasn't far to the bed. He laid her down carefully, as if she were made of blown glass and flower petals. "Do you have any pain meds?" he asked.

"I think the owners of this house had some Vicodin. Might be old, though."

"Oh. So this house isn't yours?"

She answered with a crack of laughter. "As if! Hah. This is just a house-sitting gig. The owners are sailing in the Greek islands. I'm just watering their plants."

"I see. How about a broad-spectrum antibiotic? Do they have any of those?"

"Yeah, there's something, but I think they're pretty old, too. Look through the medicine cabinet, see what you can find."

Henry rummaged through the small pharmacy in the bathroom. He found an orange prescription bottle with eight Vicodin tablets, and another bottle half full of amoxicillin capsules. It was more or less the right drug, though it had expired four months ago. He filled a glass of water and brought it out to her.

"They're old, but they're definitely better than nothing," he said. "Is tap water okay, or do you want me to run down to the fridge and get you something else?"

She gazed at the Vicodin tab he held out to her, a frown in her eyes. "I hate blunting my edge," she said. "I hate, hate, hate it."

"I'll stand guard while you sleep," he offered rashly. "There's no way I'm going to sleep tonight anyway. My brain is racing a thousand miles an hour. So go ahead. Rest."

She looked disapproving. "Henry. Come on. You got slashed, and thumped too. I saw it happen. He got you a good one to the balls."

"Not quite full on. I'm all right." He wished she hadn't mentioned it. He'd been ignoring that pain pretty successfully. Now, there it was in his groin, *whanga-whanga-whanga*, a hot red throb of pain with each heartbeat. "How about that water?" he asked. "You make a decision?"

"Tap water's fine. You're sweet, Henry."

That stung, but he swallowed it without comment. Belinda had said it so often, in that condescending way of hers. Since his catastrophe, he'd made it a life goal to root all the sweetness out of his soul. He wanted to be bitter, sour, salty. As harsh as a bout of gallstones. But he couldn't say any of this to Amber. None of his past garbage was her fault.

"Not really," he said, shaking out an antibiotic and passing it to her. "You're supposed to take these morning and night."

She contemplated the two pills in her hand. "I'll only take the antibiotic if you take one, too," she announced. "You got that same blade to your arm, right? It's only fair."

"I want to make sure there's as close to a full course as possible for you," he told her. "Your wound is deeper."

"That's not the issue," she said. "You take one, or I won't. It's as simple as that."

Her eyes were adamant. Reluctantly, he shook one of the capsules into his hand.

Amber nodded in satisfaction and tossed her pills back. She took a gulp of water, then held the glass out. "Your turn. Bottoms up, dude. We both got stabbed with the same knife blade, so we can share a glass of water, right?"

He was pretty sure her reasoning didn't pan out from the point of view of hygiene. But it was no less hygienic than kissing. People survived that all the time. He pushed the random thought away, tossed the capsule into his mouth, and took a sip, careful not to put his lips where hers had so recently been. It seemed inappropriate. In his mind, he heard Belinda laughing. *Weirdo. Sweet vanilla man.*

He swallowed. The pill stuck in his throat for a moment before it finally went down.

Amber offered him the Vicodin, but he shook his head.

"No. I want to stay awake so you can rest. It's the least I can do. You saved my life."

She rolled her eyes. "You saved mine, too," she said. "That guy would have caved in my face with his boot if you hadn't gone at him."

"But you saved me twice. And you wouldn't have needed saving if I hadn't—"

"Stop it right there, Henry. You're making me tired."

"Yeah. Right. Sorry. I'll just, um. Go. Let you rest."

"Do you have clothes in your go-bag?" she asked, looking at his blood spattered suit. "You look terrible."

"Not much. Mostly electronics," he said. "It's okay."

"Not if you need to go out. Grab some clothes from the other bedroom. At least a shirt. I think the guy who lives here is short, so his pants won't help you much."

"Don't worry about me. I'll just go and let you sleep."

He closed the door gently and went down the stairs. His go-bag lay next to the door, next to the coat that Amber had let drop. He picked up the coat and hung it on the coat tree in the foyer. There was a shelf with a big woven basket piled, strangely enough, with men's black and brown leather wallets. There were dozens of them. He flipped a few of them open. Drivers' licenses, credit cards. There was no cash in any of them.

He dropped the wallets back in the basket, feeling strange for snooping, and strolled through the house, orienting himself before setting up his computer on the kitchen table. The house made sense now that he knew she was only house-sitting. Nothing about it matched that woman, except for the busy, colorful, crowded bedroom. That was the only room that looked inhabited, with that big cluttered makeup table and mirror, the busts sporting all the different wigs, and the big metal rods on wheels for hanging clothing.

That was the costume girl's lair. Not the rest of this house, with its neutral beige and earth tones, its bland and inoffensive pieces of art. Costume Girl was chaotic, instinctive. This house felt dull and calculated, like an upscale hotel.

He opened his laptop and connected to the feeds from Victor and Belinda's. He didn't use earphones, since he had promised Amber to watch over her while she slept. Not that there was much he could do if someone did show up. He was not the warrior type. He'd barely prevailed in the stairwell, and that was only because Amber had helped him.

But he'd promised that he would stay awake so that she could sleep. That might not be sustainable for too long, but right now, he was willing to stay awake for her forever. Or at least for as long as he managed to stay alive.

Henry turned on the speaker. Amber was asleep, and no one else would overhear.

For a long time, he just watched Belinda pacing in her kitchen. She went out to the garage three times for a cigarette. Faith woke up twice and had to be soothed back to sleep at great length. Finally, Victor's car made the garage sensor switch on.

In the foyer, Victor shrugged off his coat. Then he stomped into the kitchen.

"So?" Belinda's voice was hushed. "What happened?"

"We got shellacked, that's what happened."

"What? Shellacked? But...but they're professionals! Did he take the bait?"

"Sure, he took it. We identified him, and Knox sent someone after him."

"And? Did Henry get away?"

"The guy Knox sent is dead," Victor said harshly. "Henry killed him."

Belinda gasped. "Killed? Oh, my God. Do you think...do you think that he—"

"Would kill me? Or you? Or Faith? What do you think, Bel? What exactly do you think he's saying, doing that? Do you see any other way to parse this message?"

Maybe that I just wanted to keep on living? Henry thought.

"Oh, God," Belinda quavered. "Oh, dear God."

"This will make everything harder and more expensive," Victor bitched. "I'm going to need you to go back to the bank, Bel. Knox needs to do damage control. And he has to find someone else to try again, of course. And now it'll be twice as expensive. Jesus, what a shit show."

"I'm so scared. I can't. Let's change the name on the safe deposit box to yours. I can't—"

"Don't be an idiot, Bel." Victor turned on her. "I put our future in your hands when I put your name on that safe deposit box instead of mine, so do not fuck with me."

But Belinda was beyond intimidation, blubbering incoherently. Victor shoved her up against the wall, knocking down a picture. His hand clamped over her throat. He kissed her roughly, then dragged her into the bedroom.

Henry knew he shouldn't, because it made him feel awful, but he listened to the baby monitor to see what Faith heard. It made him feel sick. Their usual aggressive, noisy sex was ramping up into something even more toxic than usual. It made him queasy that Faith was within earshot of that. But there was nothing he could do. And there was nothing to be gained from listening to any more of it.

Henry switched off the monitor feed. He couldn't feel sorry for Belinda. She'd made her bed, and damn, was she ever lying in it.

The events of the night rushed through his mind. The violence, the fight, their attacker, curled up on the black and white tile, eight floors down. But the strongest image was Amber's face as she sank down into an exhausted sleep. The freckles on her cheeks. And those lashes. They were not blonde, like she had said. They were a deep red-brown at the base.

At their curling tips, they faded to a bright, light-catching gold.

Chapter Fifteen

It was strange to be back in Vegas with no one recognizing him, fawning on him, giving him the respect he was owed. Leon had definitely liked it better before. His face itched from the fake beard. He slunk into the shadows behind the dumpster at the backstage entrance of the Magnum, where Amber had performed, as a group of women came out. He recognized a few Amber had been friendly with. Some were girls she had called on his behalf when he had colleagues from out of town and needed to organize escorts for them. Two bleached blondes, Tash and Krystal, were the ones he was targeting. Amber had called them more than once, and Leon knew where they lived, having picked up a colleague from New Orleans at their place one morning after what had evidently been a very memorable girl-on-girl performance.

One put her hand out to stop the other, pausing to light a cigarette. "Order us some Chinese, Tash," she said. "I'm starving. God, my feet hurt."

Excellent. They had ordered takeout both of the two nights that he'd been watching them, and they favored Chinese. So, he had a bag of Chinese all ready to go in the back seat of the shit-tinted Honda Civic that the US Marshals had decided that he ought to drive. Leon had picked up the food in case he got lucky.

Tonight was his lucky night.

The two women clasped hands and strolled down the alley, one smoking, the other on her phone with the restaurant. He followed them toward the parking garage where he'd left the Civic, then followed them to the Green Valley neighborhood, parking a discreet block or so away from the house they shared.

He waited as long as he could stand it before grabbing the takeout bag and going to the house. Patience had never been his strong suit. Ruthlessness, that was his gift. He had never hesitated to inflict pain when it was called for, and sometimes when it wasn't.

Keeping the brim of his hat down to hide his face, Leon scanned the block to make sure no one was watching. His pistol was tucked into his pants. Hoisting the takeout bag, he went to the door and buzzed.

One of the blondes peeked out the windowpane, then opened the door with a smile. "Wow, that was quick!"

As she reached for the bag, Leon lunged forward, shoving her inside.

"Hey! Asshole!" she yelled. "You can't just—"

Smack, he swatted the side of her head with the gun, knocking her hard against the wall. She fell to her knees with a cry, dropping the bag.

"Tash? Who's that? Did the food come?"

Krystal appeared in the entryway arch and stared down the barrel of Leon's gun.

"I have money," she said swiftly. "It's in my purse. You can have all of it."

"Fuck your purse. You." He gestured at Tash on the floor. "Get up. Both of you, go into the living room and sit down on the couch. Do it. Now."

Wordlessly, the women did as he said. They sat, clutching each other's hands. Blood leaked from Tasha's bubbling nose as she sobbed silently.

"What do you want?" Krystal's voice shook. She was clearly the tougher of the two.

Leon stared at them. "Tell me everything you know about Amber Dixon."

They exchanged startled glances. "Amber?" Tasha said timidly. "Amber's gone. A few months ago. She just disappeared. We thought she could have at least said something. But she didn't. I thought we were friends, but no goodbye. Nothing. She didn't even answer her calls and messages."

"Who did she spend time with? Besides you two."

Krystal was studying him, putting two and two together. Leon was sure that she recognized him. She was smart enough not to say it, but not smart enough to hide it.

"Amber didn't have a whole lot of close friends," Krystal said. "She wasn't into the party scene. Some of the girls thought she was stuck up. But we liked her."

"Who were her closest friends besides you two?"

Tash wiped her bloody nose on her sleeve. "Are you gonna hurt her?"

Krystal swatted her arm. "Shut up, Tash," she muttered.

Leon smiled. Sorry, honey. It was too late for salvage. Their fates were sealed. "Absolutely not," he soothed. "I'm a friend. I just need to find her. Urgently, for her own safety. So who else? What can you give me?"

Tash's gaze flicked between him and Krystal. "Well, ah… Trix," she said. "Definitely."

"Trix," he echoed. "Do I know this Trix?"

"I don't know. She was in the show with us. Long, black curly hair, big dark eyes? She and Amber were roommates sometimes, when they were between boyfriends. Then Trix got set up by that rich Japanese guy, and Amber moved in with her mobster boyfriend."

Leon saw a flash of panic in Krystal's eyes. The frantic nudge she gave Tash only confirmed that she had recognized him. "Tell me more about Trix," he said.

"Like what?" Tasha faltered.

"Last name, maybe? Family ties? Place of origin? Cup size? Whatever the fuck you know about her, you dumb bitch." He waved the gun. "Cough it up!"

Tash began to cry. Krystal shushed her sharply and leaned forward, taking charge. "I think Trix was from New Jersey. She had that accent, you know? Her stage name was Trixi Grace, but her real last name was Graziano. I think they were rich. You know, big house, the whole thing. South somewhere. In Jersey, but the nice part. She even took the guy she was seeing, well seeing on the side, down there. So I guess actually, it was kind of serious. You know, serious enough to introduce him to her mom, right? And her nephew. I overheard a call from her mom once. She was a screamer. A real piece of work. They spoke a mix of Italian and English. Or yelled, more like. There wasn't much actual talking going on—"

"So where can I find this Trix?" he said, cutting off the babbling.

"She's gone, too," Tash offered. "She left even before Amber did. Couple of days before, I think. Big problem for the show, having both of them just vanish like that."

"Why did she go?"

Tash blinked nervously. "Well, um, I was at the party, when she got the call, you know? About her boyfriend getting whacked?"

"What party? What call? What boyfriend?" he demanded.

Tash cringed away. "S-s-sorry," she stuttered. "It was, um, Monique's party. She was leaving the show. Getting married. We were all really buzzed, and then Trix gets this call, and she starts freaking out. Screaming and crying. Someone told her that her boyfriend got whacked. That she had to run away."

"So what you're saying is, this Japanese guy got whacked?" Leon prodded.

"No, no. I mean the one she was seeing on the side."

"The one she took home? To south somewhere, in Jersey?"

The women nodded in unison, and Tash continued. "Yeah. Anyhow, she takes off with the other one. Not the one who got whacked. I mean the old Japanese guy. And we never saw her again. It surprised me though. You know, that Trix went like that? She was real attached to her family. Always talking about her little nephew. Tori this. Tori that. You know, when people are like that about kids? Anyway," she shrugged. "That's all we know. Swear to God."

Leon studied the two women. Neither of them would look at him. "Did you know the other man she was seeing?" he asked. "The one who got whacked, I mean?"

Krystal shrugged. "Not really. I'd seen him pick her up at the theater a few times."

"What did he look like?"

"Short, slim," Krystal offered. "Dark. Good looking. Sharp dresser. Kind of nervy."

"Michael," he said softly.

"Yes!" Tash said eagerly. "Yes! She called him a couple times when I was with her. She called him Mikey. It was all real hush-hush because of Kenji. Then she gets this call at the party that he's dead, and poof, she vanishes."

"Do you know where? Did she go Japan?"

Krystal shook her head, her eyes big with fear. "Um. No. We don't know."

"You don't think she went home, to that place in Jersey, to see her nephew, what was his name? Tori?"

"Yeah," Tash piped up. "Tori. But no. I don't think so. I mean, somebody said she left with the other guy. Kenji. He was old, but he was loaded." She looked at Krystal. "It could be Japan," she offered.

"We don't know," Krystal said. "Sorry. We never heard from her again."

"How about this Kenji? Did you know his last name? Where did he work?"

The two women locked eyes, and both shook their head. Clearly miserable not to have something more to give him.

Leon thought for a moment. Then he asked, "What about Amber? Was Amber at this party when this Trix got this call?"

All Krystal's bravado drained away. Now, she just looked hunted. "I don't know," she whispered. "I don't remember. I was pretty toasted. Tash, too. We were doing tequila shots."

"But she knew the guy," Tash offered, ever helpful. Krystal threw her a look, but it was too late. "I heard her talking Italian with him a few times. Showing off."

Leon stared at her. "Italian? Amber didn't speak Italian."

"Yeah, she did," Tash assured him. "She spoke it sometimes in the club, when there were Italians there. Spanish, too. Felipe used to send her out to talk to them. He thought it made the club seem classier."

Italian? Leon felt a surge of rage. Amber had been able to speak Italian all along, and she had never said a word? And she had known Michael, and this Graziano bitch. Who had a nephew called Tori. Hmmm.

So Amber had warned this Trix to run away.

She'd been in on it from the start. That lying, treacherous slut. She probably understood every word Michael said in the kitchen. She'd probably already found the bonds and taken them for herself. That dirty, lying, thieving little whore.

"Mister?" Tasha trying to smile, but her voice quivered. "If there's anything we can do to help you, or, well, um. We do, like, anything. Anything you like. Anything you might enjoy. The two of us. To each other, to you. Whatever you want. We can be, you know. Really wild."

"Yeah." Catching on, Krystal hunched forward, emphasizing her cleavage. "Yeah, exactly," she murmured. "It's our thing, you know."

"Do either of you know anything more about Trix Graziano?" he asked abruptly.

Krystal shrank back. "Um," she said. "No. But I'd be happy to ask around."

Leon fired twice. The silenced bullets made a popping sound. The first hit Krystal between the eyes. The second hit her in the center of the chest. He heard Tash screaming and stopped it with two more shots. Ah, sweet silence.

In the hallway, Leon reached down into the bag of takeout and grabbed a paper napkin to use on the front door handle. He looked at the scattered cartons of Chinese food on the floor.

Might as well not leave them for the cops. That would just hand them a whole new avenue of inquiry.

Besides, being back in business made him hungry.

Chapter Sixteen

Amber was disoriented when she woke up. The light was wrong. And music was playing. Piano music, pretty and cheerful and old-fashioned. She'd slept so heavily that she barely remembered who she was for a few seconds. Then she tried to move, and gasped. Her head throbbed, her leg strung, her bruised belly ached. The night rushed back. Blackbeard. Kavanaugh's. The stairwell. She closed her eyes. Listening to the music. Someone was actually playing the piano in the dining room. It sounded nice.

She had drifted trustingly off in Vicodin's tender arms, leaving Blackbeard, no. Henry. His name was Henry. Leaving Henry to rattle around in the Grudbergs' townhouse. Henry who she had watched throw a guy over an eight-floor railing.

With your help, which makes you an accomplice. A voice in her head said. It was a disquieting thought. Almost as disquieting as the fact that she had just allowed a huge unknown with his own complicated agenda, problems, and dangers into her life. Not smart. But, she had known that last night when she started chasing him toward the restaurant.

Maybe she'd done it because Henry seemed like Leon's polar opposite. Or the polar opposite of Sid, the other contender for worst man of all time. Maybe she'd done it to get him to pay attention to her. Who knew? Who, for that matter, knew anything about Blackbeard, or Henry, if that was even his name. Certainly not her. He could be a serial killer for all she knew.

She remembered the common refrain from true crime documentaries, what everyone always said about the guy who locked you in a basement and ate your eyeballs on toast. "He was so nice. Real quiet, always kept to himself." Which described Henry to a tee. She had even told this potential eyeball eater her name. Or, at least the name she answered to most readily. Mamma had named her Annarita Rosalba. But she'd called her Ambra ever since her pale red hair grew in, and the birth-blue of her eyes turned golden. Amber had never felt like an Annarita. So when she had to pick a stage name, she chose Amber Dixon.

A soft knock on the door, made her sit up, wincing. "Yeah?"

Henry stepped into the bedroom holding a food tray. "You're finally awake. I've knocked about six times," he said. "I was starting to get worried."

"What the hell have you got there?"

"Lunch. If you can still call it lunch at four in the afternoon."

"Four?" She sucked in a horrified breath. "You mean to say that I was out for…"

"Over eighteen hours. Yes. You were exhausted. And it's well past time to take another antibiotic. It's right here, on the tray. It's supposed to be taken with food, which we didn't do last night. So I made you some lunch."

"You made food?" she repeated, stupidly.

"Chicken noodle soup. With egg noodles. That's what my mom used to make for me when I was sick, so I figured…" His voice trailed off, as he registered her expression. "I guess I could make you something else, if this isn't okay. Can I set up the tray? I found one that rests on a bed. Can I set it up for you?"

She held up a hand. "No. No, you can't."

He looked worried. "But you need to eat."

Maybe it was just lunch, like he said. He looked so clueless. Which made him even more alarming. Bringing her lunch in bed. On a tray. Chicken soup. This classic, old school pampering, it made her feel like he was making a fool of her. Setting her up to get her hand slapped.

"Thanks for making me food," she said. "But don't want to eat in bed. I'll make a mess of the sheets. I'd rather come downstairs. In any case, we need to talk."

He looked crestfallen. "Okay. I'll just bring it back downstairs, then."

"Wait. Hold on. Was that you, playing the piano?"

He looked embarrassed. "I put on the soft pedal. I'm sorry if I woke you. It's just a really nice piano, and it's been years since I had a real one, so—"

"No, no, it's okay. It was nice. I was just, you know. Wondering."

"Well. Yes," he said. "It was me. My mom insisted I learn to play. She liked those eighteenth-century opera arias." He stopped, embarrassed. "I'll just go on down and get the table ready for you."

Once Henry left, Amber got up and limped stiffly around until she found her silk robe, the one with the red poppies splashed all over it. She'd bought the robe for her Lola persona. Lola was a vain, broke, actress, well past her prime, with a strong predilection for THC gummies and sugary cocktails. Lately, though, Amber had been putting the robe on without even trying to embody Lola. She just wore it because it was cute, and it lifted her spirits.

Which was dangerous, because Amber didn't have things like favorite robes. Amber was no one. A nobody. Amber was a concept that had been deleted from the universe. That was the only way she could possibly survive this. To hide. Even from herself.

Screw it, she thought. She was just too damned tired and sore for that rigorous, hard-core bullshit today. Lola hadn't been invited to the kitchen for a bowl of chicken soup with egg noodles. Amber had. Today, Amber existed. She had already revealed Amber's existence to Henry. So there was no point in denying her existence today.

Which meant, paradoxically, that part of her could relax.

She wound the sash around her waist and, clutching the banister, made her way down the stairs and into the kitchen, a room she had so far used only for the coffeemaker. And occasionally, the fridge, to store leftover take out. A bowl of golden broth with a generous tangle of broad yellow egg noodles sat on the neatly set table. Spoon, fork, napkin, glass of orange juice, cup for coffee, and a little capsule of antibiotics lay dutifully beside it. There was a plate of buttered toast, and a bowl filled with melon chunks, grapes, and juicy bits of pineapple. Her stomach gave an uncharacteristic rumble. Fresh coffee, too. This guy. Damn.

"Wow," she said. "Where did all that come from?"

"I ordered some groceries."

She looked at him in alarm.

He raised both hands. "Don't worry. The credit card I used is in a different name than the one I used to rent the apartment where the guy attacked us. I have a few different accounts, with different names."

"Check you out," she said, impressed. "That's some smooth, super-organized next level outlawry you got going there. Leaves me in the dust, buddy."

"I do my best," he said. "Assuming you meant that as a compliment, that is."

"I don't do compliments," she said swiftly. "I've taken a holy vow. People can jack up their own damn self-esteem. Never again. I'm a cast-iron bitch from here on out."

Henry sat down across from her and sipped his coffee. "That strikes me as very deeply felt. I sense there's some history behind that."

"And you're never going to hear it because it's none of your damn business." Amber snapped. "Just because of yesterday, just because I helped you, just because you're here in this house, it doesn't mean we're besties, Henry. What's with this soup, and toast, and fruit? What's next, cookies and tea? You have your stuff, and I have mine. Let's just leave it that way."

Henry got up, took the plate of soup, and went to the stovetop. He poured the broth back into the big pot that steamed on the stove. Then he ladled up a fresh, steaming bowlful, and brought it over and placed it carefully in front of her.

"After going upstairs and back down again, that bowl just didn't look hot anymore," he said. "I won't risk serving cold soup to a cast-iron bitch. God knows what might happen to me. Eat now so you can take that antibiotic, okay?"

"Are you playing games with my head, Henry?"

"Not at all." He shrugged. "It's just lunch. No hidden meanings, no trap doors. And just so you know, I've got nothing against cookies and tea, but I actually ordered a glazed vanilla pound cake. You were asleep, or I would have asked what you liked. Next time, I can order cookies, no problem."

Laughter jolted her, reminding her that absolutely everything hurt right now. "At least you didn't make the cake yourself with your own little handsies," she said.

She caught his fleeting smile before he turned away, the first one she'd seen on his tense mask of a face. Amber looked at the steaming soup. Aw, screw it. He wasn't going to drug or poison her. She'd been unconscious for over eighteen hours, and he'd done nothing more menacing than brew coffee, get groceries, make soup, and order cake. The scary shark music could just stop playing in her head.

She picked up her spoon. Henry, who was tossing vegetable peelings into the garbage disposal, left her to it. The machine snarled briefly, chewing it all up. She hadn't even noticed there was a garbage disposal. Ms. Domesticity she was not.

She sipped a spoonful of broth. It was delicious. She'd had an iffy appetite for some time now. Ever since that night. *Michael.* The Terror Diet. Worked like gangbusters.

The broth was savory, and the chicken was tender. The noodles were nice and chewy, if somewhat awkward to eat with a spoon. Nothing on earth would get her to eat boiled chunks of celery or carrot, but the potatoes were nice. All in all, it was a great bowl of soup.

"It's good," she told him, tilting her bowl to scoop up the last of the broth and scraps of chicken.

"I thought you said no compliments." Henry took her plate and ladled more soup into it, this time avoiding celery and carrot. She didn't tell him to stop.

Amber picked up her spoon. "It's not a compliment," she said. "Just an observation."

"So a positive observation is different from a compliment?"

"Compliments are different. Compliments are meant to manipulate."

"I never knew that," he said. "I thought compliments were simply stating a truth when the truth happened to be positive. So there was a secret rule, and I never knew it. Why did no one ever explain that to me?"

"You're hurting my brain, Henry. Shut up and let me eat."

That got her another ghost of a smile. She worked through the soup and started the toast. Henry prodded the antibiotic pill. "Take it. Please."

She tilted her head, bemused. "What are you, my mom?"

"Please. Or else my brain will be all over the place, waiting for you to take it."

"So you're one of those guys. A place for everything and everything in its place."

"Yeah, I guess. When I care about something."

"Don't care about me," she said sharply. "You don't know me. You've got nothing to care about."

He shrugged. "Sorry. Too late for that. Can't I care just a little?"

She tossed back the pill, gulping down some of the orange juice. "Just don't get weird about me," she said. "I have enough problems. Understood?"

"Absolutely. I won't."

She snorted. Henry let out a strangled, choked sound which Amber belatedly realized must be laughter. Or as close as a guy like him could get to it. He retrieved one of Rayna Grudberg's pretty dessert plates, turned to the bakery box on the butcher's block, opened it, and placed a thick slice of cake in front of her.

"And what is this?" she said.

"Pound cake. Plain vanilla. Not rum, or caramel, or pecan or chocolate chip, or coffee swirl. Just plain vanilla. Because a guy has to be who he is in this world."

She pondered that as she sank her fork into the cake. "Damn, Henry. I didn't know baked goods had such deep meaning. I'm betting there's some history behind that."

He looked self-conscious. "Maybe. But it's too stupid to tell."

"Yeah, I hear you. I have history like that, too." She tasted the cake, and closed her eyes with a sigh. Just how a pound cake should be. Dense and moist but not heavy or gummy. Buttery, fragrant, melting. The glaze was light, fresh and zingy and not too thick.

"This is so good," she told him.

"You're going overboard with those positive observations," he said. "You'll turn my head."

"Oh, shut up. Aren't you going to have a piece? It'll rock your world."

He cut himself a slice and sat down. They ate slowly, savoring every crumb. When she was finished, Amber let out a sigh of contentment.

"So," she said. "Listen up. There are some things that I need to say to you right off the bat."

"Same," he said. "You go first."

Hmmm. Way to put her at a disadvantage right from the get-go. She pulled her robe around her and sat up straighter. "So, I'm sure, from my behavior, you've figured out that I have complicated problems right now."

He nodded. "Yes."

"It seems, based on what happened last night, that you have some of your own."

"Your observation is correct."

"I have to warn you. If my problems should catch up with me, and you are anywhere in my vicinity, you are meat. And I am not speaking figuratively."

"Same here. As you saw for yourself last night, when you saved my ass."

"Don't count on that happening again," she warned. "We got lucky. So, I'm just saying. Being near me is dangerous. You have been warned."

"Same here," he said. "Do you want me to leave?"

She blew out a frustrated sigh. "I don't know shit about you, Henry. Just that your hiding place got burned for you last night, it's winter, you're on the run, and you look like a puppy left out in the rain. But it looks like your enemies are too close for comfort."

"I'll leave if you want me to," he said. "I stayed last night because I wanted to look after you. Like you did for me in the stairwell. But I can go at any time."

"Thanks, but never mind last night. After the soup and the

cake, we can call it even. We don't owe each other anything. Personally, I am in no position to do anybody any favors."

"I'm not asking for favors."

"You're not? Then why are you here? What do you want?" Henry stared down, drumming his fingers on the table until she wanted to scream.

"Last night," he said finally, "after you went to sleep, I found that basket full of wallets."

Amber felt herself tense. Her head throbbed painfully. "That's my private business. You have no right to snoop. Or to make comments about it."

"I'm not judging. It just got me thinking. If that's how you choose to—"

"I don't 'choose' a goddamn thing! I do what I have to do!"

"Right, right," he soothed. "So do I. And I swear I am not judging you. On the contrary. I've been observing you for a while. I know you're a master of disguise. From last night, I know that you're brave, and that you have nerve. From the basket full of wallets, I conclude that you need money, because I'm guessing you don't pick pockets for fun."

"You're guessing correctly," she said, through clenched teeth.

"I was going to wait until you were stronger before I proposed this," he said. "But you wanted to have this talk right now, so you forced my hand."

"Proposed what? What the hell are you proposing?"

Henry exhaled slowly. "I want to hire you," he said. "I want you to use your talents to help me solve a problem I can't solve alone."

Chapter Seventeen

Henry's heart sank at the shocked, scared look in her eyes. He didn't think he could scare anyone, but somehow he'd succeeded in scaring Amber.

She wrapped her arms around her chest. "I think you might have gotten the wrong idea about me, Henry."

"Hear me out," he begged. "Let me just explain. If the answer is no, I will get my bag and walk away. I will never bother you again. I swear to God."

"I'm holding you to that." She dropped her arms and wound her hands together on her lap. "So, what's this thing you want me to do?"

"I want you to disguise yourself as my ex-wife, go into a bank, and empty out her safe deposit box."

Her jaw dropped. "Damn, Henry. That is hard-core."

"Yes," he agreed. "Yes, I know. It is."

"I'm a thief sometimes, sure," Amber said. "But I'm a very small-time thief. You get it? What you're suggesting sounds dangerous. If I get caught, I go away. Or I just die. If my enemies catch up with me and I'm stuck in prison, they'll stick me like a bug on a pin. You can count on it."

Henry considered her. "I think," he said slowly, "that with

your skills, it could be done without being caught. And, yes, it's illegal. But it's not immoral. I would be stealing from thieves who ruined my life. They framed me, and sent me to prison for their crimes. What's in that safe deposit box is mine by right."

"Sent you to prison?" Her voice cracked. "For real?"

He sighed. "Yes."

"So you're, what? Out on parole and looking for payback?"

He shook his head. "Not exactly. I never even made it to my sentencing hearing. I broke out. Or, I should say, I was broken out. By a guy I met when I was inside."

Amber rubbed her hands over her pale cheeks. "Oh, great," she murmured. "So you're an escaped con. Better and better. See what happens when I try to make friends?"

"Please, just hear me out," Henry said. "Belinda, the woman who used to be my wife? She and her lover stole a lot of money, and set me up to take the fall for it."

"This problem is too rich for my blood, Henry. Truth is, I'm a big wuss."

"Far from it!" He protested. "You're smart, talented, competent. And extremely brave."

"By necessity," Amber's voice was grim. "I've met some very bad people in my time. And I am not like them. I don't want to carry a load on my conscience, since I somehow still possess one. Inconvenient though it often is."

"I possess one, too," he told her. "And I'm not violating it, or yours, by asking for your help with this. These people destroyed my life for profit. They took everything from me, even my freedom. This is the only way I can take my freedom back."

She gave him a thoughtful, narrow-eyed look. "So you want to use me to punish your bitch ex-wife? I've heard that song before, Henry. It's not my favorite tune."

"I don't love it either, but it was forced on me. I just don't want the story to end here. With them winning, and me the chump victim, forced to swallow it and sit in jail all my life. But I'm a tech gearhead, not a master of disguise. So I need a partner with skills like yours."

"Tech gearhead, huh?" She rested her chin in her hands. "So, Henry. What would be in it for me? Hypothetically speaking, of course."

He felt a rush of terrified hope, as if he'd just surfaced from some murky underwater place and burst into light and air. "I can't say for sure how much is in that safe deposit box," he said. "They say I turned over six million dollars into diamonds. But I don't know how much they spent already, because the better part of two years has gone by. But whatever is in there? You get twenty-five percent of it."

Amber lifted her coffee, realized it was empty and set it back down. "Ah," she murmured. "I see. Twenty-five percent of a big question mark. Wow. Tempting."

He got up, grabbed the coffeepot, and refilled her cup. "We can come up with another number if the safe deposit box doesn't pay off," he assured her. "I don't have a lot of cash right now. But I have skills, and I earn well on the dark web if I hold my nose. I'm more or less an indentured servant to the guy who helped me break out of prison. His stuff takes a lot of my time, but I have other work. Hacking jobs. Surveillance stuff. Academic papers, test-taking, that kind of thing. You tell me what you need. I'll guarantee you either twenty-five percent of the take, or whatever number you come up with, whichever is largest. But if the safe deposit box is a bust, I might have to pay you in installments." He sat back, bracing himself. "That's it. That's my proposal. If you want to think about it, that's fine. Don't say no right away."

She stared into her steaming cup for so long he started getting nervous.

"So you're a techie kind of guy," she finally said.

"Yes. I designed customized databases in my former life.

For banks, hedge funds, all kinds of businesses. That was how I met my former wife. I was designing a database for a dental practice and she was getting dental work. Her boss was a former client of mine. He must have had his eye on me for a while. He came up with this scheme. She was sleeping with him the whole time."

"I can see why that might burn your ass."

"Yeah, pretty much."

"The number you want me to name," she said. "Let's call it, just for fun, a hundred thousand bucks. How long would it take you to pull it together?"

He shrugged. "I could pull together a hundred thousand for you in maybe three months, if I hustle."

"Working under a fake name? On that lam? Wow. How do you get paid? I mean, without getting caught?"

She seemed genuinely interested. Henry shrugged again. "Like I told you, I have those fake identities and bank accounts. The guy who broke me out set them up for me. He has a whole racket going. But it's a double-edged sword, since he makes me pay for it through the nose. One of the reasons I want Victor and Belinda's stash is because I'd be able to get out from under him, and get myself a valid passport. I need a clean couple of million to accomplish that. The alternative is years of drudgery doing his illegal tech stuff, and the prospect does not thrill me. The only thing that can be said for it is that it's better than prison."

"I see," she said. "Well, Henry. I appreciate your confidence in me, but I'm not loving my chances of getting paid for my labor before my past catches up with me."

"I could try to speed up—"

"Hold on. I'm not done."

He shut up, and waited, not breathing.

"I have a counter-proposal," she said. "I need help with a thing, too. There are some aspects of my thing that I just can't handle alone."

"Is your thing illegal?"

She rolled her eyes. "Does the Pope shit in the woods, Henry? Of course my thing is illegal. But it's not immoral. At least not in my view. I'll be tricking people, but not wronging them, or hurting them. The big difference is that my thing is dangerous."

He let out a disbelieving laugh. "Oh, yeah? So what happened in the stairwell last night didn't qualify as dangerous for you?"

She flapped her hand dismissively. "Nah. That guy was a pussycat. I want to get my hands on a thing that was stolen from my husband, Leon. Before he catches me and kills me."

"Husband?" he repeated blankly. "You're married?"

"Yes, unfortunately. I'm not exactly sure what the mystery item is, but it was taken from Leon, and the guy who stole it hid it in his girlfriend's family's house in New Jersey. It doesn't belong to them, they have no idea it's there, and they won't miss it if it's gone. But for me, it's the difference between life and death. So, anyhow. That's my fee, Henry. You help me retrieve the mystery item, and I'll help you with your, ah... thing."

"Why does your husband want to kill you?"

"For running away. And because I saw some things that I shouldn't have seen. Leon is a hard-core mobster. The real deal. You don't get put in jail if you cross him. He'll rip out your liver and feed it to you piece by piece. I saw him chop up a guy with a meat cleaver. Stairwell dude was just a garden-variety hit man. Leon is something else altogether."

"I see," Henry said, after a minute. "But a garden variety hit man could still have killed us."

"True," she agreed. "He definitely could have."

The question burst out before he could stop it. "Why did you do it?"

Her eyebrows rose. "I've done a lot of questionable things lately, Henry. Which one are you referring to?"

"Following me yesterday. Warning me. Jumping that guy. Almost getting yourself killed. For a complete stranger."

"I don't know." She sounded defensive. "And I mean that literally. I really don't know. It was an incredibly dumb thing to do. Most of me didn't want to. But the other part of me won. It's not like I know you, or even like you. How could I? I don't know you from Adam. But I don't hate you." She hesitated, eyeing him. "At least, not yet."

That made him laugh. "I'll try to be good."

"You do that," she said. "Maybe it's because I haven't talked to anyone for such a long time. I've been invisible. A nobody. Doing nothing but hide. But you saw me, and that made me feel, I don't know. Like you weren't a stranger. Like we knew each other. The world is shitty enough, and it would have been shittier if that guy had wasted you. I wouldn't have anyone to impress with my disguises in the Reading Room."

Henry sat without moving for a moment. Then he said quietly, "Same for me. I don't know you either. But I prefer a world that has you in it."

"Aww, that's touching." The words sounded snarky, but she was smiling. "Don't be too hasty, though," she went on. "You haven't actually heard the details of my counter-proposal yet. You might change your mind and run screaming into the night."

"I don't often change my mind," he said. "The earth really has to move."

"The earth's been shaking pretty hard for you lately, for what I can see."

He realized that he'd been staring at her lips. Their delicate, unusual shape. They were too pale. He forced himself to look away.

"Can't deny that, he said. "So? Tell me everything."

Chapter Eighteen

I t came out of her slowly, in disjointed, out-of-sequence
pieces. Everything from that hellish night in Leon's
Vegas penthouse onward. Slowly, patiently, Henry
helped her put all the broken pieces together in the right
order. Everything she said interested him. The details of
Michael's gruesome death and his babbling, nearly incoherent
confession, Trix fleeing to Japan. The US Marshals sweeping
Amber away into exile in Idaho with Leon.

Henry honed in on Michael's confession, and every detail
she had gleaned about the Grazianos. After she'd gone over
everything several times, he sat silently, his gaze faraway, but
not blank. Amber sensed a quiet, humming energy inside him,
like massive supercomputers underground, data centers that
sucked enough power to run entire cities.

Now that she had told him what she wanted to do, her
idea sounded exactly like what it was. Farfetched, childish,
dangerous, silly. She'd only tried to convince herself otherwise
because she had no Plan B. Now she was going to have to
hear him say it. That her dumb plan would never work.

Which meant she was condemned to die.

"How did you manage to warn Trix?" Henry asked

suddenly. "You said Leon took your phone when he locked you in the bedroom and went to bury Michael."

"I had Michael's phone," she explained. "I grabbed it when Leon went to take a shower and hid it in my dress that I dumped on the couch. I knew if Leon got Michael's phone, he'd find Trix right away. So I made his phone disappear."

"That was brave. He never suspected you?"

She shook her head. "Leon thought I was an empty-headed doll. I called Trix with Michael's phone, and then I threw it off the balcony. It smashed on the roof of a parking garage sixteen stories down. And there it will stay. Until the end of time."

"Good," Henry said.

"Yeah," Amber said. "And another thing. Trix called me yesterday, and got all sentimental about Michael. Said that he flew to West Palm Beach, Florida, right before he was killed. He'd told her someone down there stood in the way of their happiness, and he had to take care of it. Trix didn't know who this person was, or what problems he was creating. But Michael went to fix it in West Palm Beach."

"Got it," Henry murmured, nodding. "So, you don't know what Michael hid at the Grazianos, or where he hid it. Your only clue is this Tori's tiger thing. Correct?"

"Yup." It sounded idiotic, when it was actually said out loud.

"Maybe it's a toy, since we're talking about a kid?" Henry mused. "And you're convinced it would be in that particular house in South Cambrook, not one of their other houses, why?"

"Because Tori lives there. And it's the house Trix grew up in. She took Michael there to introduce him to her mother right before Leon killed him. But it didn't go well. Serafina called Michael a greasy, two-bit pimp right to his face. I heard all about ad nauseam. Trix was all broken up about it."

"So Michael was physically in that house, in South Cambrook?"

"Not for long. But yes, he was. I have an idea about how to get in. But I can't do it alone. Whatever I find there, I'll go with the same deal you offered me. Twenty-five percent. But I can't offer you another number and give you whichever is larger. I don't have anything much, and I doubt I can earn much more before Leon kills me. Or the Feds or the DiAngelos find me."

"That's okay. It's worth it to me to get you onboard. I'll help you, and you'll help me. It seems symmetrical, right? We'll be taking on equal risk."

Knowing Leon, Amber was pretty sure the guy was dead wrong about how equal the risk was. But she wasn't about to argue. She stuck out her hand. "Deal."

They shook, his hand pleasantly warm, her own feeling ice-cold and clammy. "So," she said. "How's this going to work?"

Henry's gaze dropped to her leg, hidden behind the glossy folds of the red poppy robe. "Depends on you," he said. "When you're strong again. When you're up to it."

"I'm up to it now," she said promptly.

"No, you're not." He frowned. "You're healing, and I am, too. We should lay low and rest for a while. Yesterday was a big day."

Well. That could not be denied. And, Amber had to admit, she was feeling a little unsteady. Cold and sweaty at once. She needed to lie down.

"We'll start on the research tomorrow, come up with a plan," he said.

"Just like that, huh?" Despite the sudden queasiness, she smiled. "Easy-peasy."

"No," he said. "Not easy. But doable. It'll be a big logistical challenge, but I enjoy those."

"Huh," she murmured. "Do you? Can I ask one more thing?"

He looked wary.

"That piece you were playing before?" Amber said. "On the piano. Will you play it again? It was pretty."

His eyes widened. "Oh. I'm not, you know. Very good."

"I don't care. I just want to hear it. You said it was an opera aria, right? So it has words, too? Can you sing them? Do you sing?"

He let out a snort of nervous laughter. "Sort of. I can try, I guess."

He stayed close behind her as they went into the dining room, ready to catch her if she fell. Henry pulled out a dining room chair for her. Then he sat at the piano and opened up a big, thick book with a pale green cover.

"I played "*Ah! Perchè non posso odiarti, infidel, com'io vorrei!*, from La Sonnambula," he announced. "By Bellini."

She was surprised. "Why can't I despise you, faithless, as I should? Really? It sounded so upbeat. What did she do to upset the guy?"

"He thought she betrayed him," he said. "I'll try to sing it, but don't say I didn't warn you."

Henry did not, in fact, have a highly trained voice. But that was okay, because she didn't have a highly trained ear. His voice was tuneful and resonant and nice, and she liked the way he sang. Simply, with energy and heart. And his pronunciation wasn't half bad. Amber liked it. For her own selfish, specific self. Not for any of her other personae. Just for her.

After he finished, she clapped. "That was great, Henry. Thanks for indulging me. I like the way you sing."

"I haven't done it in years, so I can't imagine why," he said. "You should rest. You look pale. Are you feverish? Can I take a look at the wound?"

"I'm fine," she said. "You gawked at my thighs plenty last

night. If I start to get gangrene, I'll let you know. How about yours? The slash wound, your bashed balls?"

"Fine," he assured her. "No gangrene that I can see. Can I help you upstairs? I could carry you, if you—"

"I'd rather not." She pushed to her feet using the dining room table. "Sorry to leave you with the dishes, but nobody asked you to cook, so it's your own damn fault."

"No problem." His lips twitched. "Can I ask one more question before you go up?"

She braced herself. "Sure."

"Dinner. Would spinach and ricotta ravioli be okay for tonight? With fresh tomato basil sauce? And, if so, do you prefer Parmigiano or Romano cheese?"

She shook her head as she backed toward the stairs. "Henry," she said. "Get this straight. We are not playing house."

He looked perplexed. "I just don't want to make food you won't eat."

She grabbed the banister and hung on for dear life as she started up the stairs. "Whatever is fine," she said over her shoulder. "I'm not picky. If you cook something and offer me some, I'll eat it, because I'm a natural opportunist. Just don't think I owe you anything in return. Not even cleanup. Got it?"

"Absolutely. Do you prefer white wine, or red?"

"Goddamn it, Henry," she snapped. "You're making it weird again."

Chapter Nineteen

The bottle of Burgundy breathed on the table as he tossed rock salt into the pot of boiling water. Fresh, warmed Italian bread was wrapped in a cloth. A dish of tarragon-infused olive oil sat next to it. The salad greens gleamed in their vinaigrette dressing. Henry had learned how to do all these things while he was married to Belinda.

Before Bel, he had been a Ramen-eating, Red Bull-pounding, solitary night owl whose idea of cooking was sticking a bag of popcorn into the microwave. Husbandly nesting behaviors had been a challenge for him, but he'd made an effort to adjust and improve. It was painful to remember how hard he had tried.

With Belinda, he always felt like he was taking, and failing to pass, some mysterious test, always hoping his offering would be acceptable to her. That being good, and doing it right might make being with him worth her while.

This felt so different. With Amber, he just wanted to tempt her appetite. She needed building up. She was too thin, too pale behind her complex disguises. Too light when he'd picked her up and carried her. He wanted to see her eat hot delicious meals, and enjoy them. This wasn't fawning over a beautiful woman because he was hoping to get lucky. He had been cured of that brand of dumb-assery forever. Belinda had inoculated him for all time.

Amber was different. This was a matter of self-interest. She was his secret weapon. He needed her strong, alert, and in top form.

As Henry assembled the meal, prying open the frozen ravioli he'd had delivered from a nearby Italian deli, stirring the sauce, grating the block of Romano, he thought about what he'd learned about Amber's husband. Before he turned on them, Leon Gambelli had been deeply entwined with the DiAngelo crime family. The DiAngelo's were based in Los Angeles, but they did business throughout the Southwest, and beyond. As Amber had told him, Leon had testified against the boss, Tommy DiAngelo, and also against Tommy's two sons, his son-in-law, and several others, all of whom were now in prison awaiting trial.

That meant, among other things, that Leon Gambelli was a dead man walking.

The US Marshals Service ran an excellent witness protection program. Cracking it was notoriously difficult, so the DiAngelos would look for other ways to find Leon. One of them would be Amber. Organized crime syndicates often left families, especially wives and children, alone. But not always.

He knew it was deeply unwise to open himself up to a whole new set of dangers. On the other hand, it was incredibly refreshing to think about something other than Belinda and Victor. The water in the pot was boiling energetically. Henry dropped the ravioli in and stirred gently.

"Look at you. A man of many talents."

He spun around at the sound of Amber's husky, amused voice. "Hey," he said. "I was about to call you down for dinner."

"Looks great. Can I help?"

"No, it's almost ready." He pulled out a chair for her and poured some wine into her glass. "Sit down and relax."

"I'd bet a vacation house on a beach in Baja that you've been hunting around online checking out my story," she remarked. "So?"

"Do you blame me for checking it out?"

"Hell, no." She raised her glass. "I'd expect nothing less. I don't want a stupid partner."

"I feel the same way. So I assume you've done some digging of your own," he said. "About my trial, and Belinda and Victor, and all the rest of it."

"Yes, a bit. I need to get deeper into Belinda's social media accounts. I did look through her pictures. On first glance, I think making myself look like her is doable, from a technical point of view. We have a similar facial shape, the same basic nose, similar width between the eyes. I don't see any big challenges. Did she let you in on the fact that she's not a real blonde?"

He was bewildered. "Huh? But…but she's always…"

"Nope." She sipped her wine with a small, secret smile. "Men. So easily misled."

"But how do you know?"

"Oh, I'm not being catty. Her hair looks like a million bucks. She has a great hairdresser. But I can just tell. Same way I know your hair is dyed."

"Did I do something wrong with it?"

"Not at all. I can just see it by looking at your skin tone, your eyebrows, the texture, the highlights. Don't look so shocked. You don't look bad. At least, no more than any other rumpled, bearded, wild-eyed dude in a dorky baseball cap."

He had no idea what to do with that, so he just kept busy, scooping the plump, steaming ravioli onto their plates. He ladled sauce over them generously and placed it before her. "There's Romano cheese, if you want."

"Don't mind if I do." She dusted a big spoonful onto her

ravioli and forked up a bite. "Mmm, nice," she said appreciatively. "And that means something coming from me. I'm Italian."

She laughed at the look on his face. "I know, right? The red hair and the freckles? I look Scotch-Irish, not Italian. But Mamma was from an Italian family that emigrated to Argentina after the Second World War. She fell in love with an inappropriate American businessman from Phoenix when she was just eighteen."

"Inappropriate, how?"

"He was married. With children."

"I see."

"So anyhow, he goes back to his family in the States and decides to take his nineteen-year-old mistress back with him. That was before he realized she was pregnant."

"Pregnant with…"

"Me, yes. He was a ginger. Scottish, I think. I never knew him. She tried to pressure him into stepping up to support us, but it backfired on her. He snapped, and killed himself shortly before I was born. Hung himself."

Henry looked up. "God. I'm sorry to hear that."

She took another bite of ravioli. "Never knew him, never missed him," she said lightly. "Doesn't sound like he would have been much use to me in any case. I mean, he literally preferred death to taking responsibility for me. So there poor Mamma was, a few thousand miles from home, all alone with a baby and her broken English. What a mess."

"I bet it was. So that's why you speak Italian? And Spanish too, I expect."

"Yes, and yes."

"But a name like Amber? That doesn't sound Argentinian. Or Italian."

"Annarita Rosalba DeGennaro," she told him. "Mamma called me Ambra, for my hair and eyes, so I just went with Amber. If it sounds like a stripper name, that's because it is. I was a showgirl in Vegas for more years than I will ever admit to any man. It was my stage name. Amber Dixon."

"Okay," he said.

"I'll need some help to hack into your ex's socials." Amber reached for a piece of bread. "I need to study her clothes, her makeup, her voice, her walk, everything she ever posted. But there is one thing I noticed right off the bat, in her profile pic. What's up with that baby? Is that baby yours?"

For a moment, Henry couldn't speak. "That's Faith," he said finally. "She's two and a half."

"Is she yours?" Amber asked again.

"I, ah…I thought she was. Once." He couldn't keep the bleak tone out of his voice. "She's a great little kid."

Her face tightened. "Oh, Henry," she said. "I'm so sorry. That's really awful."

"It was," he agreed. "The worst part. Besides prison, of course. Knowing that Faith has that lying asshole for a father. Victor is dead inside, and he doesn't care who he hurts. He'll hurt her. He already has, and he's only just gotten started."

Amber put down her fork, picked up her glass and swirled her wine. "I'm going to ask some really direct questions, Henry."

"Ask away," he said, raising his hands. "I'm ready."

"You told me last night that you'd decided to hang around and bully and terrorize those two because you're pissed, and they deserve it. And you've been doing a pretty good job, considering the response you got last night in the stairwell. They are reacting. But you still haven't made any big moves to get your money back."

"It's not that easy. I've been working on it."

"And taking your sweet time." She eyed him over the rim of the glass. "I just wonder if maybe you're hanging around because you want to stay nearby and look out for that baby."

He tried to swallow, but his throat felt as dry as ashes. He gulped his wine.

"Not that I would blame you," she said. "She clearly needs a fairy godfather."

Henry shook his head. For once, her golden eyes seemed gentle.

"I can't take her with me," he said. "I'm a fugitive. I'll always be a fugitive."

"Ah. So you've done the math. Which means I don't have to do it for you. No, you absolutely can't. The real question is, can you walk away? If I open that safe deposit box, and take what's in it, will you be able to haul ass without looking back? Because if you can't, we'll both be screwed. So be honest with me."

"I have to," he said. "I'll walk away. When the time comes. I swear it."

She nodded, put the glass down, and picked up her fork. "Damn, Henry. You made this sauce out of fresh tomatoes, right?"

"And garlic, onions and basil."

He was delighted to see her eat an entire plate of the ravioli, plus some salad and bread. He couldn't have hoped for better.

"Belinda grew up with a single mom," he told her. "Like you. They didn't have much money. Her parents divorced when she was twelve. She never saw her dad again."

"Was he a dickhead to them?"

"I have no idea," he said. "Belinda never talked about him."

"So he was a dickhead, then. What about the mom?"

"She died when Belinda was a year from finishing college. Breast cancer. They found it late, and she died fast. We had that in common. My mom died of cancer when I was twenty-one, so we bonded over that." He paused. "Or, at least I thought we did. She worked as a secretary and an office administrator. Belinda was Victor's office manager."

"And those guys got it on the whole time that you and she were married?"

"And before," he admitted. "He picked me out for his fall guy as soon as I took him on as a client. He sicced Belinda on me himself."

"And it didn't bother him that she was sleeping with you?"

"Yes and no," he said thoughtfully. "From what I hear through the bugs in their house, he really loves hating it. Or else really hates loving it. I can't tell which, but it's ugly to listen to."

"So you actually watch them? In their house?"

"Well, not in their bedroom. But Victor has a smart house, and I made it my business to hack into it first thing. And, I'm way ahead of them whenever they try to change their passwords."

Her eyes widened. "It's so easy, then? To hack into a smart house?"

"I don't know. It was for me. But as many people have told me, I'm not normal."

"This house is a smart house," she said. "I haven't used any of its smarts, because I don't give a shit once I set the thermostat to keep me toasty warm. But theoretically, this house would be hackable, too, right?"

"With the username and password, sure," he said. "Which makes me think of another thing. That video camera over the front door. Is that camera live? And is that video saved someplace?"

"I have no idea," she said. "I have the packet somewhere, with all the passwords and stuff. We can check. Why? Should I turn it off?"

"Yes," he said. "They could probably turn it back on from wherever they are. But if I'm going to be here while we work on these things, it might be good to just, you know. Disable it, for a while. Maybe make the video go away. Do the neighbors know your face?"

"No, actually," she said. "It so happens I have no neighbors, on either side. One of the houses has been on the market for years. The other has an absentee owner."

"Well, good," he said. "Fewer sets of eyes to notice us. Would you be willing to disable the video?"

"I wouldn't have a snowball's chance in hell of figuring out a trick like that."

"Leave that to me," he said. "I'm good at it. I've compromised Victor and Belinda's security cameras, their heating, their appliances, their electronic butler, and Faith's baby monitor. Look at this." He grabbed the laptop that was sitting on the end of the table, spun it around, and clicked open an app. Belinda appeared on the kitchen monitor trying to feed a squalling Faith while Victor watched, drinking a glass of whiskey. The kitchen was a shambles, thanks to the fire. Belinda looked like she was close to tears.

Victor stepped closer. "Here, kid. Try some of this to calm you down." He dipped his finger into the whiskey and stuck it in the baby's mouth.

Faith shrieked and writhed wildly. Belinda knocked Victor's hand away. "Don't do that!" she hissed. "That is poison for her!"

"Oh, lighten up, Bel. It's just a joke. You can't start 'em off too soon, right?"

Belinda unbuckled Faith from the high chair and carried her out of the frame.

Amber looked up, pained. "Ick," she murmured. "I've met guys like him. I see why you worry." She crossed her arms over her chest. "So why not put him away for good? Set him up, just like he did to you? At least long enough for her to mostly grow up without him around. Plant something horrific on him. Like kiddy porn."

"I thought about it," he admitted. "But even if I were just accessing that material to entrap him, I'd still be trafficking in it, and that makes me complicit. I can't do that."

"Well, hmm. That is to your credit, Henry. I applaud the sentiment, impractical though it is. Your principles might mess you up. I just hope they don't mess me up, too."

"I'll be sure not to ever implicate you in anything. I swear it."

"Aww. You know what, Henry? You're one of the good guys." Amber raised her glass. "Yay, you."

"Yeah," he said grimly. "For all the good it does me."

"Concentrate on getting your life back. Your freedom. You shouldn't risk that just to slap those bitches around. If you get caught, you're letting them win twice over." She poured both of them another glass of wine. "That's what I intend to do. I can't go toe-to-toe with Leon. He'd crush me. So I'm running as soon as I can. I'm not ashamed of it."

"Nor should you be," he said.

She lifted her glass again. "Here's to the good guys. And to freedom."

He hesitated. "Maybe you shouldn't overdo the wine. Alcohol can interfere with the function of the antibiotic, and that pill is already—"

"Henry," she said gently. "Stop right there."

"Yes? Why?"

"Don't be a pain in the ass. Toast, and drink. To the good guys. And to freedom."

"To the good guys, and to freedom," he echoed obediently.

In the silence that followed, they heard a strange, rhythmic sound coming from the computer speaker. Victor and Belinda, at it again. She was whimpering and pleading. Victor said something harsh. Loud thudding followed.

"Wow," Amber murmured. "Quite the dynamic those two have there."

Henry slapped the computer closed. "Sorry. I didn't mean to make you listen to that."

"I'm not shocked, Henry," she said, her voice faintly

amused. "Maybe you haven't noticed, but I've been around the block a few times."

"Even so, it's ugly, and Faith can hear it. That's the audio from her baby monitor. It picks up the noise from their bedroom, through two closed doors. That's how loud it is."

She looked pained. "Henry. I'm so sorry. That sucks."

He nodded. There was nothing to be done about it. No solution he could think of.

"I just don't get it," he said.

"Get what?" she asked.

"Her, choosing him when he hurts her. Going to those insane lengths for him. Hurting me, destroying me, imprisoning me. Having Faith. Hurting Faith. All to please him. When he talks to Bel, he says demeaning, hurtful things. I never..." He stopped and shook his head. "I could never have given her what she needs, if that's what she needs."

"Thank God for that," Amber said. "That shit started way back for her, Henry. You said the dad went away when she was twelve? I bet it was him. Or if not him, it was one of the mom's loser boyfriends. I bet she was a pretty little girl. Broke single moms with pretty little girls are like catnip to scumbag predators."

"Like I said, she never said much about her dad. So I have no idea."

"She might not either. She might not remember it. Or maybe she's too ashamed to think about it. Or it hurts too much. Bad memories have an electrical charge. You learn to steer around them without knowing you're doing it. They change you inside. I've known lots of girls like that. My profession is full of them."

"Girls like what? What do you mean?"

Amber looked like she was choosing her words carefully. "If someone you love uses you like that when you're small, you get snarled up inside. Good is bad, light is dark, day is night. You start to confuse being used with being loved. Once the damage is done, you have a flashing neon sign over your head you can't shake saying 'use me, use me, use me.' It's invisible to normal people. Only asshole predators can see it."

"Oh."

"Yeah," Amber said. "So, of course, girls like that get used. Sometimes, they even convince themselves that it's love. Hard love, complicated love. The harder the use, the more love they feel."

Henry held up his hand. "Don't," he said. "Don't make me feel bad for Belinda. I don't know if it was like that for her. It might have been. But it's not my problem."

Amber nodded swiftly. "Sorry, Henry. You are under absolutely no obligation to empathize with that lying skank after what she did to you."

He started to shake, and realized it was laughter, of all things. It wrenched him, like a seizure. So intense, it was painful. He hid his face in his hands. When it finally stopped, he breathed more deeply. The noisy, anxious buzz in his head diminished. He looked at Amber. "Thank you."

She nodded, and even smiled. But with his new inner stillness, he saw her differently. Despite her faint, calm smile and her startling beauty, her shadowy eyes seemed unfathomably sad.

"A broke single mom," he murmured slowly. "A pretty little daughter. Catnip to scumbag predators."

She held up her hand, shaking her head. "Don't go there, Henry."

"It happened to you, too, right? Like Bel?"

"No point in thinking about it. Or talking about it."

"Yeah, okay," he said. "But you're not like Bel at all. You're not under that spell you talked about, like Bel is with Victor. You don't have that neon sign over your head."

Her eyebrows shot up. "You don't know." She sounded faintly amused. "If I did, you wouldn't see it, Henry. Good guys never do."

"Right," he said sourly. "I'm the vanilla man."

She got up from the table. "It was different for me. It wasn't someone I loved or trusted. I knew the guy was a piece of shit. I knew it before, during, and after."

Henry regretted having walked them into this dark and thorny place. "That doesn't sound any better," he said cautiously.

"Oh, it's not." Her voice was flat and cold. "It's just different."

Henry hardly let himself breathe as her light footsteps retreated up the stairs.

Chapter Twenty

"Mr. and Mrs. Rampling, please. I think it's a poor use of our time to go through every single one of the cleaning products we provide to our—"

"On the contrary!" Henry doubled down on the prissy, adenoidal voice Amber had coached him to use. "I suffer from severe skin sensitivities, debilitating respiratory allergies, and several different auto-immune diseases. It is paramount that we research every single pollutant that a prospective cleaner might bring into our home. Just being in here now is causing my throat to close. Kindly do not tell me how to manage my own health." He buried his face in a tissue and had a fit of hollow coughing right on the spot.

"Do you need a shot, honey?" Amber, in the person of Karen Rampling, a bobbed, curly blonde with big blue eyes, a cardigan, and pearls, dug into her bag with aggressive purpose. "I have the EpiPen, if you need—"

"I won't need it if Ms. Zale would just show us the list of products and equipment that her workers use!"

Elyse Zale, dispatcher and manager of Menzies Deep Cleaning, huffed out an irritated breath, and got to her feet. "I suppose. If you insist."

"I do insist."

"Don't get agitated, sweetheart." Amber's voice was much higher and breathier than usual. "It makes your hives worse. And remember. Breathe. Slow in. Slow out."

Elyse Zale rolled her eyes as she led them out of her office and into the common area where rolling carts and shelves of products and cleaning devices were stored. "This is all the stuff we use, depending on the job," she announced. "There are hundreds of products here, sir. It would take days to hunt down all the ingredients in every one of them. I'm sorry, but I cannot do that for you."

Henry sighed, letting her know she had disappointed him deeply, and asked, "Do your teams wear a uniform?"

"An apron, yes. Why?"

"Could you tell us what detergent the aprons are washed in?" Amber asked.

Zale turned to her. "You're kidding, right?"

"Not at all. Do you have some aprons here? If I take a sniff, I can tell right away if he can be in the same room with them. Otherwise, we'll have to request the team wear no aprons. And that the cleaners wear clothing that's been washed in detergent with no surfactants. Contact with petroleum distillate or naphtha could land him in the hospital."

Zale let out a sharp laugh and jerked her chin toward the back. "Aprons are stored in those blue plastic crates on the bottom shelf, ma'am. Sniff to your heart's content."

Amber trotted purposefully toward the shelf the woman had indicated, while Henry pulled out his phone, and started snapping pictures of the shelves. "I'll do the research myself," he said. "If a product has ingredients that endanger my life, I'll take on the responsibility of finding an alternative with non-toxic ingredients. If you put us in touch with the cleaning team, we can communicate with them directly."

"I suppose that might be best," Elyse Zale agreed with bad

grace. She looked over at Amber. "Ma'am? Could you stop that, please? It's against our company policy to allow photographs in here!"

Henry began to cough. The fit escalated to choking sounds.

"Darling?" Amber hurried to his side. "Are you all right?"

"It's the benzalkonium chloride," he gasped out. "It's making my esophagus burn. I can't…breathe. I have to get out of here. Right now."

"Please excuse us," Amber said. "We have to go."

"Please. Feel free," Zale muttered, stepping to the door and holding it open for them.

Even before they reached the car service that had waited around the block, Amber and Henry began to shake with stifled laughter. Mindful of the driver, they tried not to look at each other, but the harder they tried, the worse it got.

"Benzalkonium chloride?" she whispered, wiping her eyes as they climbed into the back seat. "Is that actually a thing?"

"Absolutely. The air was thick with it. It's the active ingredient in Lysol."

"Oh, stop it, Mr. Rampling," Amber moaned. "You are killing me."

They shuddered and shook for another minute before he turned to her. "Did you get the—"

"Oh hell, yeah." Amber opened her black bag, showing him two blue and green Menzies Deep Cleaning aprons, folded and stiff with starch.

"Excellent," he said. "Brilliant work."

"Admit it, Henry," she whispered. "You enjoyed that. It was fun, right?"

He was almost afraid to admit it, but it was true. Fun, as a concept, had always mystified him. Even being with Belinda, while thrilling and exciting, had not been fun. He'd always been walking on eggshells, terrified of screwing it up. But Amber made him laugh. She was sharp in all the ways he wasn't. She'd put this scenario together, sketched out Mr. Rampling's personality, taught him his lines and changed his looks. She'd coached him into being someone else. And yes. It had been fun.

"I got pictures of their set-up," Amber said.

"Not necessary. I saw it." He tapped his head. "It's all in here."

"For real? You've got photographic memory? There were hundreds of bottles!"

"A hundred and seventy-four that I could see."

She whistled. "Shoot, Henry. That would be so handy in a casino. Ever try playing poker? Or learning another language, or ten? I bet you'd be fast."

"Maybe, but then I'd have to talk to people in those languages," he said.

Amber laughed and slapped him on the leg. She teased him all the time, but it didn't sting the way Belinda's teasing had.

Back at the Grudberg house, Henry pulled up a spreadsheet on his laptop and started typing. "The Graziano house was on the white board behind Zale's desk," he said. "A two-person team, four hours, once a week, Wednesday morning. The cleaners are Stacy Wiggins and Bryony Haner. Today is Monday, so we either do it the day after tomorrow, or we wait another week. I got into their database already, so I have Mrs. Graziano's number."

Amber looked worried. "The day after tomorrow might be premature, but I'm more scared of waiting. Plus, once this job is done, I can give becoming Belinda my full attention. I've been listening to her voice from that video that was posted online of that wedding you went to. Remember when she roasted the bride? I think I've got her down pat. Want to hear my Belinda?"

The thought made Henry shudder. "No, thanks," he said swiftly. "Hard pass."

She gave him a playful pout. "Aww. You're no fun. After all my hard work."

"It was bad enough having to video you moving like her and dancing like her," he said. "It makes my stomach clench."

"Well, I'm not doing it to hurt you. I'm just being professional. I needed those videos to compare with Belinda videos. To see how close I'm getting."

"Absolutely. Moving on. The plastic logo for the van should be ready at the printer by tomorrow. We need to shop for one of those carts, and fill it with everything Stacy and Bryony would use. Most important, we need to convince Menzies Deep Cleaning that Mrs. Graziano is canceling her appointment this week."

"Leave it to me," Amber said. "Want to hear my Serafina Graziano?"

Henry was startled. "How do you know what Mrs. Graziano sounds like?"

"You forget, I shared an apartment with Trix before we shacked up with Leon and Kenji. Mrs. Graziano used to call Trix and harass her. She wanted to know when her daughter was going to stop acting like a whore, shaking her ass in front of dogs and pigs."

"Ouch."

"Yeah. Trix would put her on speakerphone, for the entertainment value. Real character, that Serafina. So? Let's call Menzies and do this thing. I'm psyched for it."

"You mean cancel the cleaning crew for Wednesday? Right now?"

"You got a better time? Give me a fresh phone. Let me do it while I'm hot."

He got a burner from his stash. She punched in the number, then put it on speakerphone.

"Menzies Deep Cleaning, this is Elyse Zale speaking. How can I help you?"

"This is Serafina Graziano," Amber brayed in a blaring,

cigarette-roughened voice with a New Jersey/Italian accent. "I'm callin' because I don't want no cleaners tomorrow. We're leavin' today on a trip an' we won't be here. I'm cancellin'."

"Do you want to switch the day, Mrs. Graziano? When would you like—"

"Nah. I'll call you when I'm back. I don' know how long we'll be gone."

"But we have a policy of at least a forty-eight-hour notice before canceling—"

"You don' like it, I find another cleaner. You cleaners are a dime a dozen."

"Mrs. Graziano, I didn't mean to imply—"

"I'll call you. Don' call me. I don' wanna hear from you."

Amber hung up and gave Henry a triumphant glance. "So?"

He stared at her, stupefied. "That was amazing," he said. "It's like a superpower."

"Oh, I got way better than that in my bag of tricks," she assured him. "So that bit is handled, thanks to little old super-human me. That leaves one thing we haven't talked about yet, but it's crucial. Can you clean, Henry?"

He was taken aback. "Well…I don't see why not."

"Uh-oh. You have no clue, do you? Have you ever done it?"

"I understand the basic principles," he said. "How hard could it be?"

She laughed. "It's not how hard it is. It's more the quality of your energy while you're doing it. Serafina Graziano is an elderly Italian American lady with an industrial grade person-ality disorder. She is an absolute bitch on wheels. Compulsive does not begin to describe it. If she sees you in action, and we have to assume she will, she'll expect life-or-death urgency."

"I see. That's intimidating."

"It is," Amber nodded. "Believe me. Trust me, I know these women. My grandmother was one of them, minus the personality disorder. My mother would have become one if she'd lived long enough and had a nice house to keep. Who knows, I might become one myself someday, if I get lucky. So, you never cleaned before? Is that what I'm hearing?"

"Ah, no, I guess," he admitted. "Not like that. Just, you know, doing dishes, wiping down a counter, cleaning up after the baby. How do you know how to clean? Are there tricks to it? Were you ever a professional?"

She hesitated for a moment. "In a way," she admitted. "Yes. After Mamma died, I ran away from Sid, her boyfriend, and hooked up with a crew of grifters I knew from way back with my mom. I got involved with two women, Lannie and Sabine, who ran a cleaning service. It was a front. We were actually casing places for burglaries. But in the meantime, we were a valid cleaning service. We cleaned the hell out of those houses. I might even go so far as to say that we took pride in our level of service. Ironic, I know."

"Oh," he said. "Wow."

"It didn't end well. One of the burglars got caught and gave up Lannie and Sabine. I was out of town at the time, spending the weekend in Reno with some guy or other. Lannie and Sabine ended up doing time."

"And they never told the police about you?"

"No, they did not," she said softly. "Lannie and Sabine protected me."

"Are you still in touch with them?"

"Lannie died in prison, after about five years after she went in. Heart attack. Sabine got out on parole and vanished. You saw that tattoo on my back? The vine and flowers?"

He nodded. "Yes, I saw it."

"They both had that tattoo. It was a girlfriend set for them. I got it tattooed onto my own back by the same artist after they went inside. In their honor. To remember what true friends do for each other." Amber gave him a bright, let's-move-on smile. "So that was it for me. No more grifting. My mother was a grifter. She taught me everything I know, but she died in prison, too. After that, plus what happened to Lannie and Sabine, I lost my nerve. So I tried out some different things, and eventually ended up shaking my stuff at the Magnum. Where I had to paint over that damn tattoo every damn night, but whatever."

"I'm so sorry about your mother," he offered. "And about Lannie and Sabine."

"It was a long time ago," she said briskly. "Back to business. Rubber gloves, chemicals and elbow grease. But most importantly, the gung-ho attitude. Tonight, we clean."

"Will that be before or after dinner?"

"Dinner?" she said blankly. "Excuse me?"

"I used the Grudbergs' slow-cooker," he admitted. "I made pot roast."

"Oh, for God's sake. Are we planning dangerous heists, or are we playing in Barbie's Dream House? We're busy, Henry! We don't have time for gourmet meals!"

"Slow-cooker pot roast is not a gourmet meal," he protested.

"Well, I'm hungry," she admitted. "But I feel as if I shouldn't encourage you."

"Don't worry," he said. "Food will give us more energy for planning dangerous heists. And I learn fast. I'll clean like no one's ever cleaned before. It'll be fun."

"I bet you're the first person ever to use the word "fun" about cleaning, Henry."

Chapter Twenty-One

It was the smell that got her. It catapulted her straight back to that night. The yellow rubber gloves, the nose-burning perfume of the stuff in the spray bottles. There she was, shivering and almost naked, earrings swinging as she struggled to spritz and swab Michael's blood off the floor and the worktop and the cabinets.

But she couldn't. No matter how hard she tried, there was always a pinkish smear left behind. She saw Michael's head, rolling on the ground. Mouth open, eyes wide. His lips were moving, but only for her. She heard his ghost voice in her ear.

Run, you dumb bitch. Run!

I can't, she wanted to yell at him. *I can't run. I'm naked, wearing four-inch heels, and he's holding a meat cleaver. I can't!*

"Can't what? Amber? Amber! What happened? Are you okay?"

She blinked, gasping. She was crouched on the floor.

Time rearranged itself. Henry was there. Henry, her linchpin, her anchor, pulling her back to the present. The Grudbergs' kitchen. Not the blood-spattered Vegas penthouse.

He stroked her shoulder. "You kept saying "I can't," he said. "Can't what?"

"Don't want to talk about it," she whispered. "Bad memory. Sorry."

She knew he wanted to, but didn't have the nerve to close his arms around her.

"Seemed like more than a bad memory," he offered. "Do you want to stop for a while? I think I have the hang of it now. We could knock off. Have dinner. A glass of wine."

She twisted away. "No. Not yet. Let's finish the kitchen."

She white-knuckled it for a while, showing him the ins and outs of oven cleaning, how to get grease spatter off the inside of a microwave, and the best techniques for cleaning the refrigerator. Then they went back to scrubbing and spraying surfaces.

And boom, down she went again. No hallucination this time, but her blood pressure plummeted anyway. This time, she swam back into regular space-time in the Grudbergs' kitchen with her ass flat on the floor and her stomach flopping nastily.

Henry was next to her, his arms and legs around her. His chin rested on the top of her head, giving her his warmth. His body heat helped the shivering, but she couldn't speak. She just shook.

"I don't know much about stress flashbacks," he said gently. "Other than from novels and articles. But I've read that the best thing is to talk about it. Until it actually bores you."

She let out a brief, soggy laugh. "That won't happen anytime soon."

"But you could start," he urged. "Where did you go in your head?"

"The night Leon made me…" Her words trailed off. She swallowed. "He made me clean."

"Clean what?"

"Michael's blood. It was everywhere. Leon made me clean it up." She held up her hands. "Rubber gloves, just like these. A yellow sponge, like this one. But it was the smell of the spray that did it. And this kitchen is shiny white, like Leon's kitchen. I've felt tense and nauseated in here from the start. I didn't even make the connection until now."

His arms tightened. "I'm so sorry."

After a while, she found herself leaning back against his chest. The air was starting to go into her lungs again, bit by bit. Her heart slowed its frantic gallop.

"He took Michael out in a suitcase to bury him," she said. "In pieces. And locked me in the bedroom. Can you believe I lived in that apartment for months and never realized the bedroom door locked from the outside? And I thought I was so sharp."

He stroked her back.

"He wanted sex when he came back. I didn't have the nerve to say no. And it happened again, like…like Sid. When I was a girl."

"What happened?" His voice was gentle.

"Disassociation. You just float. Somewhere outside yourself. It happened again." She found herself shaking with bitter laughter. "Want to know something crazy?"

"Of course," he said. "Tell me."

"I'd been thinking about running away from him," she said. "I was working up the nerve, weighing pros and cons. I should have run sooner. But I didn't listen to my instincts."

"Of course you were hesitating," he said gently. "It's normal. Anyone would have."

"I knew they would pink-slip me at the theater soon. I was the oldest dancer in the show. I didn't want to be a casino dealer or a cocktail waitress. I was so scared of being old and broke, I actually got mixed up with Leon. And came home… to that."

Henry stroked her hair. "You're hardly old, you know."

She snorted. "Depends on who's looking."

"I'm looking," he said softly.

"I knew something was off with Leon. I knew I had to

break with him. After Sid, I could only fool myself so far about men. I shouldn't have gone home at all. But I wanted to pack my stuff. Get my clothes, my jewelry. My goddamn jewelry, can you believe it? So I went home. To a bloodbath."

"You left him the first chance you got. You're turning it around. You're strong."

She twisted until she was staring right into his bright blue eyes, moving closer. Almost as if she were going to kiss him, but she stopped. Pulling away, Amber grabbed the countertop and got to her feet. "Talk therapy time is over. We still have a lot of work to do."

"You sure you won't have a stress flashback at the Graziano house?"

"Nope. I'll just get all my ya-yas out tonight. I don't have the option of being a fainting flower. I feel better already. Good talk, Henry. Thanks. You're a pal."

"We could wait. Do it next week."

"No. If we do that, we'll burn our Menzies opening. I'm sorry I scared you. I promise I won't have a stress flashback on Wednesday. I'll be a trooper."

"Let me do the spray bottle part," he begged. "Let me spare you that."

"Nope," she said tightly. "Back in the saddle. Only way to do it."

Evidently cuddling on the kitchen floor and talking through her trauma with Henry was therapeutic, because it didn't happen again. The spray-bottle part made her queasy, but she did not faint, or barf. All in all, it was a success.

The way Henry flung himself into the task impressed her. He gave housework the same laser concentration he gave to everything he did. When she found him on his knees in the guest bathroom, scrubbing at discolored grout with an old toothbrush, she finally put her foot down. "Henry," she said. "Please. Chill. You're overcompensating."

"The more I look at it, the dirtier it seems." He wiped the tousled hair off his face.

Amber laughed at him. "Congratulations, buddy. You have just encapsulated the mechanism by which generations of women have sublimated their anxiety and dissatisfaction into endless and futile housework! Serafina Graziano will love you."

He looked worried. "That's bad, right? If she notices me at all?"

"So, don't overdo it. Do it one hundred percent. Not a hundred and fifty. Okay?"

"You said she'd want us to work with desperate urgency, right?"

"Urgency is fine. Just try not to enjoy it so much. It's kind of creepy."

His face had gone red. He peeled off the rubber gloves. "I'll just, ah, go check on the pot roast," he muttered.

Amber listened to his footsteps going down to check the dinner, hoping she hadn't embarrassed him or hurt his feelings. She knocked the guy around pretty hard, but he didn't seem to mind being teased. Or if he did, he didn't show it.

She felt stronger since teaming up with Henry. Probably it was from eating three tasty squares a day. She'd never done that before in her life, whether because of poverty, laziness, indifference, dieting, or some unholy combination of all four. Plus, she was a crap cook. She liked being pampered by Henry. Hell, she liked Henry, period.

'Trust' was a big word for a woman like her. Not really in her working vocabulary. But this just might be the closest she'd ever come to it. And after only a few days, too.

Plus, it was handy having someone so smart around. The skills she'd polished most in her life were disguises and grifting, occupations that required her to be sharp as a tack, ready to jump in any direction. But as a showgirl, geisha, and serial mistress, her job had been to look pretty, stay youthful, pump up male egos, give pleasure. It required a different kind of energy.

Men were simple creatures. Henry, not so much. There were layers to that guy.

It was obvious that he had a crush on her. But it wasn't just a sexual crush. It felt more like awed reverence. As if she were mighty and powerful, a high priestess of something or other. She reacted by teasing him mercilessly, but he was a good sport about that, too.

And he was cute, in his buttoned-up kind of way. Very cute.

So, yeah. She'd thought about it. Quite a bit, in fact. But sex could ruin everything. If she took him to bed, maybe that awed reverence and gentleness would morph right into the usual boring, possessive, condescending male bullshit. Then what she liked so much about him would be gone, poof.

Besides, she might not even be able to do the deed right now. She might glitch. Disassociate, like in the old days. Leon had summoned back all her old ghosts.

She had done what she had to do in bed with Leon, if only by the muscular automatism of long practice. She made the sinuous moves; she smiled and glowed, and even, apparently, came. She was a professional, after all.

But this wasn't a 'fake it 'til you make it' scenario. If she tried to seduce Henry and she glitched, it would be scary and traumatizing for him. He was a good guy. He deserved better.

He certainly wouldn't seduce her of his own accord. He would never push through his shyness and hesitation. She'd have to drag him through his resistance.

She was so curious. What would it be like to be with a lover who actually saw her? Even when she was dressed as an ancient crone, hunchbacked and hook-nosed, he had seen her. When he looked at her, what the hell did he see? Maybe he could show her. Point it out. Shine a light. Teach her.

What a joke, that a guy as innocent and awkward as

Henry might be able to teach a jaded old bag like her anything, especially about sex. In her vast experience, sex seldom elevated anything. She'd most likely kill that delicate, ephemeral thing she was jonesing for. She was being as silly as an adolescent girl. Which was probably the point, because her deeply buried adolescent girl self would be safe with Henry. She was trying to heal old wounds with this hopeful fantasy.

It was a lot to ask of a flawed, stressed-out mortal man, even one as unusual as Henry. A fugitive and a criminal, burdened with problems of his own. But he had dedicated himself so completely to her project. He had made it his own, giving all his brains and resources and energy to it.

Maybe he could do the same for her. She wanted to know what was down there, in her essential core. If anything still lived and breathed, or if she was nothing but an empty, blasted wreck.

A blasted wreck was not what Henry saw. She could tell by the way he looked at her.

She wanted to look into his eyes and see herself reflected back, whole and unbroken.

Chapter Twenty-Two

"So what's your name again?"

"Todd Dillon," Henry replied promptly. "From Peekskill. Living in Jersey City for the last two years. In my aunt's garage apartment."

"Good. And I am?"

"Josie Bixby," he said. "From Quincy, near Boston. You've been living with your brother-in-law in Newark."

"Good. And we are filling in for who?"

"Stacy and Bryony," he replied. "They have the flu. Stacy gave the flu to Bryony. They're in terrible shape."

She nodded. "Poor them. Let me do most of the talking. You just be the strong, silent type. Now let me get a good long look at you."

Amber cupped his face, frowning into his eyes. She'd put a sand-colored wig on him, styled in an awkward bowl cut. It made him look ridiculous. But he did not look like himself, which was the point.

Amber, too, looked completely different as Josie. Her mouse brown wig had messy, trailing wisps falling out of a tight braid to fan awkwardly over her ears. She'd put on round, wire-rimmed glasses, and accentuated the natural shadows under her eyes. She'd done something clever that canceled her lip color. She was trying to make herself plain. But that was impossible. At least in his eyes. He would always see how beautiful she was. It shone through any disguise, like sunlight through stained glass.

"Ready?" she asked. They were sitting in the rented van with the newly acquired Menzies cleaning logo stuck to the side, idling a half block down from the Graziano house.

"I was born ready," Henry replied dutifully.

Amber nodded and put the van in gear. In the Graziano's drive, she rolled down the window and rang the bell. The security camera blinked. They'd been recognized and cleared. Light flashed, the gate hummed and ground open. Amber drove on through, up the driveway, and on around the back. She pulled over behind another parked car, hoping she wasn't making mistake number one, and gave Henry a bracing thump on the shoulder with her fist. "Showtime," she said. "Knock 'em dead. That was what my mother always said when we started a new job."

"Back at you," he replied.

A large, burly security guard with a scowl grooved deep into his fleshy face came out the back door and stood there, arms over his chest. Then a thickset, middle-aged black-haired woman in a housekeeper's uniform came out, her face also disapproving.

"Who the hell are you?" she asked suspiciously. "Where are Bryony and Stacy?"

"They got the flu," Amber said. "Elyse had to scramble to find someone to cover for them. She didn't want to leave an important client like Mrs. Graziano in the lurch. Elyse told us this is an important job. I'm Josie, and this is Todd."

The woman did not introduce herself. She just stared coldly at Amber's outstretched hand.

"Um. So," Amber said. "Bryony and Stacy were in no

condition to give us any pointers about how you do things around here. Any hints?"

The woman's lip curled. "We don't like un-vetted strangers. And I don't have time to run around after you and manage you."

"Certainly not," Amber smiled brightly. "We'll be self-sufficient. May we come in?"

The housekeeper harrumphed and opened the door. Henry got the cart out of the van and followed Amber into a large, gleaming professional kitchen. It had to be a blindingly white. That was going to be hard for Amber.

"Shall we start here?" Amber asked, ever the tough babe.

"No, you will not," the housekeeper snapped. "I'm busy making ragú, and I don't need anyone messing around in my kitchen. You don't have time for the kitchen, anyhow. Mrs. Graziano just wants four hours today. Dusting, vacuuming, wet mopping, floors and bathrooms. And do the windows. As you would have known, if you'd done your homework."

"Sorry," Amber said. "Of course."

Excellent. Henry was quietly jubilant. They could mop and sweep and dust and wash windows all day with no stress flashbacks.

The housekeeper jerked her chin at him. "What's his problem? Can't he talk?"

"Sure he can," Amber said. "He's just quiet. But he works like a demon. Right, Todd?"

"Right. Total, er, demon." He nodded at the woman, then looked toward the scowling security guard. "Morning."

The man didn't answer. The housekeeper waved them out the kitchen door. "Go on," she said. "Get to work."

And so, they did. Pulling on the rubber gloves, they started in on the spacious living room, Amber vacuuming, Henry dusting and doing the downstairs bathroom.

He noticed two communion photos right away. One was of a pretty girl with a heavy mono-brow and dark eyes. The other was of a thin, pale, jaundiced looking boy. Same pose, same prayerful hands and rosary beads, same white angel robe. But the boy's tight-lipped expression screamed, *get me out of here.* He gave Amber a questioning look. She nodded in corroboration. Yep, those were Trix and Tori.

Cleaning the Graziano house was unsatisfying, if only because the place was already spotless. Not one speck of dust had been allowed to rest upon any china doll, or antique clock, or marble mantle. No streak or smudge or water stain marred the window glass. The carpets were clean, and the wooden floor was buffed and gleaming. There was no way to gauge any progress through the place, apart from the growing intensity of chemical perfumes of the products they were using. Henry and Amber's eyes watered, but rarely met. Their conversation was reduced to brief, muttered orders or suggestions.

Even so, Henry sensed the pressure building up inside her.

Two hours into doing the downstairs, the housekeeper came out, peering at surfaces and sniffing suspiciously. "That's enough down here," she announced, finally. "Go on upstairs."

Hauling the carts, Henry followed Amber to the second floor. No one would ever guess from her face, but he knew that hope and fear were vibrating through her body.

Amber started down the main corridor, glancing through open doors. They passed two guest bedrooms, an old-fashioned, wood-paneled library/office, and arrived at a walk in linen closet, its shelves stacked with sheets and towels.

"We'll need those for the kid's room." Henry pointed at a shelf labeled 'twin'.

"Good thought." Amber grabbed a set of black sheets.

The next door opened onto a large bedroom, probably Mrs. Graziano's, all snowy white lace, marble-topped dressers and antique photos. The wall over the bed was dominated by a large painting of the Madonna and Child with a ghostly cross hovering in the clouds behind them.

Amber opened the door to the next room and sighed with relief. This definitely belonged to an adolescent boy. It had a huge desk, and was lined with shelves covered with intricate Lego sculptures of famous buildings from around the world, as well as cars, robots, monsters, and spaceships from popular movie franchises.

"I don't see any tigers," Amber said. "Looks like he's not the stuffed animal type."

"Maybe it's not a stuffed animal," Henry said. "It could be a folder, a backpack, a notebook. Shall we start with the sheets?"

"Sure." She pulled back the black velour coverlet, tastefully decorated with glow-in-the-dark skulls and bones. "This is one mopey emo kid."

"I can relate to the Lego," Henry said. "I liked them too, back in the day. They calmed me down."

Once the sheets were on and the pillow stuffed into its fresh case and plumped, they spread the coverlet back over the bed. Henry took a feather-duster and handed Amber a second one. "I'll do the top shelves," he said. "You do the lower ones."

It went quickly. Unsurprisingly, there was no dust, either on the shelves or on the sculptures. Henry lifted up each separate piece of Lego, checking behind it and under it for recessed cavities. There was nothing in any of them. Amber did the same on the lower shelves, with the same results. Then she looked through the closet, which was unnaturally tidy for a thirteen-year-old boy. Nothing there, either.

They started on the desk. It was covered in heaps of notebooks. Seventh-grade math, English and Social Studies. Pages filled with doodles and drawings of animals and comic book characters, interspersed with a couple of buxom naked ladies, which were not half bad.

Amber's face was tight with misery. "Zip," she muttered.

Henry was pushing the bottom drawer closed when he felt it catch. "Wait," he whispered. "There's something here."

She crouched next to him as he pulled the drawer out and felt above it. "There's an envelope taped to the bottom of drawer above," he told her as he delicately loosened the tape and pulled out a thick cardboard mailer. Henry passed it to her. "You should do the honors."

Amber gulped as she reached inside, pulled out the contents, and fanned them onto the floor.

Pornographic magazines.

Henry leafed through a couple, just to be sure, but there was nothing of any interest in them. He slid them back into the mailer, and tucked the envelope back where he had found it, pressing the tape to the drawer above.

"I knew it was too good to be true," Amber whispered. "I knew it."

They both heard the ominous thud-thud-thud, clopping steadily toward them.

Amber bounded toward Ettore's bed, flinging off the cover. Henry pushed the drawer closed and seized the feather duster just in time.

Serafina Graziano smacked the door open, her expression thunderous. Amber was bent over the bed, tucking in the sheets she had just pulled loose. Henry was gathering up the notebooks he had scattered over the desk.

"Who the hell are you two clowns? And what are you both doin' in the kid's room?" she demanded, her voice sharp with suspicion. "I don' like strangers in my house. And there ain't enough work in this bedroom for the both of youse anyhow."

Fishwife. That was what his mother used to call women with that scratchy, braying voice. Though, to be fair, his mother, the elegant and classy Faith Devlin, had been a dedicated librarian whose favorite phrase had been "shhhh."

"I was just doing the bed," Amber said. "And my colleague—"

"I can see what your colleague's doin' with my own eyes, honey. Nothin'. That's what he's doing. Wasting my time and money, eh? Were you two getting up to something naughty in here?"

"No!" Henry said.

Mrs. Graziano summed him up in a glance. "Oh, ho! It speaks!"

"I assure you, we are completely professional, Mrs. Graziano," Amber assured her.

"Oh, are you? Well, I liked the other two girls. They didn't go snuggling up together in the bedrooms. You there." She waved at Amber. "Go do the bathroom across the hall. Your boyfriend can finish up Tori's room. Move your butt."

Amber shot him an eloquent glance as she grabbed her cart and rolled it out.

"We are actually finished in here," Henry said. "I could go and do the other bathrooms in the main bedroom—"

"You know what my mamma taught me when she taught me how to clean house?" Mrs. Graziano marched over until she was terrifyingly close to him. "She made me pull every piece of furniture away from the wall to clean behind it. Do you know why?"

He tried not to let his gaze drop. "Ah, no. Why?"

"Because God sees everywhere!" she said triumphantly.

He shook his head helplessly. "I'm not sure what you mean, ma'am. Do you want me to move the furniture and clean behind it?"

"Are you deaf? Or just stupid?"

What followed was the strangest twenty minutes of his life. Under Serafina Graziano's watchful eye, Henry moved both of the dressers away from the wall, vacuumed behind them, and mopped as well. Then came the couch. Then the bed.

He had tugged the large wooden book shelf at the head of the bed loose from the wall, and was bending to dust behind it, when he noticed something. A cheap plastic box frame had slid between the bed and the wall.

Henry picked it up. A pen, ink, and chalk rendering of a tiger's snarling face stared up at him. Its fangs were bared. Its golden eyes looked like they were aflame.

His heart hiccupped. Then it started to gallop. Looking at the wall, Henry noticed the protruding nail at the same moment he realized the box frame was heavier than it should be. Something was inside it.

"My Tori did that," Mrs. Graziano said proudly. "Last year. He's a good boy."

"He's talented," Henry said, meaning it. The drawing was good. He hung the picture back on the nail.

"You see?" Mrs Graziano sounded vindicated. "If those lazy, worthless girls were doing their jobs, they woulda found Tori's picture and hung it back up months ago! I'm gonna tell 'em about it when they come back."

"You definitely should," Henry said.

She harrumphed. "I better go check on your girlfriend. Make sure she's not slacking off. You gotta watch cleaners like a hawk. Those sonzabitches will rob you blind. Start on the other bedrooms! And remember! Move all the furniture! Got that?"

"Yes ma'am," he said dutifully. "Absolutely. Every single piece."

The second she stepped out the door, Henry pulled out his phone and snapped a picture of Tori's tiger. Then he took it down and pried the cardboard back off the frame.

Inside was an old, faded manila envelope, crumpled and water-stained. Henry lifted it out. Whatever was inside was thick and heavy. Henry tossed the manila envelope into the trash bag hooked to his cart, making sure it was buried under old Kleenexes and toilet rolls. Then he pressed the picture back into the frame and returned it to the wall.

The last forty-five minutes of the shift were agony. Henry

couldn't so much as whisper to Amber. Serafina Graziano followed them the entire time, criticizing everything they did. When it was finally over, and they were packing the carts into the back of the van, he turned to her.

He checked to be sure that the housekeeper and the security guard had gone back into the kitchen, and whispered to her. "Amber. I have to tell you something. I—"

"No, you don't. You don't have to say anything."

He was taken aback by her tone. "But I—"

"I just can't right now, Henry. Sorry." She pulled open the van door. "You don't deserve it, and I don't want to be a bitch, but not right now. Get it?" Turning her face away, she climbed into the passenger's seat, tossing him the keys. "You drive."

Unhooking his precious garbage bag, Henry tucked it behind the seats before climbing behind the wheel. Amber stared out the window as they rolled down the drive. Once out of the gate, Henry headed for the dumpster in the back of a strip mall where they had decided to dump the van logo, the aprons and cleaning supplies. When they got there, he killed the engine, and tried again. "Amber—"

"Henry, what part of shut-the-hell-up do you not understand?"

"You're throwing a tantrum," he said. "Stop acting like a baby and listen to me."

She rolled her eyes. "What could you possibly have to say to me about that stupid, risky, expensive, useless thing we just did that I would want to hear?"

"Well," he said, twisting around and grabbing the garbage bag, "For one thing, I could tell you what happened in Tori's bedroom after Mrs. Graziano kicked you out."

"Given the volume of Serafina Graziano's voice, I heard most of it," Amber said. "The old hag's last pleasure is bullying people and riding their asses. God help poor little Tori. What the hell are you doing rooting around in that garbage bag?"

"I need to show you something." Henry stopped rooting. "The old hag wanted me to move the furniture." He handed Amber his phone. "And a picture had fallen down between the bed and the wall."

"What am I looking at?" Amber took the phone grudgingly. "What the hell is this?"

"Just look. Calm down for a damn second and look."

She stared down at the tiger image on his screen and gasped. "Henry! Did you…?"

"Of course I did. The second Mrs. Graziano left the room. It was in the frame, between the picture and the backing." He pulled the manila envelope out of the garbage and held it out to her. "The picture was too heavy with the envelope inside, so it had fallen down behind the bed."

She took it almost reluctantly, staring at it with frightened eyes. "Is it…"

"I don't know. I didn't dare check. I'd hate for you to be disappointed again. But it should be you who does the honors."

"I'm not sure my nerves can take this kind of honor," she told him.

"Just one more time," he coaxed. "The odds are in your favor. It was behind Tori's tiger. X marks the spot. Go for it."

As Amber undid the clasp, the entire fold, rotten and dusty, came off in her hand. She reached in and pulled out a thick sheaf of paper.

Not papers. Bearer bonds. Each redeemable to the U.S. Treasury. Each one worth a hundred thousand dollars. Amber rifled through them, counting. "Holy shit," she said, her voice shaking. "If these are valid, then there's…there's over ten million bucks in this envelope."

"I bet they are valid," Henry said. "Leon killed for them. Michael risked his life for them. They're legal tender."

Amber crumpled the two bonds on top. Her shoulders shook.

"Are you okay?" he asked, alarmed.

She didn't answer. Henry waited for a minute. She let go of the crumpled bonds, smoothing them with her hands. When she finally looked up, her eyes were burning, just like the tiger's in Tori's drawing. She was wearing brown contacts as Josie, but somehow, he still saw that tawny gold shining through.

"You could have just taken these." Her voice was jerky. "Why didn't you?"

He just stared at her, dumbfounded. "Huh?"

She flapped her hand. "Don't play dumb with me."

"I never play dumb. When I'm dumb, I promise it's for real. But I don't get why you're angry. I thought you'd be happy. Isn't this what you wanted?"

Tears blurred the makeup around her beautiful eyes. "You don't get it," she said. "I wasn't even in the room when you found this envelope. I would never have known it existed. Why didn't you just keep your mouth shut and take the money for yourself?"

Henry hesitated, sensing that his answer was a turning point in his life. If he could be smart enough to solve this riddle, then the troll under the bridge wouldn't eat him. He'd be allowed to cross the river and have everything he'd ever longed for. Even the things he'd never dared to long for.

But he wasn't smart, at least not in that way. The only answer he had for her was the raw, unvarnished truth.

"We had a deal," he said. "And I would never do that to you."

"Why not?" she demanded. "I might have, in your shoes."

"I doubt that very much."

"You'd be as dumb as a rock to doubt it. I was raised by a con woman. I spent my childhood on the grift."

"That's where you're from," he said. "It's not who you are. And I want you to have those bonds."

She shook her head. "Goddamnit, Henry. I just don't know what to make of you. I don't know what to think."

"It's a fair trade," he assured her. "I'm glad this came through for you because what I need from you, pretending to be Belinda at the bank? It's a big ask."

"Oh, please. Get real." She hefted the envelope. "This is ten million bucks!"

"Great," he said. "I'm glad for you. I hear it's convenient to have rich friends."

She let out a laugh. "I can't believe you found it," she said. "We went through that place with a lice comb."

"I had divine help."

"Huh? How do you figure? I never would have pegged you as the religious type."

"I'm not," he admitted. "But Mrs. Graziano said something that made all the difference."

"Yeah? What did she say?"

"She said God sees everywhere."

They stared at each other and started to laugh.

Chapter Twenty-Three

Amber's mind buzzed all the way home. She was euphoric. Amazed, they had pulled it off, and anxious to figure out what was going on in Henry's mind.

There had to be a self-interested reason for what he'd done. She'd survived this long was because she always figured out all the angles before whoever she was dealing with copped to the fact that she had a brain. Of course, the difference was, she had never tried to hide her brain from Henry. Maybe because they saved each other's lives that first night.

Then there was the issue of sex. Men were irrational about sex. That was a given. But for God's sake, not to the tune of ten million bucks.

Another part of her wondered, almost fearfully, if she dared take his gesture at face value. He might still be hoping to get lucky, of course. She wouldn't blame a guy for that. But he had never made a move on her. Not even a lascivious glance.

After a lifetime of lascivious glances, that was a notable thing.

After they dropped the van, they made their way back to

Manhattan. On the cab ride back to the townhouse, Amber spotted a gourmet deli. "I want to buy a bottle of good champagne," she told him.

Henry looked dubious. "I'm low on cash. I have some academic papers to write that will top us up. But we've been so focused on this thing, I haven't looked at them yet."

She sighed. "Ironic, isn't it? With all this money?"

"Yeah," he said. "The bonds are useless for incidentals. And you're in no position to redeem them right now. We have some Prosecco, I think. We'll celebrate with that."

"I can get a hold of some more cash, too," she said, as the cab stopped in front of the Grudberg house. "Same way I did before I met you."

"Please, don't," he said. "It's too dangerous. I'll make enough to keep us going."

She waited until he finished paying and they got out of the cab to answer. "That's very tough and heroic of you, Henry, but I'll decide for myself."

"Of course you will," he agreed.

"Oh, shut up," she said. "You're no fun at all to fight with."

"The last thing I want," he said as he followed her up the steps, "is to fight with you."

"I know. You just want to serve me cookies and tea."

"Guilty as charged. Speaking of which, I'm starving. Shall we throw that steak in the fridge on the grill? The potatoes are all ready to go into the oven."

"I'm up for eating if you're up for cooking," she told him. "Just take off the Todd wig and the glasses before dinner, okay?"

He pulled off the wig and glasses, letting his shaggy dark mop spill out. Amber took them and ruffled his hair. "That's better."

"Take off your disguise, too," he said. "Not that I have anything against Josie."

"Will do." His smile made her eyes sting. She fled up the stairs as if pursued.

In any other situation, she would be one hundred percent sure that he was putting on this sweet, innocent, ingenuous act for some crafty reason. Running some kind of scam. After all, it was ten million dollars. He couldn't really be just handing it to her like that, could he? Unless he was playing a really long game. Longer than she could imagine.

Closing the door to her bedroom, Amber spread the bearer bonds across the bedspread, just to make sure they weren't a fever dream, and finally allowed herself to consider the terrifying possibility that Henry was for real. She counted the bonds again. He really had kept faith with her. So keeping faith with her had been more important to him than money.

That made him seem so vulnerable. It scared her to death for him.

Damn it, she could not be scared for Henry, too. She couldn't be canny and hard-nosed and worldly for Henry and for herself at the same time. She only had so much of that to give.

Amber sat at the vanity for a long time in her panties and camisole, finger-combing the pin-curls from under her hairnet, swabbing off the dulling makeup she'd used for Josie until she was down to brass tacks. Just her own pale face, spattered with reddish freckles. Her eyes looked hollow and shadowed. Nothing to distract from the visible signs of encroaching age. Crows-feet at the corners of her eyes. A pucker above her lip.

She felt the urge to smoke a cigarette, but she didn't keep them on her. Cigarettes were only for certain characters she played. They weren't part of the basic, no-frills Amber. Cigarettes came in a kit that was bought separately. All the extraneous stuff did. The clothes, the wigs, the nail polish, the lipstick colors, the shoes, the sparkles. They were all kits, each making up another person, another story she did not have to own, or feel, or take responsibility for. Without them, Amber

Dixon, formerly Annarita Rosalba DeGennaro, was as bare and flat and blank as a paper doll.

But Henry did not see her as flat. He'd looked into her darkest places. Mamma dying. Sid and his friends. Sabine and Lannie. Leon with his meat cleaver. Years of strutting her stuff on stage with a big, bright smile, pretending to be someone who didn't have to remember. And Henry still looked at her as if she were beautiful.

It occurred to her that she'd never been intimate with a man as herself. She'd always been someone else. Fun-loving, undemanding, carefree. The perfect girlfriend. She stood up, peeled off the camisole and panties, and stared at herself, trying to see the woman reflected in the glass. Not the paper doll who was always ready to adapt into whatever she was required to be.

She looked okay, all things considered. The tits were holding up well, if a bit deflated from the fugitive diet. Her ass was flatter, too. Her muff was a bit overgrown, since Brazilian waxes were strictly part of the mistress/geisha/showgirl kit, which were no longer in her budget.

It would be a tricky business, figuring out how to be just plain Amber.

She thought about mascara and lipstick, but decided against them. It wasn't right for tonight's honest vibe. But the poppy-splashed robe was a big yes. She had claimed that garment as hers. It was a start. She'd build from there.

The aroma of steak and potatoes was rising up the stairs. Dinner was ready.

She did a couple of pumps of scented body lotion, rubbed it in well, and pulled on the robe, tugging the sash tight. She had no idea what she might end up doing in the next couple of hours.

But whatever it was, she would smell nice doing it.

Chapter Twenty-Four

Henry heard a sound and turned to see Amber standing in the kitchen doorway.

For a second, he was almost transfixed, his breath stopping at the sight of this improbably bright, glowing creature. Then he shook himself and opened the freezer to pull out the Prosecco he'd been flash-cooling.

"To a job well done!" He poured two glasses of the pale, sparkling wine. "And to Mrs. Graziano," he added, handing her one. "For her well-timed lesson in practical theology."

"I owe you, Henry," Amber said, raising her glass to him. "For all time."

He shrugged, suddenly embarrassed. "Just until you help me with my thing. Then we're square. No debts. Just friends."

"Friends," she echoed. "And don't forget to factor in, on top of the people who are already trying to kill you, you've now put yourself squarely on the shit list of a psycho-killer." She smiled at him. "Stick with me, babe, and things will never be dull."

"I'd stick with you in any case," he blurted. In the silence that followed, he started to panic. "Damn," he said. "Did I just make it weird again?"

Amber swallowed a gulp of her Prosecco too fast, and the bubbles made her cough. "Little bit," she gasped out.

"Sorry. Sit down." He waved at the set table. "I just need to get the potatoes."

"Stop," she said. "Stop being so goddamn nice."

He went very still "Why? What does it hurt?"

She shook her head. "It just makes me afraid for you, okay? You're too easily exploited. Like with Belinda. You'll just get used again. Like I used you today. You let me do it. You're still letting me do it. Lying down like a carpet for me to walk on."

He pulled out a chair for her. "Let's discuss this after you have some food inside you," Henry said. "You were too nervous for breakfast and too busy for lunch. Eat, for God's sake. You're in a state."

She flopped down with a huff of nervous frustration, cradling her glass, letting him heap food on her plate. She actually seemed to calm down as she ate. Not that she would ever admit such a thing to him.

"Do you feel better?" he asked a few minutes later.

"I'll feel better when you take your twenty-five percent," she said.

"I told you. All I want is to——"

"Sharpen up!" He was surprised by the edge in her voice. Amber pointed her fork at him. "Don't let anyone else screw you over, you hear me? It's a bad habit. It's lazy, and it's sloppy. And it stops right here. Take the goddamn money you're owed."

"So." Henry put his own fork down. "Let me see if I understand this. Shoving two point six million dollars down my throat is supposed to teach me how to be selfish? Ouch. Stern, harsh Amber."

She glowered at him. "You should have learned this from your ex. I shouldn't have to teach it to you again. People will use you. It's a natural law. They can't help it, Henry. All human interactions are based on that. Even the good people. Even the sane ones. Even us."

"So you following me, jumping that guy in the stairwell. You were just using me?"

"No. That was a momentary lapse of judgment. Me being too curious for my own good. Chalk it up to my weird personal pathology, okay? Not to the natural laws of human interaction."

He fiddled with a potato. "I like your weird pathology."

Amber let out an explosive breath. "Stay on subject, Henry. Didn't you tell me that the guy who broke you out of prison has you pinned down with debt? Then there's the passport that you need. Will those two things cost more than twenty-five percent of those bearer bonds?"

He was taken aback. "Ah, no," he admitted. "Actually, that would cover it, and then some."

She looked triumphant. "Well, take it! Pay him off. You're free. Hurray."

"Let's just hold on a little longer," he said. "Let's see what's in that safe deposit box. If it's enough so I don't have to touch your stash, then I would rather—"

Amber slammed her hand down onto the table, rattling the plates and making the wine glasses wobble. "God damn it, Henry, there you go again."

"Calm down," he said gently.

"I can't! You're making me nuts!"

"You know, my mom had really high standards when it came to ethics," he said.

"Did she?" Amber snapped. "What does that have to do with any of this?"

"Her father, my granddad, died on the beach in Normandy. Her uncle was a firefighter. Her other uncle was a cop. Their folks came over from Ireland. They all ended up in service of one kind or another. So did she, in her own way."

"How is this relevant? Let's skip the history and genealogy lecture, Henry. I'm not in the mood."

"She used to say that everyone has to serve," he continued, ignoring her. "Whether it's their family, their friends, their country, the world. She was very high-minded that way. She said that service is the highest calling there is. Service that asks nothing in return."

Amber made a dubious noise. "Sounds like an invitation to let yourself get taken."

"I guess it can be, but not when it's done on purpose. With purpose. And because you care deeply for the other person, or people. Because you feel connected to them. They say we're all connected to everyone else. I don't feel it. But I wish I did. It would make it easier to be, you know. Selfless."

"You lost me, Henry." She sounded almost angry. "This shit is way above my pay grade."

"I was willing to serve Belinda and Faith," he said. "That blew up in my face. But I'm willing to try again. I'm willing to serve you. I feel connected to you. And I don't want to use you. I really don't. I want to cherish you. You've been used enough."

Amber wouldn't meet his eyes, but her face went pink. "Ten million bucks really takes the sting out of it, buddy," she said. "Rest easy, okay? I'm feeling cherished as hell."

He laughed, but the laughter died quickly. "You could walk away with your money right now," he said. "But I really, really hope you don't."

"I won't."

She stared across the table at him. The moment felt almost ceremonial, buzzing with all the possible meanings of their words. Henry felt his face get hot. He hurried to fill the silence.

"Oh," he stammered. "Yeah. I just got a message from that Craigslist guy up in Sorenson. Just before you came down. He'll sell us the car we need for the bank thing. Could you drive up with me up tomorrow morning? I'll need you to drive the other car to Milton."

"Happy to," she said. "Staying busy keeps me calmer."

"And another thing. After you told me about Michael going to West Palm Beach before Leon killed him, I thought I'd check out people who went missing in the West Palm Beach area around that time. There were a few. Nothing struck me, but now that we know what Michael was hiding, I see it in a different light."

"Yeah? What light?"

"One of the missing guys was named Frank Holstein," he said. "Seventy-six years old. He's been retired for eight years. Lives in a gated community in West Palm, plays golf. You know. Then, the day before Michael flew back to Vegas, Frank disappears. His wife and daughters are frantic. They never found a body, or a note. There was no reason for him to leave that they know of."

"Okay," she said. "So what makes Frank Holstein relevant to us?"

"Frank had a long career in Washington, working as an IT specialist in the Bureau of the Fiscal Service. Which is part of the U. S. Treasury."

She inhaled sharply. "Oh! You think Holstein must have been on DiAngelo's payroll? That he was supposed to send up a red flag if anyone tried to cash one of those bonds?"

"Exactly. Michael must have killed him. That's what he went to West Palm Beach to do. Michael wanted to redeem the bonds and run. And if Holstein was dead, DiAngelo would never get notified about the bonds being cashed."

"That poor guy. And his poor family," she said. "With no clue."

Henry nodded. Then he got up and started putting plates in the sink.

Amber pushed her chair back and began collecting the salt and pepper, the butter dish. Henry was intensely aware of every tiny sound she made. Her bare feet on the tiles. The shush of silky fabric around her body. He could smell the body lotion she had used, humid and warm and sweet.

He didn't dare turn around. His stupid, inappropriate feelings would be written all over his face. They were his cross to bear. It was unfair to inflict them on her. Embarrassing for them both. Guaranteed to make it weird. He focused on the steak platter, washing and rinsing as if the world depended on it.

Amber put her hand on his shoulder. Slowly, gently, he laid the platter down on the counter before he dropped it.

"Henry," she said, her voice low. "Turn around. Please."

He turned, bracing himself. Her beauty disoriented him. Every detail of her was even more wonderful when she was this close. All the gold tints and textures.

"Amber," he said, just to feel the word in his mouth.

She put her hands on his shoulders and rose onto her toes to kiss him.

He froze, but she grabbed the back of his neck and pulled him down. The moment felt miraculously sharp. The silky softness of her lips brushing his. Her sinuous body, graceful and pliant against his own. Her chest brushing his chest. Her warm breath. She coaxed his mouth open and flicked her tongue against his.

"Amber." His voice was so unsteady, he barely recognized it. "Are you sure?"

Her nails dug into his hand. "Do I look unsure?"

Then they were kissing wildly. He forgot all about not being smooth, not having any moves, not knowing what to say. He was just desperate to touch her and taste her. Feel her, lithe and strong and hot under that smooth, silky wrap.

She started in on his shirt buttons before she pulled him out of the kitchen. They went down the hall, and up the stairs, tossing things along the way. His shirt, his belt. A shoe. In the bedroom, she jerked down his pants and briefs. Henry gasped as she stroked and squeezed him.

"Amber." It was all he could say. Acknowledging her existence, hardly believing this was real. It was so improbable that someone so rare and brave and fine walked this earth at all. Let alone that she was touching him.

She pushed him down onto the bed, tossed open the comforter, and coaxed him onto his back. She tugged the sash of the robe loose and spread it open, showing him all her shadowy glories before she clambered over him, straddling him. The poppy strewn silk spread over them both like a mantle. The tender, inner heat of her body against his made his heart gallop.

"You want to serve, Henry?" she demanded, holding his gaze.

"Yes," he said. "God, yes."

"Good." She gave him a luminous, secret smile. "Then serve me."

Chapter Twenty-Five

They lay facing each other, smiling and tongue-tied and shy. The robe was twisted around her shoulders. Their hands were knotted, her thigh still draped over his. For years, Amber had made a living displaying her body, but she'd never felt naked until now.

Henry's eyes were soft. Another part of him decidedly wasn't. She explored it with her hand, making his breath catch.

He cleared his throat. "Are you, ah…"

"Satisfied?" Her laugh felt free and full and easy. "I'm getting there." She grabbed his shoulders, encouraging him to roll on top of her.

He obliged, but his eyes looked worried. "Really? Already?"

"What's this?" she teased. "Are you unwilling to serve? Are you already spent?"

"Never," he said, and she laughed, showing him how she wanted it.

The second time was slower, longer, languorous. It was so different when she was not looking for ways to speed everything up. Now it was the opposite. She enveloped him like a cloud, with wild feelings storming crazily through it, and he held her, never wavering, never losing focus. Never letting her down.

Afterward, while Henry dozed, she got up, twisted her hair into a knot and took a shower. She pulled on sweatpants and a hoodie, draping one of the Grudbergs' cashmere afghans around her shoulders.

His face was so different in sleep. His mouth, usually a tight, tense hyphen, was relaxed. Pink and sensual. Look at her, mooning like a ninny over a sleeping man. Amber silently laughed at herself and opened her iPad, scrolling through her news feeds, and suddenly stopped cold, staring at a headline from yesterday that appeared halfway down the page.

No Leads on Double Homicide of Magnum Theater Dancers.

She clicked on the article, her heart racing.

Naomi Carlsbad, stage name Tasha Starr, and Christine Webber, stage name Queen Krystal, were found murdered three days ago in the house they shared in the Green Valley neighborhood of Las Vegas. Gang involvement is being considered as a possible motive, though the investigation is ongoing. Anyone with information is invited to call the tip line below.

Tash and Krys? They had been the closest thing she had to friends besides Trix.

A gang hit? No way. That was bullshit. Tash and Krys had gone much farther down the spectrum of performative sex work than Amber had ever wanted to go, and they were deep into the party drug scene. They loved getting high and living large. But Amber had never heard of them stepping on anybody's toes, overreaching, power-grabbing. That just wasn't who they were.

Panic fingered the back of her neck. Tasha and Krystal had been tight with Trix. Trix had even let herself be seen with Michael with them. If Leon had come to Vegas looking for Amber, digging for clues, the first people he would go after would be Krys and Tash. And they would lead him straight to Trix.

Leon was supposed to stay in Idaho. Sneaking off could ruin his deal with the Feds. He had good reason to kill Tash and Krys, just to cover his tracks.

"What is it?" Henry's voice, rough from sleep.

She held up the tablet with a shaking hand. "Friends of mine in Vegas." Her voice didn't sound right. "We were in the show together, at the Magnum. They were shot in their home. Three days ago."

Henry took the iPad, read the article, and looked up at her. "Do you think that it was Leon?"

"Yes," she said. "Leon knew they were my friends. They were Trix's friends, too. If he asked the right questions, they might have told him about Michael. He could make the connection to Trix's family."

He put his hand on her leg, stroking it gently. "I'm sorry about your friends."

She stared down at the smiling professional photographs of Tash and Krys. "Did I do that to them?" She looked at Henry. "I mean, it's me he's chasing. But they're the ones who are dead."

"No, you did not do that," Henry said. "That was Leon. Nothing you could have done at any point would have changed anything for them."

"They were harmless, drug-addled bubbleheads, not king-pins in some criminal syndicate." Amber shook her head, tears blurring her vision. "No one but Leon would have any reason to kill Tash and Krys."

"It's not your fault," he said again, more forcefully this time. "You're just trying to stay alive."

"Easy for you to say." She clutched the blanket around her shoulders. "If he goes for Trix's family, they're screwed. If he asked Krys and Tash about me, they would have told him about Trix. Where she's from. If he was pointing a gun at them, they'd have told him anything they could think of."

Henry scooted closer, putting his arms around her.

"I have to warn Mrs. Graziano," she said. "You still have her number, right?"

Henry nodded, tightening his embrace. "Yes, I have it. But is now the time? Right after we scam their cleaning service? She's probably already found out we were fakes. You really want to double down now?"

"Now is the only time! It may already be too late. She has to get that poor kid away from there. We can't make her do it, but we can warn her. I owe Trix that much." Amber was scrabbling at her discarded clothes, looking for the burner she'd used before.

"No, no." Henry plucked it from her hands. "Not that one. I'll get you a fresh one. Hold on."

He got up, pulled on his pants, and left the room. Amber closed her eyes. She'd spent a lot of time in Tash and Krys's living room. She could see it all. Leon. That old, puffy green couch. Blood matting the perfect blonde waves of their hair.

Henry returned, handing her a phone. "I programmed the number in already."

"Thanks," she murmured.

"Keep it quick," he said. "Use a different voice. She'll remember Josie's."

Amber nodded. Her hands were shaking so hard she could barely hold the phone. A gruff male voice answered. "Who is this?"

"A friend." She made her voice low and gravely, gave it a

New Jersey accent. "I have an important warning. For Serafina Graziano only. Let me talk to her."

"Give me the message. I'll pass it on to her."

"No." Amber tried to keep the shrill anxiety out of her voice. "No. I have to speak to Serafina myself," she repeated. "You put her on, or you'll be sorry. It's a matter of life and death."

There was a pause. Then a grunt. Then Serafina's grating voice blared in Amber's ear. "Who the hell is this?"

"I'm calling to warn—"

"I ain't listening to no warning unless you introduce yourself, bitch."

Amber thought fast. "Remember when your daughter Trix came home a few months ago with that no-good boyfriend Michael, and you said he looked like a greasy little pimp? Well, you were right. He's got Trix in a crapton of trouble."

"What do you know about my daughter? Do you know where she is?"

Amber had her now. She lowered her voice. "Pay attention, Mrs. Graziano. Listen very carefully. Michael stole something from a very dangerous man named Leon Gambelli. Trix is safe. I promise you. But Michael is dead. Leon killed him. And Leon thinks Michael might have left what he stole in your house."

"In my house? What do you mean? Where is Beatrice?"

"Gambelli is a very dangerous man." Amber took a breath to calm the tremor of her voice. "He worked for the DiAngelos. If he thinks have what he wants, he'll kill you, and he'll kill Tori. That's what I'm calling to tell you, Mrs. Graziano. If you want your grandson to live, then take him and run. And I mean, right now."

"The DiAngelos?" The tone of Serafina Graziano's voice changed completely. "Who the hell are you?"

Serafina was a tough old bird. Amber knew that from

Trix's stories. She deserved a chance. Amber just hoped that she would take it and run with it. "I'm a friend," she said. "Just a friend who wishes you well."

"And my Beatrice?" Serafina Graziano's voice was quieter now, calculating. "Do you wish her well, too? You swear to me my Beatrice is safe? She's not dead?"

"I swear." Amber could hear the old woman breathing raggedly. "Run," she said again. "Please."

She ended the call and burst into tears. "I shouldn't have taken the bonds," she said as Henry pried the phone out of her hand. "I might have killed them. If Leon gets to them, they'll have nothing to give him."

"They wouldn't have anything anyway," Henry said. "They couldn't tell him what they didn't know. And even if they had the bonds and handed them over, he'd still kill them. You know he would. You just gave her the only chance she's ever going to get. And you did not rob her. The bonds were never hers. You've done everything you could do to help." He rubbed her back. "Breathe," he urged her. "I'm going to get rid of this phone. This one's done."

Amber closed her eyes again and saw the sad-eyed, peaky little Tori, defenseless and scared. She pictured Serafina backing away from Leon, eyes full of fear. Tash and Krys, blood matted in their beautiful hair. She heard the *thunk* of the cleaver and heard Michael's howl of agony. She saw the blood dripping down the kitchen island in a thick, steady crimson stream.

"Breathe. Breathe, Amber. You're here with me. It's okay."

She felt her forehead pressed against Henry's warm chest. He was stroking her back again. Gentle pats. Not grabbing, not squeezing. Giving her space to breathe.

Her heart slowed. Her fingers twined with Henry's. His were warm. Hers were clammy, ice cold and clutching, pulling at him like clammy, strangling vines. "Sorry," she whispered.

"It's not your fault," he said gently.

"You keep saying that."

"Because it's true. You never hurt anyone, or cut anyone or shot anyone. You're just staying alive any way you can. And I want you alive. I want more than just that for you. I want you safe. And comfortable. Happy, even."

She snorted, against his chest. "Don't go crazy on me, Henry."

His arm tightened around her shoulder. "It's what you deserve," he said, smoothing the hair off her forehead. "You're brave, and kind."

"Yeah? So? Even if that were true, no one gets what they deserve. You didn't, right? Was your kindness ever rewarded? Your service?"

He thought about it. "Maybe not by Belinda, no. But what just happened to me here, with you?" He blew out an expressive breath. "That was pretty damn rewarding. We're still in the game, Amber. We're still fighting. There's still time for us to get what we deserve."

She was wracked by silent, tearful laughter for a moment. "Wow, Henry," she said, sniffling. "That was super-inspirational for an escaped convict. Are you a life coach now? Giving me a pep talk?"

He gave her a narrow-eyed look. "Is it working?"

She laughed. "Maybe. It made me laugh. And I'm not having a panic attack right now. So I'll just go out on a limb and say yes. It appears to be working."

"Good. That's the best I could hope for."

Amber stood up, shrugging the blanket off her shoulders. "Come on," she said. "We have work to do. Leon is going to crawl down our throats any minute."

"So you're sticking around?" Henry looked as if he were bracing himself.

"Hell yeah," Amber said. "I'm not going anywhere until we get your diamonds back from that skanky bitch and her douchebag boyfriend."

Chapter Twenty-Six

Joseph Knox sat in his car and stared at the unprepossessing building on the edge of Hell's Kitchen. It was in a state of sad decay, balconies rusted, the façade grimy. The scaffolding that had been erected to fix it looked weather beaten too, as if someone had started work, run out of steam, and couldn't even be bothered to take it down.

He'd got copies off the security cameras, and been through the place about a hundred times since Tim Burdell had taken his swan dive down the stairwell, and he still couldn't figure out what the hell had happened. The whole shit-show had been a huge surprise. When Joe had checked Henry Devlin out at Kavanaugh's, the guy had looked nervous and frightened. No trouble at all. Cowering under that flat cap, he hadn't exactly presented as a problem for a nasty battle-hardened combat veteran like Burdell. If Joe had thought differently, he would have sent more guys. Who'd have thought that a tough bastard like Tim Burdell would meet his mortal end at the hands of an egghead like Henry Devlin? Go figure.

Joe flicked through the still images he'd pulled from the tapes, going floor by floor, waiting for a flash of insight. He'd flashed his PI badge and talked to some of the residents, but he hadn't learned much. Nobody had seen or heard a thing. Maybe having murders outside your door got to be like living beside a railroad yard. After a while, you didn't hear the train whistles anymore.

He pulled out a tablet and ran the speeded up security tape once again. This time, though, he paused it at one of the flickers of action. He'd seen the footage before, but something made him slow it down and look at it again. This was the guy he'd seen on the eighth floor. He looked familiar.

He was very tall. What hair he had left was longish and blonde. He was wearing a puffy tan coat as he stopped and banged on the door of Apartment 807. When nothing happened, he yelled and banged again. Then he pulled out his phone and made a call, but no one picked up. He dropped the phone back in his pocket and walked away. That had been two days ago. Late afternoon, right around now.

Joe picked up the still photos and leafed through them, and there he was again. Same guy, walking away from 807, looking pissed. He looked at the date stamp. Sure enough, yesterday, right around the same time. Somebody was looking for the occupant of 807 and not finding him. Could 807 have been Henry Devlin's apartment?

Joe got out of the car and trotted across the street. A little old lady with a shopping trolley was trying to get out of the building. Knox held the door for her like a perfect gentleman before he ducked inside.

He headed straight for Apartment 807, which was directly across from the stair railing. The door was scarred and scratched. A good kick would cave it in, but picking it had been faster.

Pointless, though. Henry Devlin wasn't there. He hadn't left much behind, either. Just a bunch of electronic shit. He would take it all and get his people to comb through it, but Henry Devlin was smart enough not to leave any breadcrumbs. He'd bet money on that.

He went to the railing and peered over again, all the way down to the shadowed well of the basement where Burdell had met his end. When he'd been here before, there had been people around. Cops. Looky-loos. He crouched and studied the floor, going tile by tile.

And there it was. The tiniest little brownish smear, barely the length of his pinky nail, staining what was left of the grout. He looked around. Near the wall, at the head of the stairs, someone had wiped up a mess, but not carefully enough. Because this was not dirt or dust or ash or grease. It was blood.

Joe took out his phone, photographed the stain and was just slipping in back in his pocket when the elevator dinged. The thing was usually broken. It clunked loudly as the door ground open.

Two people got out. The woman wearing headphones turned left and disappeared down the hall. The tall guy in the tan coat went straight to 807. And he already looked pissed

Joe pretended to tie his shoe as the man banged on the door, huffing and muttering, then calling. "Hey! Raymond! It's Anselm! What the hell, man? I got work for you! And you're already late on the last ones! Open up!"

Joe stood up. "Excuse me," he said. "I wonder if you're looking for the same person I'm looking for."

Anselm wheeled around, alarmed. "Are you a cop?"

"God, no," Joe said, with a big friendly smile. "Far from it."

"Do you know Raymond?"

"I don't know Raymond, but I think we're talking about the same guy. He's done some jobs for friends of mine in the past. I need him to do one for me. But I lost my phone with all my contacts in it, so I thought I'd come looking for him here.

You don't have his number, or know where he is, do you? It's kind of urgent."

"What kind of job?" Anselm asked.

"Physics. Electrical engineering stuff." Joe was spit-balling, working off the profile he'd been given of Devlin.

Anselm's eyes lit up. "Ah. Then Raymond is definitely your man."

"Good. That's great. So, you can put me in touch with him? Like I said, time sensitive."

Anselm's eyes went crafty. He smelled a little ripe, like he hadn't taken a shower in a few days. "Well, that depends. I'm his agent, see?"

"His agent? So you want your cut?"

"Yeah. Of course. I mean, Raymond's not out there pounding the pavement for work, is he? He isn't even answering his goddamn door!"

"Are you sure we're talking about the same person?" Joe asked. "Maybe there's a mistake. Tall guy, skinny, dark brown curly hair, a beard, caved-in cheeks, blue eyes?"

"Yeah, that's Raymond. No mistake. He's an odd duck, but he's brilliant. He owes me some academic jobs, and then he just up and disappears. I mean, like, without getting paid or anything."

"So you don't even know if you'll be able to get in touch with him?"

"Oh, no. No, not at all." Anselm pulled out his phone and waved it. "I'll text him. Don't worry."

"How much would an academic job cost?" Joe was genuinely curious.

Anselm's eyes gleamed. "It depends. Raymond kind of goes case by case, according to the amount of work he'll have to do. But he's expensive. Twenty-five K, minimum."

Joe stifled a burst of laughter. "Hmm. Pricey."

"Just because it's Raymond. You can find someone

cheaper if the work doesn't have to be, you know. Exceptional."

"If Raymond's so exceptional, why isn't he in a lab at some university, winning a Nobel Prize for his contributions to humanity?"

Anselm looked affronted. "How the hell do I know? He didn't say, and I don't ask. Life gets complicated sometimes."

"Right," Joe murmured.

"Is this thesis for you? Not to be rude or anything, but I don't know how credible that would be. You look a little long in the tooth for this kind of thing."

Joe smiled over clenched teeth. "It's a graduation present for my godson," he said smoothly. "Can I have Raymond's number?"

"No, but I'll take yours." Anselm's voice was lofty and officious. "I'll tell him about the job, and he'll call you if he's interested. That's how it works."

Joe briefly considered throwing this dumbass over the stair railing, too. But that would be counterproductive and unwise. "I could pay more, if necessary," he said. "A lot more. Money is no object. I want only the best for my godson. Tell Raymond that. But I'll need to meet him face to face."

Anselm's face fell. "That might be a deal-breaker. Raymond hates that."

I just bet he does, Joe thought. He pulled a pen and a blank card out of his jacket pocket, wrote the number of one of his burner phones, and held it out to Anselm.

"Ask him," he said. "Meeting him in person is non-negotiable." He slid five crisp twenties out of another pocket. "This is for you. Just tell me honestly. How good is this guy, really?"

Anselm looked dazzled. He took the money and leaned close enough that Joe could smell his breath, and a nasty whiff of body odor. "Well, get this," he whispered. "The first time he wrote a computer engineering thesis? The guy's thesis advisor took it and published it in his own name right away. Patents pending, lawsuits, too. A big, hairy mess, and all because of geeky old Raymond showing off. I had to tell him to tone it down a notch. Be a little less brilliant. Best not to attract attention, you know what I mean?"

Joseph Knox smiled at the guy. "Oh yes," he said. "I know exactly what you mean."

Chapter Twenty-Seven

The next morning found Amber and Henry on the highway, speeding toward an appointment in Sorenson with Leroy Badner, the owner of the junker car Henry had found on Craigslist. Amber wore the black Shearling coat that was part of the Trix outfit. She'd chosen it because it was the warmest thing she had, but it occurred to her she actually liked it. For herself. Like Lola's poppy robe. Like the opera tune. It was an Amber coat, not a Trix coat.

"I hope the Grazianos left town," she fretted. "I wish I could call and check."

"You gave her fair warning. What she does with it is up to her. She knows the risks."

"She's also a stubborn, crotchety old woman. I probably will be like that too, if I live that long."

"You will live to be absolutely ancient, if I have anything to say about it."

She shot him a teasing glance. "Then you better stop feeding me all that bacon, buddy."

"We're doing a hard, high-stakes job, so we need to run on

very heavy fuel. As soon as we get through this, it'll be grilled chicken and steamed broccoli only, I promise."

She laughed at him as she sipped strong French roast coffee with a shot of heavy cream out of her travel mug. "Amen. Speaking of which, we need some more of that vanilla pound cake."

"Do you want to try another flavor? Rum pecan, chocolate swirl?"

"Nope. I know what I like. Why try to improve on perfection?"

Amber was trying hard, but this morning, she couldn't make him smile, no matter what. "What's wrong?" she asked. "Are you upset?"

"I'm worried," he admitted. "I don't want to involve you in this anymore. It's ugly."

"Don't be silly. You found my bearer bonds. You put yourself in Leon Gambelli's sights for me. I've put you in far more danger than you're going to put me in."

He looked unconvinced. "I want to be clear on this, Amber," he said. "I'm dead serious. If we get caught, I am the one who takes the fall. You hand them my ass on a plate, understand? I am a vicious escaped convict. I abducted you, bullied you, threatened you, beat you. Whatever awful thing you can think of. Make it convincing. I'll play right along."

She laughed. "You really think you could sell that? Henry, the evil constrainer?"

"Sure. I've been listening to Victor. It's like taking a master class."

"But it won't be necessary. You want to know why?"

He shot her a quick ghost of a smile. "Tell me why."

"Because I am freaking amazing at what I do. This will work. I won't get caught. You won't have to play the monster. It's all going to be fine."

"I would play the monster for you," he said quietly. "I'd do anything for you. I'd jump in front of a bullet for you, if I was quick enough."

She frowned at him. "Don't say things like that. It's bad luck. You're no good to me dead."

"Okay. Sorry." He put on the turn signal. The roads grew narrower with every turning as they approached the small town of Sorensen. Beyond it, the GPS more or less quit, abandoning them on a dirt single track that threaded its way through a leafless gray forest. Amber read the directions the seller had given them.

"There," she pointed. "You missed it."

"What?" Henry slowed the car.

"We just passed the ruined cabin he talked about. There's the big rock. That's Leroy Badner's driveway."

Henry backed up.

"What are you doing?"

"Parking behind the cabin," he said, pulling in. "You wait here. I'll walk to his place. I don't want him to see you."

"I'd rather we stayed together." She reached for the door handle.

"Me, too," he said. "But you're not in disguise, and you're very memorable. It's better he just sees me. I'm a total nobody. Invisible. You are not invisible at all. Please. Just wait in the car, okay?"

"Okay, okay," she agreed. "Go buy the car. Good luck."

As he leaned awkwardly to kiss her, her heart twisted, all hot and tender. She grabbed the back of his neck, pulled him close, and gave him a sensual, clinging kiss that promised all possible worldly delights later, in the privacy of her bedroom. And she genuinely couldn't wait to follow through.

"Hurry," she said. "I'll be sitting here, chewing my nails."

Henry slid out, closed the door and vanished into the trees. Amber settled in to wait. The car was stuffy after the long drive. She rolled down her window. Wind rustled the branches, bringing with it a cold, earthy smell of pine and rain and rotten wood. Restless, she climbed into the driver's seat, flipped the ignition and turned on the radio. She found a station with some good indie pop. When it broke for news, she reached to turn it off, then her hand froze.

"...arson," the newsreader was saying, "and a suspected double homicide in South Cambrook, New Jersey. The victims appear to be two adult males. The investigation is ongoing."

Amber scrambled in her bag for her iPad. The signal wasn't great, but it was good enough, and the story was exactly what she feared. Late last night, the Graziano house in South Cambrook, New Jersey, had burned to the ground. The firemen had pulled out two bodies, both male. Serafina, Tori, and the housekeeper weren't mentioned.

She should have expected it, but even so, her hands were shaking and her ears roared. Please, God, let Serafina and Tori be alive and free and a long way from Leon. She wondered if the bodyguard she and Henry had met at the Graziano house the day before was one of the men who had died.

She shoved the car door open and threw up the breakfast Henry had insisted she eat.

Amber heaved until she was empty, coughing and spitting. Then she found a bottle of water in her bag, rinsed her mouth, and pulled out the spare burner Henry had given her. She had to concentrate to remember Trix's number. Given Trix's shaky state, Amber was not convinced that telling her friend what had happened was a good idea, but she didn't feel like she had a choice.

Trix answered on the first ring. "Who's this?" Her voice was sharp.

"It's Amber." She took a breath. "Did you hear about your Mom's house?"

"You mean, my family's security staff getting burned to death and my childhood home getting torched? Yes, Amber. I fucking heard about it."

"Look, I warned your mom last night. I told her to run with Tori. And I didn't hear them say anything on the news about bodies of a woman, or an adolescent. So I think they got away safe." Amber was not sure she thought any such thing. But she wasn't about to tell Trix that. "I know this is bad. But for God's sake, stay put. It's safer if you—"

"Too late for that, girlfriend. I'm in New York."

Oh, shit! Amber closed her eyes. "New York? Trix, you are out of your mind! I told you to stay in Tokyo!"

"You told me? Really? Well, guess what, Amber. I'm royally sick of being told what to do. Kenji had business in New York, so I just thought, hey. I have business, too. So here I am. We're in the Swann. Very swank and exclusive. Penthouse suite."

"But, did you get in touch with—"

"My mom? No. Her cell goes to voicemail, so I called the house last night. Angelo said she was gone, and that Tori had left with her. That was thanks to you, right? You scared them away?"

"Yes, thank God!" Amber said sharply. "Tash and Krys are dead, Trix. Do you hear that? Leon got to them. And I am sure he was coming for your mother and Tori. So you better believe I scared them away. I just wished I'd scared whoever those two guys at the house were away, too. Did you tell this guy Angelo where you were staying?"

Trix faltered. "Not exactly. I just gave him the number of the hotel. So he could give it to Mamma when she called."

Panic exploded inside her. "Then get out of there!" She was shouting now. "Quick! Now!"

"But, we're in the Lapis Lazuli suite. It's—"

"Jesus, Trix! If those guys had the number of the hotel, then Leon has it, too! Run!"

"Don't yell in my ear." Trix's voice was petulant. "The security guys at the house, Angelo and Matteo? They practically raised me, Amber. They would never just hand me over to Leon like that."

Amber closed her eyes and spoke slowly. "They were tortured, Trix. That's what Leon does. They wouldn't have had any choice. They told him everything they knew. Leon knows where you are!"

"Yeah. Locked up tight in the Lapis Lazuli suite with Kenji's security guy. My boyfriend is the CFO of a huge bank, Amber. He travels with his own private bodyguard. But you probably wouldn't know that. So chill, okay?"

Amber opened her eyes and stared at the scraggly trees and the ruined cabin. Why was she surprised? Trix was Serafina Graziano's daughter, after all. Stubborn to the end. If only she were smarter.

"In the meantime," Trix said. "We have to discuss that thing, remember? Did you find it? Do you have it?"

This was where things got sticky. Amber considered lying. Just saying no, she hadn't found a thing. But Henry hadn't lied to her, or stolen from her. So she couldn't lie to Trix either. Not without dishonoring Henry's gesture.

"Yes, Trix," she said. "I did find it, thank God."

"Great. So?"

"It's not safe for us to meet," Amber said. "And there's no time. You should leave right away. We'll have to wait until we—"

"Wouldn't that be convenient? Run away, Trix! Run off to Japan! Don't come, don't call, don't ask! It's too dangerous here, where all the money is!"

Amber made a huge effort to keep her voice calm. "I just want you to be safe."

"I have protection already, okay? Don't worry about me. What did you find?"

"I can't talk about it on the phone. I promised you half if I found anything, and I am not going to screw you over. So drop the attitude."

"Yeah. Having my boyfriend chopped into pieces and my family home burned down really does a number on my attitude. If you have it, then we need to meet. Right now."

"I can't now," Amber said. "I'm out of town, taking care of a thing."

"What thing?" Trix's voice sharpened. "What are you doing?"

"Nothing that concerns you. I'll be back this afternoon. I'll come see you then."

"With the money? It is money, right?"

"Yes," Amber muttered through her teeth. "It is money."

"Okay." Trix's voice changed, brightening as if a switch had been flipped. "Good. Just make sure to call before you come. Kenji doesn't like surprises. Remember, the Lapis Lazuli suite. On the top floor. Kenji's coming. Gotta go."

Amber sat staring into the gray tangle of bare branches, fighting the temptation to fling the phone into the woods and never call that snotty bitch again. Trix would never find her, after all. She wasn't smart enough.

She rubbed a hand across her eyes, which were hot and gritty. Here she'd been, busting her ass and Henry's, trying to keep that whining piece of fluff safe and do her a multi-million-dollar favor, which Trix had not earned in any way. She had contributed nothing to this project. Zilch. Zero. Amber had only promised her half the money to shut her up and calm her down. And because she'd felt guilty for shoving Trix off to Tokyo with Kenji, where she had clearly been miserable.

At the time, she'd never dreamed she might actually get lucky.

She couldn't tell Henry about her promise to Trix, either. She didn't want to crack the brand new trust they'd found, but on the other hand, she hadn't lived the better part of thirty-seven years without learning that when something needed doing, you didn't waste time asking for a man's approval or

WARREN ADLER & SHANNON MCKENNA

permission. This stupid situation was her own fault, and she had to fix it.

Plus, if she gave Trix her share now, Amber wouldn't have to figure out how to move large amounts of money through the international banking system. As Trix had just pointed out, she had a banker boyfriend. No. The sooner she got Trix her share, the sooner Trix would go back to Japan, far from Leon. It was the best place for her, whether or not she hated it.

And here she was, up on her high horse, telling poor Trix what was best for her. Hypocritical as hell. She hadn't been able to stomach being Leon's bed toy, not even to save her own skin.

They said that no good deed went unpunished. But damn, being punished for this particular deed really stung.

Chapter Twenty-Eight

Buying the junker car took longer than Henry had anticipated. Leroy Badner was a garrulous old guy with a wispy beard yellowing at the ends. He hadn't talked to anyone in some time, and wasn't about to surrender the opportunity now.

The car ran okay, and looked pretty ordinary, despite its advanced age. Which was important, because Henry had to be able to drive it at least as far as Milton and leave it across the street from the coffee shop without attracting any attention. After that, it was all over for the twenty-eight-year-old bronze Taurus sedan. The end of its earthly sojourn was at hand.

But he couldn't tell any of that to Leroy, so he had to bear witness to the whole complicated sentimental history of the car; its colorful passenger list, the babies conceived in its back seat; the contraband hauled in its trunk.

He test-drove the Taurus along the dirt road, careful to turn left out of Leroy's drive, away from the ruined cabin and Amber, since the old geezer had insisted on coming with him to continue his monologue. When they got back, Leroy insisted on serving him a cup of foul coffee and a lecture on all his various conspiracy theories.

Leroy had gotten into chemtrails and aliens when Henry finally pleaded an urgent appointment. He handed over a fat envelope of cash, grabbed the title and ran. He'd be driving unregistered and uninsured, which was a big risk, but if the cops took notice of him now, the legal status of the car he drove would be the least of his worries.

The engine sputtered as he pulled out of Leroy's driveway. He rattled and bumped over the washboard roadbed to the mossy cabin.

Amber got out of the rental car as he pulled in behind it. She smiled at him, but she looked pale and pinched.

"Are you okay?" he asked.

"Fine," she said. "Just a little nervous, being left in the spooky woods by myself. I'm no nature girl. What now?"

Henry studied her eyes. Something was off, but he couldn't tell what. "Now I set up the device," he said. "It won't take long. I've done most of it already."

And it didn't. The small explosive device was already assembled. Henry had bought it from one of Ivar's contacts, using up almost all the money he had left. The guy had shown him what to do. It was pretty simple. Just a miniature bomb.

When Henry was finished, he put it in a paper grocery bag and set it gingerly on the Taurus' passenger seat. It took him only another two or three minutes to switch the Taurus' Jersey plates out for a Louisiana set he'd stolen from a long term lot on the lower West side.

He turned to Amber. The look in her eyes made him uneasy. "What happened?" he asked. "Is something wrong?"

"Yes." Her voice was bleak. "I heard the news. There was a fire last night in South Cambrook, New Jersey. It was probably arson. The Graziano house was torched. Two bodies were found inside, both adult men."

Henry blew out a careful breath. "I see. But not Serafina? Or Tori?"

"No mention of them. But Leon has arrived. That was his calling card." She made an impatient gesture. "Let's move, for God's sake. This place makes me itch."

"You drive the rental, and I'll go ahead in the Taurus. So if it falls apart, you can scrape me off the road," he offered.

Amber didn't smile back at him.

They were halfway to Milton when one of Henry's phone started chirping out text messages. One eye on the road, he fished it out of his pocket and glanced at it.

Anselm, of all people. He was going to have to break it to the guy that he had better things to do than write theses for cheating grad students.

Three texts had come in, one after the other.

CALL ME

IM SERIOUS VERY GOOD JOB $$$

CRAZY GOOD MONEY CALL QUICK$$$

Henry glanced at the GPS. He had to clear the decks. It was best to get rid of Anselm now. All he needed was to get pulled over for driving and dialing with a bomb in the front seat. But there was nobody around. He hit the return number.

Anselm picked up on the first ring. "Raymond, my man!"

"I don't have time for writing papers right now, Anselm," Henry said. "Or for taking tests. Sorry, but I'm in a big crunch on another job. You'll have to find somebody else for the gigs you gave me the other day, too. I won't be free anytime soon."

"No way, man! You can't do that to me!"

"Yeah. Sorry. But I am. No choice."

"Hear me out, hear me out, man! This is a graduate thesis on some physics shit for this guy's godson, and he says money is no object! I shot out twenty-five K. You know, just for shits and giggles? And dude, he didn't even blink! So I figured, you can bump it up to, I don't know, maybe forty-five K? Hell, try fifty!"

"Huh." Henry thought for a second. "Sounds too good to be true."

"No! I saw this guy with my own eyes. Definitely an asshole, but he has money to burn, and he wants the very best. So jack it up as high as you dare and grab this!"

"Did he give you any more detail? Parameters, topic, source material? Anything?"

"He said he'd tell you all that when he meets you."

Henry stiffened. "I don't meet anyone. Didn't you tell him that? That's why I have you. What do you think I pay you for?"

"To find you the work, my man! I do my magic and you do yours! Reciprocal magic! You need me, I need you! But this guy has to meet you in person, or the deal's off. You can't say no to this one, Ray. It's too big."

"Did you check him out?"

"He said his name was, ah. Let's see here, he gave me a card." Henry could hear Anselm shuffling around. "Steve Smith," he said. "Right. Steve Smith. He left you a phone number."

Henry groaned. "Steve Smith? Come on! Anselm, there are probably thousands of Steve Smiths in the tri-state area. Give me more. Town? Profession? Company name?"

"Sorry, Ray. He didn't say much. He was maybe late forties? Tall, big shoulders, receding hairline, fish-belly skin with spots. Big nose."

"There are probably hundreds of Steve Smiths in Manhattan alone who fit that description!"

"Stop bitching and just meet the guy," Anselm coaxed. "See if he's for real. What could it cost you? The price of a cup of coffee and a few minutes of your time."

Or my life. Henry fought his spiking anxiety. Anselm was right. He couldn't afford not to check this out. There might be nothing of value in Belinda's safe deposit box, and he needed something to bring to the table in this budding thing with Amber. She wasn't the avaricious type, but still, he wanted to protect her, keep her comfortable, give her a real shot at a new life. With him.

If she wanted such gifts from him, of course. Maybe he was getting ahead of himself. But ahead was exactly where he needed to be, if this was going to work. If he had a shot with Amber, he was taking it.

Also, his standard for the comfort and safety of potential hotels and rentals had just shot way up in cost. He could stay in a grubby, bug-infested hotel alone if he had to, but he would never bring Amber to such a place.

"When does he want to meet?" he asked.

"Soon as possible." Anselm couldn't keep the eagerness out of his voice. "Now, if you can."

"Can't now. I could this afternoon."

"Where?"

Henry paused. "I'll text him a location when I'm back."

"Why so coy? Let me just tell him where to go! It's not like you're James Bond!"

"Just text me his number, Anselm."

Anselm did so, grudgingly, and Henry closed the call. Just a few more miles now. He had lived farther up the train line with Belinda, but they'd known people from Milton, and he really did not want to run into any of them.

Henry made his way to Belinda's favorite coffee shop, Beans & Brew. To his relief, nothing much had changed on the opposite side of the street. There was still nothing there but a chain-link fence in front of an abandoned construction site. The fates were with him today. Henry pulled in to a parking spot right in front of the coffee shop window. He pulled on his baseball cap and tugged it low over his forehead before he got out, locked the Taurus and walked away, head down, shoulders slumped.

Amber's car was two blocks down. Henry got in. "Done," he said.

"Great. Shall I drive? Or do you want to?"

"Please, you drive," he said. "If you don't mind."

His phone vibrated. Anselm again, sending the number plus dollar signs and exclamation points. "When we get back, I need to run an errand," he told her.

"Yeah? What kind of errand?"

"A potential client. I found this guy through a man I met in prison. He throws me work sometimes. The client wants me to write his grad thesis for him. My guy thinks the client could cough up a lot of money, but he wants to meet in person, which I hate. But I don't want to blow off an opportunity for this much fast cash."

She glanced at him. "You don't think the timing is a little suspicious?"

"Of course it is. But everything feels suspicious now. And it could be legit. I've written a bunch of these before. It's not that hard, and it's good money. Besides, if the safe deposit box turns out to be empty, we're going to need some cash."

We. He realized he was saying "we." As if they were partners. He braced himself for a takedown about making assumptions. Making it weird.

"You know, Henry, it occurs to me that, aside from being a skank, Belinda's not even a good gold-digger," Amber said. "She played her cards all wrong, if she wanted to be filthy rich."

He looked cautiously over at her. "You think?"

"I definitely think. That boyfriend, Victor or whatever his name is, is just a hollow man. But you? You are the real deal. You can do crazy tech stuff that can pull down real money. She just didn't see it. Dumb cow. Her loss."

He laughed. "I hope you're right. But her loss is your

gain." He shot her a glance. "I mean…I hope her loss is your gain. If you want to gain it."

Amber concentrated on the road. "We'll sort out those details later," she said. "Let's just stay focused on what we're doing, okay?"

"Of course," he said swiftly.

It wasn't the wholesale slap-down he had feared, but it kept him tongue-tied on the drive back.

Amber pulled the car up in front of the townhouse and double-parked. "Are you driving to your appointment?" she asked. "Or walking?"

"I could walk, but I'd be happy to park the car for you," he offered.

She got out and fluttered her fingers in farewell. "All yours, then," she said. "See you later."

He watched her go up the steps and into the house, back straight, hair like pale fire against the black Shearling coat. Snug jeans. High-heeled boots. Miles out of his league. Belinda had been, too, but Amber had a blazing, ethereal soul quality he'd never even imagined existed before he met her. Now, he was continually amazed by it.

He parked the car the first place he could find and got out, pulling out his phone. Fortunately, he was still tricked out as Todd, with a fake nose, weird hair, cheek padding, and mouth prosthesis. Even his beard had been trimmed into a different shape. He punched the number Anselm had given him into a burner and sent a text.

> Raymond Wise here. Meet at Finch's Diner in 20?

Henry included a link to the restaurant's website. It was barely a minute before the phone chirped.

> See you there. Steve S.

Henry stared at it for a minute, remembering what Amber had said about convenient timing. About it being too good to be true. Then he thought about fifty grand and set off on foot.

He got to the diner with a couple of minutes to spare. Finch's was a grubby, no-frills kind of place. He ordered coffee and a sweet roll and waited. Minutes crawled by. An old lady came in and ordered soup. A couple of construction guys had grilled cheese sandwiches. No one else came in. Steve Smith was seven minutes late.

Another minute…then another. He thought about texting again, but the hairs on the back of his neck were standing up.

This had been a mistake. He was being greedy, looking for shortcuts, trying to get into a woman's good graces. All deadly traps. He should know better.

He dropped money on the table and walked out, hunching and shambling to make his body move differently, like Amber had taught him. A cab cruised by with its light on. Henry lunged for it.

The driver was bewildered by his instructions. Down to Battery Park, then up the East River Drive to Harlem, circling around, trying to spot the tail he knew had to be there.

Finally, he told the driver to take him back down to the West 4th Street subway station. When they got there, he shoved cash through the window at the driver and bolted, running down the stairs through the tunnel. Anyone following in a car would lose him. Anyone jumping out of the car to follow on foot would have to fall way back or get spotted.

As he ran, Henry pulled out the burner he kept for Anselm and tossed it into a trash can. One source of income gone. His resources were dwindling. He was now really hoping that Belinda had something juicy in that safe deposit box, and not just because he wanted the satisfaction of taking it from her.

Now he wanted something for himself. That changed everything.

———

Joe Knox had shoved cash at the driver, jumped out of the cab, and run into the subway, following Henry.

Henry was pretty sharp. He had run a pretty good SDR. A proper surveillance detection route could take all day, but he hadn't done badly with the time. Joe Knox was just better. And he'd been ready.

Devlin was pretty good at disguise, too. Knox had taken a couple of minutes, when he first spotted Henry, to decide that the dude with the hair and the cap and glasses really was him.

Now, he hung back, keeping Henry fifty yards in front of him, picking up the pace only when Henry headed up to street level.

Coming up onto the sidewalk, Joe spotted Henry watching the subway exit from the shadows at the end of the block. Joe crossed the street, went into a bodega, bought himself a cup of coffee and a pack of cigarettes, and walked out again. As he'd hoped, Henry was gone. Joe ran across the street to where Henry had been standing. He looked left, then right, and spotted Henry striding westward. *Yes.*

Henry wove through the quiet residential streets. After about twenty minutes, Joe watched him run up the steps of a nice townhouse and let himself in. Well, well, well. Mr. Devlin had come up in the world from that grubby rat-hole in Hell's Kitchen.

Victor would be pleased at this development. A good thing, considering how hard he was squeezing the guy.

Chapter Twenty-Nine

Amber had been surprised by her unexpected stroke of luck. With Henry out on his errand, she didn't have to lie, or sell the idea, or argue about whether Trix was entitled to a portion of the bonds or not. She didn't have to debate about the danger of what she was about to do. It didn't matter financially from Henry's point of view, since she'd already decided that Henry's twenty-five percent came right off the top. She would split the remainder with Trix. Three point nine million was plenty for anyone. Even Trix would have a hard time blowing that much money.

Then again, maybe not.

Not that she had to ask permission from anyone. But she owed Henry a hell of a lot. He'd have his cut, along with her eternal gratitude, respect, and even, well...she barely dared to think it. She had to sneak up on it. Turn her face away. Play it extremely cool.

Trust. There, she said it. She trusted Henry. She actually did.

For just a second, she felt like a hopeful young thing, her life ahead of her. Ready to conquer the world, because anything was possible when you loved someone.

Love. Whoa. That was another concept altogether. Trust was an iffy enough proposition. And honestly? Right now, she didn't have time or the energy to think about either one of them.

Amber ran upstairs to change. Today's look had been fine for the woods, but it would not do for the Swann Hotel. The place would be thick with security cameras. The disguise that made the most sense was to be Trix herself. She was already staying there, so her presence would be unremarkable.

Amber counted out Trix's share of the bearer bonds, put them in an envelope, and zipped it into her big black bag. Then she tugged on a gray plaid miniskirt and white silk blouse. Trix dressed more conservatively when she with Kenji. Amber added some fake diamonds and her Trix wig, fluffed up on top to give her extra height. Then she went to work on the nose, the fuller cheeks, the dark contacts, new foundation and fresh makeup. She decided on low-to-medium heels. They suited the Swann. And they were better for running, if, God forbid, she ran into Leon.

A cab stopped for her quickly and ran her uptown and over the park to the East Side. Amber took a deep breath as she stepped into the lobby of the Swann. Leon aside, the biggest challenge was directly in front of her. The penthouse suites in places like this cost a fortune and had the security that went with it. There was no way she was getting anywhere near a dedicated elevator without a code or some kind of key card. Spotting the executive floor reception desk, nothing more than a thin slab of marble with a young woman in a black suit standing behind it, she adjusted her stride and embodied Trix with her most petulant face. The trick would be to do this quickly. Shock and awe. That was her battle plan.

The young woman, whose blonde hair was scraped back in a ponytail so tight it looked painful, smiled as Amber approached.

"Hey," she said, her voice sharp with irritation. "I was

down in the spa, and now I can't find my key card for the elevator. The name's Graziano, Beatrice Graziano. Lapis Lazuli. The penthouse suite."

"Of course, Ms. Graziano." Blonde Ponytail was glancing at something under the desk, probably a still from one of the security cameras, or a scan of Trix's passport, to see if the woman in front of her was who she said she was. Amber held her breath and crossed her fingers.

The clerk pulled out a drawer, looked up and gave her an ingratiating smile. She'd passed the test.

There was an electronic swipe, a click, then a card slid over the desk. "So sorry for the inconvenience, Ms. Graziano," the clerk said.

As if it were their fault. Wow, being that rich must be fun. "Thanks." Amber palmed the card.

She sashayed into the busy lobby, looking for the elevators and pretending that she knew where she was going. Amber didn't know how many penthouse suites there were, but she was the only person in the elevator. Even so, she studied her boots and let the long black curls hide her face from the flat, round eye of the security camera. There was no reason to tempt fate.

A minute later, the doors slid open, and Amber stepped out.

Through the glass wall of the lobby, she saw the city laid out like a map. The door of the Lapis Lazuli suite was straight ahead. Someone inside the suite was probably already watching her on a security screen. She hoped it was Trix, not a bodyguard, wondering why there was suddenly a second Beatrice Graziano outside the door. Or worse, Kenji, wondering why his girlfriend suddenly had an identical twin.

She took a deep breath and pressed the bell.

She couldn't hear it ring, but then again, the door looked about three feet thick. Nothing so vulgar as a peep-hole or a fisheye. When nothing happened, she pressed it again. By the third time, what had been mere anxiety was blossoming into fear.

Trix had known she was coming, and that she was bringing a shit-ton of money with her. There was no way Trix would blow her off today. Something was wrong. She looked at the key card in her hand.

She could just walk away. Keep the damn money. Get back in the elevator. Get out of here. *Get back to Henry.* Forget about Trix, who wouldn't follow advice and keep herself safe. It was probably too late to save her now, anyway. But Trix was her friend. Annoying, clingy, entitled, but she'd always been there for Amber. They had weathered storms, helped each other through tough times, had a lot of laughs.

The last thing in the world she wanted was to see what was behind this door. But she couldn't just walk away. She hoped the sweat on her palms hadn't messed up the electronic code as she held the card to the keypad. The light flashed green, and the locks clicked.

Amber gave the door a little push. It swung a couple of inches and stopped. She pushed again, then took a deep breath, and peered around it. A man was sprawled at the entrance to the suite. Oh God.

She couldn't see much of him, but he was big, and wore a gray suit. Kenji's bodyguard. She shoved at the door with her shoulder, forcing open a narrow space so she could slither through. She had to look down to step over the body.

There was a bullet hole in his forehead. The contents of his head were splattered across the opposite wall.

The hallway was short and wide. The door to a black and white-tiled powder room stood open. It was empty. Amber forced herself to step into the living room. A second man lay face down on the oriental rug. Kenji. She'd met him once or twice. His suit was still immaculate, but his silver hair was matted with blood. He, too, had been shot in the head.

Beyond the living room, the suite had a dining room, a

butler's pantry, a single staff room and two full guest rooms. Doors stood open. Sound-proofed, plush, exclusive, the place was utterly silent. CNN played silently on a big TV screen in the dining room.

Amber found Trix sprawled across the huge blood-drenched bed that stood in the center of the master suite. She froze at the sight of her friend, letting out an involuntary sound, as if she'd been kicked in the belly. Oh, God. Oh, babe. No.

For a second, she just stood there, staring, unable to move. Then she fled.

Amber dodged Kenji's body as she sprinted back across the living room. She clambered over the dead bodyguard and slithered back through the door. She'd half expected to find it locked, to be imprisoned in there with the bodies, the blood. She started to lunge for the elevator, then stopped. She had no idea how long they had been dead, but it couldn't be long. There were cameras everywhere. She'd been seen coming up. She couldn't undo that, but it was probably wiser not to go through the lobby again. She looked around, frantic. There had to be fire stairs.

The door was behind a large potted palm, and so discreet that Amber barely registered the regulation Fire Exit sign. She pulled it open and started down, clutching her bag and the bannister. There were cameras here, too, but fewer of them. Amber kept her face averted, letting the wig fall over her features. Somewhere around the fifth floor, a door opened and closed below her. She paused. There was the sound of voices, but no one came onto the stairs.

By the time she finally got to the ground floor, she was hot and cold, sweaty and winded all at once. Her knees wobbled. The fire door opened onto a quiet side street.

Amber stumbled out into the damp chill and walked away, blindly. It was her fault. She hadn't made Trix understand how vicious Leon was. What else could she have said? What else could she have done? Why wouldn't Trix understand? Why were people so fucking stupid?

She walked down to the Grudbergs' house in Chelsea, the black bag with Trix's bonds clutched to her chest, barely aware she was holding it. It was a minor miracle she hadn't dropped it in the Lapis Lazuli suite.

The only reason she still held it was because her hands wouldn't unclench.

Chapter Thirty

W hen he came home to find Amber gone, Henry lurked near the window for hours, anxiety rising inside him. By the time he finally saw her coming down the street, he was frantic with worry.

He was out the front door and halfway down the steps when he saw the look on her face. He stopped, horrified.

She was clutching a black handbag to her chest as if it was a dead infant. In her black wig, with mascara smeared down her cheeks, she looked like a survivor staggering out of the smoke and dust-choked wreckage of some terrible disaster.

"What happened? Amber, are you okay? Are you hurt?"

She looked at him and blinked. "Henry?"

He seized her shoulders. "What happened?"

She shook her head, looking over her shoulder. "Not here," she muttered. "Inside."

Fumbling for his key, Henry helped her up the steps. As soon as the door closed behind them, she slumped against him.

"What happened?" He bent to look into her face, but she turned away from him. "Amber? Do you want something to—"

"No," she said. "I don't want anything. I just want to go up to my room."

"Let me help you." Jesus. Had she been attacked? Mugged? Worse?

She didn't have the energy to protest as he scooped her into his arms, and that scared him more than anything. He carried her upstairs and into her bedroom, slipped off her coat as she sat down on the bed. Henry and scanned her for injuries, but couldn't see so much as a scratch. What the hell had happened?

Amber dropped the black bag, peeled off the Trix wig and flung it across the room as if she couldn't bear to touch it. The fake eyelashes were next, then the weird silicone thing on her nose.

"You've got heterochromia iridum," Henry said.

"Huh?" She blinked up at him. "Come again?"

"Sorry. Your eyes. One is dark and the other's gold."

"Yeah. I was crying. The contact must have washed one out." She plucked the remaining lens out of her eye and flicked it away. When she looked back at him, two golden eyes stared out of the mask of streaked makeup.

"Let me get you a glass of water," he said.

Henry got the makeup wipes while he was at it. As soon as she'd drunk the water, he sat down beside her and began gently swabbing the black streaks and smudged foundation. "Tell me what happened. Did someone hurt you?"

"Trix came to New York," she told him.

"Wait." His hand stopped. "Didn't you say she was in Tokyo?"

"She was. She was supposed to stay in Tokyo, where she was safe. But she didn't. She tagged along with her boyfriend to New York. They were staying at the Swann."

"Why didn't you tell me you were meeting her? It's not safe! We should have gone together!"

She looked away from him, picking at the coverlet. "I

knew it wasn't a smart thing to do, but I had to do it anyway," she said, finally. "I figured you'd be dead set against it, and frankly, I didn't have the energy to argue with you."

Henry was dismayed. "For God's sake, I'm on your side! I wish you'd trust me."

She still would not look at him. "Henry, I do my best," she said. "I really do. But with my history, it's one hell of an ask." There was a quavering edge in her voice. "If wishes were horses, okay? But they're not horses. And I went through hell today, so do not fucking start with me."

He nodded and lowered his voice to a mild, soothing tone. "What was this hell you went through? Just tell me what happened."

"I went to see Trix at the Swann," she said dully. "I dressed as her, so there wouldn't be any record of me on the security cameras. I got a key card, said I'd lost mine. When nobody answered the suite door, I used it to get in." She shook her head. "Like I didn't know what I was going to find."

"And?"

She let out a hitching breath. "Leon had been there. I tried to warn Trix, as soon as I knew she was in New York. But she wouldn't listen. He killed them. All of them. Trix, Kenji. Their bodyguard."

"Oh, my God."

"Yeah. Trix had been trying to get ahold of her mother. Serafina wasn't answering her cell, so she called the house. Serafina and Tori were already gone, thank God. But Trix gave one of the security guys the hotel number to pass on to her mom. Leon must have tortured it out of them before he set the fire."

"Why?" Henry was unable to keep the frustration out of his voice. "Why did you meet with her? You knew it was dangerous."

Amber hesitated. "I was going to give her a cut of the bearer bonds," she admitted. "I promised her that I would share. I figured, if she had them, she'd leave, and she'd be safe. Or safer, anyway. But Leon got there first."

"You promised Trix a share of the bearer bonds?" he asked, dumbfounded. "Why?"

Amber shrugged, a little angrily. "Mostly because of a dumb thing I said to her the night Michael was killed. I told Trix I'd look for Michael's haul, whatever it was he'd stolen from Leon, and if I found it, I would split it with her. So we could both get out of this trap, you know? Of being kept women who don't dare grow old? Plus, I was scared and lonesome, and even if Trix was sniveling in a luxury penthouse in Japan while I did all the work, she was still my best friend. We were like partners, sort of. And I owed her, since I was the one who convinced her to go to Japan to be Kenji's concubine, even though I knew she didn't want to. I felt bad about that, but she was safer there. Then again, she'd still be in Tokyo if I hadn't dangled all this money in front of her. Miserable, but still alive. So I guess I killed her, too. I killed them all. Fuck's sake, Henry. I killed everyone."

"No, you did not," he said firmly. "Don't do that to yourself."

"He cut her to pieces." Amber stared at him with bleak eyes. "This is what happens when I try to share. Tash and Krys, shot in the head. Trix, butchered. Those guys at the Graziano house, tortured and incinerated. It's like a curse. God knows what'll happen to you."

"Nothing will happen to me. Listen to me." He cupped her cheek so that she couldn't turn away from him. "Nothing will happen to me. I will be fine. And so will you. You are not the curse. Leon is." He waited until she nodded before he let her go. His mind was racing now, processing the new information. "Did Trix know where we're staying?" he asked.

Amber shook her head. "No. I didn't tell her. I said I'd go to her."

"Good. Do you think you were followed?"

"Well, I certainly wouldn't have made it back here if I had been."

Her snappish tone encouraged him. That was a definite improvement. "Right. So you walked back?"

"Yeah. I came out a fire door, not the lobby. I didn't see anyone." She gave a mirthless little laugh. "I wasn't really looking, to be honest. I probably wouldn't have known my name if you'd asked me. But if Leon had seen me, he wouldn't have hesitated. He would have taken me, and I would be dead. So, no, I don't think he saw me." She bent to retrieve the black bag, unzipped it, and pulled out an envelope. "These were for Trix. I'd promised her half, but I cut your twenty-five percent off the top first. Three point nine million for her."

"But she didn't earn it," Henry said, before he could help himself.

Amber let out a harsh laugh. "Oh no? You think? You should have seen what he did to her."

"I'm so sorry, Amber. But I don't understand. I truly do not get why you would risk your life to give away almost four million dollars to this woman. Why did you do that?"

"Do you want to know?" she asked, her voice almost belligerent. "Really?"

"Yes, really! Please. Explain it to me!"

She clapped her hand over her mouth. For a second, he thought she was crying. Then that she was laughing. Then he realized it was some terrifying hybrid emotion.

"It's because of you." Her voice was tight, quavering. "This is your fault."

Henry stared at her. "Me? What do I have to do with it? I didn't even know you were going to do it!"

"It's you, Henry," she repeated. "I admit, it started when I promised to share whatever Michael had stolen with Trix if I found it. But I might just as easily have broken my promise and kept those bonds for myself. I could have reverted back to my old con woman ways, lying and stealing and scamming and whoring like I've always done. But then I met you, and started hearing all your high-minded nonsense about service to your fellow man, right? And suddenly, I'm wanting something better. Something more. Because if a person isn't making a goddamn effort to be better than they were before, then what is the point, right? So there it is, since you asked. I did this stupid thing because of you, Henry. You're a very bad influence on me. You make me want to be a better person. But it blows up in my face. People die. And it's my fault."

She covered her face with her hands and dissolved into tears. Henry wrapped his arms around her shaking shoulders, racked with guilt and conflict. Here she was, trying to be a better person at such a terrible cost, while he was becoming a worse one. Manipulating her into risking prison, and for what? For nothing more important than money. Payback. Revenge on Belinda and Victor.

That was not the way to treat someone he loved. And he did love her. He knew that now, with absolute clarity. The bewildered lust he'd felt for Belinda wasn't even on the same scale.

"Amber?" he said.

"Yeah?"

"The thing tomorrow, the coffee shop? I'm calling it off. We're done."

She jerked up, her eyes wide, as if he'd slapped her. "What? No fucking way! I've been working my ass off on this! You can't cancel it!"

"It's too dangerous," he said. "I'll figure out another way to make money. You need to take your money and go into hiding. Get out of the country. I'll get you a passport somehow. At least go to Mexico. You can't stay here. Leon is hunting you, and he will never stop."

"But what about your diamonds? What about those assholes robbed and defamed you? You think I am going to let them get away with that? No way! Fuck them sideways, Henry!"

"It's too dangerous."

"Well, too bad! Because I am doing it anyway."

"I am the boss of this job," he said. "It's my call. I do not want to use you. You're too important to me."

"Oh, fuck you! You patronizing jerk!" She jerked away from him. "Don't be stupid. We've come all this way. We've made all this effort. You've already compensated me a thousand times over. We do this thing, then we blast on out of here!"

They were staring at each other like two cats with arched backs when a phone buzzed. She stared down at her coat, which lay on the bed. The horrified look in her eyes chilled him.

"Who has the number for the phone?" he asked cautiously.

"Trix," she said in a small voice. "Only Trix."

"She'd gone, Amber. It's not her." He said it just because it seemed like it needed to be said.

"Yes," she whispered. "Yes, I know. So. The only other people who might use that number are the police, if they found the crime scene. Which I doubt, since housekeeping won't be in until tomorrow. Or else…"

"Leon," he finished.

They stared at the coat, the phone still ringing persistently from inside her coat pocket.

"Is there any reason to answer him?" Henry asked. "I could talk to him. See if I can find out something about his intentions."

"No." Amber reached down and retrieved the burner phone from her coat pocket. "I'm the one who has to talk to him."

"Speakerphone," Henry said quietly.

She nodded, pushed the button, and answered. "Who is

this?"

"You know damn well who, bitch."

Amber seemed to curl around herself at the sound of the harsh, grating voice. But when she answered, her voice sounded steadier than Henry expected. "Hi, Leon," she said. "You've been busy."

"You thought you could cheat me, didn't you? Just like Michael."

"You didn't have to hurt Trix," she said.

"That's on you. You shouldn't have involved her."

"I didn't involve her. I just tried to un-involve her, that's all. I told her to run away. She had nothing you needed. She knew nothing you needed."

"Oh yeah? Tell me something, Amber. Why didn't you tell me you understood Italian? You knew what that little shithead was squeaking about when he forgot his English. And you chose not to tell me. You played dumb. You fucking little liar."

"I didn't understand very much, actually," she said. "It was Calabrese dialect, *stretto stretto*. Plus, I was afraid more people would get hurt. Guess I was right."

"What? Like those two sluts in Vegas? They told me Michael had a girlfriend. This Trix. That she was your bestie. Your ex-roommate. They told me she had a nephew, little Tori. And they told me you spoke Italian. If you'd been straight with me from the start, Amber, your slut girlfriends would be shaking their tits in the Magnum as we speak."

"You didn't have to hurt them," Amber repeated.

Leon let out an ugly laugh. "Hurt them? Hah. What I did to them is nothing compared to what I'm going to do to you. I've learned from my mistakes, see? I'll keep you alive a whole lot longer than Michael. I practiced on that bitch at the hotel. Trix took longer than Michael, in case you're interested. It was tough keeping her quiet, though. She was a squeaker."

Amber's face was chalky white. Henry reached for the

phone, but she slapped his hand away, put her finger to her bluish lips, and shook her head.

"What did she tell you?"

"Everything she had to tell," he said. "She said she was coming to get her bonds. The ones Michael hid in her mom's house. I'd already figured that part out, from the whores in Vegas. Then she told me you found them first. My guess is, she was coming to steal them back, right? Because you fucked her over too, Amber. You'd walk over somebody's face in fucking stilettos to get what you want. I know all about you."

"No," Amber said softly. "You're wrong. You don't know anything about me."

Leon laughed. "We'll see, baby. We'll see. Because, I'm coming for you, Amber." His voice hissed through the phone. "I'm coming for you, and I'll keep you alive for days."

"Goodbye, Leon." She closed the call and sat there, breathing fast and shallow. "Trix didn't tell him," she said finally, her voice a thin wisp of sound.

"Didn't tell him what?" Henry asked.

"I told Trix that I'd come to her this afternoon with the money, but she didn't tell Leon that. If she had, he would have waited for me there. But she didn't tell him. She saved my life."

Henry sat next to her and took her hand. "I'm so grateful to her. And so sorry."

The words felt hollow. He wanted to say more, but this was not the time to burden her with his feelings. He took the phone and started to pry it open.

"Stop!" She snatched it back. "Don't touch it!"

"You don't need to listen to any more of his filth," Henry said. "I don't think he knows anything that's of any use to us. So why keep it?"

"We should never throw away a line of communication! This is our only way to reach him!"

"Right. An open line to the devil. We want to maintain that exactly why?"

"I don't know yet!" she snapped. "I haven't thought all the thoughts yet, Henry! I'm not like you. I have to think one thought at a time, and they have to take a number and get in line!" She paused and took a breath. "We might want to manipulate him. Misdirect him, fool him, bait a trap, who the hell knows?"

"Yes," Henry said, slowly. "God, yes. That's exactly right. You're brilliant."

"And don't I know it. I'm not giving up on your diamonds, though. If you don't want to help, fine. I'll do it myself." She put a hand up before he could say anything. "Don't try to stop me because it will be a waste of your time. But if you help me, it'll be quicker and safer. Then we can leave. I don't know about you. But I feel a powerful urge to be somewhere else, and it's getting stronger by the minute."

We. She had said we. Henry could feel his heart hammering. "We'll discuss it in the morning."

"We will do no such thing." Amber shook her head. "There is nothing to discuss. It's a done deal."

"Now is not the time for this fight," he said. "Not when you're exhausted. Let me bring you something to eat. You should probably—"

"No. You are not going to distract me with food. And there will be no fight, not now, not ever. I'm going to take a shower. This conversation is officially over. We'll get up tomorrow and do exactly as we planned."

He stared at her. She stared back. He wasn't going to convince her of anything tonight. "I'll give you some space," he said, finally. "Tell me if you change your mind about eating."

He went downstairs, wishing he knew how to comfort her, or that he could transform himself into an invincible warrior to protect her. But he had nothing to work with but his brain.

That, he would put entirely at her service. As long as he drew breath.

Chapter Thirty-One

Henry waited until he heard the shower before he pulled out the bearer bonds. He took a photo of the top one, emailed it to himself, opened his laptop, downloaded it, and posted it on the dark web.

Certain cardinal points were becoming clearer as each minute passed. The first was that Leon had to go. To prison or to hell, preferably the latter. Running from him for the rest of their lives was a non-starter.

Henry alone didn't have the muscle and the savagery required to come down on Leon, but Tommy DiAngelo, Leon's old boss, definitely did, and so did the Feds, if they could catch him. Leon was slippery, but if he could be pinned down some place far from Amber, the DiAngelo crew and the Feds, either alone or combined, might be enough to finish him.

He sat there staring at nothing in particular, watching scenarios play out in his head, and had a flash of inspiration. He could point them all at Victor. Why not? Leon, the DiAngelo's, the Feds, all at once.

He could kill several nasty birds with one big, terrible stone.

He pulled out the phone he used only for Ivar, pulling up the last Mirror, Mirror alibi video he had just completed. He sent it to the encrypted server on the dark web, waited for a few minutes, and called Ivar's number.

"Hey there, Hemlock." Ivar insisted on using the nickname he'd given Henry in prison. "Anselm has been bitching about you. You disappointed him, and a disappointed Anselm is a real pain in my ass, so thanks for that."

"He almost got me killed," Henry said. "Tell him to leave me alone. Forever."

"Your own fault for being a cash cow. You got him spoiled. And you made the same mistake with me. Your bad, Hemlock. What can I do for you?"

"Did you get the video?"

"Yes. Payment has been applied to your debt, unless you're broke and need me to throw some coin your way for incidentals. As always, beautiful work. You make me look so good. You know I'd pay you a king's ransom if you'd sell Mirror, Mirror to me outright. Then you'd never have to bother with these stupid little videos ever again. Wouldn't that be nice?"

"No," Henry said. "It's too dangerous."

"Aww. Hemlock. So burdened by morality. Don't you trust me?"

Henry carefully ignored that question. "I need to ask a favor."

"Shoot."

"I need another high-quality passport like the one you said you had made for me. As soon as possible. For a woman. I'll get you a photo."

"A woman, eh? These things don't grow on trees, you know," Ivar bitched. "When do you need it?"

"Yesterday."

"Well, of course you do." Ivar made a humming sound. "The good stuff takes time. I have to contact people. And obviously, you'd have to make it worth my while."

"I'll pay you back every last penny I owe you tomorrow morning early," Henry said.

Ivar paused, startled. "Oh, yeah? Where the hell did you find all that cash?"

"I keep myself busy," Henry said. "And I have another favor to ask. I need a phone number for whoever does the books for Tommy DiAngelo. A direct line."

"DiAngelo?" Ivar's voice lowered to a hiss. "The LA DiAngelos? What the fuck do you want with them? They'll eat you for lunch. Hemlock, tell me you're joking."

"No," Henry said. "That's what I need."

"Do you intend to sell Mirror, Mirror to them? I promise, I will pay more."

"I am not selling Mirror, Mirror to them or to anyone. This is something completely different. I have my reasons, and they won't affect your bottom line or create competition for you. I give you my word."

"You're nuts." Ivar's voice was grim. "Those people are not to be fucked with."

"I know that," Henry said.

Ivar let out a dubious grunt. "I'll see what I can do," he said, and the line went dead.

Henry put the phone down and double-clicked the folder where he had collected all the videos Amber had used to study how Belinda moved, spoke, smiled. He opened one from the Whitten Burbank Art Institute Gala, which Belinda and Victor had attended last summer. Posted on Facebook and Instagram, it featured Victor and Belinda on the dance floor. Belinda wore a low-cut, backless dress. Until just a few days ago, watching that video had made him burn with rage. Now he watched it with a cool, detached eye.

After studying it, Amber had put on a slinky gown, heavy makeup, and high heels and imitated Belinda's dance routine. Which made it even easier to find clips to feed into Mirror, Mirror.

When Henry was finished a half hour later, Amber had replaced Belinda on the dance floor. He now had an airtight video of Victor Shattuck dancing with Amber Dixon, complete with her tattoo. As he worked, he gamed out every possible move going forward, seeking one that ended with himself and Amber, alive and free.

He set about linking that video to every reference to Victor he could find. He didn't need to convince forensic experts with this video. Just Leon, and the DiAngelos.

His dedicated Ivar phone vibrated. Henry looked down and saw two messages. The first was a phone number. The second said:

> Domenico D'Amato. Watch yourself. Do not involve me.

Henry took a moment to gather his nerve. He was flying blind on a handful of hopeful assumptions. One, that D'Amato didn't know that Tommy DiAngelo's inside Treasury guy, Holstein, was already dead. Two, that Michael killed Holstein to stop him from alerting Tommy if any of the bearer bonds were redeemed. He had no proof of these things. They were still just a story he had told himself. A plausible one, but still. He could be wrong. In a million different ways.

But being with Amber made him bolder, and fortune favored the bold. Henry chose a fresh burner, and typed in a brief text to the D'Amato number.

> We need to talk.

Then he went back to fine-tuning the Amber/Victor video. Ten minutes later, the phone chirped.

> who is this

Henry took a deep breath.

> Frank Holstein

The response came a few cautious minutes later.

Treasury guy. Heard you disappeared down in Florida. Eaten by alligators.

> I'm still here. Alligators everywhere.

Henry tapped.

> I don't dare poke my head up.

How do I know it's you, Alligator Lunch?

> They're cashing in those bonds. Take a look. Sending a link. Note the serial number.

There was another pause, then,

Congratulations on not being dead. What do you want?

> Protection for myself and my family.

After a few minutes, D'Amato responded.

Who is cashing them?

> Victor Shattuck, from Milton, Connecticut. That's all I know.

The next pause was even longer, but he still held his breath until D'Amato finally texted back.

Okay. We'll be in touch.

And then, a second later:

Watch out for alligators.

He could hardly believe what he'd just done, but it wasn't as if it put Amber in any more danger than she was already in. Leon fully intended to torture her to death.

He just wished it was his own face that he could put out there to draw the attention of evil men seeking to devour. But no one gave a damn about his stupid face.

Only Amber's gorgeous smile could launch a thousand ships.

Chapter Thirty-Two

Amber looked into the kitchen. "It's late. You should get some sleep. Big day tomorrow." She gave Henry her most menacing look.

"I can't sleep," he said. "I'm plotting our escape."

"Oh, yeah?" She came in and pulled out a chair. "That sounds promising. Tell me more."

"Well, Leon has got to go, for starters."

She cleared her throat. "From your mouth to God's ears. So what's your cunning plan?"

"To control the narrative. I'm letting it be known that Victor has your bearer bonds."

Her eyes widened, impressed. "No shit. How?"

"I contacted Domenico D'Amato, Tommy DiAngelo's numbers guy. Told him I was Frank Holstein. Remember the Treasury guy who disappeared, down in Florida? I sent him a picture of one of the bonds, making sure the serial number was crystal clear and told him Victor is redeeming them."

Amber nodded slowly, impressed. "Henry Devlin, that is diabolical. How did supervillain Victor get the bonds?"

"You gave them to him," he said.

She blinked innocently. "Me?"

Henry nodded.

"Why on earth would I do that?"

"Because you're crazy for him," he said. "You two are having a wild affair."

"Ewww." Her mouth tightened in distaste. "I'm displaying my usual stellar judgment in men, I see."

"Yup." Henry double clicked a file and Amber watched herself tango across the screen with Victor Shattuck.

"Holy shit," she said. "Did you use—"

"Mirror, Mirror? Yes. I want Leon to come down on him. And Tommy DiAngelo's guys, preferably all at the same time. They can tear each other to pieces. I have invited them all to a bloodbath, but you and I won't be attending."

Amber thought for a minute. "Bold," she said finally. "But risky. Hard to control."

Henry shrugged. "Who's trying to control anything? Let 'er rip."

"What about Belinda?"

He looked uncomfortable. "I hope she'll be okay. I think Victor is the real monster here. She's just weak, and damaged, and a shitty mother. But I'm not going to hold back for her sake. She didn't hold back for mine. Want a cup of tea?"

She laughed. "A cuppa to murder by? Why am I not surprised at that question. Yes, please. I'd love one."

Henry switched on the electric kettle and found a couple of teabags. "There's one more thing we need to do," he said. "And you're the only one who can do it. Milk and honey?"

"Sure." She accepted the mug of tea and sipped it "So? What do I have to do?"

"It's about those FBI agents, the ones who got Leon to turn on Tommy DiAngelo," he said.

"Larry Wojniac and Steve Daly. Not my favorite guys. What about them?"

"Why didn't you like them?" Henry sat down opposite her, cradling his own mug.

"Well, they took me for a brainless slut, for one thing," she said. "I'm used to being underestimated, but these two were awful, especially Wojniac. Daly wasn't quite as bad." She shrugged. "I liked the US Marshals better."

"Do you still have their phone numbers?"

Amber nodded. "Actually, I do. Or at least, I have Wojniac's card. It was in my purse when I ran away. Why?"

"These guys could bait the trap for us. You could call them, come clean about Michael's murder, say you were terrified of Leon—"

"I absolutely was," she said.

"Right. So tell them that's why you ran, and then you tell them about all the other people we know Leon has killed. Five today alone, which puts him in mass murderer territory. Then, suggest this. You give them Trix's number, they contact Leon, tell him they know where you and your lover Victor Shattuck are, and that they will share this information in exchange for two-thirds of the bearer bonds. Which he will take from you after he kills you."

"Excuse me for seeing some flaws in this," Amber said. "The very idea of sleeping with Victor Shattuck is nasty as hell. And I may not have cared for Wojniac and Daly, but they weren't bent."

"That doesn't matter, for our purposes. This is just a lure to get him in the right place so the Feds can nab him or the DiAngelos can kill him. They don't have to be bent. Leon just has to believe they're bent. And he will. That's how his mind is wired."

Amber slowly finished her tea as she pondered his words. Then she put her mug down, and stuck out her hand. "Okay," she said. "I'll make the call. On one condition."

Henry looked like he was bracing himself. "What?"

"I will do everything you say on the condition that tomorrow, we go ahead exactly as planned, with no more arguments from you. We get that safe deposit box key from Belinda. I insist on that."

Henry looked miserable. She just stared at him, implacable.

"Shake on it," she said.

"Deal," he said, finally. "Provided you eat something."

Amber rolled her eyes. But he did shake her hand.

Five minutes later, when Henry put a plate of generously buttered sourdough toast down in front of her, Amber stared to laugh. "Henry, you're never going pass for a ruthless, scheming criminal with this toast and tea schtick. It's really off-brand."

"So nobody's perfect. Just please. Indulge me. Eat."

She did, and as usual, she found she was starving. When the toast was gone, she went upstairs and rooted through her bag for Wojniac's card. She brought it downstairs to the kitchen. She had to do this fast, before she lost her nerve, but as she reached for the burner on the table, Henry stopped her hand. "No," he said. "You can't use one of those. They can triangulate it almost immediately. And there's the metadata."

"Even with burners?"

"Even with burners." He clicked around on the computer. "We'll use an app. It makes it way harder, and I have a VPN on this. If and when they get that far, it will look like you called from Helsinki."

"But he can't see me?"

"Of course not. I disable the cameras on my computers anyway. Voice only. Here," he held out his hand for the card. "Give me the number."

They sat side by side in front of the computer as Wojniac answered, his voice thick with sleep.

"Who is this? This better be fuckin' good. It's three in the morning."

"Special Agent Wojniac?" She made her voice wispy and ultra-feminine.

"Yeah?"

"This is Amber Dixon, Leon Gambelli's wife. Do you remember me?"

There was a pause. "Of course I do." They heard muffled sounds, heavy breathing as he got out of bed and went into another room. "Ms. Dixon? You still there?" Wojniac sounded wide awake now.

"I sure am."

"Are you all right? Are you in immediate danger?"

"Um. No. At least I don't think so."

"Okay. It is good to hear your voice. We've been worried. You put yourself in real danger, running away from the safe house, Ms. Dixon."

"You think that living with Leon wasn't dangerous?"

Wojniac cleared his throat. "Ah. My apologies."

"Yeah, right," Amber said. "I didn't call to discuss my marital problems, Agent Wojniac. I'm calling to tell you that Leon has slipped the leash. He's on a rampage. Those two girls in Vegas? My friends, Krystal and Tasha? He shot them. Just like he killed Michael Basile, and I know he did, because I saw him do it. That's the only reason I ever stayed with him. I was terrified. It's also the reason that I ran as soon as I got the chance. Just since last night, he burned down a house and killed two people in Jersey. This afternoon, he killed three more people in a New York City hotel. And he's just getting started."

"You say you saw him kill Basile?"

"Michael Basile, yes. Leon made me clean up the blood afterward. I was so scared of him it took me months to work up the nerve to run away."

"Could you show us where Michael Basile is buried?"

"No. Leon locked me up and disposed of the body without me."

"That's a shame. And the other people you're talking about? Krystal and Tasha?"

"That was in Las Vegas, four days ago. Five now. He went to them to find me. I don't know who was supposed to be keeping an eye on him, but they aren't doing a great job. Last night, he killed two men at a house owned by the Graziano family in South Cambrook, New Jersey. This afternoon he tortured Beatrice Graziano to death, and shot her boyfriend and his bodyguard in the Lapis Lazuli suite at the Swann Hotel in Manhattan."

"I see," Wojniac said. "Just a moment, please." They could hear him writing, taking notes, probably texting on another phone, initiating a trace and triangulation to pinpoint her location, which would be useless, thanks to Henry. "This is really specific, Ms. Dixon. Amber. Can I call you Amber? You want to tell me how you know? And why he'd do all this?"

"He's trying to find me. He thinks I have six million dollars in bearer bonds that he considers his. He killed Michael Basile for stealing them. And I know this because he told me."

"He told you? Leon Gambelli? Your husband. You've seen him?"

"No, of course not. I'd be dead if I had. He called me a couple of hours ago."

"And you say he's in New York?"

"He was today."

"Do you know where he called from? Any idea?"

"None," Amber said. "But I do have a number where you can reach him."

Wojniac was silent for a moment. "Frankly, I doubt Leon would take my call."

"He wants those bearer bonds," Amber said. "He's been after them for years. Ten point four million, stolen from Tommy DiAngelo. Now Leon is convinced that I have them."

"And do you?"

"Sadly, no, but try to tell Leon that. He won't stop until I'm dead. But I can give him to you. He'll meet with you, if you tell him that you know where I am. Me and my boyfriend, Victor Shattuck. I don't want Leon to kill him, either."

"Why would we tell him that?"

Amber rolled her eyes at Henry in exasperation. "So you can do a deal with him," she said impatiently. "Demand a cut of the bonds. A big enough cut so that he'll believe you. Half, two thirds, something like that, in return for handing over me and my boyfriend to him. He'll go for it. Trust me. He's hungry for blood. And those bonds."

Another long silence. "Where are you, Ms. Dixon?" Wojniac asked.

She let out a crack of laughter. "You don't need to know that, Special Agent Wojniac."

"And you think he'd believe that we're that dirty?"

"Yeah," Amber said. "He'd believe it. Listen up. I'm going to read you the phone number."

She heard a rattle and rustle as he groped for a pen. "Go ahead."

She recited the number, slowly and clearly. "Do it soon, Agent Wojniac," Amber said. "Real soon, before he kills someone else." Then she nodded at Henry. He hit a button and killed the call.

"So? What do you think?" she asked.

"You were perfect," he told her. "You dominated him with grace and style. Now, we see what happens."

She reached out and took his hand. "Big day tomorrow. We should get some sleep. Tomorrow's make-up takes hours to apply."

"And I have to go out before we leave," he said. "To pay my guy and get my passport, with my cut of the bearer bonds. If you're absolutely sure about that."

"I am," she said. "And I'm delighted to hear it."

Amber felt his hand clasp hers. They walked upstairs side by side, hands fingers twined.

Chapter Thirty-Three

Tommy DiAngelo sat staring through the bullet-proof glass at his accountant, Domenico D'Amato, a short, thick-necked guy with a greasy comb-over. Tommy's lower back throbbed. It was all these goddamn hard chairs. Your tax dollars at work. Couldn't the government even make a goddamn decent chair? It put him in a foul mood.

He picked up the handset, wiped the mouthpiece with a Kleenex, and said, "Gimme some good news, Domi."

"I got interesting news," D'Amato answered. "Not sure quite yet if it's good."

Tommy shrugged "So? Like I got a choice. Go ahead. Entertain me."

D'Amato leaned forward, dropping his voice, all but whispering into his handset. "You remember, how after that thing with Ferdie, you wanted us to set up some system so we'd know the minute anybody got lucky?"

"I remember that," Tommy said. "What are you telling me?"

"Well, we found a guy to flag the system for us. You remember."

"Yeah. I know."

"Anyway, he retired a few years back, but he's still got his finger in the pie. Knows people who know people, has access to the system. Couple of months ago, I hear he's gone missing down in Florida. Anyway last night, some guy texts me. Says it's Holstein. Says he's in hiding because somebody's trying to kill him. And here's the interesting part. He also says one of the ah, items, showed up. Sent me the picture and everything. It's one of yours. Serial number checks out."

"No shit." Tommy sat forward in his chair, back pain forgotten. "Who cashed it?"

"Some hedge fund asshole I never heard of. I looked him up. One Victor Shattuck. Old money prep school type. Lives in Connecticut. Thinks he's God's gift."

"So, how did he get his hands on it? What's the connection?"

"Well, that's interesting, too. Found some footage of him, on, you know social media. Dancing at some art museum fundraiser."

"Yeah?"

"Yeah. I'd have brought my phone in to show you, but you know how they are about these things. Anyway, she's a looker. Real distinctive. A redhead, wearing one of those backless dresses. I never can figure how those damn things stay on. Anyway," D'Amato waggled his eyebrows. "You know the most distinctive thing about her? She's got this tattoo. A vine with these purple flowers going right down her back. Remember that broad?"

Tommy sat forward. "You are shitting me."

D'Amato shook his head. "Sound familiar?"

"Yeah. I met her in Vegas last year, at that party. Topaz, Crystal—"

"Amber. She was a showgirl when she married our mutual friend. She got tired of him though. Who can blame her. He's an asshole. She disappeared about three months after we had our little problem. Now she's popped up again. The lovely

Mrs. Gambelli, doing the dirty two step with the hedge fund guy who's cashing in those things we talked about."

"You sure it's her?"

"Oh, I'm sure. You can take it to the bank. Pun definitely intended."

Tommy drummed his fingers on the grubby counter. "So our friend robs me, then Michael robs him, then this Amber robs us all and runs off to bone this hedge fund clown, and they start doing the two step and cashing those things like it's nothing." He looked up. "Pretty stupid. Feels like a trap."

"Maybe. Maybe not." D'Amato shrugged. "People do stupid things when there's lots of money involved."

"That they do," Tommy agreed. "Reach out to the guy. Let's see how stupid he is. Set up a meeting. If it's all over fuckin' social media, I'm sure our mutual friend will want to meet him, too. Maybe catch up with his wife. It'll be a big old happy reunion. You can all catch up. Shoot the shit."

Domi smiled widely. "On it, boss."

———

Wojniac got a call on the way to the airport. He fumbled for the cell phone, cursing. "Yeah?" he barked, just missing a Toyota Camry that swerved in front of him.

"You alone?" The voice was hushed, but he still recognized it.

"Pauly? Yeah." Wojniac flipped the Camry the bird and changed lanes. "Tell me."

Pauly had been his snitch in DiAngelo's crew for almost two years now. He was nowhere near as senior as Leon had been, but the info he gave was usually good. He was always a little squirrelly, but today he sounded even more jumpy than usual.

"I gotta be fast. Something's going down. We're going to New York after some guy named Victor Shattuck. He's shacked up with Leon's ex. And he's cashing in bearer bonds. That's what they say."

Well, damn. So Amber had been telling the truth. It was actually happening. "The trace on your phone?" he said. "Hit it when you land. I need to follow you."

"You know that if they find it, they kill me. You got my back, right?"

"You know it, buddy," he said, hanging up.

He was late by the time he parked. Daly was already through security and waiting at the gate for him. Wojniac was out of breath. His wife was right, he had to quit the cheese steak, or he'd keel over, never mind fail the next physical. Quantico seemed like a lifetime ago. Then again, so did the rest of his life.

The line was starting to board when Daly walked up and handed him a phone. "Take a look."

As they shuffled forward in the economy line, Wojniac watched a few seconds of video. Two attractive people in evening wear danced to a swing orchestra. The woman was a redhead with a movie-star body and a flowery tattoo trailing over her back. When they stopped, she gave the crowd a dazzling smile.

"That's our girl," he said, his voice reluctantly admiring. "Always lands on her feet."

"Sure does," Daly said, taking his phone back. "Let's hope her luck's not about to run out. Shattuck looks like an asshole."

"Leon Gambelli was an asshole," Wojniac observed.

"No kidding. Maybe it's her thing."

Wojniac pulled up his boarding pass on his phone. "I just heard from Pauly. Those bearer bonds? The DiAngelo crew is going after them."

Daly nodded. "No surprise. Your guy lined up?"

"I sure as shit hope so. There might be a lot of loose money flying around." He glanced at Daly. Ahead of them, a man complained that the scanner wouldn't read his phone. The gate agent sighed and held out her hand.

"Loose money," Daly said softly. "Bonds, shit like that. They can get lost."

Daly passed his phone over the scanner and started down the jetway. Wojniac scanned his own boarding pass and fell into step beside him.

"Counting things like bonds can be a bitch," he said. "You know, in the heat of the moment."

Daly nodded. "Especially if no one knows how many there were to start with," he said. "Whatever happens, as long as we get that asshole Gambelli back in the bag, I'll be satisfied."

Wojniac shrugged. There was no reason not to be a little bit more than satisfied.

Chapter Thirty-Four

Leon stopped as Trix's phone vibrated in his pocket. He pulled it out and frowned. It wasn't Amber. Curiosity won over caution. "Who's this?" he snapped.

"Hello, Leon."

Leon recognized Wojniac's voice and looked around the room, panicked. "How the fuck did you get this number?"

"Your wife called us." Leon could hear the smile in Wojniac's voice, and it bugged him. "She wants us to keep you from cutting her and her new boyfriend to pieces."

"Lying bitch. What new boyfriend is that?"

Wojniac ignored him. "I heard on the grapevine that she's come into some serious money."

"She told you that?"

"Of course she didn't tell me that. She's not an idiot. Why did you run, Leon? I thought we had a deal."

Leon laughed. "Yeah. Right. Some deal. Shit house, shit job, shit town. Really warms the heart, after putting my ass on the line against a shark like DiAngelo. You guys really know how to show a guy that care. Next time, say it with flowers."

"At least you weren't in jail," Wojniac pointed out. "But

maybe you should have been. Those showgirls? The Japanese guys, in New York? The Graziano bodyguards in Jersey. Michael Basile? Jesus, Leon."

"I didn't kill anybody. That bitch is a professional liar, and she's trying to fuck me up. She hates my guts."

"Yeah, maybe," Wojniac said. "But, liar or not, she's the one with the bonds. With our contacts, Daly and I could track her down for you. If you felt like it."

"If I felt like it?" Leon stopped pacing and stared at the phone. "What the fuck do you mean?"

"I'm talking about you working with us again," Wojniac said. "If we find the bonds, then you, me and Daly split them three ways. If you were smart enough not to leave fingerprints and DNA in your last crime spree, we could probably get you back into WITSEC."

"Not in Idaho," Leon said swiftly.

"Definitely not in Idaho. Hawaii, maybe."

"And the money?"

"We'll get it to you. All you have to do is testify against DiAngelo, just like you agreed to. But this time when you're done, you'll be much richer. Everybody wins."

"Except Amber. And the boyfriend. Who the fuck is this boyfriend? Lying slut."

Wojniac rolled his eyes at Daly. "Leon, it all falls apart if you start killing people," he complained. "Come on, it's the best deal you're ever going to get."

"Go fuck yourselves."

"Okay," Wojniac said agreeably. "Good luck finding Amber on your own. There are a lot of people looking for her. People who have more info than you. How long do you think your baby doll will stay ahead of a pack of hungry dogs like that? They'll eat her alive, Leon."

"Assholes," Leon growled.

"Text me." Wojniac gave Daly a thumbs up and ended the call.

Leon threw the phone on the floor. He paced around the room some more. Then he sat down on the bed, pulled open his bag and pulled out the small plastic clamshell. Inside, three loaded syringes nested in foam slots. There were four slots. This missing syringe was in that suitcase with the rotting pieces of Michael Basile, now buried deep in the Nevada desert.

The three remaining would be plenty to do the job. He closed the case, retrieved the phone from the floor, and texted Wojniac.

> **Where and when?**

Chapter Thirty-Five

Amber studied herself from every angle in the standing mirror. She used a hand mirror to get the back of her head, checking for false notes. She hadn't done a deep backstory on today's persona, usually her strong point. She'd been too shocked by Trix's death, and too short on sleep.

Mamma would have scolded her for being sloppy. Mamma believed in deep backstories. Mamma probably would have been a very talented and convincing actor, if she'd been given half a chance at a profession like that. But she hadn't. She'd made the best of it, and used her talents as best she could.

Today, Amber was Amy Grezynski. She'd chosen a fat suit, but not the pear-shaped Donna one. This one was blockier, thicker in the shoulders. Amy was single, in her early forties. She wore patterned leggings under her plain brown jersey dress, and a beige and white polka-dotted scarf. Amy's eyes were green, since the brown contacts were lost. Amber had slicked her eyebrows down and painted them over, with a thinner eyebrow painted on in a high, arched line that had been fashionable twenty years ago. She had spots on her chin and wore round wire-rimmed glasses. Her hair was a long, mousy bob with blunt, too-short bangs. Amy Grezynski was a burnt-out, disillusioned social worker whose last job had ended badly due to incompatibilities with her boss. She hadn't had the heart to find a new job yet. She lived alone, on unemployment, with four cats.

Amber had designed Amy to be completely unthreatening to Belinda, since Belinda struck her as one of those women who automatically distrusted other women, especially pretty ones. Amber had come to this conclusion after studying the roast-the-bride speech from the wedding that had been posted on Instagram. The roast had been full of veiled, competitive snark. The bride had been forcing herself to smile. Her own fault, Amber thought, for picking that snotty bitch to be her maid of honor, but still. Belinda was one spiteful cat-bitch.

She triple-checked her big tote, which had five different purses packed into it. Belinda's socials and her online shopping accounts had yielded some hints about her possible purses, but nothing definitive, so Amber had included five options. She hoped one of them would match. Her look was completed with a black quilted winter coat which closed just a little too tightly over Amy's belly, making the zipper bulge and strain.

As a persona, Amy was still a little green, but she wasn't going to be using Amy long term. There would be no lingering. They did this job, then they scrammed.

The front door opened as she came down the stairs, letting in Henry and a gust of frigid air. It was freezing outside. He was bundled into his coat and hat. He stopped when he saw her, mouth open. Amber still got a kick from the startled look Henry gave her whenever she showed him a new persona.

"Whoa!" he said. "Who's this?"

"Meet Amy Grezynski," she said. "Sit down with her for a while and she'll tell you all about her food intolerances. Garlic and onions, to start with. They make her burp something fierce. And when they get further down the tubes, things get really crazy."

"I don't know how you do it. You're so beautiful, but you just, I don't know."

"Switch it off?" She laughed at him. "Yeah, of course, because it's all smoke and mirrors to begin with. So did you see your guy? Did you give him the money you owed him?"

"I did," Henry said, unwinding his scarf. "He wasn't happy."

"Geez. What kind of sourpuss is unhappy with a big pile of money?"

"One who wants Mirror, Mirror. Or at the very least, who wants me chained to a computer and running it for him indefinitely. He wasn't expecting his good thing to end quite so soon."

"But he gave you the passport?"

He pulled out the little navy booklet out of his pocket and handed it to her. She opened it up, admiring it. "Benjamin Glass, huh? Not bad. That name fits your vibe. Better than my last alias did. Can you believe the US Marshals decided I was supposed to be Mary Agnes Hinkley?"

He laughed. "Oh, man. That's bad."

"Tell me about it. Congratulations, Mr. Glass," she said, handing the passport back to him. "Aren't you happy?"

"Not yet," he said. "It won't do me any good unless you have one, too. It might take him weeks to come through, and we can't hang around here for weeks. Or even one week. We'll have to have it couriered to us somewhere. That's risky."

She shrugged. "I'll muddle along with Trix's license for now. So. Are you all set?"

"No. We'll have something to eat before we go."

His look dared her to argue, so she followed him into the kitchen, and waited while he made her a plate of scrambled eggs with a buttery English muffin, just the way she liked it. Funny how Henry knew these things better than she did.

She'd never paid much attention to what she liked and what she didn't. Her own preferences were at the bottom of her priority list, if they were on it at all. It had always been more important to keep her characters' likes and dislikes consistent.

But Henry had paid attention to how she liked her toast, her eggs, her coffee. Pretty much everything, really. Damn. At this rate, she might even become one of those high-maintenance, demanding women. Who knew.

They picked up the rental car. Amber drove so Henry could monitor Belinda on the laptop on the way. When they arrived, Amber and Henry parked under a tree near the coffee shop waiting for Belinda, who had struggled to get the fussing, whimpering Faith into her car seat. Amber watched the icon that represented her car, holding her breath, hoping Belinda would be true to habit. That today would not be the day she did something different and random. Otherwise this drama would have to repeat itself over and over until they got lucky. Amber was eager to wrap it up. The stress was eating at both of them.

Belinda stopped near the day care center. They waited for the ten minutes it took her to get Faith settled. Then the vehicle began to move again. The corner of Fairway Street and Washington Avenue was the moment of truth. If Belinda turned right on Fairway, she was stopping for coffee. If she went straight on Washington, she was driving directly to the office. She was late, so it was a toss-up.

The icon slowed at the intersection…and turned right.

They both exhaled. Amber gave Henry a big smile and a high five, her pale lips stretching over Amy's unfortunately large buck teeth. "That's my cue."

He leaned forward and kissed her gently, careful not to smear her makeup. "Thank you."

The kiss moved her, which made her want to toss a snappy comeback back in his face. She stopped the automatic defense mechanism just in time. She patted his cheek. "Right back at you, buddy."

Amber let Amy's flat, fleece-lined, rubber-soled snow boots dictate how she walked as she made her way toward Beans & Brew. The front of the coffee shop was painted a pale purple with deep purple trim. Flower boxes piled with snow lined the windows. Belinda's car was parked down the street. Near, but not too close to the ancient Taurus that she and Henry had left here yesterday. No other car was near it, thank God.

The coffee shop was filled with the usual crowd such places attracted. A few people writing on their laptops. A business meeting in a corner. A hushed lovers' quarrel was taking place near the bathroom, while a few middle-aged ladies gossiped by the window.

Belinda stood staring up at the menu, her lips flat and pursed, as if she'd eaten something sour. She was using her Coach bag. Hurray. More luck. There was an exact match for that bag in Amy's tote.

Belinda didn't look good. Her make-up was perfunctory. Her hair, which clearly had not been blown out, looked frizzy and stiff. She stared at the cookies, lemon bars, loaf cakes, and brownies with blank eyes. Her face was blotched and puffy, and she wasn't even trying to hide it.

Henry's campaign of low-level terror was working. Not that Amber was sorry for her. It wasn't as bad as what Henry had experienced in prison. That was for damn sure.

The line inched forward. Belinda ordered a caramel latte with whipped cream, drizzled with caramel syrup and sprinkled with toffee bits, because clearly, it was just that kind of day. When it was her turn, Amber ordered a dark-roast and a piece of loaf cake, if only because it reminded her of Henry serving her tea and loaf cake that first weird day they spent together. Vanilla man, Belinda had called him. Hah. She had no idea what she'd given up. She'd probably never seen Henry at all.

Women. The stupid shit they did to themselves.

She found a table near Belinda's, nibbled her cake, and watched Belinda stare blankly out the window. She looked so exhausted that once again, Amber almost felt sorry for her. Almost.

Belinda might not have masterminded the plot to disgrace and destroy Henry for money, but she had consented to it. She had played right along and put up no objections, so to hell with her. She was no-account trash. She deserved any and all pain that came her way, and then some.

Amber sent a text to Henry.

> Send the video.

From where she sat, she could hear Belinda's phone ping. Belinda looked at the notification, debating whether or not she gave enough of a shit to open it. *Look, you dumb cow. See what you traded in your vanilla man for.* Finally, Belinda fumbled with her phone and clicked the message open. She stared at the subject line they had chosen.

> Look at what he is hiding from you.

It would obviously be stupid to play it. Almost as stupid as it was irresistible. No warning about the dangers of scams or malware could win out against the mortal fear of a woman who already knew she was going to be betrayed, and suspected that she deserved it.

Belinda touched the screen as if it might burn her. Her mouth fell open as she watched the video. The super-cuts version of Victor's prostitute party. Amber had straw-bossed Henry into editing it down from the original long and deadly boring hour and twenty minutes of video down to a punchy six-minutes of highlights. Victor getting blown, first by one, then by another naked girl. Victor sandwiched between a girl on her hands and knees, and another girl skillfully stimulating his ass with a vibrating sex toy. Victor, pumping energetically away at this one or that one, in various positions and combinations. Then came the shower sequence. It was a large shower. All three girls fit into it. They had used a lot of that clip.

When it finally ended, Belinda was frozen stiff. She didn't even put the phone down. She just sat there. Amber wanted to yell at her to stop feeling sorry for herself. She had no goddamn right. *That's what you put Henry through hell for. Hope that guy is all you dreamed of, honey.* She checked one last time to make sure that no one was standing anywhere near the old bronze Taurus. Then she texted Henry again.

Now.

Amber counted the seconds, heart in her mouth, hoping Henry hadn't screwed something up with his wires, that the detonator wasn't—

Boom. The car's windows blasted out. Flames licked out of the openings. Windows rattled. People jumped, gasped, screamed. The lovers huddled on the floor, arms clamped around each other, their argument forgotten. Everyone bolted to the window to stare at the burning car.

Belinda, too, had jumped up, the blast shocking her back to life. As she jostled her table, tipping over her coffee, Amy/Amber leaped into action. Pulling the Coach bag out of the tote and slinging it over her shoulder, she hurried to Belinda's table.

"Omigod, are you okay? Did you burn yourself? I saw your coffee spill on you! Are you hurt? Here, sit down!"

Belinda sank back into her seat, eyes brimming. "I'm, ah, okay," she mumbled. "I think."

Amber slid into the chair beside her, neatly knocking Belinda's purse into her big, wide-open tote bag. She grabbed a handful of the useless little table napkins and mopped at the lake of coffee that was now dripping down onto Belinda's lap.

"Oh! Your beautiful coat. It'll be ruined! I'll run to the bathroom and grab some paper towels," she babbled anxiously. "They're way more absorbent than these stupid things. Hold on! I'll be right back!"

She dropped her own Coach purse onto the chair, grabbed the tote and sprinted for the bathroom, which was blessedly free. Everyone was staring out the window at the Taurus, burning merrily away.

Inside the bathroom, Amber rummaged through Belinda's purse, looking for the red satin-covered case Henry had told her about that Belinda used for her small things. Inside it, oh joy, she found the key to the safe deposit box. Amber left in its place the one they had found at the junk shop, decorated with a grubby Minnie Mouse toy. She put the satin case back in the purse, zipped it closed and dropped it back into the tote. On the way out, she remembered to grab two huge handfuls of paper towels. The whole operation took less than a minute, from closing the bathroom door to opening it once again.

Amber/Amy galloped valiantly back to Belinda's table, dumping her own Coach bag onto the floor again as she attacked the puddle of coffee. She leaned deep into Belinda's personal space to dab in vain at her ruined clothing. Her silk blouse, her woolen skirt, her camel coat, all of it was coffee-soaked.

"Oh, dear," she fussed. "Do you need ice? Did you get burned?"

Belinda looked hazy. "I'm okay." She rubbed at the silk blouse plastered across her bra. "I have to go home and change. I can't go to work like this." She looked up into Amber's eyes. "Wait," she said, in dawning horror. "Wait. I can't go back there at all! Ever! I can never go back there now!"

"Well, I mean, you'll have to change your clothes, but your

boss will understand, right? I mean, a car blew up! I think we all spilled our coffee, metaphorically speaking!"

"My boss," Belinda echoed. "My boss. That filthy, lying son of a bitch."

She started sobbing. Amber took the opportunity to retrieve Belinda's purse and put it on the chair again. She tucked her own decoy into the tote and zipped it up. "I really don't know what's going on with you," she said earnestly. "But whatever it is, I'm really sorry."

"Me, too." Belinda mopped at her reddened eyes with a paper towel. "I mean, it's like a sign, you know? That car blowing up, right in front of me, right after I see…"

Amber waited a few beats before she prompted her. "See what?"

"Nothing." Belinda stood up, shrugged her coat on, grabbed her purse, and shoved Amber aside in her hurry to get to the door. "Get out of my way," she muttered.

Amber watched her through the crush of people at the window as she trotted unsteadily to her car, her coat flapping in the cold wind. After she left, Amber sat there just long enough to finish her cake, and left. She did not want to be there when the police arrived.

Henry was waiting four blocks away. The car was blessedly warm when she got in. She felt cold from the inside. Almost as if she wanted to cry. But for what? For Belinda? No. She should be feeling righteously triumphant.

Henry pulled out onto the street. "How did it go?"

"Smooth as silk," she said. "I got the key. No problem."

He glanced over, alarmed by the flatness of her tone. "Are you okay?"

"Not really, but it's not your fault. You let me off the hook ten different times. I insisted. It's just…oh, whatever. My defenses were low. Some of the ick seeped in through the cracks. It happens. You can't do stuff like this without getting a little stained."

"I'm sorry."

"She deserved it," Amber said. "And we did her a favor by showing her that tape. If it breaks them up, that might give Faith a fighting chance, right?"

"Right," he said.

"But this is my last grift. After the bank thing, I am officially retired. Forever."

"How about you retire today? Forget the bank. Let's just pack and go."

"After all this trouble we've gone to?" Amber said. "Not a chance."

When they got back to the city, Amber headed upstairs to put the final touches on tomorrow's final performance, Belinda Devlin, the man-eating minx. She'd spent every spare moment for the last several days studying videos of Belinda. She'd spent hours pondering the clothes, styling the wig. She put it all together and realized that she looked more fresh and turned-out than the real Belinda had looked this morning. But that was probably okay. Belinda's guy at the bank would only ever have seen her at her best.

Over the years, Belinda's lips had been injected with too much collagen. It gave them that weird, pendant downward pull, tricky to fake. Amber stared into the mirror, pouting aggressively. She was going to need a ridge of putty on her gums to push the lips out more, and lip plumper to make them swell. She'd draw the lip-line bigger. She'd need some cheek-packing, too, since Belinda's face was rounder. Belinda's nose was tip-tilted, so she'd picked out a latex prosthesis. She would have to delicately glue down the outside corners of her eyes to get that sleepy, sensuous look. She had painstakingly painted on the thick arched eyebrows, even though they would be mostly hidden by the shaggy bangs that framed her face.

The rest would be all nerve and attitude. God knows, she had plenty of that.

Chapter Thirty-Six

Henry had not expected the conversation between Victor and Belinda about the sex tape to be so painful to listen to. The crying, the swearing. More than one plate and vase had been shattered. It was a good thing Faith wasn't toddling yet, because the house was a death trap of glass and ceramic shards.

Belinda was packing her suitcase while yelling at Victor on the phone. Henry was listening through the Bluetooth in his car.

"...this is his thing, Bel! His area of expertise! He deep-faked me with Mirror, Mirror, babe! You should be smart enough not to fall for it!"

"Deep-faked you, my ass," Belinda snarled back. "Does Henry know what your dick looks like? How your chest hair grows? The surgical scars on your knee from your ski accident in high school? Henry couldn't deep-fake that, you lying bastard. You've been fucking around the whole time, right? Of course you have!"

"Belinda, I'm coming home. We'll talk about—"

"Don't bother. I'll be gone. I don't want to see you ever again."

"We have to talk!" Victor bellowed.

"There's nothing to talk about. The video showed me everything I needed to know. I've been packing my stuff—"

"Belinda, calm down! If you freak out, it means he won!"

Belinda sniffled. "No, Victor, it means you lost. And I mean everything. Don't call me again. I'm blocking you."

She ended the call. Henry could still hear Victor snarling and cursing, as well as the sounds from the baby monitor, as Belinda blundered around in her bedroom. Her sobbing got louder as she came into the nursery to gather up baby gear. He heard the sound of a big zipper closing, then *thump-thump-thump* as she dragged the thing down the stairs. He caught a glimpse of her in the kitchen and then in the garage, where she heaved the massive suitcase into the back of her car and opened the garage door.

After Belinda's car pulled away from the house, Henry turned his attention to Victor. He had been waiting for the right moment to seize control of Victor's car, but he'd kept putting it off. It had such an end-game feel to it. But if this wasn't the end-game, what was?

At least he'd driven Belinda and Faith away from Victor. They even had a home to go to, ready and waiting for them, the one he'd bought for her when they got married. She owned it, free and clear, and she could find another job and face life as a single mom, like millions of other women. Maybe she would even pry child support out of Victor. If only she could keep herself and Faith away from that bastard. If that was the only real thing Henry had achieved with all this effort, it would all be worth it.

Benjamin Glass's passport sat next to the computer, taunting him. It was useless unless Amber had one, too. It was good that he'd taken Ivar by surprise with the payment, leaving him no time to plot some way to delay him, or manipulate him into doing more Mirror, Mirror work. He couldn't force Henry without kidnapping him. Ivar might actually be capable of that, if enough money was at stake. But he would have to psych himself up for it, and luckily for Henry, he hadn't had the time.

He returned his attention to Victor's car. He could lock the doors and drive Victor into a concrete piling at high speed. But it wouldn't give him the same thrill of furious pleasure that it would have before meeting Amber. He followed Victor's progress as he pulled in, then raged through the house, yelling for Belinda, breaking everything that was breakable. In the nursery, he caved in a pretty little wooden toy kitchen set that Belinda had set up for Faith with one vicious kick.

Well, hell. Henry had finally succeeded in destroying Belinda and Victor's relationship just in time to realize that he no longer gave a shit. That was ironic.

Victor appeared on the kitchen monitor, a bottle of whiskey in one hand and a silver flask in another. He filled the flask and slid it into the pocket of his winter coat. A muscle twitched in his clenched jaw as he stomped out to the garage.

This was the moment. Henry entered the commands that would allow him to seize control of the car. He needed Victor and Belinda otherwise occupied while Amber did her thing at the bank. After that, those idiots could implode any damn way they liked. He wouldn't even look back to see how they did it.

Faith. His chest twisted. He wouldn't look back at Victor or Belinda. But he wouldn't be able to stop looking back at his little girl.

———

That whining little *bitch!* Victor was so angry. He would cheerfully wring Belinda's neck, and her squalling little brat's neck too, for good measure. He pulled out the flask and took a swig. Something crunched under his foot as he accelerated through the Chilton Estates, tires screeching. There was broken glass in his pants' cuff, for Christ's sake. Belinda had made him do that. And Henry. Goddamn them all.

When he found Henry Devlin, he would come down on that scrawny little geek-ass motherfucker so hard. He would crumple him up and wipe the floor with him.

He called Belinda again. It went straight to voicemail.

Victor doubted that she'd go to the house she'd shared with Henry. It depressed her, which was why he'd moved her into his place in the first place. She'd taken the passports. Hers, Faith's. His, too, which was a serious problem. The thieving bitch might be setting him up. He wanted to call Knox, but he was nervous about Henry listening in.

Victor stopped at a drugstore, bought a burner, and charged it as he drove around, checking hotel parking lots for Belinda's car. After he'd tried the Marriott and the Indigo, he headed for the downtown Hilton, getting progressively angrier as he drove. He couldn't let Belinda just walk away. It was too late for that. She knew too much. And she was stupid enough to hurt herself for the sake of hurting him. Or even for no reason at all.

He took another swig of whiskey. "Henry Devlin!" he yelled. "I know you're listening to me, you conniving little motherfucker. I am going to find you, and you're going to wish you'd stayed in prison! When I get my hands on you, dying will look good! You hear me, fuckwit? I will *end* you!"

As he spoke, his car began to speed up. Victor jammed his foot on the brake. The car did not respond.

Holy shit. The car. It was possessed. Like something out of a horror novel. That crazy freak had hacked his fucking car.

A red light glowed ahead. Victor's car sped up, turning into oncoming traffic. Terrified drivers braked, swerved, and sideswiped each other trying to get out of the way. Horns blared, people yelled. Victor howled and clawed at the locked door as his car sped down the avenue, darting and swerving. Finally, it made a sharp left, tilted on two wheels, thumped back down and sped toward the...oh fuck. No, no, no. That was the police station.

He tried instinctively to brake, even though it was useless. His whole body arched in desperate effort as the car lurched up onto the curb and smashed into a light pole.

The crash was huge. Metal grinding, glass shattering.

When Victor finally opened his eyes in the ringing silence that followed, he was pinned behind the airbag. Car alarms rang in the distance. People were shouting. He must have cut his head because blood was dripping into his eyes. Something wet was spreading across his lap. Jesus, was it blood? Had he cut a femoral artery? Or pissed himself?

No. The distinctive smell hit him. Single malt whiskey, the remains of the flask, had spilled all over his crotch.

People gathered around the twisted frame of the car. Faces peering in. Concerned faces. A lady cop, Latina, hair braided tightly back, frowning. "Sir? Can you hear me?"

"It wasn't me," he told her. "There's a guy stalking me. My wife's ex. He hacked my car, and he drove it right through all the lights. I had no control at all. He drove it right up into the light pole. He was trying to kill me. I swear to God, it was him."

"Don't worry about that now," she said through the broken window. "An ambulance is coming."

"It wasn't me," Victor's voice sounded tinny to his own ears. "It wasn't me."

"Okay, sir," she said. "Calm down. Breathe. The medics are on the way."

Chapter Thirty-Seven

"So? Do I pass?"

Henry's body tightened at the sound of Belinda's voice. Well, not Belinda. Amber being Belinda. Brace himself as he might. He wasn't prepared for what he saw when he turned around. Amber didn't just look like Belinda. She had become Belinda, down to the last detail.

His ex-wife's kittenish face and turned-up nose. Her plump, glossy lips. Her arch smile. Her beautiful, expensive clothes. He remembered that rust-colored suit with the short skirt, and the boots she wore with it. He knew the black silk blouse. The hint of cleavage. The mane of thick, streaky blonde hair.

It was incredible, masterful work. And he hated it.

"It's amazing," he told her. "You're a genius."

She spun around, smiling, so like Belinda it made him shiver. Watching him, the smile faded. Under the make-up, the green eyes narrowed. For an instant, he glimpsed Amber and felt a surge of relief.

"What's wrong?" she asked in her own voice. "You look a little green. Are you okay?"

"Nothing. I'm fine. You just look exactly like her, and it's a shock, that's all. Sorry."

Amber was everything that Belinda wasn't. Everything he respected and admired, trusted, longed for, craved. He had taken that treasure, and asked it to dress up as trash.

That could not be good, in the grand scheme of things. That could not bode well for their future, now that he'd realized, to his surprise, that he still wanted one.

Amber's bigger, wider smile flashed across Belinda's face. "Let's hope the guy in the bank tomorrow morning feels that way, too. Shock and awe is the plan."

"Are you sure you want to do this?" Henry couldn't stop himself from asking, again. "I don't need this anymore. I really don't. We could jump ship right now. Tonight. We have enough money. This was all about spanking the two of them, to even the score, and that's done. I'm already satisfied."

"Well, damn, Henry," Amber pushed the Belinda hair out of her eyes. "You might suddenly be above it all, but I'm invested now. I want to see this through. Plus, I've pumped a lot of time and work into this project. To say nothing of money. And those two losers? They were bad to you, Henry. Selfish and wrong and evil. Stop agonizing. Let's do this thing."

"Okay," he said reluctantly. "But we'd better do it fast. Things are heating up."

"Why? Did you stir the hornet's nest again? You bad boy? Tell me."

"I, ah, hacked Victor's car," he admitted. "Drove it into a street light in front of the police station. While he was drinking."

"Whoa!" she said, impressed. "Nice!"

"He was yelling, telling me how he was going to destroy me." Henry shrugged. "I couldn't resist."

"Why would you resist?" She laughed. "They didn't."

"It didn't make me feel better," he said. "I'm glad this is almost over."

"Me, too." Amber glanced at her phone. "It's late. Want to go upstairs and consolidate our bond? I have a few tricks I could show you that would consolidate the hell out of it."

He hesitated. "I'm always up for consolidating our bond. But would you take off Belinda first?"

"Oh, God, yes. I'm not a total pervert. Give me a few minutes, and I'll be all Amber again, and oh, so ready for you." She turned in the doorway. "And Henry? One more thing."

"What's that?" he asked.

"Victor and Belinda did not destroy you," she said. "I've known a lot of destroyed people. More than my share. And that's not you. You are as far from destroyed as they come."

He sat there, thinking as he listened to Amber going up the stairs. Before, he hadn't cared if karma slammed him. His heart was already broken, his life already ruined. He didn't have any further to fall.

All that had changed now. He was flying so high, the ground was miles below his feet.

But gravity was still as merciless as ever.

Chapter Thirty-Eight

The appointment Amber had made with Derrick Berman at the bank in Weybourne was for one o'clock. They were there a few minutes early. A muscle pulsed in Henry's jaw. She reached to touch his hand. It was ice cold.

"Don't worry," she soothed. "I know what I'm doing. It's all going to be fine."

He nodded. "I know. I just wish it was me."

"Well, that's sweet. But it can't be you. You can't be Belinda."

"Remember," he said. "If this goes sideways, and you get arrested, you know what to say. I forced you to do this. I beat you, threatened you, terrified you, day in and day out. Yada-yada. You know the drill. Got it? That's what you say to them. That's the story. Clear?"

"Clear," she echoed, smiling, then remembered, and switched to Belinda's narrower, more pouting smirk.

"Swear it," he said. "You cannot leave this car until you swear it."

"Oooh! you've been working hard on your mean, mean motherfucker persona—"

"Please, Amber. Please just swear to me."

She leaned over toward him, smiling. "I'd kiss you, but I worked too hard on this make up. Okay, I swear it. You, Henry Devlin, can be the sacrificial lamb and take away the sins of the world. But it won't come to that. Because this will go smooth as buttercream frosting." She patted his knee. "Chill, babe. We're at the finish line. Excuse me while I freshen my gloss." Amber dug into the Coach bag which had served so well the day before, pulled out a tube and slicked on another layer of lip goo. Then she reached for the door handle. "Showtime."

"Knock 'em dead." Henry told her, forcing a smile.

She minced toward the bank in her high-heeled Belinda boots. It was 12:59. Right on time. This was a smallish suburban branch, so it didn't take long to find Derrick Berman. She'd checked out his headshot on the website. A short guy with a slight double chin, curly black hair and an impressive nose. The only thing she didn't know was whether or not Belinda used his first name. Best to use none at all.

"Hi there!" she said, walking into his office. "Thanks so much for making the time!"

Derrick Berman jumped up and turned to face her, holding out his hand, all smiles. "Belinda! I hope I didn't keep you waiting."

"Oh, not at all, Derrick," she assured him. "I just got here now."

"Can I get you coffee? We have pastries."

"No, thank you, not today. I'm sorry, but I'm in a bit of a rush. Could we get right to it?"

Derrick produced the form for her to sign and date. It wasn't hard. Belinda's initials and the times and dates she'd checked the box in and out ran down the page, so Amber just copied them. Forgery was one of the skills her mother had insisted upon. She pulled out the key she'd taken from Belinda at the coffee shop and followed Derrick into the vault room.

He inserted his own key next to hers, pulled out a large box. She followed him to the secure cubby, basically a closet with a desk and chair.

"Just give a holler when you're ready," he said, setting the box on the desk.

"Sure thing!" Amber waved as he closed the door.

For a second, she stood there, her heart thudding. Then she sat down and opened the deposit box.

She let out a sharp hiss of appreciation. Belinda and Victor had been busy. The box was stuffed with fat blocks of banded cash, all hundreds. Close to a million, maybe. Three small velvet sacks were squashed down the side. Amber plucked one out and untied the silk knot.

Diamonds. Small, glittering, perfect. Who knew how much they were worth? She had no idea, but it was a lot. The box was filled with money and gems that had been bought with Henry's life, reputation, freedom, future. And not one shred of remorse from those blood-sucking bastards.

They would be sorry now. And Henry would have something concrete for his effort and trouble, if she had anything to say about it.

Time was passing. She looked fine for the cameras, but it was best not to linger. Besides, Henry was out there having a slow-moving heart attack, poor guy. She pulled out the canvas tote she'd folded into the purse, and packed the cash and diamonds into it. Then she closed the deposit box, and opened the cubby door. "All set," she said, stepping out.

Derrick, who had been lingering over by the pastries, dusted the powdered sugar off his hands.

"Great," he said, hurrying over. "Let's just get this put away, and you're on your way."

He collected the box, and she followed him back into the vault as he slid it back into its place. She handed him her key. Derrick fished his out, turned them both, handed hers back, noted the exit time, and that was it. All done.

She fluttered her fingers at the bank tellers with an arch smile, and left with a toss of her blond locks and a saucy twitch of her ass. So far, so good. Shoulders back, chin up. She looked at Henry, who was gazing at her from the car with that bright, hungry gaze of his. She gave him a thumbs-up and a smile.

But not Belinda's smile. This time, the smile was her own.

Chapter Thirty-Nine

Victor was ready to stab someone by the time Reggie, his lawyer, got to the hospital to pick him up. A night in the trauma center was probably better than a night in the drunk tank. They hadn't handcuffed him to the bed rail or anything. But he was due in court later today, and that burned his aching ass.

Henry Devlin would die for this. Watching him do so would be enjoyable and cathartic. That was about the only thing that cheered Victor up.

"Look at it this way," Reggie droned on. "You didn't kill anyone. Some cars were smashed up, but no one was badly hurt. Scrapes and bruises. You've never had a DUI before. Not so much as a parking ticket. We'll get this down to a misdemeanor. There might be some community service time. But we can probably sue the manufacturer. Big time. These smart things are total bullshit. Just make sure, when we get in there, to be contrite. I know the judge. She loves contrite."

Victor growled. He wanted to squeeze Henry's neck until his eyes popped and his face turned purple. He wanted to feel the bones splinter and tendons snap under his hands.

He looked like shit. They'd cleaned him up, and Reggie had brought him clean clothes. But his forehead was bruised. They'd shaved some of the hair away to stitch the top of his scalp where it had collided with the roof light. His nose was swollen, and he had two black eyes from the air bag exploding in his face. And his ribs were cracked. It hurt to breathe.

"Let's go," he grumbled.

The nurses insisted on the obligatory routine about riding in a wheelchair to the hospital entrance. Insurance. Fucking insurance. Reggie pushed him to the elevator, then out the big revolving doors. Much as he hated the wheelchair, standing up and walking to the car was no fun, either. Everything hurt.

Reggie kept glancing at him nervously on the drive home. Like he needed anything else to piss him off.

"What?" he snarled. "Spit it out!"

"Okay. For starters, your car is totaled."

Victor sighed. "No surprises there."

"Nope."

"Your blood alcohol wasn't that bad. But they charged you with a DUI. So, like I said—"

"I was not drunk! I had one sip from my flask! Maybe two. The rest spilled in the wreck!"

"Which happened right in front of the police station. Like I said, be contrite, and I can probably get it down to misdemeanor. But I'm worried about you. Okay? You turned into oncoming traffic, jumped the curb, and probably would have gone right into the goddamn police station if you hadn't hit the streetlight. So, I gotta ask. What's going on with you?"

"I told you, Reggie. But you don't seem to be listening," Victor said grimly. "It wasn't me driving. It was that geek, Henry Devlin. He hacked my goddamn car. I know he did."

Reggie just kept driving, his mouth tight. He did not look over or meet Victor's eyes.

"Holy shit," Victor said slowly. "You don't believe me.

Reginald, we have known each other for years. I may be an asshole, but I'm not a stupid asshole. I would never do a thing like that deliberately."

"He hacked you," Reggie said slowly. "Vic. Seriously?"

"You know it's possible!" Victor bellowed. "Like these goddamn self-driving cars that go crazy and run over dogs and kids and shit! That's what happened to me!" He stopped, panting for air, which hurt. "I am telling you. My fucking car was possessed. You cannot possibly think that I would lie about this."

"Of course not," Reggie's voice was soothing, as if he were talking to a lunatic. "But you've been under a lot of stress, since Bel's ex escaped from prison, and the baby, and all that. It's understandable if you—"

"Stress? You think what just happened is me being stressed? I am telling you, Henry Devlin did all of this. That's his plan. To destroy me!"

"And why would he do that?"

"Because he's jealous," Victor bellowed.

Reggie looked at him out of the corner of his eye, and looked away quickly. "Okay. If you say so. But you also need to call your office."

Victor groaned. "Why? Is something wrong there, too?"

"They know you've had a car accident, and won't be in today. But your secretary was in tears."

"About me?" Victor found that hard to imagine. He was not Iris's favorite person.

"No." Reggie stopped for a light, one that Victor had plowed through yesterday. "She said she's been getting threatening phone calls and messages. 'We know where you live' kind of calls."

"What?"

The light changed. Reggie sped up. "Is there something you're not telling me, Vic? Because if so, well..."

"Wait, what? Now you think I'm mobbed up, as well as crazy?" Victor slammed his hand on the dashboard and immediately regretted it. His fingers were like the rest of him, swollen and sore. "It's fucking Henry again! I know it!"

"Call them. Okay? Just tell them what to do. They're floundering."

"Fine," Victor snapped. "Fine. I'll call them."

"And remember," Reggie said, dropping Victor in front of the house. "Court this afternoon. I'll pick you up. Contrite. Work on contrite."

Victor watched him walk away before he stomped into the house. His head hurt so badly he almost couldn't remember the key code. At least fuckwit Henry hadn't changed that. Yet. He could still get into his own house.

The place was a mess. Broken shit everywhere. He'd have to get the cleaning service again, which would cost a fortune. Victor found some Excedrin, swallowed three dry, peeled his clothes off and hobbled into the shower. His body throbbed like a rotten tooth.

As soon as he was out, dressed and feeling halfway human, he called the office.

"Hey Iris," he said to his secretary. "I'm home. Reggie said you had some kind of a problem? What's going on?"

"Oh, my God, Victor! Oh, my God! Your phone's been ringing nonstop. It's this scary guy who keep saying you have to meet with him about some bearer bonds!"

"Calm down, Iris. Bearer bonds? What people? Did they identify themselves?"

"No! I told them I didn't know anything about it, but they just keep calling!" Iris wailed. "I put it straight to message. But in the last message they left, the guy said, "tell that bastard I know where he lives. I know the car his wife drives. I know his baby's daycare center. It's in his best interests to call us back right now."

"Bearer bonds?" he repeated, baffled. "Are you sure these people said bearer bonds?"

"Yes, of course I'm sure! You should call the police, or the FBI. I was just about to call them, but I was waiting to talk to you before I—"

"No!" Victor barked. "Look, Iris. Calm down. I know this is upsetting. But I'm sure this is a prank. Kids. You know."

The following silence suggested that Iris did not know. " You honestly don't know what they want?"

"I haven't got a clue, Iris. I don't have any bearer bonds. I never have. If they call again, say that and hang up. But there's one more thing. I need you to call Belinda for me."

"Why? Isn't she with you?"

"No," Victor said. "She's not. We had a fight. Bel's not taking my calls. But yours would get through. On the off chance this isn't a prank—"

"But you said it was! You said you had no idea—"

"I know. And I don't. But somebody ought to just give her a heads up. Just on the off chance. She should know. That they mentioned her car. And the baby's day care. Tell her that."

"But she always gets huffy with me when I—"

"Come on!" he barked. "Her baby is being threatened by criminal goons, and you don't have the fucking nerve to call and warn her about it?"

"Okay. Fine. Fine." Iris huffed. "I'll call her."

Victor thanked her and hung up. Yesterday's cold coffee was still in the pot. He poured some into a mug, and stuck it in the microwave. As he slapped the door shut, it occurred to him.

That prick Henry was probably watching him at this very moment.

"Henry!" Victor yelled. "You peeping Tom dipshit! Are you listening? You are not going to win this! Go on, hit me, fuckwad! Give it your best shot! Asshole!"

Snap. The microwave stopped humming. The LED lights on the appliances switched off all at once, like a constellation of stars winking out.

Victor pulled out the cup of coffee, which was still stone cold, and threw the mug across the room.

Chapter Forty

Her baby is being threatened, and you don't have the fucking nerve to call and warn her about it?

The words rang in Henry's head, twanging like discordant strings being plucked all at once. Sitting in the car parked down from the bank, he stared at the open laptop. The monitor was open on Victor's kitchen.

What had he done? Faith was just a baby. And the DiAngelos were threatening her.

Henry realized that he had buried everything he felt for his daughter under his landslide of hatred for Belinda and Victor. He had compartmentalized her so completely, divorced her from Belinda and Victor so totally, that he'd never even thought about the consequences of siccing Leon and the DiAngelos on them. Faith. His baby girl.

Victor didn't give a shit about her, so she would be useless to Leon or the DiAngelos as leverage. But they didn't know that, and they wouldn't figure it out until it was too late for Faith.

Belinda was sloppy with her internet hygiene. A chronic over-sharer. It was one of the few things they had genuinely argued about. Faith was dangerously easy to find. He'd always hated that.

Movement caught his eye. For a second, he saw Belinda walking out of the bank. But it was Amber, waltzing along in those fur-trimmed boots, clutching the camel coat around her in the icy wind. She gave him a swift thumbs-up and flashed her gorgeous smile.

Henry stared at the tote bag she was carrying, and what they were doing here came back in a blinding rush. He had actually sent Amber into that bank to impersonate his wife and steal whatever was in that bag. That the theft was morally justified meant nothing in the eyes of the law. Just like the fact that Victor didn't give a shit about Faith meant nothing to Leon and the DiAngelos. Faith and Amber were the only two people on earth he could honestly say he loved, and he had just used them both.

He had put them in danger. Which made him a total asshole. An irresponsible fuckwit.

Amber opened the door and got into the car. "Jackpot," she crowed, hoisting the tote onto her lap and cradling it like a baby. "Just like you thought. Diamonds! Cash!" Grinning, she unzipped the tote, and held the top open so he could see. "I crushed it, if I do say so myself," she said, zipping it back up again. "Poor little Derrick was eating out of my hand."

"So it all went smoothly?"

"As buttercream frosting, just like I said." She glanced at him. "Henry?" Her eyes narrowed. "Are you okay? Shouldn't we be speeding away from here toward the highway?"

"Yeah." He started the car. "Yeah, of course. I'm, ah, glad there was something worthwhile in the box. After all the trouble you went to."

Amber shrugged. "Why shouldn't those two dirt bags bankroll our new lifestyle as mysterious and deeply tanned expats, living in a deluxe beach house with no visible means of support? Subsisting on fine cheeses, raw oysters and fresh fruit?"

He tried to smile as Amber put on her seat belt. She placed the bag stuffed with cash tenderly at her feet and frowned at him. "What the hell is up with you?"

"I was listening to a conversation at Victor's house. His office got some calls about the bonds. Scary calls."

Amber's eyes widened. "Oh? Good. So it's working. Like you hoped. That's what we wanted, right?"

"No," he admitted. "They threatened Faith."

Amber stared at him. "Well, shit, she said after a minute. "That is bad. They should send the kid away. Not that anyone would take my advice." She looked around at the street, the bank on the block behind them. "Um. Don't you think we ought to get out of here?"

Henry put the car in gear, then put it back in park. He shouldn't ask this of her. It was dangerous. Too much.

Amber read the plea in his eyes and turned to look across the street. Three buildings up, barely a block away, there was a bright yellow house. A mural with rainbows and unicorns, a knight, a dragon, and a princess had been painted on the side of the building. Above it, smiling bumblebees held a banner that read, Busy Bees Daycare and After-School Program.

He saw her eyes go wide the minute that realization dawned. "Oh, my God," she said. "Henry. You have got to be fucking kidding me."

"I'll give you everything you got out of the safe deposit box if you help me now," Henry said. "Every last thing. Faith is in danger. I did this to her. And I have to fix it."

"What good will your hot diamonds do me? This is kidnapping, Henry! She's a baby! They don't let that slide! Everyone will be on Victor and Belinda's side, and you will look like a psycho who snatched an innocent little girl to do God knows what to her, purely out of revenge. And I'll be right in the middle of it. No, I'll be in jail. For life. Except it'll be a short life, because I'll get shivved in the shower. Inmates hate bitches who mess with kids. And this is way riskier than the bank. Derrick saw Belinda once in a blue moon. At that place, they see her twice a day!"

"I swear. Like I said. If they get us, this is all on me. It was my idea, and I coerced—"

"Oh shut the fuck up, Henry," Amber snapped. "You're so full of shit." She glared at him. Then she grabbed the Coach bag, opened the door, got out, and stalked off toward the daycare.

Chapter Forty-One

The freezing wind was making her eyes tear up. Amber dug in her purse for a Kleenex. The mascara was waterproof, but it would still run, and if she wasn't careful, she'd lose a lens. Then she'd be kidnapping a kid while sporting one green eye and one yellow one. Pretty fucking memorable.

She was being such a baby. Come on. What did she expect? Henry was getting what he could while the getting was good. That was what people did. They used each other. Even if they loved each other. Especially then. And Henry was no saint. No genius, either, exposing his baby to Leon and the mob like that. A boneheaded move if there ever was one.

Then again, she'd played her part, and she hadn't exactly thought about it, either.

Damn. Kidnapping was a logistical nightmare. You couldn't stash the stolen item in a vault. You had to feed it, give it water, food, a place to pee, a place to sleep. Keep it from yelling, freaking out, fighting back. As crimes went, it was very labor intensive. She wanted no part of it.

Amber squared her shoulders, took a deep breath, and flounced up the walk and into Busy Bees.

The front hall had been turned into a lobby. Cubbies were filled with mini boots. Tiny coats hung on a rack. Kid's drawings, bunnies and dogs and stick figures covered the walls. The young woman behind the desk gave her a puzzled look.

"Mrs. Devlin? You're early. Is everything okay? You look, um, different."

Amber beamed. "Yes! Thanks for noticing. I just went to the salon. Got my hair done."

"Oh. Well. My compliments. You look very nice."

"Thanks!" she said in her best Belinda voice. "So we've had a sudden change of plans. We're going on a spur-of-the-moment trip. We're taking off in about an hour, so I need to pick up Faith now."

"I wish you'd called before." The woman looked disapproving. "We just got Faith down for her nap, and it took some doing, let me tell you."

"Believe me, I know," Amber said. She looked around. "Is her stroller around here somewhere?"

"Usual place," the woman said, getting to her feet. "Right where you left it this morning."

Amber put on her best condescending-bitch smile. "Could you bring it out for me?"

The woman rolled her eyes, but she complied, thank God. She disappeared behind a swinging door with more cartoon bumblebees on it. These were holding their fingers up to their lips and saying, Shhh! Quiet Room. A minute later, she reappeared, a toddler, whom Amber assumed had to be Faith, squirming wildly in her arms.

At the sight of the stroller, Faith let out a squall that made everyone jump. Amber had no idea what to do with the stroller, but she had to get out of here. She grabbed Faith. The bewildered toddler flailed and shrieked, trying in every way possible to rat Amber out for her subterfuge. Too bad, kid. Being preverbal sucked rocks.

"Could you help me with the stroller?" Amber yelled. "She's so fussy. Teething, I think."

The woman sighed and threw her a look that made Amber think perhaps neither Faith nor Belinda were her favorite clients. "Sure," she said, grudgingly.

The woman cranked and jerked the device into a useful shape and Amber fought to strap the kid into it. It was like wrestling a rabid raccoon. Faith, listless though she looked, had a tough, wiry strength in her tiny frame.

It took all three of them to get the kid into her stroller, and four more kids were wailing from the nap room by the time Faith was properly restrained. Still more were shrieking when Amber finally pushed the wailing child out the door. The staff were clearly grateful to see them go. They hadn't copped to Amber's disguise, but Faith certainly hadn't been fooled.

Henry leapt out of the car as they came down the street. Not the smartest move, considering the security cameras probably watching, but there was no way Amber could have gotten the kid into the car by herself.

"Here." She shoved the stroller at him. "There you go, buddy. Have at."

Henry swiftly unbuckled the screaming child and lifted her writhing body. "We have to get her a car seat," he said. "It's not safe to just throw her into the car. We have to—"

"Not safe? Seriously, you have the nerve to say that to me right now?"

He had the grace to look shamefaced. "We need stuff. Diapers, wipes, juice—"

"There's a few diapers in the stroller pocket. That'll tide you over." She took care to say 'you,' not 'we.' There was no 'we' in this equation.

Henry lifted the trunk, shook the stroller shut with one deft, expert jerk, and stowed it, single-handed. "Since we don't have a car seat, could you sit in the back with her until we get to the—"

"Oh, hell, no. I'll drive. You sit in the back with her. Stay down low so no one sees you. Get reacquainted. Good luck with that."

To his credit, Henry got into the back seat with without argument. Amber tossed her purse onto passenger seat the seat, did a quick check to make sure the tote was all zipped up, and took the quickest route to the highway, hoping to God the cops did not see them. The kid howled energetically, mile after mile.

Her happy buzz was gone. Before, things had been complicated. Now, they were really complicated. They were fugitives, marked for death by multiple killers, carrying stolen bearer bonds, dirty cash, hot diamonds, and a stolen toddler who produced sounds at a decibel level she had previously only imagined. So much for flying under the radar. With this one move, they had pushed their luck too far. Or rather, Henry's luck. Their luck was no longer linked.

And she had a sinking feeling that her own luck had just run out.

Chapter Forty-Two

"But...but that's just not possible," Belinda said blankly. "I wasn't here before!"

First, Derrick looked distressed. Then he looked defensive. "Yes, you were, Mrs. Devlin. You stood right there an hour ago and asked for access to your safe deposit box, which I gave you. You left about fifteen minutes later. Here, look at the log." He tapped the paper. "Look. See?"

He showed her a form that some woman had scrawled her own name on. She shoved it back. "That's not my signature, and I wasn't here!"

Derrick looked at her as if she were a madwoman. "Then whose do you think it is?"

"Not mine!" Belinda yelled. "Because I wasn't here! Did she show you any ID?"

"No. Of course not. You never do, because we know each other!"

"You don't know shit!" Belinda shrieked. She scrabbled in her bag, found her passport and slapped it down on the desk in front of him. "You have been scammed, you idiot! That woman was not me!"

"Good afternoon, ma'am. What seems to be the problem

here?" It was an older woman, the branch manager. She had cold eyes and a tight, nervous smile.

Derrick turned to her. "One of our clients came in here about an hour ago, Belinda Devlin," he told her. "I was the one who opened her account and rented her a safe deposit box last year. Now this woman just shows up and tells me that she is Mrs. Devlin, which frankly, doesn't track. She's nothing like the Belinda Devlin that I know, and I never—"

"So just look at my passport, already! I need to get into my safe deposit box, if she hasn't emptied it already! What kind of bullshit bank is this?"

"This woman probably stole Mrs. Devlin's ID," Derrick said, his eyes flicking over the document and then at her tousled hair, her blotchy face, tear-reddened eyes, and rumpled sweatshirt. "This is definitely not the Mrs. Devlin I know."

"You lying piece of shit!" she hissed. "You're just covering your own ass!"

"Ma'am," the older woman said. "Please don't use that language on the premises. If you continue to make a scene, I'll be forced to call the police."

Belinda let out a cackle. "The police," she echoed. "Hah! Wouldn't that just be a hoot." She dug into her purse, feeling around for the satin case where she kept it. "I don't know how she got in. I keep the key with me. I have it right here, so…"

Her voice trailed off as they looked at the key she held. This key had a grubby, painted rubber Minnie Mouse figurine dangling from the ring. It swung back and forth with the force she'd used to whip it out of the case.

"That does not look like our key, ma'am." Derrick's voice was triumphant.

Belinda forced her mouth to close, each new thought displacing the last in her head. This could be Henry. Or Victor. That lying, cheating son of a bitch Victor. He'd gotten sick of her at last. He'd found some whore who looked like her, and he'd hired her to clean out their stash. Maybe he was setting her up the way he'd set up Henry.

She turned on her heel and walked out, across the lobby, past the staring bank tellers, out into the icy wind. As soon as she'd closed the car door, she turned on her phone and called Victor.

"Bel!" He picked up even before it rang. "Thank God! Where the fuck are you? I've been trying to—"

"You piece of shit. You're setting me up, aren't you? You took all the money! You're trying to offload me! You're going to leave me to take the fall, like we did to Henry! Right?"

"Bel. Bel, calm down. You're being crazy. I need to tell you something important. I've been trying to call, but you've had your phone off. I asked to Reggie to call you, and Iris—"

"I'm not interested in talking to Reggie or Iris. Did you hire some bitch to clean out the safe deposit box? Did you?"

There was a pause. "What?" Victor's voice went low and tense. "What the hell are you saying?"

"It's over, Victor. You know what? I don't care anymore. Fuck whoever you want for as long as you can, because I'm turning you in, you scumbag son of a bitch. What we did to Henry was shitty and wrong. And you know what? It feels good to say that out loud. I'll confess everything. I'll tell everyone what a dirty, scheming thief you are—"

"And do time yourself, for being my accomplice? You think you could handle prison, Bel? I'm telling you right now, you can't. So forget the crisis of conscience, okay? Shut up and listen! We are in a shitload of trouble. I don't know anything about the safe deposit box, but mobsters are threatening us! They called here to threaten you and Faith. That's what I have been trying to tell you."

"Mobsters?" Belinda held the phone away and stared at it before she put it back to her ear. "What the fuck did you do, Victor?"

"Nothing! I swear. It's Henry. He's set us up so that it looks like we stole money from one of the families. Something to do with bearer bonds."

"Bearer bonds?" she echoed stupidly.

"Yes. Some shit about bearer bonds. I have no idea, I swear. Is Faith with you? Bel!" He shouted when she didn't reply. "Is Faith with you?"

"No. She's at daycare. Like always."

Victor grunted. "She might not be there when you show up. And if you're going to fall to pieces on me like this, maybe it's just as well. They're fucking welcome to her, if you want to know the truth."

"Wha...what?" She swallowed hard. "What the hell do you mean by that? Who's welcome to her?"

"I think you know." Victor was using that soft, taunting voice that made her belly clench. "I liked partnering with you, Bel. But I did not enjoy being a threesome with that screaming parasite. She ruined our lives. Admit it. We were better off before."

Belinda's mouth worked. She was shocked speechless. "But...but...you told me to—"

"Yeah, yeah. I told you to go ahead with the pregnancy. I didn't know how bad it would be, okay? So sue me. So if the mobsters take her, and she's not at the daycare anymore when you get there, well... problem solved, right? We'll be shocked and sad. Everyone will feel so sorry for us. Such a tragedy. Robbed of our only child, etc."

She dragged in a shuddering breath. "You are such a fucking monster." She tossed her phone onto the seat as she sped through the streets toward Busy Bees.

When she got there, she slipped on the icy walkway outside and stumbled through the door, thudding painfully down onto one knee. The new girl behind the desk, Holly? Jessica? That was it, Jessica, was staring at her.

Belinda felt her heart stop when she saw the confused look on the girl's face. Oh, shit. No.

All at once, every ounce of love for her whining, obnoxious, difficult, beautiful, perfect baby girl rose up in her throat and threatened to throttle her. "Where is she?" she demanded. "Where's my baby?"

Jessica was already backing toward the swinging doors, hands up, shaking her head.

"Where is she?" Belinda barely recognized that scratchy roar as her own voice.

Children were crying. The director, Mrs. Harvey, was reaching out to touch her and then yanking her hand away, as if Belinda were on fire. Which seemed about right.

"Don't tell me. Let me guess," she snarled. "Some bitch who looks just like me just walked in here and took my baby. Am I right? And you let her do it!" Her voice rose to a shriek. "You just fucking let her do it! I paid through the nose! I trusted you to look after her, and you just handed her over!"

"But…but she looked just like you," Jessica said, sounding lost. "She could have been your twin! She was identical. Except that she looked, ah…" Her voice trailed off.

Better. The unspoken word hung in the air.

"Jessica." Mrs Harvey was fighting to remain calm. "Dial nine-one-one."

"Yeah," Belinda said. "You do that. And right after that, you'll be hearing from my lawyers."

She stumbled out of the door. Her ears roared so loudly, she barely hear Mrs. Harvey standing outside the door in the freezing cold, calling her name.

Belinda got back into her car. When Henry had first broken out of prison, she'd fixed tracking devices, those little button things that talked to your phone, onto Faith's stroller and car seat. She'd never told Victor, because he would have called her paranoid, and she was so fucking done with that.

It wasn't paranoid. In fact, it was the smartest thing she'd ever done. She pulled out her phone, scrolled to the app, and switched it on. At first, nothing happened. Then a map loaded. In the middle of it was a little red dot, moving slowly. Faith's stroller, heading south on the Interstate toward the city.

Belinda started the car. She was going to kick some ass, get her baby back, and run as far from this place as she could go.

She was ready. Packed already, passports and everything. She just had to get her baby back from that thieving whore before Victor caught up with them, or the mobsters did something horrible to them.

The mobsters were welcome to Victor, however. Good fucking riddance.

Chapter Forty-Three

Victor walked across his backyard, carrying the cheap drugstore phone he'd bought the day before. When he was far enough away that he was sure whatever listening devices Henry had inside couldn't pick him up, he punched in Joseph Knox's number.

"This is Joe Knox," the private investigator said. "Who am I talking to?"

"Victor Shattuck. I'm in a situation. I need your help."

"Okay. Where are you calling from? Is this a secure phone?"

"I'm outside my house and it's a piece of shit I bought yesterday in a drugstore."

"Good enough. Shoot."

"You said you know where Henry Devlin is staying? And that you were getting in touch with a guy who could take care of it?"

Knox paused. "All true," he said finally. "But it doesn't happen overnight. You're going to need to be patient."

"No time for patience," Victor said. "It has to be today."

"Then you're talking to the wrong guy."

"You're not getting it" Victor said. "I'm take care of this

320

myself. Believe me. I'm not outsourcing a goddamn thing. I just need to know where he is."

"Victor," Knox said, handling him. "Slow down. We can get this done. I know you are angry. But you're not a professional. This guy is dangerous. Truly."

"Don't fucking handle me!" Victor yelled. Then he added, "And don't tell me he's dangerous. He's destroyed my entire life. Yesterday, he tried to kill me. I don't have time to be patient. I'll pay whatever you need."

"Okay," Knox soothed. "Okay, I get it. How do you want to do it?"

"You're going to get me a gun. Unregistered. With a silencer."

There was a long pause. "It'll cost you," Knox said finally.

"That isn't a problem. I told you. I don't care."

"Calm down. I'll text you how much money you need to bring. Then hire a car. A cab, a limo, a rideshare, whatever. Get out at Washington Square Park, and call me again. I'll pick you up and take you right where you want to go."

Five minutes later, the crappy little phone chirped. The dollar amount the man had texted him was eye watering.

Victor went into the garage, threw aside a stack of tarps, shifted a workbench and opened the safe that even Belinda didn't know about. There was just barely enough left in it. He found an old duffel bag, back from when he used to go to the gym, and put the money, a baseball hat and an extra sweater in it.

Then he pulled up the rideshare app and ordered up a car.

Chapter Forty-Four

Wojniac's phone buzzed. The text was from Pauly, who had spent the night and all of today with the DiAngelo crew, discreetly watching Shattuck's house.

> Shattuck on the move.

> Following.

"He's moving." Wojniac put the car in gear and glanced at Daly, who was sitting in the passenger seat. "You monitor Pauly on your phone."

"I don't like it that the DiAngelos will get there first," Leon growled from the back.

"Chill." Daly shot the guy an impatient look. "They're the ones leading us to Amber, so there's not a hell of a lot we can do about it."

"You really think this guy knows where she is?"

"DiAngelo seems to think so," Wojniac said. "And Shattuck is the only guy who ever redeemed one of those bonds, according to Pauly. So yeah. I think he's going straight to her, and so will we, if we follow him."

"Is he fucking her?"

Daly shrugged. "I assume so. But that's not our concern."

"I'll decide what concerns me. Let's get the fucker. After he hands over the bonds, I'll make him eat his own balls."

Chapter Forty-Five

Amber kept trying to catch Henry's eye in the rearview mirror, but no dice. He was deeply absorbed in a complex conversation with Faith, conducted in coos, grunts, and peeping sounds. The baby had her grubby, drool-slimed fist wound into his beard and was pulling on it. She stared earnestly into his face, like the world depended on whatever senseless nonsense he spewed. As if Henry was her savior, her knight in shining armor, who would make everything okay.

Hah. Poor kid. Amber had fallen into that trap herself, and had less of an excuse than Faith, being almost thirty-seven, not two. Henry's soft, wondering look was infinitely seductive. She knew that look. How irresistible it was.

"We're almost to the bridge." Her voice was sharp, trying to snap him back to the real world. The one where about twenty people wanted to kill them and they'd just stolen a shit-load of cash, diamonds, and a baby.

"Okay," Henry murmured. "I can hardly believe it, but it feels like she actually remembers me."

Oh, please. Amber's eyes were sore from rolling. By the

time she found parking three blocks from the Grudbergs' house, Henry was tickling Faith, who was giggling madly.

They walked back to the house; her carrying the tote bag of cash and diamonds, which he'd evidently forgotten all about. Him carrying Faith and the stroller, oblivious to her and everything else in the world. Inside, Henry took the baby up to the bed Amber had been using, stroller still under one arm. Amber watched from the door as he changed her.

"I should probably keep her in the stroller to nap," he said. "Just in case we have to move fast, and she's still asleep."

"Go for it," she said coolly.

If Henry noticed her frigid tone, he didn't show it. Instead, he got to work padding the stroller with one of the Grudbergs' very expensive afghans and nestling Faith into it, weaving her hands through loops and straps, and snapping all the buttons together as if he'd been doing it all his life. Then he jiggled and jostled the stroller, crooning until Faith's eyes drooped. She fell asleep in second. Henry tucked her up in the folds of the blanket so she looked like a little burrito with a head.

"I need to return the rental car," he whispered. "We were probably caught in God knows how many cameras driving it. We need a new one from another rental place, and a pack of diapers, and some wipes, and some baby-friendly food. I'll take care of it as fast as possible." He glanced over his shoulder at her. "Are you ready to leave?"

"I have some packing to do. I was too distracted yesterday."

He nodded. "Do it fast. You can keep an eye on the baby, too?"

She gritted her teeth. "You keep an eye on her. I'll rent the car. With cash."

"You can't. They won't take cash. You can't rent without a card." His voice was apologetic. "I'll be quick. I should have rented two cars this morning. It would have been smarter."

A lot of things, Amber thought, would have been smarter. Drawing the line at kidnapping, for instance.

"I'm sorry," he said. He had an uncanny, no scratch that, fucking irritating, ability to know what she was thinking. "I'm so sorry about all this. I know it's a really hard left turn, but I—"

"Spare me. Whatever clever speech you've dreamed up, I don't want to hear it. Go get the car and get your ass back fast, because I am not cut out for babysitting. Is that perfectly clear?"

"She's sleeping, Amber," he protested. "She's harmless."

"Hah. Right. Go."

A couple of minutes later, Amber heard the downstairs door close. Peeking out the bedroom window, she watched as he vanished down the street. When he was gone, she stared at the sleeping toddler. That kid terrified her. So this was why she had never been even minimally tempted to reproduce, and had always made a big deal about taking precautions. In fact, she'd been obsessive about it.

The world was just too dangerous. She could barely keep her own self alive and kicking. Forget being responsible for a helpless, flailing creature that couldn't talk, or listen to reason, or take instruction. One who couldn't or wouldn't shut up on command, and regularly made sounds as loud as a train whistle.

Amber packed quietly, in mortal fear that the little gremlin would wake up while Henry was still gone. Only the items and the personas which had proved most useful went into the case. She left Betty Lipschitz behind completely. Partly because the costume was so bulky, and partly because she didn't want Betty's mildewed coat stinking up the rest of her gear. Her favorite make-up, latex, facial prosthesis, and dental inserts all went in the suitcase.

Looking around, she realized that she was leaving way too much information behind for the Grudbergs to puzzle over when they came home. But it was too late to clear it all out and leave the house as she found it, which was the professional, courteous thing to do.

They shouldn't even still be here. They should be speeding down the highway, halfway to nowhere. Unencumbered, rich, and free. The world at their feet.

Now they needed to stop for diapers, wipes, a car seat, a sippy cup. She'd been telling herself a romantic story about her and Henry, wild and on the run. A modern-day Bonnie and Clyde minus the multiple homicides and the rain of bullets, and hopefully with a much happier ending.

Who knew what went on in Henry's head? Now he had his baby back, his priorities would shift. She wasn't exactly a maternal role model. Even if she'd wanted to be. A thieving, aging ex-con artist, ex-showgirl, ex-mob moll. Her resumè did not scream 'nuclear family'. Even one that was on the lam.

Looking at the little clock on the bedside table, she felt a blind impulse to run. She could have, but now she was chained to a goddamn sleeping baby. She couldn't just abandon the poor kid. Faith's skinny face was wizened, like a monkey's. Hadn't they been feeding her?

Amber returned to her packing, taking care to get the second suitcase out without making a racket. She had no idea how long toddlers napped. She'd probably traumatized the poor kid, snatching her out of Busy Bees like a raptor snagging a rabbit. She'd be punished for it when Faith woke up and found Henry not here. Hoo boy, would she ever.

Amber had just got the last suitcase down into the entry, wincing at every scrape and bump, bracing for a shrill yell of rage from the bedroom when the doorbell rang. The buzz made her practically jump out of skin. Henry must have forgotten his key. He had the timing from hell today.

She glanced at the little monitor screen, which was blank, of course, because Henry had disabled the video camera. She yanked open the door. "It's about time you—"

"Fucking *bitch!*" Belinda screamed, leaping at her.

Amber tumbled backward and fell onto the suitcases, knocking them over like dominoes. "Whoa! Back off!" she yelled.

"Back off? You took my money! You took my diamonds! You took my baby!"

As the furious woman leapt on top of her, punching and flailing, Amber decided that the list got Belinda's priorities about right. Baby a distant third. She landed a punch to Belinda's throat that made the other woman gasp and cough.

"You didn't seem all that interested in her, to be honest," Amber panted, scrambling to her feet.

"You don't know shit about me or my baby! Did Victor hire you? Or Henry? You fucking whore! Where is she? I know she's here! Where is Faith?"

Amber ducked a wild, pin-wheeling slap, but Belinda caught some of her hair. Amber replied with a finger stab to the eyes. Belinda squawked and lunged again. They pitched over, rolling on the carpet, scratching and slapping and grappling. Amber finally managed to get on top, at the price of a knee to the belly that knocked the air out of her. God, the woman was strong. She saw where Faith's crazed raccoon energy came from. She held Belinda by the throat as Belinda scratched, punched, flopped, bucked.

"How did you find this place?" she gasped.

"Did you think I wouldn't put trackers on my baby's stuff, you dumb bitch?"

Yeah, they definitely should have thought of that. Amber got in an uppercut beneath Belinda's chin, which knocked the other woman back for long enough that she could crab-walk sideways and get to her feet. Backing away, she grabbed one of the irons from the fireplace and held it like a spear.

"Get back!" she gasped out. "And shut up! You'll wake the baby!"

"*My* baby!" Belinda grabbed a brass lamp from a corner

table and brandished it, looking Amber over. She laughed, sounding shrill and crazy. "She's my baby, and don't forget it. So you're the slut Barbie version of me, huh? Did you steal my clothes right out of my closet?"

"No, just your husband," Amber shot back. "The good one. Not that perverted troll that you traded him in for. You picked the wrong guy. You dumb cow."

"Where is she? If you hurt her, I'm taking you to fucking pieces!"

"Hurt her?" Amber paused, startled. "You mean Faith? Why on earth would I hurt Faith?"

Belinda let out a sobbing, breathless laugh as she swung the lamp. "Don't play dumb. I know they're paying you to hurt me. But I'm going to take my baby away from all this. You can all just fuck each other over for the money if you want to. I don't care. Just leave us alone. Forget that Faith and I exist. That's all I want!"

Belinda swung the lamp. Amber blocked with the fire iron, but staggered back, knocking two of the Grudbergs' family gallery of photographs off the wall. They shattered at her feet. She regained her footing and lunged before Belinda had time to wind up with the brass lamp again. Barreling into her, Amber knocked the woman backward.

They landed together on the coffee table. The glass broke with a crash. The wooden table frame crunched and buckled beneath their weight.

In the stillness that followed, Amber took stock. She didn't think she was sliced open, or bleeding out. Belinda, however, was not moving. There was a lot of blood on her face.

Amber pushed herself up, glass crunching beneath her palms and knees. She touched Belinda's throat, and felt a rapid, fluttering pulse. She was all cut up, but not dead yet. The room was cold. The front door was still open. Cold wind swept across the floor and ruffled the curtains.

Belinda's eyes and locked onto hers. Amber felt the woman's muscles tense and bunch.

"Stop," she warned. "Don't move. You're lying on a pile of broken glass. You'll bleed out."

"Doesn't matter," Belinda croaked. "Help me up. I want my damn baby back."

A strange clarity settled over Amber as she stared into Belinda's tormented eyes. She remembered the look in her mom's eyes when she was trying to find a way to get them away from Sid. That wild desperation.

"I didn't hurt your baby," she said. "I would never hurt her. I only took her because Henry begged me to. To keep her safe."

"Henry." Belinda laughed, then stopped, wincing. "God-damn Henry."

"You can't blame him," Amber said. "He sicced those people on Victor. Then he found out afterward that they were threatening Faith. He didn't do it to punish you. He did it to be free."

Belinda stared at her, a long, searching look. Amber nodded. "Don't get me wrong," she said. "He's disgusted with you. But he mostly wants to punish Victor."

"Good," Belinda spat. "Victor is a fucking monster."

"And you're just noticing this now?" Amber couldn't stop herself.

They stared at each other for a long, charged moment before Amber reached out, cautiously.

Belinda hesitated, then took her cold, shaking hands. It was hard to grip, both of them freezing, shaking, slippery and bleeding. Finally, Amber managed to help Belinda sit up, then roll onto her knees, and get to her feet. She shook glass from her hair and brushed it off her shirt. She was still dripping blood steadily, and her face was chalky white beneath the smeared blood.

"Where is Faith?" Belinda asked.

"Like I said," Amber replied. "Upstairs in her stroller, asleep. Perfectly fine."

Belinda's lip quivered. "I can't let Henry take her away. She's my baby."

"I can't let you take her now," Amber said. "Wait for Henry. Talk to him. It's not my decision to make, after everything that's happened between the two of you. God knows, he's not in a good place to keep a baby. But he was afraid she'd get hurt. We didn't take her to punish you. I swear to God."

Belinda snorted. "And the diamonds?" she croaked. "Was that to punish me?"

"Oh, come on. Do you blame him? After what you did?" Amber couldn't keep the edge from her voice.

Belinda shook her head. "No. I'm sorry now," she said dully. "If that's any comfort to him. I'm sorry. I'm sorry as hell about all of it. All I want now is Faith. She's all that matters now."

"Let me call him. I'll tell him to get back here and deal with this."

Amber knew what Henry would do. He didn't really have a choice. He wasn't Faith's biological father. He would be heartbroken, but he would hand the kid over, and probably fill Belinda's purse with diamonds or cash for the kid's upkeep, too.

Selfless, ill-advised generosity was a tricky personality trait in a boyfriend, but that was why she loved him, so she just had to suck it up.

As Amber reached for the phone, Belinda said, "I bet he told you he was going to cut you in, right? That you two were going to live happily ever after on the beach somewhere?"

"That's none of your business," Amber said crisply.

Belinda gave her a pitying look. "Oh God. You really think he's coming back, don't you? Jesus, girl. You're almost as gullible as me."

"Of course he's coming back." Amber's gaze flicked to the shelf where she'd put the satchel with the bearer bonds.

The satchel wasn't there. The shelf was empty.

Belinda nodded knowingly, wiping blood from her mouth. "Yeah," she said. "Yeah. I know that look on your face. What did he say? That he was going to get some stuff for the baby? That's a classic."

"He'll be back," Amber said stiffly. "I know he will."

Belinda shook her head. "Welcome to the Gullible Sluts Club." She sounded exhausted. "Membership costs you everything you have."

Belinda dragged herself upstairs to find Faith while Amber searched for the bonds. She looked in the living room, the kitchen, the dining room. She opened every drawer, every cupboard. The fridge, the freezer, the breadbox and the oven. The linen closet, even the washer and dryer. When she opened the recycling bin, the book of opera music was right on top. The cover was missing, but the book was still folded open to *Ah! Perchè non posso odiarti, infidel, com'io vorrei!*, the song Henry had sung to her that first day they spent together.

Why can I not despise you, the song asked. Huh. She'd probably learn how pretty damn quick.

Slamming the bin shut, she ran upstairs, dripping blood on the carpet, and searched the cupboards and shelves. Incredible that the kid could continue to sleep through all this. Though come to think of it, that kid had slept through some godawful ruckuses before. Maybe she'd trained herself to screen it all out. Yay for coping mechanisms. But she didn't have time to empathize with Henry's little gremlin right now. She searched the bathrooms, walk-in closets, chests of drawers, bookcases.

She found the satchel in the room that Henry had used before she dragged him into her own bed. It was empty.

Well, fuck. She went into the bedroom where Faith was still fast asleep, head in her stroller. Belinda stood by the window. She turned around, eyes wide with alarm, putting her finger to her lips.

"What?" Amber hissed.

"Victor! He's out there. On the street. We have to hide Faith. He hates her. He told me he wanted the mob to kidnap her. She's not safe with him." Tears ran down her bloodied face. "I'll go downstairs and slow him down. Take her, please!"

"Take her where?" Amber was already struggling with the buckles and straps, bending to lift the sleeping toddler.

"Up onto the roof! I'll say you and Henry left town already and took the baby with you. Go!"

Amber went. She ran up the top flight of stairs and paused on the landing. She needed to hear what was going on.

She sank down onto the bottom step of the last ramp of stairs, out of sight, jiggling the baby and listening with all her strength.

Chapter Forty-Six

The gun felt heavy and reassuring in Victor's cold, sweaty hand, shoved deep in the pocket of his long coat. Good as his word, Knox had driven him straight to the townhouse. It had been clear as soon as they saw it that something had happened, or was in the course of happening. The front door was wide open.

"Looks like someone might have gotten here already," Knox mused under his breath. "How many enemies does this guy have?"

Victor's jaw cramped. "I'm his worst. That son of a bitch is mine."

"Fine. Then go for it, tough guy. Lead the charge."

Victor ran up the stairs, peering into the house. There was no sign of anyone moving. Knox followed a few steps behind, walking more softly. Victor crept into the foyer, pointing the gun swiftly in one direction and then the other, as he'd seen cops do in movies, but there was no one to be seen.

The foyer was crowded with big suitcases which lay strewn every which way.

"Don't touch anything," Knox warned. "You didn't bring gloves."

They entered the living room. The place was a shambles, broken glass everywhere, furniture overturned. One more step, and they both stopped short at the gruesome apparition swaying at the bottom of the stairs. It was Belinda, bloodied and slashed, with blood-stiffened hair. Her eyes looked wild. Her nose was bleeding so heavily, her mouth, chin, and chest were a wet, grisly red.

"Victor," she whimpered. "Victor. Oh God, Victor. Help me."

Victor recoiled a step. "Bel? What the hell happened?"

"They beat me! They cut me! They took my baby and left with all the money! All the diamonds!"

In a flash of brutal clarity, Victor saw how it would play out. He could try to retrieve that stupid, squalling brat who made his life a ceaseless hell of sleepless nights, constant inconvenience, and tedious arguments. Or he could let the baby go. Try to recuperate what he and Belinda had been pre-Faith.

But Belinda in this state, blood-smeared, wild-eyed and desperate, repelled him. She was deranged, degraded. She was damaged goods. She would sink him like a stone.

He looked over at Knox. "She told me she'd roll over on me," he said. "Just this morning."

Knox tut-tutted under his breath. "Problematic."

"I don't suppose you'd, ah…" Victor trailed off, eyeing Knox suggestively.

Knox let out a sharp laugh. "That's about what I figured. You don't have the nards for it. You should have waited for my guy, Vic. I tried to tell you."

"It was Henry I wanted to kill," Victor retorted. "I'd rip that asshole apart with my bare hands. But I didn't anticipate, you know. This."

Belinda looked wildly back and forth between them as his meaning sank in. "Victor, no! You can't be serious! I would never hurt you! I love you!" Her eyes widened, panicked, as he pulled the gun out of his pocket. "No! Don't do this! I was really angry when I said that today, about going to the cops! I wouldn't ever do that to you! I was at the end of my rope!"

Victor tasted something corrosive bubbling in the back of his throat and blocked her words out of his mind. She held her bloodied hands up, trying to shield herself, crying and pleading. He looked to Knox for guidance, courage, permission.

Knox shook his head. "This is not what I signed up for," he said. "I'm out of here. Don't contact me again, Vic."

He walked out swiftly, and Victor was alone with his dilemma.

He lifted the gun again, trying to steady it. He had to just shut a door, and let some other part of him do what needed to be done. Belinda's babbling voice rose in volume and pitch, pleading. He wanted to make it stop. Needed to make it stop.

A muffled *pop*, the silenced gun spoke.

Belinda fell backward. Glass crunched and tinkled as she fell. He felt nothing, looking down at her twisted body, her blank eyes. The red, jumbled mess where her mouth used to be. He turned away and vomited all over the pink and cream Persian carpet.

Victor wiped his mouth, panting. None of this felt real. It felt like a fever dream, jagged and overexposed and incoherent. Chunks of his life remixed into an awful, bewildering kaleidoscope.

And he wasn't even done. He still had to kill Henry. He wondered, in a frantic, disordered way, if he could somehow make it seem as if Henry had killed Bel. It would make sense, after all. He had stolen her baby.

And suddenly there were voices, footsteps. Men he did not know, with hard, cold eyes, boiling through the door and into the room. Surrounding him.

Chapter Forty-Seven

Amber crouched against the wall at the top of the stairs, holding Faith in one arm and her pocket makeup mirror in the other, angling it downstairs to try to make out what was happening down there.

Belinda was dead. Now still more men had muscled their way into the house. One of them was holding a gun to Victor's head. She knew Victor from Henry's computer. But who were these other guys? The DiAngelo crew?

Miraculously, Faith was still asleep. Through a catfight, broken glass, a gunshot, a shakedown. Even her own mother's murder hadn't woken the kid.

Amber considered her options. All of them were bad. She had no bargaining power now that Henry had fucked her over. All she had was a baby, and the goons would assume that the baby was a lever to move her. Which, in fact, she was. Amber did not want to watch anyone hurt a little baby.

Victor was after Henry, and he had problems of his own. He probably didn't even know she existed. But the DiAngelos knew all about her. Henry had made sure of that.

That realization tore open a black hole inside her, of anger, hurt. He'd done this to her deliberately. He had put her in this hellish position on purpose. Faith, too. There was no way down those stairs and past those men.

Belinda had been right about the roof. It was her only option. But with the rain and the cold wind howling around her? And Faith, meek and quiet and good as gold? Brilliant plan. Keep 'em coming, Einstein.

She closed the mirror and edged backward off the landing. The carpet in the hall was thick. She tiptoed up the staircase toward the door to the roof terrace. She unlocked the door with her heart in her throat, and slowly pulled it open.

Icy air whistled and blew through the crack in the door. It was frigid up here. Arching over the baby, Amber thanked God for the Grudbergs' cashmere fetish. She tried to shelter Faith from the wind, shivering. *Please, baby. Don't wake up yet.*

Chapter Forty-Eight

I n the living room, Victor stared at the men surrounding him. There were four of them, all pointing guns at him. All expecting something from him, although he had no idea what.

"Yeah, this is Shattuck," one of them said. "The dipshit who's cashing the bonds. Damn. What the fuck happened to you, man? Did someone run you over with a bus?"

"I'm not cashing any bonds!" he said frantically. "I don't know anything about any bonds!"

"Shut the fuck up, asshole." The guy who spoke was obviously the leader. "Did I tell you to talk?"

Victor's throat made a thin, high-pitched sound as he sucked in air. "N-n-no."

"I'm guessing…" The tall guy gestured toward Belinda with his gun. "That bloody mess over there must have been the showgirl."

Victor stared at Belinda's body, then looked back at the four men. "Showgirl?"

"Drop that gun you got there," the tall guy said. "Drop it on the floor and kick it toward me. Nice and easy."

Victor did. The gun hit the floor with a thud. It spun a little as he kicked it.

"Better," the tall man said. "So tell us. What's with the dead blonde?"

"Who are you?" Victor demanded. "What do you guys want from me? I never did anything to you!"

The tall man let out a theatrical sigh. "Okay, so we'll do this a different way. I'm going to tell you what happened here, and you're going to tell me if I'm cold, warm, or hot. Ever play this game?"

"Please. I don't know anything about any bearer bonds—"

"Shut the fuck up. I go first. So this is what went down. The dead chick is Amber Dixon, right? Hard to tell, when you shoot 'em in the face."

Victor started to protest. Then he thought better of it and just nodded.

"So, she gets you to help her cash the bonds, then you fuck her over because you don't want to share. Am I right? Because you're a bad, greedy shithead. Am I warm? Hot?"

"Look," Victor said. "I don't know anything about bonds. I mean, of course I know about bonds. I run a hedge fund. But I don't know anything about these bonds. I—"

"Looks like we have to do this the hard way." He nudged Belinda's foot with his shoe. "I see you're familiar with the hard way, judging from this poor bitch. I saw her on stage once. She was something else. Now look at her. All because she insisted on the hard way. Women. So hard to reason with. But you're not dumb like that, are you, Victor?"

Victor felt the room closing in around him. "I'm not dumb at all. I'd tell you if I knew anything. I'd tell you anything. Give you anything. I want to live, I swear to God."

"Where are the bonds, Shattuck? Are they here? In this house?"

"What bonds?" he wailed. "I don't know how to give you what you want!"

"Keep it down, asshole!" the tall guy hissed. "Let's take him to the warehouse." He looked around at the other three. "Tony, tape him up. Pauly, check through those suitcases, just in case, and make sure nobody else is in the house."

Victor snorted back the tears that were running into his nose as Tony stuck a rubber ball in his mouth and snapped a gag tight behind his head. The tall man took one last look at Belinda.

"What a fuckin' waste," he muttered.

Chapter Forty-Nine

Wojniac watched the DiAngelo's come out of the house. They'd been sitting in the SUV with binoculars trained on the place for what wasn't actually very long, but felt like hours stuck in the car with Leon. They'd brought a third set for him, in case he identified somebody interesting, but he was too busy bitching and moaning.

"They're coming out," Daly said. "Taking Shattuck to the van."

"About time." Wojniac lowered his glasses. "We're in business."

"No." Leon said, from the back seat. "We can't go. Amber's not with them."

"Leon," Daly sighed, reaching for his seat belt. "Don't be difficult. We can't —"

"I need to see if Amber's in the house before we go anywhere," Leon insisted. "We get her, then we follow them. That was the deal. Remember?"

"Look. I know you're obsessed with this woman, but she's not the priority here," Wojniac said. "If they're taking Shattuck, they either have the bonds already or they believe he knows where they are. Shattuck is the key. If we lose them, we—"

"You won't lose them. You have a trace on your fucking snitch. We'll catch up with them, no problem. We get Amber first."

Wojniac frowned over his shoulder and started up the car. "We'll get the Amber later. It's more important to—"

He was cut off by a bright, fiery point of pain in his neck. It spread fast, burning like a wasp's sting.

Wojniac tried to raise his hand and swat the thing, but he couldn't. He managed to turn his head just enough to see a syringe sticking out of Daly's neck.

Daly's eyes met his as he sagged in the seat belt. The last thing Wojniac was aware of was his door opening and Leon reaching across him, killing the ignition. Leon grabbed the keys and groped for the phone that ran the app with Pauly's trace.

Then everything faded away.

Chapter Fifty

Amber prayed to every fates, angel and benevolent spirit she could think of for the kid to not wake up, while wondering if it was normal for her to sleep this heavily, in the cold, in the wind and the rain. If something could be wrong with her.

Later, for God's sake. One disaster at a time.

She crept over to the street side, cuddling the sleeping toddler and peering down into the orange glow of the streetlight that illuminated the sidewalk in front of the house. Waiting for that last guy to finish searching the upstairs.

A couple of minutes later, he came out and ran toward the van. He got in, the headlights flicked on, and they drove away.

Tears of relief sprang into her eyes. Her knees went weak. Oh yes, yes, yes. Eternal gratitude sent up to the skies, going up now and forever.

Then another tall, broad figure stepped out into the pool light on the sidewalk by the steps, and looked up at the house.

Leon.

At that moment, Faith woke up and let out an ear-splitting yell.

———

Leon slammed the car door shut and felt for his gun. Then he remembered that they hadn't let him bring one. He could take one of theirs, but he didn't really need a gun to deal with Amber. He wasn't interested in shooting her.

He had slower, juicier things in mind.

He checked the tape stuck to his chest that held the last syringe, pried it loose, and stuck it into his pocket. He would bet good money that Victor Shattuck was not the key to those bearer bonds. The key was Amber. His beautiful, treacherous Amber. He'd never loved her more than at this moment. For a second, he looked up at the house, almost imagining he could see her. That their eyes were meeting like star-crossed lovers.

Then he ran up the steps, and in through the open door. "Hi, honey! I'm home!"

He had to climb over a bunch of open suitcases in the foyer. He strolled through, looking at the broken glass, trashed furniture, a pool of vomit. Big battle here.

He had a bad moment when he saw the dead woman crumpled on the floor, but a closer look reassured him. The dead girl's eyes were green, not Amber's dreamy gold. But he ripped open her blood-soaked blouse to check her tits, which were impossible to mistake. Just to be sure.

The dead bitch's tits were not half bad, but she was no Amber. Plus, there was no crawling flower vine tattoo over her chest and shoulder.

Leon cocked his head. There was a strange noise up there. Shrill, like a car alarm, but less regular. It seemed to be coming from directly above him.

Abandoning the dead woman, he ducked into the kitchen. It was shiny, white, like his and Amber's Vegas apartment. Same layout, with a central island. It gave him a pang of nostalgia.

So did the meat cleaver, which was right where it should be in the knife block. Wasn't that just fucking appropriate as hell. He swung it experimentally, slicing the air as he climbed up the stairs.

———

Amber froze at the toddler's wail, wasting precious seconds. Now what? Abandon a two-year-old to Leon's tender mercies? Dart like Spider Woman onto the neighbor's roof so she could run away over the housetops? And to where? To the end of the block, and a sheer drop three stories down to the street?

Maybe she could bang and pound and beg at every access door. Could the people in those houses even hear someone howling and pounding on their rooftop terrace doors?

She lay the baby gently down onto the wet wooden planks of the terrace. God, she should have brought a fire iron, a knife, a lamp, a pair of scissors. Anything. She grabbed one of the metal deck chairs, and tried to wedge it beneath the door handle, because this door only locked from the inside, of course. It was just her fate to be stuck on the wrong side of door-locking mechanisms with Leon Gambelli.

The chair was a crappy aluminum thing, so Amber kicked it aside and grabbed a wooden Adirondack lounger that worked better. She had just gotten it jammed in when Leon started banging on the door.

She backed away, putting herself between the door and Faith. The door shuddered and rattled.

Bam. Bam. Bam. He was enjoying this. *Bam!* The chair jolted loose. The door burst open.

Leon seemed huge. A being made of shadow emerging from the depths of hell. He stepped out, groped for a light switch, and flipped it on. She and the wailing Faith were flooded in cold, unwelcome light.

Amber blinked. Leon's thinning hair had grown out and was sticking up every which way. A meat cleaver gleamed in one hand. He held a syringe in the other. He grinned, lurching forward.

"Hey, beautiful," he said. "Did you miss me?"

Chapter Fifty-One

I t had taken Henry forever to find a parking place for the new rental, an eternity of searching and circling. He'd been forced to wait at the car rental place, too. Their computers had gone down, and he had been stuck at the end of a long, angry line. He could feel the frustration buzzing in the air, like one of those dreams where you can't do anything right. For hours.

Finally, he found parking, grabbed the bag of supplies for Faith, and locked the rental.

They should have been long gone by now. Every second that passed, their risk went up.

Halfway down the block from the house, he saw a man slumped in a parked car. Henry stopped on the sidewalk and took another look. Not one man. Two. The car was a normal SUV, nothing extraordinary. The two guys were apparently asleep. He couldn't see them well, what with the tinted windows and the fact that they were parked between street-lights, but they did not look like the kind of men who slept in their cars. Nor did the car look like the kind of car people slept in.

The strangeness of it ratcheted up his anxiety. Then he

got to the house and saw that the door was open, and his anxiety soared right up off the charts.

Henry sprinted up the steps and crept inside, barely breathing. Amber's suitcases had been pawed through, and stuff had been tossed every which way. Broken glass crunched under his feet. He smelled vomit, and a hot, meaty smell. Blood.

He sidled into the front living room. The place was wrecked. Furniture was broken, the coffee table was smashed, pictures had been knocked off the wall. Then he looked toward the stairs.

He sidled into the front living room and let out a cry of horror when he saw the fallen woman crumpled on the floor. He ran to her and fell to his knees, broken glass crunching under his weight as his world shattered—and then he saw the ripped blouse, the green eyes.

Belinda. Not Amber.

He sagged over her with a long, ragged shudder of guilty, horrified relief. He was truly sorry for her, and sorry for whatever part he'd played in what had happened to her, but they had driven him to it. He could repent later, grieve later, process his conflicting feelings later. Right now, he had to find Amber.

Far above him, he heard a shrill baby's cry, and a man, laughing crazily.

The DiAngelos? Leon?

Henry ran into the kitchen and grabbed the first thing he saw that could serve as a weapon. A heavy marble rolling pin. He hefted it, swinging it as he ran up the stairs.

Chapter Fifty-Two

"We meet again! Hearts that beat as one!" Leon's high-pitched laughter sounded manic, untethered to anything he said. "We're linked, you and me, even though you fucked me over. I loved you, and you screwed me, so I have to kill you now. I don't want to, but you put me in that position, you know. You made me do it."

"Well, you haven't done it yet, Leon." She tried to make her voice soothing, but it wobbled uncontrollably. "And you don't actually have to. It's not necessary."

Faith redoubled her screeching. Leon made a sound like a wounded bear. "Would you shut that thing up? My head is splitting!"

She nudged the stroller back, glancing behind herself to gauge how close she was to the roof's edge. It was only a few feet away, and there was no protective ledge to block the wheels. "She's just a baby, Leon. She doesn't know any better."

"We could have had a baby," he said. "If you'd been good. We could have had a beautiful baby together. Fuck, that thing is loud. Make it stop. Throw it off!"

"We could still have a baby," Amber said. "I'd like that."

"Just make that sound stop!" he roared.

"I know you're mad at me," she said. "I know I was bad. But don't hurt the baby, Leon. Okay? You don't have to hurt her. Just forget she's even here. Pretend it's just you and me. She can't even talk yet. She'll never say a word. She just wants her mamma."

"Mamma, huh?" He lurched closer, and she skittered back, agonizingly aware of that long fall backward into the well of darkness that lay behind her. "Is that dead bitch downstairs her mamma?"

"Yes, she is."

"Did you shoot her?" he asked. "Didn't know you had it in you. My little Amber. A murderess."

"I'm not," she said, as if it mattered what he thought of her. "Someone else did that. We had a catfight, pulled some hair, broke some glass. But I didn't kill her."

His smile was grotesque and terrifying. "You don't have to lie to me," he told her. "I don't care if you're a killer. I'm a killer, too, you know."

"I know." She forced out the words through shaking lips. "I know that."

"I'm going to miss you so much, Amber, baby," he said wistfully. "You filthy, lying, thieving slut. I'll miss you like hell."

"You don't have to miss me," she told him. He was close enough now that she could smell his breath. Faith evidently smelled it too, because she screamed louder.

"If you don't throw that noisy little shit off the roof, I will," he said.

"I'm so sorry about the bearer bonds," Amber said, hoping to jolt his mind onto a new track.

Leon shrugged. "Just give them back to me, and we're good, baby."

"I can't," she admitted. "The guy who was helping me

stole them. And he split." Even now, with Leon about to throw a baby off a roof and chop her to pieces, it hurt to say it. Her voice actually quavered. Not just with fear, but because Henry had broken her heart. When Leon cut her open, he'd find it all in pieces.

What a shitty way to go. She didn't deserve this. Much less little Faith.

"You shoulda stuck with me, babe," Leon said. "You would have had it so good."

"I know." She inched back slowly, staring at the syringe glittering in his hand. The terrace light lit up the evil-looking yellowish stuff in the chamber. Leon would stab her with that, and she would wake up like Michael, duct-taped to a table somewhere. The long fall backward into the dark would be a better way to go. But what about Faith? Could she just leave her? Or worse, take her along? Dear God.

Over by the door, shadows flickered. There was another silhouette.

It was Henry's tall, rangy form, but she did not let herself to look at him or even think about him. She saw him out of her peripheral vision and pretended with all her strength that she didn't.

So Henry had not run out on her. That was wonderful. And that was terrible. Everything was a million times worse now she knew that Henry was for real. No bullshit, no lies, no games. All heart.

That was wonderful, but it was not good news. Because of that quality, he would die right in front of her, because that was what the world did to good people. A guy like Henry couldn't face down a guy like Leon. Leon was wired up to kill, like a dog in a fighting pit. It would happen, and she would have to watch it.

Henry inched closer. And closer. He was raising some club-like object on high, loading his swing, but she didn't dare identify what for fear of tipping Leon off.

Leon caught a flicker of movement at the last moment as the club whipped down. He lurched sideways, the rolling pin glancing off his shoulder instead of smashing his head.

Amber leapt for Faith as Leon howled, swinging the meat cleaver. Henry jerked back, the blade *whooshing* past his face. He swung again, but Leon slammed his boot into Henry's belly. Henry hit the terrace with a grunt. The rolling pin flew from his hand, hit the planks, and rolled. Amber grabbed it and swung it as hard as she could. She caught the blade of the meat cleaver and sent it flying.

Bellowing in rage, Leon smacked her flat with his massive, heavy arm, and for a split second, the world wavered, darkened. Then it roared back. The sound of Faith's thin, high shrieks was like a hot needle that swelled and receded and swelled again.

Amber blinked and saw Leon lunging for the baby. Henry tackled him and brought him down with a huge, rattling thump, making the plank flooring shake. Henry hung onto Leon's legs desperately as Leon tried to kick him off.

The cleaver lay a few feet away, catching the light. Amber went for it.

Everything came together, laser-sharp. Leon's hairy, thick wrist, his fingers, reaching out for Faith like some grotesque parasitical vine. Every part of her was a unified lethal weapon, and the cleaver was the business end, whipping down in a savage blur—

And chopping off his hand.

The hand rolled a few times, and came to rest palm upward, fingers curled up. Leon lurched and staggered away, his face a mask of disbelief.

She advanced on him with the cleaver. Leon backed away, his white-rimmed eyes darting from her face to the blade, back and forth as he clutched his bleeding stump. He was near the edge, but not looking at his feet.

For a split second, his eyes met Amber's. Then he pitched over backward, disappearing into the dark.

There was a clattering crash below as he landed on the Grudbergs' patio furniture.

Chapter Fifty-Three

Henry got up first, swaying like a tree in a high wind. He staggered to his daughter and scooped her up into his arms. The little girl grabbed handfuls of his shirt, hanging on like a monkey. Almost immediately, she stopped screaming, and rested her head against his chest, sucking her thumb.

Amber crawled to the edge of the roof and peered over, not quite believing it. Had the impossible actually happened? Was Leon really gone?

"Wait," she croaked. "Wait. Is this real? Am I awake?" She half expected to see him climbing up the side of the building with one hand.

Henry kissed the top of Faith's head. "Maybe." He said, his voice a breathless croak. "We should ask ourselves that when we're in the car, speeding away."

They stared down at the bloody, disembodied hand that lay on the terrace boards. Henry nudged it gingerly with the toe of his foot toward the edge until it slid over and fell to join its source material. They both waited for the clattering *thud*.

She and Henry stared at each other. Her throat was tight and hot. He kept swallowing.

"You came back," she whispered. "You came back for us."

"Well, of course, I came back. I'm just so sorry I took so long."

She got to her feet and threw herself at him, hugging him and Faith together. The three of them stood there, shivering in the icy wind until Henry finally said, "Come on, let's go inside."

He took the baby. Amber gathered up the bloodied cleaver, the syringe, and the rolling pin and followed him down the stairs, clutching the banister to keep from stumbling.

They avoided the living room and Belinda, and went straight to the kitchen where Henry ran her a glass of water, then drank one himself. They sank into chairs, all three of them still shaking and stupefied. Faith kept her face pressed against Henry's chest, which now sported a large drool spot. Henry did not notice or care. He just cuddled Faith and held Amber's hand, his breathing still rapid and uneven.

"We'd really better get going," he said finally.

"I agree," she said. "We certainly can't stay here. There's a cadaver in the living room and another one on the back patio. So we're murder suspects now, right? On top of everything else?"

"We'll see," Henry said. "Let me think about that."

She snorted with slightly hysterical laughter. "Think away, smart boy. When have I ever tried to stop you?"

"I'm so sorry I wasn't here when he came. I should never have left you two alone."

"I'm grateful you weren't here," she told him. "You would have been killed. This place went nuts after you left. Everybody showed up here looking to kill somebody."

He looked at her, startled. "Oh. So it wasn't just Leon, then?"

"Oh, God, no. First Belinda showed up. We had words."

"You talked with Belinda?"

"Yeah. She had some choice things to say to me, but she

mostly just wanted her baby. Then Victor showed up, and Belinda panicked and said I had to take Faith up on the roof. That the baby wasn't safe with him. And damned if she wasn't right. That bastard shot her. In cold blood."

"God." Henry's voice was colorless.

Amber nodded. "I know. Then the DiAngelos showed up. They took Victor away with them, so it looks like your crafty ruse worked. And after all of that, Leon showed up for the grand finale."

"But...but how did Victor and the DiAngelos not see you? Where were you? On the roof?"

"Upstairs, and on the roof, yes. They didn't even know Faith and I were here. Somehow, she stayed asleep. For most of it, anyway."

"Thank God," he said. "Thank God."

"No kidding. But listen. Before all this, I searched the house for those bearer bonds. Which, oddly enough, had vanished from where I left them."

He drew in a breath. "Oh, no. I should have said something."

"Yes, you definitely should have," she agreed. "Did you hide them? Or take them with you?"

"I hid them." He had the decency to look sheepish. "I took the banded cash in my bag because it's bulky and hard to hide. But the rest of it, I just hid right here. I meant to say something to you."

"That would have been nice," she said crisply. "Belinda said some stuff about the perfidy of all men, and I looked over at the shelf, and voilà, they were gone. Suffice to say, not a great moment."

"I hid them before I left. I didn't say anything because you were so angry about Faith, and I just wanted to get on the road. I didn't expect it to take so long to rent the damn car."

"So where are they?"

Henry got up, Faith still clamped to his chest, and went to

the piano in the dining room. He came back with the volume of Italian songs and handed it to her.

"They fit perfectly into the book cover," he told her.

She opened it, staring at the sheaf of bonds inside. "I saw the music book in the recycling bin," she said. "It was open to *Ah! Perchè non posso odiarti, infidel, com'io vorrei!* and I thought, check that out. A song about an unfaithful lover."

"Actually, in the story, Amina didn't really betray Elvino." Henry's tone was careful. "It was all just a big misunderstanding."

"Hmmph." She frowned. "Still, maybe Amina should have communicated better. Amina should have gotten out ahead of it beforehand, just to prevent any weirdness."

"Absolutely," he agreed. "Won't happen again."

"Good. How about those diamonds? Where did they disappear to?"

Henry opened the cabinet under the sink and pulled a wet, heavy diaper wrapped in diaper tape out of the garbage bag. He hefted it, giving her one of his sweet, fleeting smiles. "Voilá," he said. "Diamonds."

She shook her head with a smile of reluctant admiration. "Henry Devlin, you are one sneaky guy."

"When I need to be. Which is not with you. I will always be straight with you. Always."

She let out an unsteady breath. "It's been a bad night all around. But thinking that you took the bonds and ran out on me? That was the worst."

He looked appalled. "Leave without you and Faith? What would be the point? I might as well drive off a cliff and be done with it. Hold Faith for a second, would you? I have to go check on something. In the living room."

Amber stared at him. "Huh? Why?"

"I can't take Faith in there," he said gently. "You know that."

"Right. Of course can't. Sorry," She held up her

arms, bracing herself for Faith's train-whistle noise as he passed the baby onto her lap.

But it didn't happen. Amber held the little girl awkwardly. She was small, skinny, nervy, and surprisingly strong. Faith stared up at Amber with big, thoughtful dark eyes that reminded her of Henry's. Then she grabbed Amber's tangled hair, yanked on it, and babbled something. It sounded like a question, but Amber didn't speak the language.

"Sorry, kid," she said regretfully. "I got nothing."

Faith touched her cheek and cooed something that sounded reassuring. She had that wide-open, trusting look on her little face. No idea what a mess she was looking at. No idea that Amber was stained, soiled, marked. Scrawled all over in blood, like vicious graffiti.

She wanted to wash it all away and start over. To have never seen what she'd seen, or done what she'd done. But there was no way back from it.

Suddenly, to her horror, she was hugging Faith close and crying like a baby.

Chapter Fifty-Four

H enry started by going outside to check on Leon, just in case the man was still alive. He turned on the patio light, flinched, and flicked the light off. No need to look any closer.

He went back inside and picked through the shambles of the living room until he found Belinda's purse. As he rifled through its contents, plans formed, shifted, and reformed in his mind.

By the time he came back into the kitchen, Amber was bouncing Faith on her lap.

"Belinda was running away," he announced.

Amber nodded. "Yeah, she told me that. She said that Victor would hurt Faith."

"Her documents are all here. Hers and Faith's passports. Victor's passport, too. Maybe to keep him from following her. She had their birth certificates, the deed for the house I bought for her when we were married, their social security cards. Investments. Insurance."

"I see. And this is relevant why?"

"I'm not sure yet," he admitted. "But I feel as if it is somehow."

Amber's face was an ashy gray, her lips colorless. He got up and put on some tea. "Belinda had her car keys in her purse," he said. "Her car must be parked outside somewhere."

"Yeah? So?"

"We could leave in her car," he said. "It's a good car. A Toyota Gamma. Only a few years old. I bought it for her myself. And it'll have a car seat for Faith in it already."

Amber looked dubious. "Seems weird, to take her car. And risky. Won't they put out an APB for it as soon as they find her body?"

"Maybe," he said. "Maybe not."

"They will as soon as they identify her," Amber said.

"Could be difficult, if the house should blow up."

She gasped. "The Grudbergs' house? My God, Henry. Are you serious?"

"I'm sorry, but it's just a house," he said. "There's no one living on either side at the moment. No one will be hurt. This house, versus our lives? Our lives win. Hands down."

"Whoa," she whispered. "You're ruthless, Henry Devlin. But what about DNA, dental records and all that forensic stuff that they do now?"

"Fire pretty much destroys DNA," Henry said. "And besides, they won't have any reason connect that body to Belinda. They'll connect it to you. Do you have dental records someplace?"

"No," she said. "Dental care was scarce in my life. I got my teeth cleaned and whitened from time to time when I lived in Vegas, but I've never had an X-ray."

"I designed the database for the dental practice Belinda used," Henry said. "That's how I met her. She doesn't have any hardware in her mouth. No implants, no capsules."

"They won't get much info out of Belinda's teeth after what Victor did to her."

"True. And my hope is that they won't compare anything at all. They have no reason to think that body belongs to anyone but Amber Dixon. The FBI knew you were there. They knew that Leon was coming for you, and that he was obsessed with killing you. Why would anyone think of Belinda when they find that body?"

Amber bit her lip. "I don't know. But I do know that, no matter which car we take, we need to get moving. DiAngelo's people will come back here, once they realize Victor is useless."

Henry put a cup of hot, sweet, milky tea on the table in front of her. "Drink this. Then we'll get you and Faith and all the bags into Belinda's car."

Belinda had been lucky in her parking spot, if in nothing else. The car was right around the block. Henry put the bags and the stroller into the hatch back, and tucked Faith into the car seat. Amber climbed in front to find that Belinda's car had a wealth of useful goodies in it. Packs of crackers, juice boxes, more diapers, all scattered amid a heap of twenty-ounce empties from the Beans & Brew.

"Wait here," Henry told her. "I won't be long."

He ran back to the house, and went through every room, making sure all the doors and windows were tightly shut and sealed. He went to the back patio and dragged Leon's big, heavy body inside, trying not to look at the grisly sight as he did it. Then he steeled himself to go back out with the flashlight and find Leon's hand. His gorge rose as he picked it up. It was chilly, clammy. He laid it by Leon's arm.

When all that was done, Henry put two metal travel cups and several spoons and forks in the microwave. Then he found the gas line, and cut it.

The rest he would do remotely, from hundreds of miles away, with the smart-hub.

He closed the front door to the sweet, sickly scent of propane, and locked it, apologizing in his mind to the Grudbergs. Thanking them for the shelter their house had given. Hoping they had good homeowner's insurance.

Henry ran around the block, boots pounding, cold air burning in his lungs, trying to get the propane stink out of his nose. He got into the Gamma, grabbed Amber's hand and squeezed it.

She squeezed back. It was a wonderful sensation.

By the time they hit the George Washington Bridge, Amber and Faith were both fast asleep. Henry drove, wide awake, his mind buzzing steadily on, compiling a list of the toddler gear they had to acquire while thinking about the next phase of their project. A phase he had not allowed himself to hope for until all the dragons were slain. Their future life. Because incredibly, they still had one.

So many possible paths from here, but his mind was rattled by images of terror. Leon dragging Faith's stroller toward the edge. Belinda, lying dead in the broken glass, her beautiful face destroyed. Victor, tortured by the DiAngelo crew, caught in a chain of events that Henry had set in motion.

This was a harsher punishment than any he had ever envisioned for Victor. A long and horrible ordeal, and nothing but an unmarked grave at the end of it.

Still. Victor had shot the mother of his own child in the face. To hell with him.

Seldom was karmic justice served up so swiftly and so efficiently.

It was past dawn when he stopped at a budget hotel somewhere in Maryland and nudged Amber's arm. Henry apologized when she jerked awake. "Sorry. I didn't mean to startle you. Let's get a room. You bring the bag. I'll bring Faith."

He unhooked the car seat. Faith continued to sleep soundly under the fuzzy cashmere blanket, their only memento of the Grudbergs' house. He lay the sleeping child on one of the two beds while Amber lay down the other bed, watching him.

When he sat down, opened his laptop, and started typing, she said, "Shouldn't you try to rest?"

"Just a couple of things to take care of."

"Yeah? Like what?"

His fingers clattered over the keyboard. "I met Belinda at the dental practice. I was working on their database. I still have the override codes. In my head."

"Oh. So…what are you doing?"

"Trolling the patient database for a candidate." He looked up at her. "Right now, I'm looking at Cecilia Turturro, of McCurdy Ridge. She seems ideal. Had a root canal done four years ago but has no dental prostheses with serial numbers. Sadly, she also died of leukemia last year, so it won't inconvenience her if I switch her records out for Belinda's. Just in case they do get interested in the body at the Grudbergs'."

"I thought there wouldn't be much left of it?"

"There won't. Nor Leon's, either. But it's better safe than sorry, right?"

Amber rested her head on her elbow, watching him with her beautiful, thoughtful tiger eyes. "Huh," she said. "I guess it's lucky I've never had any dental work done, right?"

"Very lucky." He opened Belinda's bag and pulled out a handful of documents. "Here's your passport. Brand new, never used, since Belinda was afraid to fly. Here's your birth certificate, and a deed to your house, the one your no-good jailbird ex-husband bought for you. Here's your bank account info, records of a couple of CDs and investments, credit cards, and insurance. Hello, Belinda Devlin."

Amber sat up. "Wait, wait, wait," she said. "Just slow down, Henry. Wait a damn second, here."

"Why? It's all right here. Everything you needed. A new identity, free and clear." He lay down another passport, and a crisper, newer birth certificate. "And this is your daughter."

"Whoa!" She held up a hand. "What about Amber?"

"You'll always be Amber to me," he said. "But that

woman was tragically murdered by her husband, Leon Gambelli, last night. May she rest in peace with the angels."

"You really think I could just take Belinda's identity, just like that? You think this could work?"

He pointed at the computer. "Once I remotely turn on the microwave that's filled with silverware and stainless steel, and a spark ignites a room full of propane gas? Ka-boom. It will definitely work."

She shook her head. "Henry," she said, her voice shaky and muffled. "This is all so sudden."

He let out a snort, and for a few minutes they traded smothered, helpless bursts of laughter, trying not to wake the baby. Soon Amber's laughter morphed into that hybrid laughing/crying thing she sometimes did. It didn't scare him anymore. He just pulled her close. He was bigger now than he had been before. He could get his arms all the way around any feelings she might have.

Amber sniffed hard and looked at him. "Let's keep one thing straight," she said.

"And what's that?"

"I'll take Belinda's official identity, because I have to," she said. "But I won't spend my life pretending to be her. I won't go blonde, or wear green contacts, or try to talk like her or smile like her. I'm just me now. Plain old Amber. I'm all done assuming other people's personalities. I'm spending the rest of the time I have left just figuring out who Amber is. That's plenty for a single human life."

"That sounds good to me. But I know exactly who Amber is." Henry got up and came to sit beside her. "She's my lover. My best friend. My bride, I hope. If I get lucky."

"You're such a romantic," she whispered.

He stroked the top of her head and kissed it. "Where you're concerned, definitely. Hey, something funny just occurred to me."

"Yeah? I could use something funny."

"If I could just stay Henry Devlin, I would already be married to you," he said. "Belinda filed for a divorce while I was in prison, but it hadn't been finalized yet."

She snorted. "No shit. That is funny. So I could inherit Belinda's husband as well as her daughter."

"But I'm not Henry Devlin anymore," he said. "I'm Ben Glass now. Which means I can marry you again."

"Aw." Her gaze fell, but he could see that she was smiling. "Well, then. Now that I think about it, wedding vows strike me as an item best not recycled."

"So, ah…" Henry paused. "Is that a yes, then?"

She shrugged. "We still have a few details to hammer out."

"Yeah? Tell me what they are. We'll make an itemized list. Knock them off one by one."

"Well, for one thing, Faith has to know," she said. "What happened to her mamma, I mean."

"That could be awkward," Henry said slowly. "When she's older, maybe?"

"Her mother stood up for her," Amber said. "She died for her. She defended her daughter from a monster."

"And you defended her from another monster."

"Sure, but that's not my point. Her sacrifice should be honored. It means something to know that your mom cared about you that much. She has to know about it. I insist on that. For both their sakes."

"Okay. Once Faith can form complete sentences, we will discuss ways and means. Anything else?"

Amber gave him a doubtful, sidewise look. "Um, yes. I appreciate the offer, but are you really sure about this? One hundred percent? In case you haven't noticed, I'm not exactly the maternal type."

"You're not? Facing down Leon Gambelli and his meat cleaver? Keeping him from throwing Faith off the roof? That's about as maternal as it gets."

She made a doubtful sound. "Well, in a primal sort of way,

I guess. Like a mamma grizzly. But you won't find me in the Mommy & Me swim class, or doing story hour at the library, or bringing cookies to the bake sale to benefit the soccer team. I'm just not the type."

"Screw the soccer team and the swim class. Faith would be incredibly lucky to have a mamma grizzly. There's never been anyone like you in the world, Amber. You're not a type. You're one of a kind."

Amber let out a short laugh. "So is that a good thing or a bad thing?"

He lifted her hand to his lips. "It's a true thing."

After a few minutes, she was sniffling again. "Stop it, Henry," she snapped. "You're making me leak. Enough of your sappy, manipulative bullshit."

"Will you give it a shot? Please?"

"Fine," she said tartly, grabbing a tissue. "Go ahead. I'm on board. Belinda Devlin, here I come."

Henry grabbed the laptop, and clicked into the Grudbergs' smart-hub, found the microwave, set the timer, and toggled the switch to 'on.'

Epilogue

El Paso-Cuidad de Juarez Border Crossing
El Paso, Texas
One Month Later

The green Toyota Gamma had been waiting for almost an hour in the Texas heat before the line finally inched forward enough so it was their turn. The woman driving rolled down the window and presented the three passports with a friendly smile.

The female border agent smiled back as she looked them over and peered inside, checking faces against passport photos. Cute family. Pretty blonde mom at the wheel. Handsome, dark-haired dad in the passenger seat. Cute-as-a-button little toddler girl in the back, all dressed up in a fairy princess dress complete with a sparkly tiara, a jeweled necklace and a wand tipped with diamond stars that glittered just as brightly as the gems scattered across her puffy skirt made of rainbow-colored tulle. She held up a start-tipped magic wand, and waved it purposefully.

The border agent laughed at the spectacle, charmed. "So

what is the purpose of your visit to Mexico, Ms. Devlin? And how long will you be staying?"

"Three weeks or so. We're driving down to Mérida for my niece's *quinceañera,* then heading to Tulum for a little beach time."

"I see that Miss Faith here," she glanced at the passport, checking the name, "is already dressed for the party!"

"Oh, you bet. Overdressed, even. Diamonds galore. That's just who she is."

The border agent laughed as she turned to scan their passports. When she handed them back, she waved at the little girl, who was solemnly sucking on her thumb, still clutching her wand. "Aren't you the little magic princess, all dressed up in your sparklies!"

The little girl smiled and swished her wand once again.

"Yes, she does love her diamonds," the blond woman said, laughing. "Whoops, look out! I think she just put spell on you. No worries, though. Looks like a good spell."

The woman passed the passports back. "Not a moment too soon," she said. "I'll just sit back now and wait for my luck to change. Thank you, your magical highness! And you're quite right in your wardrobe choice. A girl can never have too many diamonds!"

The little girl giggled and swished her wand wildly.

The border agent was still chuckling as the car pulled away.

THE END

A Note from the children of Warren Adler

Thank you for down loading this book. Help us keep our father's memory alive by leaving a review on **Amazon** and **Goodreads**.

It makes us feel so proud knowing people are still reading our father's books - and introducing his work to a whole new generation!

For complete catalogue including novels, plays, and short stories visit: www.warrenadler.com

Connect with us on:
Facebook —www.facebook.com/warrenadler

About the Author

Acclaimed author, playwright, poet, and essayist Warren Adler was best known for "The War of the Roses," his masterpiece fictionalization of a macabre divorce adapted into the BAFTA- and Golden Globe–nominated hit film starring Danny DeVito, Michael Douglas, and Kathleen Turner. Adler's internationally acclaimed stage adaptation of the novel premiered on Broadway in 2015–2016.

Adler also optioned and sold film rights for several of his works, including "Random Hearts" (starring Harrison Ford and Kristin Scott Thomas) and "The Sunset Gang" (produced by Linda Lavin for PBS's American Playhouse series starring Jerry Stiller, Uta Hagen, Harold Gould, and Doris Roberts), which garnered Doris Roberts an Emmy nomination for Best Supporting Actress in a Miniseries.

Adler's works have been translated into more than 25 languages, including his staged version of "The War of the Roses," which opened to spectacular reviews worldwide. Adler taught creative writing seminars at New York University and lectured on creative writing, film and television adaptation, and electronic publishing. He lived with his wife, Sunny, a former magazine editor, in Manhattan.

Printed in Dunstable, United Kingdom